# ZOMBIE ROAD

## CONVOY OF CARNAGE

### DAVID A. SIMPSON

Wise Pug Publishing

# ALSO BY DAVID A. SIMPSON

Zombie Road: Convoy of Carnage

Zombie Road II: Bloodbath on the Blacktop

Zombie Road III: Rage on the Rails

Zombie Road IV: Road to Redemption

## ANTHOLOGIES

Tales from the Zombie Road: The Long Haul Anthology

Undead Worlds: A Reanimated Writers Anthology

Treasured Chests: A Zombie Anthology

Splintered Dreams: A Guide to the Apocalypse

**Zombie Road**

**Convoy of Carnage**

**Book 1**

Is a work of fiction by

**David A. Simpson**

Copyright © 2016 David A. Simpson
All rights reserved.
ISBN-13: 978-1520479989

ISBN-10: 1520479980

*Zombie Road*
*Convoy of Carnage*
*A two fisted trucker tale*


*To my dearest partner in life, the nitpicky, OCD, grammar Nazi, Robin.*

# PROLOGUE

"If you would, have a seat here, Sir," the man indicated a comfortable chair pulled up to a simple plank table, "we can get the microphone set up for you."

He sat heavily and looked around his living room, at all the people gathered and watching him, most of them with various instruments to aid in the recording process.

"What do want me to say?" he asked, a little uncomfortable with everyone standing around, more than he was used to seeing high in the mountains. Especially in his own home.

"You were a hard man to find. We have talked to everyone else we've been able to contact about the early years," the smiling man said. "This isn't really an interview, we just want you to tell us what you remember. Just tell us a story like you were talking to friends. Tell us what you can, and with the trove of video we found from one of the survivors, we hope we can assemble an accurate picture of the times."

"You understand, it's kind of hard to separate the legend from fact after all these years, right?" he asked, "I can't tell the difference in what was real, and what I remember as real, sometimes."

"Yes, Sir. It has been a long time, but we're pretty sure we have all of the facts correct. We just want to add the human side of the story wherever we can. We want to get a feel for the people who were there, how they felt, and why they did some of the things they did."

"Is this going to be a movie or something?" the old man asked.

"We don't have that kind of technology, not to do it properly. We hope to lay out the definitive history of the Fall in a book, perhaps two or three if we have gathered enough of the human element to tie all of the dry statistics together. We hope to write a compelling story, not another history book."

The old man smiled. "Well, some of the things I remember, nobody will believe anyway. It's all true, but some of it may not have happened."

He took a sip of water and started talking.

THE THREE FLAGS TRUCK STOP

**Day 1**
**September**

Gunny came through the glass doors of the garage and into the long corridor that would lead him to the dining area of the Three Flags Truck Stop. He had just brought his old Peterbilt into the bay for an oil change and was now looking forward to the morning's first cup of coffee and whatever the breakfast special from the kitchen happened to be. He glanced to his right when the gym doors opened, and a heavily built man came out, a towel draped around his neck, wiping the sweat from his great bald head.

"Hey, Tiny," he said in greeting. "You eat yet? I'm headed for chow."

Tiny, ironically named because of his bulk, flashed a smile that seemed to glow out of his ebony face. "Hey,

Gunny," he rumbled. "Yeah, headed there myself. Something wrong with your Pete?"

"Nah. Just a service. Tommy put one of the mechanics on it. You and Scratch still running veggies out of the valley?" asked Gunny.

They walked down the long corridor, catching up on each other's lives since they had last crossed paths a few months prior. They ambled by the various shops and stores of the old Truck Stop, most still closed at this early hour. The barbershop, the laundromat, the Cutting Edge knife shop, the CB shop, the freight brokers' offices and Doc's Place, among the many that catered to the professional drivers. Old Cobb gave these little shops low rental rates because of the smell of 90 weight gear oil, and the sound of impact wrenches was more prevalent near the workshop.

The Three Flags Truck stop had been around almost as long as the highway it was named after. Route 395, at one time a main north-south road, ran from San Diego all the way up to the Canadian border. Thus the three flags designation of the three countries it joined together.

The truck stop had been established in the 50s by Old Cobb's dad, a World War 2 vet who went on to drive trucks after the Big One and saw the need for a good place for truckers to refuel both themselves and their rigs. The land was cheap up north of Reno, it was nothing but scrub, and no one else wanted it. So using the benefits of his G.I. Bill, he bought nearly 200 acres along Route 395 and business was good.

He expanded rapidly during the boom years of the 50s and 60s, buying up used army Quonset huts for his buildings and simply putting in long banks of government surplus windows on one side to let in natural light, so they wouldn't feel so claustrophobic. He used a small airplane hangar as his main building and had a wing off of one side for his mechanic shop and a wing off of the other side for his wife's diner.

His wife ran the kitchen, Cobb ran the workshop and he hired other vets, many of them damaged from the war, to help him run his business.

When the new freeways came in, business slowed. They managed to hang on, but there were some lean times for a number of years. When Cobb Jr. took over when he retired from the Marines, he brought the old truck stop into the modern times. He convinced some of the local artisans and vintners to sell their wares to draw in tourists.

With some internet advertising, and savvy marketing as the oldest Truck Stop in Nevada, it became THE place to stop and see a little roadside Americana. There was a huge junkyard out behind the shop where wrecked and worn-out trucks sat, dating all the way back to the 40s and 50s, from their towing and recovery service.

He even had a half dozen of those trucks with the big sleepers moved up to a little area where he cleaned and polished them so they looked like new. He ran some electricity for heat and air conditioning, then rented them out on Airbnb for $40.00 a night. Old Cobb laughed all the way to the bank. It was a family business and the pride they took in it showed in a lot of small ways.

As Gunny and Tiny made their way through the Quonset hut they saw Cobb coming out of the shower area, pushing a mop and bucket. "Cobb, when you gonna put in some moving sidewalks like they got in Vegas in this place?" Tiny grumbled. "It's gotta be a mile from the gym to the diner."

Old Man Cobb squinted at him through his one good eye. With a grizzled voice that was partly from Lucky

5

Strikes, and partly from a piece of shrapnel to the throat he had picked up in the Khe Sanh Valley, he spat out, "Looks like you could use the exercise, Squib. But you Navy boys ain't used to that."

"Morning Cobb," Gunny said, grinning at the age-old rivalry of the Services.

"Gunny," Cobb nodded. "You need to hit that gym, too. You're getting as flabby as him."

"I'm just going after some breakfast, maybe next time," he said, knowing full well he wasn't planning on lifting lumps of metal anytime soon.

"He gets plenty of exercise, Navy Style," Tiny grinned. "We called 'em 12-ounce curls," as he mimicked drinking a cold beer.

"Yeah. I can see. Looks like you had plenty of burritos to go with those brews," he added, poking at Tiny's not so tiny stomach. "Speaking of food, Martha's been making up some blueberry pies and pancakes last couple of days, got a crate of fresh ones that "fell off the truck". Make sure you try some."

"Thought you said I was fat," Tiny said. "And now you want me to eat pie?"

"Well don't eat none, then," Cobb rasped out, "I'll just tell her you think her cookin' ain't no good."

Tiny threw his hands up, aghast. "Don't you dare, Cobb! You tell her that, she won't feed me for a month!"

Cobb laughed quietly and shooed them on, "Go on, get out of here. Can't you see a man's trying to work," he said and turned back to his mopping. "And walk on the edge near the window, it'll be dry by now," he barked out.

They continued, taking a left into the main hut that was massive enough to have an old airplane suspended from the ceiling, with a rounded height of more than 30 feet. It housed the tourist attractions and the video arcade, along with the souvenir shops and main C-store that sold everything you would expect in a well-stocked convenience store and tourist trap.

There was a pretty good selection of trucker-related items, too. Electronics and load straps and log books, along with the audio books, DVD multi-packs and rattlesnake eggs.

As they passed the arcade, they looked in and saw an intense young man wielding a plastic shotgun, blasting away at never ending hordes of Zombies. They looked at each other and smiled.

Gunny opened the door and they both shambled toward him, arms outstretched, moaning in their best zombie wails and groans, "Brains!"

He spun like lightning, twisting at the waist, feet never moving, orange plastic shotgun to his shoulder. "Boom Boom! Dead, you flesh bags!" he yelled out, targeting each one of them, then turned back to his game, but it was too late. The screen was counting down, demanding more money if he wanted to continue.

"Awwww, piss!" he said in aggravation. "I was on the last level before the Boss Fight."

"C'mon Scratch," Gunny said. "We just saved you from yet another slow, painful death. Besides, Martha's got blueberry pancakes."

"No thanks to you two ass wipes," he grumbled. "You're buying. This damn game cost two bucks to play. Cobb's getting rich off of me."

"Where you running today?" Tiny asked, changing the subject.

Scratch put the plastic gun back into its holster and turned, grabbing his jacket off of the unused Pac Man machine with the metal claw from his prosthetic left arm. "Supposed to take this load of winter squash down into Sacramento, but dispatch has me in a holding pattern here. They want to verify with the warehouse before they send me in."

"Verify what?" Tiny asked. "Either they ordered them or they didn't. What's so hard about that?"

Scratch stopped at the glass door Gunny was holding open and looked at them. "Haven't you heard what's been going on?" he asked.

They looked at each other, then back at him. Tiny shrugged, "No. I don't watch the news. Is it that Mecca thing?"

"That Mecca thing," Scratch snorted. "That happens every year."

Gunny said, "I've been on a Louis L'Amour binge this week. Got a bunch of audio books from the library when I was home."

"Geez," Scratch said and shook his head. "You two hermits ever get out of your trucks and talk to people?"

"I don't like people," Tiny quietly rumbled. "I don't even like you. You're ugly and your mother dresses you funny."

They were walking through the tourist areas, making their way to the doors of the diner, Scratch's metal arm fully exposed in his short sleeve shirt, jacket slung over his shoulder.

A young college-aged couple, with their carefully matched second-hand store clothes and scarves, looked at them in indignation. They were browsing the authentic Navajo jewelry and heard what Tiny said. They saw the young man's missing arm and shot daggers at the big man for being so insensitive.

Tiny didn't notice, Gunny didn't care, and Scratch was used to it, people taking umbrage on his behalf since he "was a cripple". But they were all former servicemen. Navy, Marines, Army...it didn't matter. If you weren't continually insulting each other, it meant you didn't care. He was like most people with a disability, just wanted to be treated like one of the guys.

"C'mon. It'll be all over the news in the diner. Man, something is making people go crazy. There have been riots in nearly every city. Hell, it's worldwide according to Alex. How long since you turned on your radio?"

Gunny was starting to get an uneasy feeling in his gut. He thought, wracking his brain, when WAS the last time he had watched the news? He'd left the house a little over a week ago, had talked to his wife Lacy a few times, and got onto his teenager about homework and chores once.

He really hadn't had the radio or CB on, except for traffic checks, since he picked this load up in Maine. More than a week. He'd been burning through the days listening to tales of the old West and gunslingers and Indian raiding parties. Warriors of yesteryear. He got like that sometimes, "one of his moods", as Lacy would say. Just wanting to shut the world out and live in his own bubble. The news was always the same anyway. Always depressing.

A cop shot someone and there were protests in the streets.

Some terrorists blew something up.

Some politician was doing shady stuff.

Stocks were up.

Stocks were down.

Some celebrity was getting married or divorced.

The war in the Middle East never ended.

North Korea was saying they were going to nuke

somebody.

It seemed that the only thing that changed was the names of the people involved. But riots in every city? The last news he had watched back home, that all the talking heads were excited about, was the big announcement by the Salaam meat packing factories.

It was a Muslim owned company and they were going to start selling pork products to the world during this year's Hajj. This was to show the world that "Muslims were a peaceful people and were in opposition to the terrorists."

But in reality, Gunny figured it was just a way to get their Halaal products on the store shelves without any back-lash from people who didn't want to see them at the local grocery. They were going to release all these pork products when most of the Muslim population in the world went to Mecca for their pilgrimage. Probably so some high Imam would calm the masses and tell them Allah said it was okay.

Kind of like Jesus did in the New Testament, when he told the Israelites it was all right to eat pork.

Gunny figured it was just a marketing move. It didn't matter what your religion was for a multinational corpora-tion. In the end, it came down to making money. It was all about the bottom line. But if it brought Islam into the 21$^{st}$ century, he was okay with it. Maybe it would help stop ISIS. Give them one less reason to chop your head off.

He didn't hate all of the Muslims like some of the vets did. Even though he'd killed his fair share of them, he'd met a lot of good folks over there. But were people so pissed off about it, they were protesting in the streets? He doubted it. It wasn't that big of a deal.

That was capitalism. Maybe it would bring the price of bacon down. He knew Scratch wasn't prone to hysterics, even though they had only known each other for a few years. He'd lost his arm in Afghanistan when a couple of AK rounds had done too much damage to repair.

That story came out late one night at the poker table behind the mechanic's shop, the one the tourists didn't go to, or even know about. As old soldiers tend to do when they were together and the whiskey flowed, the talk turned to war stories and battle scars. Scratch said they had been under heavy fire after multiple IEDs had trapped his convoy.

Even with his arm half blown off, the bone shattered to fragments, he was still able to man the .50 while the medic put on a tourniquet. That was one cool customer, Gunny had thought as he lost another forty bucks. But if his tales were coming from Alex Jones, then maybe they could be dismissed. Everybody knew Alex tended to add a lot of hyperbole to the facts, right? I mean, he was famous for all his conspiracy theories. He didn't talk about aliens or chupacabras. Mostly politics and corruption. And corrupt politics. So he had plenty to talk about.

As they headed to the diner, Scratch filled them in on what little he had heard. "People are acting weird, man. It all started a few days ago. It's like somebody spiked the water with bath salts, or Flakka, or Spice, or something. People are, like, eating peoples' faces. It's mostly in the big cities, but I read on the net that it's all over the place."

"Ahhh," Tiny said dismissively. "It's gotta be just hype, just another internet thing."

They passed the Missing Man table that was cordoned off with velvet ropes that Cobb had probably stolen from a bank somewhere, and they all fell quiet for a few paces. All three paying a silent tribute, in their own way, to the empty chair.

The small round table draped in a white linen cloth had

been there ever since Gunny had discovered this out of the way truck stop. When he first saw it, he knew he was at a good place. The chair at the table was empty, symbolizing all the soldiers who would never be coming home again.

The red rose in the vase was always fresh, never plastic. The lemon slice and the salt on the plate, representing bitterness and tears of the family, were changed twice a day by Martha herself.

There were a couple of Honor Boxes hanging on the wall. Cobb's dad's, Cobb's and his son Tommy's. The flags in them tightly folded into triangles, the medals proudly displayed.

If you knew how to read them, one look and you could tell the type of man you were dealing with. Old Cobb put on a crotchety and cantankerous attitude, a crusty old bastard who only cared about making money, but when you looked at his medals, the silver star, his purple hearts, his drill instructor's ribbon, it told a different story. A story of heroism and bravery. Of sacrifice for his fellow Marines.

If you watched him around his wife or grandkids, you saw the soft side of him. He might treat drivers like they were raw recruits on their first day at Parris Island sometimes, but he never barked at her.

Behind the Missing Man table, there were three rifles, bayonets affixed, muzzles down in a small rectangular plot of dirt with the period correct battle helmets perched atop the shoulder stocks.

There was an M1 Garand, an M-16 and an M-4, each representing their own era of American Fighting Men. Behind that, in a sturdy case against the wall, was a glass-fronted box half-filled with coins with "All proceeds go to the Veteran's" written across the front of it.

There was an O scale train track that ran right over the

top of the box and around the entire circumference of the diner, near the ceiling. It wound its way through the walls, into the main Quonset hut, and down to table level in an area near the arcade room.

Cobb had cleverly modified the trains to look like semi trucks and the tracks to look passably like roads. So instead of train yards modeled on the extensive tabletop layout, there were buildings and loading docks and model trucks and cars in the miniature town. He had built a funnel for pocket change on the loading docks so the children could drop in their coins.

When one of the semi trucks with the custom made hopper came by, it would trip the lever dumping the money into its trailer. The trucks ran in a continuous loop around the C-store and over the Missing Man table, where they would trigger the bottom release and dump their load of coins into the box for the Veterans.

The kids loved it. They followed their chosen truck around to watch it dump, squealing with delight, and ran back to parents asking for more change. The parents didn't mind, it kept the kids busy so they could browse and it was for a good cause.

Cobb liked it because it kept a steady stream of money coming into the box, and he gave it to where it was needed. Whether to the POW/MIA groups, the Wounded Warrior Project, or to some vet whom he knew needed a little help.

It was too early for the kids to be up and active, so the trucks rolled quietly by on their never-ending journey as they entered Martha's Diner.

Cobb's Vietnamese wife's real name wasn't Martha, though. When Gunny had asked Cobb what it really was one day, he growled out that he couldn't pronounce it and it sounded like Martha, so that's what her name was. And that

Gunny should mind his own business. And he should see the barber over in Driver's Alley 'cause he was looking mighty scruffy. And that his truck was dirty and he needed to take that rolling scrap heap around to the Truck Wash to get cleaned up some so as to quit disgracing his parking lot with it. Then he walked out of the diner, saying something to her in very fluent Vietnamese.

The café was already starting to fill up with the early birds. There were a few dozen people in the main dining area. Families with sleepy-eyed kids, or couples on scenic day trips up into the mountains. Guests from the Airbnb trucks. A group of cowboys at the counter drinking their coffee, a couple of bike riders wearing full leathers with their crotch rockets parked out front, getting ready to go carve up the mountain.

It was going on 7:30 and the "Professional Drivers Only" area was already half full with men working on their breakfast platters and bottomless cups of coffee, although the conversation was sparse. Gunny knew most of them by name, or at least their CB handles, and there were nods of acknowledgment and half raised coffee cup salutes as they made their way over to a booth by the windows looking out over the gas pumps.

They were a motley looking bunch, the men and women in the driver's area. They weren't scary looking men in an outlaw biker gang sense, but these were, indeed, some quietly hard men. Most were 40ish, calloused hands and laugh lines. Cowboy hats or steel toed boots. Jeans, of course. The type of men who held doors open for people, whether man or woman. Men who would say please and thank you and Ma'am.

Men who would apologize if they bumped into you at a crowded bar, or offer to buy you another drink if they spilled some of yours. But men whose hold on their bottle would innocuously go from a grip to sip beer, to a grip to wield a weapon, if you were unwise enough to push the issue into a confrontation. Men who wouldn't back down.

Owner operators, most of them. Men who owned their trucks and took pride in them. Spent money on extra lights and lots of chrome. These men hauled heavy and oversize, live cattle and swinging beef. They were the guys who strapped loads of steel with 100-pound tarps and logging chains in blistering July heat. They slung iron and rolled through the mountains on chained up tires when the snows were piling up and the other drivers were hunkered down in the truck stops.

Most were bearded, tattooed, and former military. Men who couldn't stand being cooped up in an office or warehouse. Men who wouldn't tolerate having a boss looking over their shoulder or telling them what to do. Some because that's just how they were built, some because they suffered varying degrees of PTSD and knew they were better off away from people, for the most part.

Men who got out of the service and couldn't hold down a normal job, so they turned to trucking. The career choice had probably saved a lot of marriages, also. A team of psychiatrists would have a field day, diagnosing them with everything from oppositional defiant disorder to excessive patriotic zeal.

America had been at war in the Middle East for over 20 years and nearly everyone that sat in the driver's area had done his time over there. They'd seen death up close and personal and now they knew the importance of living life, not just going through the motions.

They rode America's highways and saw what there was to see, getting off the four lane and onto the small roads whenever they could. These were the men who took the time to stop and help a stranded motorist change a tire or give them a ride to the gas station. Some of the older guys had even taken part in the Trucker Wars back in the 70s. They were the old school Knights of the Road, who tolerated all the new laws and regulations that came down every year when they were tolerable, and ignored them when they weren't. In short, they were men who could take care of business, and it didn't matter what that business might be.

The few ladies in the crowd were just as tough, if in a different way. They had to be in order to be accepted. Their nails weren't long and painted; their hair was usually short or in a ponytail. They had to be able to drive better than most men because when they pulled up to a dock, more often than not a small crowd would gather to watch them back in. Some expecting them to take five or six attempts to get it right so they could look at each other and smile knowingly.

G unny slid over against the window and Scratch plopped down beside him, leaving Tiny room to spread his bulk out on the other side of the booth.

"Check that out!" Scratch pointed out the window to a gleaming red Ferrari parked at the main entrance. "Man, I'm gonna have one of those someday."

"You gonna be as big an ass as he is?" Tiny asked. "He's in the handicap spot."

"Maybe he's got a dose of Affluenza," Scratch laughed back.

Gunny grabbed the menus slotted behind the condiments rack and passed them out, announcing, "I'm having the special, and I don't care what it is. It's always good."

The TV was usually muted, with the weather channel on, something that affected all of the drivers. Today the volume was up, not loud, but enough to be heard over the quiet clinking of silverware and coffee cups, and they turned to watch as they settled in.

It was a local channel, the Reno Morning Show, which usually didn't cover a lot of hard news. It was the early morning friendly banter, cooking tips, and today's weather show, with a healthy dose of celebrity gossip thrown in.

There was a banner running across the bottom of the screen stating 'viewer discretion is advised' and they kept using the same footage over and over of some extremely violent protesters or rioters attacking people. It was a long distance shot and shaky, but it got the point across.

It was brutal to watch and it left the three speechless for a few moments. When the show hosts came on again, they were talking about out of control gangs and police budget cuts, and whatever else they could come up with off the top of their heads when they really didn't know anything. The two local personalities seemed completely out of their depth, trying to cover something so deadly serious.

"Damn," Tiny said quietly. "You see that guy just body slam that girl? It had to break bones. That hurt me just watching it. I didn't take hits that hard when I played ball. And we had pads on."

"Yeah. That ain't normal," Scratch said.

"Why don't they have CNN or Fox on?" Gunny asked.

"The feed is out," Scratch said. "I asked the same thing when I was in here earlier. None of the cable channels are working."

Gunny fell silent, just watching the film loop and ignoring the chatter of the anchors and their guests. "You see that?" he asked suddenly, "Watch in the background, to the far left. See that body with the guts hanging out. That guy is dead. Has to be. Now watch."

The body was still as they stared at the TV, the camera fully zoomed in from a balcony overlooking the street from the looks of it. It was shaky, the operator obviously frightened. The main focus was of some guy in a suit jumping up from yet another bloody man writhing on the ground. He plowed into a screaming woman at full bore as hard as he could, knocking her out of camera view.

But in the corner of the frame, just for a scant second, the gutted man in the background started to sit up. The film ended abruptly and started looping again.

"Dude, that's whack! Why did they cut it there?!" Scratch demanded. "I'm telling you, man. Alex is right. They're covering something up!"

"It probably just got way too bloody, they can't show that stuff on TV," Tiny said. "It was rigor mortis, or something. Or somebody grabbing him. Folks with their insides hanging out don't sit up."

Kim-Li rattled a plate of toast and three cups down on the table and started filling them with from her coffee pot.

"You boys know what you want?" she asked, whipping out her order pad, her perky Midwestern accent a surprise to anyone who had never heard her speak before. Most people assumed she would sound like she looked. Vietnamese. "Hey, did you see Jimmy Winchell over there?" she continued, not giving them a chance to speak and obviously excited, pointing with her pencil to a handsome thirty-something cowboy sitting with a few of his friends at the counter.

"Well, I'll be," said Gunny. "He's on tour? Is he playing in Reno?" Quickly shifting mental gears from weird news footage to everyday small talk.

"I don't know, I can't ask him that," Kim said, slightly flustered.

It was obvious to all that she was crushing on him.

"Who's Jimmy Winchell?" Tiny and Scratch deadpanned.

"Tiny, you ain't got no excuse, I know you like country music and Scratch, well, your brain is melted from all that heavy metal screamo noise you listen to," she scolded them. "He's only the biggest country music star ever!"

"Bigger than Johnny Cash?" asked Scratch.

"Bigger than Charlie Pride?" Tiny joined in.

She gave them the stink eye and they bantered back and forth for a few minutes while she took their orders, then she was off to freshen up more coffee cups and take care of her other tables.

"Better not let Old Cobb catch you staring at his grand-daughter's ass," Tiny told Scratch.

"I wasn't," he quickly said, turning back to face the table. "I was checking out the Super Star."

"Uh huh," Tiny laughed.

Gunny sighed heavily and glared at his phone. When he felt them looking at him, he glanced up. "I can't get through. Was going to call home, see if the Mrs. has heard about any of this stuff down near us."

"Try texting," Scratch said while stuffing his face with buttered toast. "That is, if you know how. It will go through even when voice won't."

Gunny gave him the bird then opened the messenger app on his phone. He sent a quick note then got busy buttering his own toast.

Tiny grunted and set his phone down. "I can't get through either. Who's your carrier?"

"Verizon," Gunny said. "You?"

"AT&T," Tiny replied, opening a jelly packet. "I got plenty of bars, strong signal. The call won't go through, though. I'm getting an 'all circuits busy' message."

"I didn't even get that," Gunny said. "Just rang a few times and disconnected."

Scratch dug his phone out of his pocket and tried to call his dispatcher again, but also got nothing. "They don't pay me to sit around, I need to know what they want me to do," he said. "I'll run this freight in, I ain't worried. Some jacked-up crackhead tries to mess with me, he'll meet Mr. Hook." He snapped the claws on his left arm together quickly.

"What you gonna do, clap at him?" Tiny asked.

"Stick your finger in there and feel the clap," Scratch retorted, holding the ominous looking claw wide open.

"No thanks," Tiny said dryly. "Ol' lady would kill me if I came home with a case of V.D."

Gunny laughed, shook his head. "You walked right into that one," he said.

They passed the time waiting for their breakfasts, watching the looping newsreel and speculating about what was going on. They overheard snatches of conversation from other tables with the same questions and concerns they all had.

Gunny turned in the booth, addressing the next table over, "Hey, Firecracker. Did you just come up from the Shakey?" He knew the man had a dedicated route running raw cabinets from LA to Salt Lake City every week. He figured if there were madness going on, it would be heaviest down there.

"Yeah I did, Gunny. But there wasn't anything going on down there when I left yesterday. I mean, anything worse than normal," he amended. "That where you headed?"

"No, I'm going to the Gay Bay. This news has got me starting to get worried now. Wondering if it's safe to get in."

"Can't say, man, I'm headed to Salty City. Maybe check with Wire Bender, see if he has contact with anybody there."

"Good idea," Gunny said. "I'll check after grub. Thanks."

"That IS a good idea," Scratch chimed in. "When does he open up?"

Nobody wanted to drive into a city that was having riots in the streets and road closures from protesters. They all remembered Reginald Denny, the driver who was dragged out of his truck and pummeled mercilessly during the L.A. Riots years ago. All of it caught on film and played over and over again, until it was ingrained in every trucker. If a situation like that came up, lock the doors and hit the gas.

"He'll probably be open by the time we're finished eating," Tiny said. "He keeps early hours. Half the time, he just racks out on that cot he has set up in there."

Out of the window, they saw the County Sheriff's car pull past the gas pumps and into one of the parking spots in front of the building.

"Good, maybe he knows what's going on," Tiny said and heard the same thing chorused from a few of the other tables at the window. A lot of the drivers had tried their phones and only a few had gotten through. It was troubling, and the concern in the room was starting to ratchet up.

Kim-Li brought their plates over and passed them out, then started refilling their cups

"Hey, this ain't that Haji Bacon is it?" Scratch asked, eyeing it suspiciously. "You can take it back if it is, I ain't eating that crap."

Kim cocked her head and looked at him hard, never

spilling a drop going from one cup to the other with the steaming coffee pot.

"You forget where you're at, Scratch?" she asked. "You think Pawpaw would serve that here? And you owe a dollar to the cuss jar."

"What?" he spluttered. "Crap's not a cuss word!"

"That's two bucks, and yes, it is," she smiled sweetly. "Everybody's learned not to curse in here anymore, so we've expanded the unacceptable words list."

"Damn, that's extortion," Scratch said under his breath, digging out his wallet to put the money into her outstretched hand.

"Three bucks. Want to go for an even five?" she said, snapping her fingers. "I've got my eye on a new purse I need."

He just smiled grimly and made a zipping motion across his lips as Tiny and Gunny snickered at him. He held up his claw to them as she walked away and asked, "Guess which finger I'm holding up right now?"

The sheriff's deputy came in, looking a bit harried, and quickly walked up to the counter. Martha was behind it at the coffee urns, filling up another filter with fresh ground. She glanced over her shoulder and asked him in her accented English, "You want brak-fast?"

"Not today," he said. "Can you give me a dozen sausage and egg biscuits for the office? I've called everyone in and some of them just got off shift an hour ago."

Martha yelled back to Cookie, who manned the grill. "You hear?" she asked. "Chop chop! Make first!"

"Coming right up," he hollered back over the din of the sizzling griddle and the dirty dishes being loaded into the dishwasher.

Deputy Billy Travaho was a lean, rangy man. Sun

baked by the Nevada summers, his Shoshone tribal features were prominent. His jurisdiction in the county covered everything from just north of the densely populated Reno area, all the way up to the Oregon border. Nearly 6,000 square miles of sparsely populated and rugged terrain.

The sheriff took care of business in the cities of Reno and Sparks, south of them. Everything else Travaho ran as he saw fit from his office just a few miles from the Three Flags. It was a quiet job for the most part. The occasional domestic dispute, or marijuana operation up in the mountains. He had grown up just down the road from the truck stop, and old Cobb had given him his first job washing trucks when he was 14.

He knew about the illegal poker games in the back rooms. The working girls who sometimes drifted in, plying their trade among the truckers. He knew about the bare-knuckle cage fights in the junkyard that drew in the Reno crowds, where some pretty substantial sums changed hands. He knew the truckers used this route to get around the California inspection stations.

He knew all these things and a little more, but turned a blind eye. He usually didn't put too much effort into the little things. The deputy leaned his back on the counter, sipping the coffee Martha had brought over to him while he was waiting for his breakfast biscuits.

He recognized Jimmy Winchell sitting a few stools down and smiled at him. "Mr. Winchell," he exclaimed. "I saw the tour bus. Welcome to Nevada. You guys doing a show in Reno?"

Jimmy put on his patented "aw shucks" smile that had graced his platinum selling albums, stood and walked over to the deputy, holding out his hand. "Yes, sir," he said as they shook. "We have one this evening, but with all this craziness going on, do you know if they are shutting down big events? I can't seem to get through to our manager." He nodded his head at the phone lying on the counter top.

"I honestly don't know," Billy said. "I haven't heard anything like that yet, but we're just now starting to get reports of some attacks in Reno. I've called all of my deputies in and I should know more when I get to the office."

The entire diner was listening and a few drivers called out questions. "Have you heard anything about Sacramento?" "Are they shutting the highways down?" "Is it some kind of terrorist attack?"

Deputy Travaho held up his hands in front of him. "Hold on, fellas," he said. "I haven't heard anything except a few isolated reports from Reno. That's all my radio picks up. I won't know anything else until I get to the office. But as it stands right now, it's just a few incidences. Nothing to get too worked up about, and no, I don't know what is behind it all. Could be just a bad batch of Mexican drugs, or mass psychosis. Remember those German nuns back in the 15$^{th}$ century who started biting everybody?"

Nobody did, but a few of the drivers laughed at this. Some of them knew Billy from the old days, when he would wash their trucks and continually stump them with weird trivia questions.

Peanut Butter and Butter Cup were in a booth near the counter and the older of the two ladies, Peanut Butter, as the drivers all knew her, asked him if he'd heard anything about the governor declaring a state of emergency. And if he did, would trucks still be allowed on the roads. They had a load of livestock on, they couldn't wait for days for things to settle down. They didn't carry extra feed or water.

Again, Billy reiterated that he didn't really know

anything yet. He'd have someone call and let them know more once he got to the office. The conversations among the drivers started back up again and they speculated about things no one really had any answers to.

Tiny and Gunny turned back to their plates before their food got cold, Scratch was texting on his phone again. They heard a dull thumping sound before they looked up to see a blacked out Chrysler 300, complete with huge rims and skinny tires, pull up to the gas pumps closest to the building. The heavy thumping bass beat must have been deafening inside the car.

"Yo, I got 15s banging: they can beat a man up," Scratch rapped, throwing his best hand and claw gang signs.

Tiny just shook his head. "And he's gonna wonder why he gets pulled over," he said. "Disturbing the peace, if nothing else."

A skinny black man with braids and beads in his hair jumped out, nearly dancing to the beat, which continued on after he shut off the car and swiped his card to start fueling. He was wearing his saggy pants so low, most of his skinny rump and brightly colored underwear was showing. His gold chains, the sideways hat, the silver teeth and neck tattoos announced to the world he was ghetto and proud of it.

A white cargo van with ladders on the roof pulled into the last island and a couple of guys in paint-stained pants got out and stretched, started filling their own gas tank, ignoring the young black man dancing to his music.

Most of the drivers had noticed the ghetto gangster because of the thumping bass vibrating the windows of the diner, and were half-jokingly laying odds on how long till he got pulled over for driving while black. Gunny went back to his blueberry pancakes. He had better things to worry about.

The two motorcycle riders had finished their breakfast and had walked outside to their bikes, talking and strapping on their helmets.

"Going to be a good day for a ride," Gunny commented. "If Billy is bringing in all his deputies, they have the road to themselves."

Tiny harrumphed. "They can have it. You know they'll be running a hundred miles an hour through those curves. Gimme my old Harley any day. Slow and easy."

"Shit," Scratch said, quickly looking over his shoulder to make sure Kim hadn't heard. "They'll be going a hundred before they leave the parking lot."

The deputy had paid for his dozen breakfast biscuits and was trying to get out of the restaurant without being rude, but still trying to answer some of the questions, when Cobb stumped in and cut everyone off. "The man said he don't know nothin' more than what he's already told ya, so shut yer gobs and let him get out of here and do his job," he rasped.

Billy smiled and nodded his thanks, pushing open the door and walking into the C-store, headed for the main doors out to the parking lot.

The two motorcycle riders, fully kitted up with their helmets and leather gauntlets, took off out of the lot with a little too much throttle than was strictly necessary, anxious to start carving the winding mountain roads. Especially now that they knew the sheriff's department wouldn't be on patrol. It was going to be a glorious early fall day.

The bikes were running beautifully, the police presence was at a minimum, and the Go Pro cameras were turned on. What could possibly go wrong?

2

Sara, on her CBR, couldn't help but feel the awesomeness of the day coming on. Her riding buddy was on a GSX, a bike equal to hers. She had a full tank of gas, it was perfect fall weather, and there were a hundred miles of curves to conquer. She had been riding all her life, starting on mini bikes and dirt bikes when she was a kid growing up on the farm. As a woman, she had a hard time finding other females she could really tear up the roads with.

She knew plenty of girls that rode, even belonged to a group that would tool around on day trips, and they were fun, but none of the other girls she rode with liked to really rip through the mountain roads at 150. Most of them had probably never had their bikes much past the speed limit.

So she rode with guys. Most were cool after they saw that she knew how to handle her bike, it wasn't all just show. Today she was riding with a guy she had met at the bike shop. He seemed nice, wasn't pushy. Cute, too. She'd reserve judgment until she saw how he handled that big GSX, she thought.

She gave the throttle a quick blip and brought the front wheel up a foot or so, enjoying the feeling of power and control. Whatever the morons in the city were all worked up about didn't affect her in the least. She just wanted to ride. To lean hard and drag her knee through the twisties, to see the white dotted lines on the road become a solid blur when she hit 140 in the straights. To feel the scream of her engine between her legs. To hear...."*WHAT THE?*" was all she had time to think before she was tackled off her bike and slammed to the ground by a screaming woman in a house dress and a curious red blotch splashed all over the front of her flapping gown.

She had come out of nowhere it seemed, launching straight at her while her front wheel was still hanging two feet off the ground. The force of the impact ripped her off the bike, her hand twisting the throttle full to the stop as she flew backward with the gnashing and screaming woman tearing at her as they were flying through the air.

She was like a rabid dog, lunging at her face, scrabbling with her hands and feet to get up to her neck. Sara's bike wheeled the rest of the way up and over as they left it, and she heard the instant revs of the engine to 10,000 rpms and back down again. Heard the crunch of breaking plastic as it slammed onto the asphalt, sliding toward the high desert scrub on the side of the road.

They hit the road hard, Sara's helmeted head bouncing and her Kevlar-lined leathers rasping across the blacktop and into the sand. She wasn't hurt by the fall, just stunned and trying to wrap her head around the fact that she had just been body slammed at 40 miles an hour, while riding a wheelie, by a raving lunatic. The leathers and helmet were designed for things like this... well, not exactly like this, but for taking an impact with an unforgiving surface and allowing the wearer to walk away unscathed.

The crazy lady didn't slow down one bit when they finally stopped sliding, just attacked with more ferocity than ever, snapping her jaws, raking her already broken fingernails over her leather, trying to find something human to sink her teeth into. She was all knees and elbows and fingers, everywhere, all at once.

Sara felt panic racing through her head. This schizoid kept trying to bite into her face and neck, but the helmet and support collar she wore wouldn't let her. Did she scream? Probably. She tried to push the flailing woman off, but she was like an octopus, my God, how many arms and legs did she have?

She was all over her, roaring in her face, bashing her teeth against the helmet trying to get at her. She could see her nose break, up close and in bloody 3D, as she once again smashed into her faceplate. Her hands pulled and clawed at Sara's jacket. Every time she managed to push her away she came back in, twice as vicious. A pulling, grasping woman-thing trying to tear through the leather and padding of the one-piece suit she wore. Sara knew she screamed that time, and mindless survival adrenaline kicked in.

A blind urgency to get this thing off of her overrode everything else. She no longer saw her as the 100-pound Mexican woman, maybe on drugs, maybe just crazy. She saw a monster trying to eat her face, she saw childhood nightmares had become real.

Her fight or flight animal brain engaged and she started punching the woman in the side of her head with her carbon fiber reinforced leather knuckles. She struggled and tried to roll her off, but the madwoman's strength was unreal, she ignored Sara's bashing on the side of her head and sank her teeth into the neck collar again, this time getting a solid mouthful and shaking her head back and forth like a dog with a blanket. The collar ripped clear of her neck, the Velcro fasteners coming free.

Sara's blind terror ratcheted up another notch. She had to get this thing OFF! The next lunge would tear her throat wide open. She got a handful of the woman's flying black hair as she spit out the neck collar, but the leather of her gloves was slick, not doing a very good job of holding her head back, they were slipping and she was lunging with inhuman strength.

The banshee saw the unprotected skin of her throat and screamed again, diving in to tear it open. Then Brian was there, ripping off his helmet and using it as a weapon. He smashed it into the side of her head at a full run and a crushing swing, hopping over the two flailing bodies as it dove for Sara's neck.

With the momentum of the devastating head blow and her own adrenaline-jacked strength, Sara was finally able to shove her off and scrambled to her feet, breathing hard, her eyes finding Brian's, both of them with stunned looks on their faces.

"What the fuck!" Brian yelled "Dude... what the actual fuck?" he whispered, almost to himself, staring dazedly at the blood splatter on his helmet. Sara was starting to get the shakes. She looked over at the inert body of the slim Hispanic girl, sprawled where she had fallen. Her head was caved in on one side, blood trickling out of her nose and mouth into the sands. Grayish bits poking out of the crack in her skull.

"Oh man. Oh man. Oh man," he whispered. "Oh man. I didn't mean to kill her, Sara." He sat down abruptly, like his legs had just come unhinged.

"It was self-defense, Brian. She was trying to rip my throat out," she said unevenly, trying to get her breath back, her hands shaking as the adrenaline fled her system.

"It was all so fast..." he said. "I mean, the way she took you off your bike... It looked like she was trying to eat you. I didn't mean to kill her."

"Maybe she's not dead," she said, a quaver in her voice, and started to walk over to her to see if there was anything she could do, but stopped after only a step. Her head was crushed. Horribly misshapen. Her brains were leaking out.

Sara was an EMT for Saint Mary's Regional in Reno and she knew dead when she saw it. That poor woman was definitely dead. She looked away, flipping up her visor and breathing deeply to get fresh air before she got sick. She was used to seeing blood and the aftermath of violence in her job, but not used to having any of it perpetrated on herself.

She looked instead at her bike. It was laying on its side a few feet off of the road and she started toward it, trying to clear her head. She had to step away; her stomach was really churning around the sausage and eggs she'd eaten.

The back of the truck stop they had just left was still visible, only a few hundred yards down the road. This was all so surreal. They would have to get that cop that was there, explain what happened. They hadn't meant to hurt her, everything happened so fast. Surely they wouldn't get arrested for this. It was an accident, and that girl had been seriously whacked out of her gourd.

Brian looks messed up. Geez, is he crying? Maybe he's going into shock. All these thoughts, and more, were rattling through her head as she picked up her Fireblade. It was a big bike and heavy, but she stood it back up the way she had learned years ago, using her legs, and checked the damage. It still looked rideable, just some of the plastic scratched and cracked. The sand had saved it from any real damage.

She wondered if it would start. She'd never laid a fuel-injected bike down before. She knew from riding old dirt bikes, growing up on the farm in Idaho, that they were hard to start once you laid them down. You would have to kick it over a few dozen times to get the carburetor primed and working right once you fell off after trying something stupid.

She looked over at Brian as she pushed the big Honda back onto the asphalt. He seemed out of it, just sitting there in the sand at the side of the road with his head down. Could they really had been enjoying breakfast just a few minutes ago? A lifetime had happened in the span of time it took to watch a few commercials on TV.

"Brian," she said, but stopped when she heard an eerie, quiet, howling behind her. She jerked her head around, thinking, *"God, there can't be another one..."*

But there was. Two of them, running at full speed straight toward them, coming from a mobile home that was set back into the high desert at the end of a long unpaved driveway. They looked like kids, maybe ten or twelve, still in their pajamas.

"Brian!" she screamed this time, jabbing at the starter button of her bike. Nothing happened, not even a click. *"Shit, shit, shit!"* the front part of her mind screamed while the more rational part yelled, *"Neutral safety, idiot!"* She swung her leg over, pulled the clutch lever and jabbed the button again in a single, practiced, motion and the bike fired to life.

"Brian!" she yelled again. "We gotta go! There's more of them!"

The rational and thinking part of her brain was trying to

come up with a reason why this was happening. The woman had maybe been zonked on Spice or something, but kids? No way. But there they were, tearing across the scrub-covered sands, heedless of the thorny bushes shredding their feet, hands outstretched and as crazy as the woman had been. Meth Lab gone bad? Homemade PCP disaster?

The survival part of her brain was saying, *"Who gives a shit, get the hell outta here!"* She turned to look at her newest friend, whom she'd only known for a few weeks. The guy she thought was cute and had admired his bike. The guy who had just saved her life.

He was still just sitting there beside the dead woman, staring at the sand between his legs. Is it shock? The two kids were fast. How could they be so quick? They were at a full sprint, but faster. No time to get Brian's bike picked up and started. She yelled again, "Brian! Get on, man. Get on! They're coming!"

This time Brian looked up from the ground and saw Sara shooting over toward him, fear on her face. He saw the two kids coming straight for them, running right through cactus and tumbleweeds, not even noticing the damage it was doing to their bare feet. He jumped up and started to run away from them, blind panic pushing his body to flee, not even hearing Sara's screams for him to get on the back of the bike.

The truck stop loomed in the distance.

It would be safe there.

He had to get inside.

That cop was there.

He would help him.

He would know what to do.

He had to get there.

So he ran like he was back in high school, running

sprints. No thought of getting his motorcycle. No thought of just hopping on the back of Sara's bike. Pure, blind, terror. He had seen what that woman did, tearing into Sara like she was some mad demon.

He couldn't take that.

No way.

Those two little monsters weren't going to do that to him.

He had to run.

He had to make it to the restaurant.

He had to get inside.

He ran, arms pumping, feet pounding the pavement, blind to anything else except the safety of the truck stop.

Back to the diner.

Back to people.

Back to that cop.

Sara rode up beside him, yelling, "Get on! Get on!" But it was useless. Brian was in full panic mode. Sara looked back at the kids. They seemed to be gaining ground, but they were only about a hundred yards to the corner of the truck stop. Maybe another fifty to the entrance doors. She did some nano-fast calculations. Brian could make it if he kept the speed up.

Without another second's thought, she twisted the wick and leaned into it, keeping the front tire firmly on the ground. She was up to 80 miles an hour and then hard on the binders, leaning into the parking lot. As she shot toward the front doors, she locked the brakes, then let the bike crash to the ground once she had slowed enough to hop off and into a full run.

The cop was there, just coming out of the door with a bag full of biscuits, and watched in stunned amazement as the pretty little biker with the form fitting leathers threw her bike down. Sara ran toward him, yelling and waving her arms, past the shocked faces of everyone looking out the windows of the diner.

Billy Travaho reacted quickly, the bag of biscuits fell to the ground. One hand dropped down to the butt of his gun and unsnapped the safety strap in one fluid motion. The other halfway across his chest, ready to go into a two handed shooter's stance, if need be. The kid was yelling something and pointing back the way she had come.

Had the other rider already crashed his bike? Did they need an ambulance? But when his eyes darted back up the road the way the kid was pointing, he saw the other biker running like his hair was on fire and a couple of Mexican kids chasing after him.

He relaxed his hand on the gun, letting it slide back down into the holster. Something was wrong, that was evident, but not deadly force wrong. But all the same, he didn't snap the safety strap back into place.

The music from the Chrysler was still blasting, and Billy couldn't make out what the girl was yelling. Dead woman, drugs, kids trying to kill them...

The other biker had just rounded the corner of the building and was tearing across the parking lot toward them. He looked like he was running for his life, Billy mused, taking in the big picture, assessing possible threats like he'd been trained to do at the academy. Right now, it looked like his biggest threat was the two bikers. Something was wrong with them. Had they accidentally killed a woman down the road? Caused a wreck? The biker that had ridden in was close enough now that Billy could hear her over the racket coming from the Chrysler's over-amplified sound system.

"The kids!" she was yelling and gesticulating wildly, "The kids are trying to kill us!"

Billy heard this, but couldn't process it. The two little tweenagers, still in their pajamas, were trying to kill somebody? It was laughable. But this was no prank. The fear in this woman's face was real. And she had just dropped a $10,000-dollar bike on the ground like it was her brother's ratty old Schwinn.

The young biker still had her helmet on and it looked like there was blood on the visor. Billy was trying to understand her, but the words just didn't compute. The kids were on drugs. The kids were dangerous. The kids were crazy. The kids were trying to kill them.

He put a hand up and started to say, "Just calm down and tell me what happened, " but the words didn't even get a chance to form on his lips. He was looking at the other running biker and watched in disbelief as the little girl sprang at him from at least 10 feet away, landing on his back and driving him down into the asphalt.

The girl was snarling like an animal, and the man who fell was screaming through a bloodied face. She tore into his neck with savagery more befitting a fighting dog, than anything human. Gouts of blood shot out as she tore a chunk of meat from the back of his head, ripping away a strip of his hair with it.

At the same time, the other kid, a boy of no more than 10 or 11, had veered off toward the gas island and was aiming straight for one of the painters standing next to the cargo van. The kid didn't even slow the slightest, just tackled the dumbfounded man to the ground and started biting at his face.

Billy had his gun out of the holster and was running

toward the little girl, who was going in for another bite, ignoring the flailing hands of the man on the ground.

His mind was racing, *"I can't shoot from here, she's moving too fast, and the way he's thrashing around I'd probably put the bullet in him. Shoot a little girl? I can't kill a little girl."*

He wished he had a Taser, but his department didn't carry them.

"Get inside!" he bellowed, to no one in particular, and everyone in general. "Get in the building!" It was the only place he could think of for safety until he could figure out what the hell was going on.

As he ran up to the struggling pair on the ground, intending to pull her off, she sprang at him, arms fully outstretched, aiming for his face. Her mouth flew wide open, a chunk of flesh torn from the biker falling aside, ready to tear into him. Billy realized too late he was in trouble. She would be on him before he could level his gun. She plowed into him, her uncannily powerful legs propelling her the distance between them, and she was gnashing and clawing at his eyes instantly.

He managed to get his off arm between them as he fell over backward and she clamped her jaws down on it, instead of his face, but she didn't seem to care. She ravaged it with abandon, shredding open the shirt sleeve and digging her incisors all the way to the bone. He yelled in surprise and pain and brought his service revolver up to her side, just below the rib cage, and pulled the trigger twice.

Reaction, not thought. Years of training, muscle memory, and redundancy without thinking.

He heard other shots going off, over near the gas island. The rapid fire sound of someone with an automatic, and trying to empty the magazine from the sounds of it. He expected the little girl to go limp, to fly off his arm from the impact of the two .357 hollow point rounds blasting into her at point blank range.

She didn't even register the slugs, other than a jerking of her body. She dragged her head back and forth, trying to tear the chunk of flesh from his arm, ignoring the little holes in her left side and the two gaping holes in her right, from the bullets' exit. He was on his back, her on top, his arm in agony and he could hear himself screaming at her. Incoherent nothing words of rage and pain.

He was bringing the revolver back up again to empty it into her when he saw a heavy work boot connect with the side of her head, breaking her jaw and her hold on him. She tumbled off, but was back on all fours, turning to attack again, crouched to spring, spittle and teeth flying from her broken mouth. Billy shot her in the face and she dropped like a sack of potatoes. He turned to see who had kicked the girl off of him.

Gunny was in a protective stance over him holding out a hand, palm toward him, in a "be still" gesture. In the other he held a black pistol, covering the area over by the gas pumps where he was intently staring.

## 3

Gunny had been in the diner finishing up his breakfast as Old Cobb had basically told everybody to shut the hell up so the deputy could leave. He watched the bikers pull out and smiled as he saw the girl on the Honda goose it a little and bring the front wheel up as they went out of view past the end of the building.

"Cool," Scratch said. "I wonder if I could rig a bike up to work with this hand somehow." He held up his hooks and examined them, turning them, thinking of some way he could modify the artificial limb to work a clutch lever.

Gunny thought for a minute then said, "You could always hook both brakes up to the foot pedal, put the clutch over on the right side."

"How would I give gas then?" Scratch asked.

"Lord, Gunny. Don't encourage the boy," Tiny rumbled. "He'll wind up losing his other arm."

Scratch ignored him. "Do they make automatic bikes?" he asked. "I wonder if I could get Kim to go riding with me."

"Boy, when are you gonna work up the nerve to just ask her out?

39

You two been dancing around each other for months," Tiny said.

"I don't know, I will. Just waiting for the right time," Scratch mumbled, looking almost embarrassed, very unlike his usual bombastic self.

Tiny knew what the problem was. The arm. Scratch carried on like he didn't care, like his mechanical arm was better than the old one he had. Like nothing bothered him. Tiny knew Kim didn't care about it, or he was pretty sure she didn't, but you can't tell a young buck things like that. Tiny didn't have the words. No one did. It was a thing Scratch just had figure out for himself.

He looked over at Gunny, saw he was staring at something out of the window. The gal on the Honda was flying back into the parking lot, hell bent for leather. She let the bike just fall over as she jumped off and ran to the front of the building. "What the..." Scratch started, then trailed off.

Tiny turned in his seat to get a better view of what was going on, as were some of the others in the booths. The girl was running wildly toward Billy, arms flailing and pointing back toward the road. She was yelling something, but no one could hear over the constant thump, thump, thump of the bass pounding out a steady beat.

Gunny saw the other biker come around the corner of the building in a full sprint, two ragged looking kids in pajamas screaming after him, arms outstretched. They all watched in horror as the little girl leaped like a leopard taking down prey.

Watched her land on the man's back and drive him into the ground, then tear a chunk of flesh out of his neck, spraying blood and ripping skin. All actions ceased.

Martha's eyes were wide as she stopped in mid-pour of a coffee at the counter. The diner went silent, only the muted droning of the TV and vibrations of the bass in the windows. Forks of food and cups of java held in limbo, halfway to the mouth. The country musicians at the counter had spun on their stools and like everyone else, just stared, dumbfounded.

A mother had covered her child's eyes. It was like a snapshot, everything frozen in time except for the splash of coffee overflowing the cup being poured by Martha. Then a plate shattered on the floor, dropped from Kim-Li's hand. That was the catalyst that broke the spell. Somebody yelled out, "Charlie's in the wire!" As Scratch bellowed at the top of his lungs, "Hajji at the gate!"

These both were triggers, deeply ingrained in many of the men there, and movement was instantaneous and unthinking. They both meant the same thing, from two different generations of warriors. They both meant death was right here, right now and if you didn't want it to be you, you'd better move right this instant.

No hesitation.

No consideration.

Move or die.

Those words demanded action. Those words meant the bullets were about to fly, the bombs were about to explode and if you faltered for even a second, it would be you the Captain would be writing home to your loved ones about.

Old Cobb's drill sergeant voice came booming out as he sprinted to the missing man table, and the three rifles with their bayonets in the dirt, "Secure the perimeter!"

Booths were emptied. Chairs tipped over backward as men jumped to their feet, old habits and training springing to the front of their minds, no matter how many years it had been since they had last heard a Sergeant's bellowed orders.

Cobb's was the voice of command that would not be

ignored, a ringing voice that filled the vast spaces of the Quonset hut, drowning out all others.

"Kim, on the roof!" he roared, grabbing the Garand and tossing it to her as she came running over. "Pick your targets, only 8 rounds." He grabbed the M-4 and threw it to Scratch as he flew by, already out of the booth and at a full run, close on Gunny's heels.

"Front door!" he said and Scratch grabbed it with his good hand, never breaking stride. Cobb glanced around quickly, at the men in his diner, taking in everything with a well-seasoned eye. Many had guns in their hands, pointed at the floor, facing out, searching for danger. For targets. They were unsure of exactly what to do, but ready to do it, whatever it was, now that old Cobb had established command.

"Griz, Jellybean, get down to the shop, secure the doors," he barked out at the two men closest to him that were armed.

They took off at a sprint.

Peanut Butter had her pink Lady Smith 9mm drawn and Cobb yelled at her to go wake up Wire Bender, make sure no one in the parking lot got out of their trucks. He sent others out to rouse the sleepers in the Airbnb trucks.

Cobb had an eye on the parking lot during all this and saw the painter go down under the assault from the pajama-clad kid. He'd watched Billy Travaho put two rounds in the little girl, and Gunny boot her in the face, and all it did was piss her off. He didn't know what was happening, but he knew there was going to be some more killing going on.

The trouble from the cities had come to the high desert. Old habits came back instantly. Stay alive first, figure it out later.

"You two, front door with Scratch," he pointed out two

more men he saw had their side arms drawn and ready. "Martha, lock the back door!" he yelled over to the counter, where she had returned after seeing her granddaughter climb the ladder in the back of the kitchen to the roof.

Most of the civilians, as Cobb thought of them, were still at their tables, staring in disbelief at what was going on. At all of these nice truckers suddenly running around with guns like it was a war zone. Wasn't it against the law to just carry a gun around willy nilly? They had seen the attacks, the blood, and the viciousness. But the police should handle these drug addicts, not a bunch of armed truck drivers.

"Someone dial 911!"

"Has anyone dialed 911?" they asked each other.

Mothers soothed crying children, frightened by the shouting, who didn't know what was going on, but felt the tension and fear in the air.

Cobb didn't know what it was, what was happening, why little kids would attack like he had just seen. But like some of the other combat vets in this room, he remembered children with grenades in Vietnam, and children with suicide vests in the Middle Eastern wars. *"Better safe than sorry,"* he was thinking. *"Better too much than not enough."*

He had known a lot of the truckers carried, had seen the printing of their various firearms over the years against their untucked shirts. Knew they were a breed apart and tended to ignore the rules, or bend the laws. Men who had seen shots fired in anger, and never wanted to be defenseless.

A balding man stood up and tried to make his voice heard over the din of the others in the dining area, over the crying children and frightened voices of women. "See here, all these guns are scaring people," he said. "Is all this really necessary? Someone should just call the police."

Other voices chimed in and Cobb heard things like

"overreaction" and "must think they're back in a war zone" and "PTSD."

Cobb glanced at him briefly and dismissed him as unimportant to the mission right now. That was to make sure those kids, or whoever sent them to attack, didn't get inside his building. That was number one priority. Nothing else mattered. He racked the bolt on the M-16 clone and stepped into the main building, hurrying for the front doors.

4

L ong Dawg was doing it right. The bass was pumping, his fingers were jumping. He was gassing up the Whip for the last time today. The long night's drive would be over soon, the run up from his home turf in LA was just about finished.

Obeying all the traffic laws, cruise control set three miles an hour over the speed limit. Everything was going according to plan, and no one had screwed anything up. This was it. The big one. The score that would get him out of the mean streets and onto easy street. It had taken him long years to get this far.

Careful planning, slow climbing, trust building. Learning to speak enough Nahau to communicate with the farmers when he was a translator down in El Salvador for Uncle Sugar. Knowing the right people, saying the right things, being cautious in a world where you could lose your head, or wind up in prison doing hard time for even the smallest of mistakes.

Loose lips sink ships, as they say. He wasn't a dealer, he was a business man and he only dealt with other business men. Supply and demand. He had spent every dime he had on this run. His bank was dry.

If something went wrong and he lost the shipment, he wouldn't even be able to afford a pack of smokes in jail, let alone hire a decent attorney. He wasn't a mule. He wasn't carrying for somebody else. This score was all his. All the risk, all the profit. Go big or go home, right?

Three hundred and sixty pounds of the finest and purest uncut, unmolested, cocaine money could buy. Close to three million dollars, in unmarked Benjamin's, would be his in a few more hours.

He had started with 500 pounds, gotten at great risk and great expense from contacts he had made in Comalapa when he was stationed there. But paying the fees, and sharing the wealth with the right people, ensured it got to him unscathed. Don't get greedy. A night time boat ride around Guatemala and into Mexico. A long drive up through the country and dozens of trips back and forth with his drones out in the middle of nowhere.

Then it was into LA, where he recruited his best friend and cousin to help him with the final phase of the plan. Now, finally, almost to where the man with the briefcases full of money was going to meet him. A man Long Dawg had been doing business with for years now, and a man he trusted. A man who wouldn't double cross him because he was under the impression that Long Dawg would do this again next year when the new crop came in.

But this was it for him. One and Done. Three million was enough to retire on, if he was smart. He wanted out of this life. Wanted out of South Central LA. Wanted his mom to not have to struggle anymore. He wanted a good neighborhood, a place near the water, maybe get his Car Audio business started.

It was a good plan. A perfect plan. A solid plan that had contingencies for contingencies. A plan he had begun working on when the Army had sent him to a remote little drug intervention place down in El Salvador, simply because he was fluent in Spanish. When he showed up, nobody knew what to do with him because they were expecting a Hispanic guy who could blend in.

Long Dawg did not blend in.

They assigned him to a desk, told him to keep out of the way, so he did. Drew his check each month and tagged along with some of the CIA guys and Rangers when they went out on drug raids. Some of it got pretty hairy, but he learned the native farmers' language, he'd always had a knack for picking up things like that. When he went back after his time with the Army was up, he started making deals. Started doing a little business.

He looked up from the gas pump he was bobbing at and saw a roaring little Mexican kid smash into Mario, standing in front of the van, driving him down on the concrete.

The plan! No!

"Mario!" he yelled, just standing there, pump nozzle in his hand.

The kid tore into Mario's screaming face and ripped a great chunk of his cheek off. His fingers and thumb stabbed into Mario's eyes and deep into the sockets for something to give him a firm grip to hold on with as he tore the flesh loose. Mario batted at him ineffectually, blinded and screaming incoherently. Long Dawg's cousin was at the back of the van, pumping the gas and he yelled out also. The kid sprung at him. SPRUNG AT HIM, like Spiderman or something, and they disappeared out of sight behind the painter's van, Jimmy screaming as loud as Mario had.

Long Dawg's seconds of hesitation were over. He pulled his Beretta and ran past Mario, who was still screaming, or trying to, with all the blood clogging his throat and half his face missing. He rounded the back of the van, maybe he could save Jimmy from that crazy little bastard. But what he saw stopped him in his tracks.

Jimmy wasn't yelling because he had no throat. The kid was ripping at it, blood was spraying, a long white.... some-thing.... in his teeth as he jerked around and looked straight into Laurence's eyes.

Long Dawg was gone. Mamma's little Laurence stood there looking at a horror he had never even imagined in his worst nightmares. Not even the ones where he was back in South America that woke him up in sweats and night terrors, images of Cartel mutilated bodies fresh in his mind again.

The kid sprang at him and the Beretta answered. The 9mm rounds peppered the kid as fast as he could pull the trigger, sending him sprawling backward a step with each impact, keeping him dancing and upright. The fifteen rounds were down the pipe and the slide locked back in seconds, the kid finally slumping to the ground near Jimmy's still form.

Laurence stared through the gun smoke curling up from the end of the barrel at something that just could not be.

It couldn't. But it was.

The kid wasn't dead. He had just emptied a full mag into him, Laurence knew most of them hit, hell it was nearly point blank. He saw the kid's body jerking like he was being electrocuted, but he... it.... was still trying to crawl toward him. He could see chunks of his backbone sticking out where at least one of the rounds had shattered it. There wasn't even that much blood, just the big holes in the kid's pajamas.

Long Dawg started backing up. He had heard the cop scream for everybody to get in the building, and had seen the old white guy jump back into his minivan and smoke his tires as he sped away from the pumps. He looked around, stunned to indecision, not knowing what to do first. Mario was still moaning, but Jimmy looked dead. The little kid was still trying to crawl toward him, the cop was screaming like he was being eaten, too, and the damn little kid was still coming at him.

Mario was a mess, trying to stand. The cop said every-body get in the store. He couldn't leave in his car, he needed to get the van out of here. The van had the coke in it, disguised in paint cans. And that damn little kid was getting closer. He turned to run to Mario, but some beardy ass trucker was there helping him up, yelling at Long Dawg.

"What?"

"Turn that shit off" he bellowed at him, a wave of his gun at Long Dawg's Chrysler, supporting Mario on his other arm. Laurence looked at him then at his car. "*Right,*" he thought. "*Right.*"

"*The music.*

*Turn it off. So we can hear.*"

He didn't particularly like it so loud, anyway, it was just all part of the plan to draw any attention away from the van and onto him.

He looked back at the kid still crawling toward him, with its broken back and one shattered arm and fifteen bullet holes in him.

The trucker had noticed and was staring at it with his head cocked to one side, like he was trying to figure out what the hell he was looking at. Laurence ran to his car and hit the stereo remote, silencing the thundering subwoofers instantly. The quiet was worse.

He could hear the rasping and hissing of the thing as it doggedly kept coming at him. He grabbed a spare mag out of his console and jacked it in, letting the slide go home, but before he could shoot it another 15 times, the trucker loosed one round to its forehead and it dropped.

Still and silent at last.

Mario was blubbering now, holding his hand over the missing parts of his face, his blind eyes squished and running down his one cheek. Laurence felt ill. His head was light. He leaned back against the car, afraid he was going to pass out.

"Just breathe," the trucker told him. "I need you in the game. This ain't over yet."

Across the parking lot from where the big rigs were parked, a man was looking toward them. It was obvious he had come from the trucks to see if he could help, but had just stopped in place, unsure whether to continue or run back to the safety of the parking lot when the shooting had started. It had all happened so fast. A minute or two. No more.

He stood there, a big tire thumper club in his hand and yelled over, "What's going on?"

Gunny ignored him. "Here," he said to Long Dawg. "Come here. Help me with this guy. You know him?"

"Yeah. He's blood, " he paused, wincing at his choice of words. "Yeah, I know him."

"There's a doctor's office in the truck stop, get him back there, somebody can try to get the bleeding stopped," Gunny said, handing him off to the skinny black man and getting them started walking. "I'll check on that other guy," but he had seen the death rattle in the man's feet as they protruded out from behind the van. He knew that shake. He'd seen it before. There wasn't anything he could do. He looked back toward the entrance of the truck stop, where everything had just started a minute ago.

Cobb had come out and was helping the bleeding biker back into the shop, hustling him toward Doc's little office in Driver's Alley. The girl that had been on the big Honda had wrapped something around the deputy's arm, and with a couple of the other truckers' help, they were headed back inside.

He saw Scratch with an M-4 at the front door, holding it open for them, waving the black kid and that poor guy with his eyes gouged out, to hurry up. Gunny gave his head a rueful half shake. Who woulda thunk it? Ol' Cobb's gun decorations weren't just decorations, after all.

"Watch out!" Kim-Li yelled from the catwalk on top of the main Quonset hut and pulled the Garand up to her shoulder.

Gunny followed her line of sight and saw the man who he had just watched die bounding across the parking lot. The trucker with the tire thumper was no longer in a state of indecision.

When he saw a man with a ripped open neck, wearing a white pair of painter's overalls splattered in blood, bounding towards him using hands and feet like an animal, he turned and ran. The safety of his truck was close, he could see it idling in the quiet September morning and he didn't know exactly what was happening, but he knew he didn't want any part of it. He ran.

But not fast enough.

Gunny took off after them, but knew he would be too late to do any good. There were other truckers he could see, peering out of their windshields, having been awoken by all the gunfire. A few of them took in the situation instantly and reacted just as quickly. "*No!*" Gunny thought as he ran. "Stay in your truck!" he yelled, but knew they wouldn't hear him over the idling diesels. They didn't know the situation. They hadn't seen what he had just witnessed. They only saw some thug chasing down one of their own. And that just wouldn't do. Their good hearts were going to get them killed.

He couldn't take a shot at the painter, it was too far for his pistol and a fast moving target. He wished Kim would fire, but knew the angle was wrong, she might hit the fleeing trucker.

Or maybe she couldn't force herself to shoot a man. She was just a kid. She was a great shot, had the trophies to prove it, but paper targets just weren't the same. She hadn't seen the man die, he had been under the fuel island canopy. She didn't have all the facts. Nobody did but him. And he still didn't know shit. Just what his eyes had seen and even though his logical mind was screaming in protest, his battle mind was coldly processing everything. It was coming to a conclusion that was impossible. Didn't matter. He was acting on it until proven wrong.

Bootleg DVD sellers you thought were friendly's, that had IEDs in their boxes, was impossible to imagine, until it happened. Little kids you had just given a candy bar stabbing you in the belly with a dirty knife was impossible, until it happened.

Mothers strapping bombs to their 8-year-olds sending them laughing and smiling into the middle of your team was impossible, until it happened.

And zombies were impossible, until it happened

# 5

The truck driver almost made it to his rig before he was brought down in a heap, sliding on the gravel, screaming in fear, pain and panic. He turned and tried to fight using his tire thumper and the other drivers were there almost instantly, pulling at the bloody painter.

But they didn't know what they were dealing with. They had brought a pool noodle to battle a Nuclear Armada, in Gunny's mind. The painter was a whirling dervish, biting, ripping, tearing, not caring who he bit, only that he bite to draw blood. To taste the sweetness of man's flesh. By the time Gunny had crossed the parking lot to kick it square in the face, knocking it off of the man on the ground, the other four had already drawn away. They were in a state of disbelief at the ferocity of the attack, all of them with gashes and bites. Deep scratches and chunks of flesh missing from arms and legs.

The thing on the ground wasn't finished, but it was stunned, if only a little. Gunny kicked out again, his heavy boot bouncing its head on the wheel of the rig the driver had been trying to climb into. Then he stomped down hard on its neck as the head hit the gravel and held it long enough to put a 9mm round into its snarling face. Gore splashed out of the back of its head and it went still instantly. The other drivers stared at him, all of them breathing hard, stunned looks on their faces.

"What...?" one of them started to ask, but couldn't finish the thought.

They were all bleeding, breathing deep. A little shell shocked in the quiet rumble of the big diesel beside them and the sound of Wire Bender shouting over the CB. "Stay in your trucks!" He was yelling. "And somebody blow your horn to wake everybody else up!"

There was a cacophony of sound as a dozen trucks blasted air and train horns. Some of them had just witnessed what had happened and the radio lit up with chatter, everyone talking over everybody else.

"What... "the man started again. "What the hell's going on?" He was bleeding freely from a set of nasty looking scratches across his bare chest, one of his nipples was nearly torn off.

"Zombies," Gunny panted.

The four of them stared at him. It was too unreal to be true. To unreal not to be true. Gunny knew two of them, the others he may have seen in passing. He couldn't recall.

The man on the ground was moaning and holding his chest that was bleeding through his fingers. He had half a dozen bites on him. Gunny stepped off the dead painter and put a little distance between him and the men.

"Hold on," Ozzy said. "Zombies?"

"Bullshit." one of the drivers Gunny couldn't quite place said. "No such thing. Hopped up on Angel Dust is a better guess."

"Open your eyes. Look." Gunny pointed to the

painter, to his ripped open neck that was missing half of the throat and larynx. "I don't care how many drugs you do, you don't get up and try to eat people after that happens to you. And I just saw that guy pumping gas. He was normal. Until he was killed by that little Mexican kid."

He was trying to explain. Trying to reason it out in his own head. Trying to figure out if what he was saying was even possible, let alone true. "I saw that kid take fifteen rounds to the chest and still try to bite me," he said. He was waiting for someone to play Devil's Advocate. Someone to tell him that he was wrong. That the black kid had missed all those times. That what you saw, you didn't really see. But no one did.

Gumball looked like he was going to hurl. He was taking deep, slow breaths and all the color had drained out of his face. "I got bit," Ozzy said. "Does that mean I'm supposed to turn into a zombie?" he asked, eyeing the Glock in Gunny's hand.

"I don't know," he replied. "All I know is what I see. You saw it, too." He ran his hand through his sandy blonde hair that was getting too long again, curling just above his collar. They were all staring at him. It was hard to think straight with all the noise. Some ass was still blowing his air horn, trucks were firing up, and everybody's radios were cranked up loud.

Drivers with linears were walking all over each other, trying to find out what was happening. Some of the trucks were starting to pull out, air brakes hissing as they were released. "Let's get this guy inside, back to Doc's office," he said and motioned to the man on the ground.

"Doc ain't here this early," Gumball said, wrapping his bleeding arm in his T-shirt, a grimace of pain on his face.

"And he needs an ambulance, not some old sawbones that gives physicals."

"Phones are dead," Gunny said, bending over to help the fallen man stand up. The smart part of his brain was screaming, *"Be careful! Blood! Don't get any on you! Get out of here while you still can! Run!"*

The other part that had been trained from birth to be kind to animals, to be a gentleman, don't hit your sister, open a lady's car door, you'll stand before God someday, never leave a fallen brother on the battlefield, help the helpless... that part was overriding the selfish part of him.

It was making him do what he thought he must. Making him try to help the other man to his feet. But the man had stopped moaning and his hands had slid away from his bites and lay still in the gravel. Gunny stopped in mid-bend. The wounds hadn't seemed that bad at first glance, but he did have a lot of them. His face and arms had chunks missing. His chest and neck. And there was a lot of blood on the ground.

*"Run! Run! Run!"* his mind screamed. He looked at him, at his face, at his mangled lip, his torn cheek. He was still. His chest wasn't moving up and down. Was he still breathing? No way was he going to give CPR. No way. He couldn't hear him breathe but who could hear anything with all the trucks and horns and radio chatter and...

The eyes sprung open. Black. Pupils fully dilated. Only the slightest orb of blue around the edges. Gunny reacted immediately, springing backward and bringing his gun up in the same motion as the creature that used to be a man uttered a guttural sound and bounded to his feet. The other men ran as the thing sprung at Gunny, who was pulling his trigger as fast as he could.

The Glock was pumping 9mm bullets into the flying

form, spent brass skittering across the gravel. The lead passed right through him, ripping muscle and tissue and organs, shattering bones then punching into the truck beside them. The rounds didn't send it flying backward, they barely slowed its forward momentum.

The thing slammed into him before he could get the gun high enough for a headshot. Panic had caused him to react, but not fast enough to put it down with a brain scramble. He knew that worked, he had just done it to the painter and the little Mexican kid. He had seen Billy drop the little girl with a shot to the head when two to her body didn't even faze her. It didn't even know it was shot and Gunny hadn't been lucky enough to sever its spine.

He went with the attack, falling back, rolling to his left, letting the thing's inertia and weight carry it away from him and slam into the hood of the big rig, head first. Gunny let go and spun away, toward the door, opening it and slamming the creature in the face as it recovered and lunged again. Its feet flew out from underneath it and it fell over backward as he scrambled into the cab of the still idling truck.

He slammed the door behind him, frantically looked for the lock button. He stared at it through the window as it jumped and clawed trying to get to him, not even registering the five or six holes he had pumped into it. Its intensity was unnerving. It slammed itself mindlessly against the truck over and over, denting the metal, breaking its fingers and teeth as it chewed and clawed.

There was the distinctive sound of a heavy caliber rifle report and Gunny stared through the windshield at Kim-Li, on the catwalk above the main building. She was aiming toward the road and he followed her gun to see a small crowd of sprinters running toward the truck stop, some bounding on all fours like animals.

One of them toppled and fell to the ground. It looked like the man who had just left in the minivan when all this started. Was she shooting at people? Real people? But he saw clearly, then. The blood, the way they were running and keening. Not people. Definitely not. They had been heading in his direction, but when they heard the crack of the rifle, they turned en mass toward it. Toward the truck stop. "Oh shit," Gunny said aloud. Everyone in the diner was at the windows, staring out at the running horrors.

The windows.

At the speeds they were running, and total indifference to their own injuries, they would hit those windows and shatter right through them.

Gunny hit the brake releases, slammed the rig into 3$^{rd}$, stomped the pedal and grabbed the air horn. He heard more reports in quick succession as Kim fired up the few rounds she had. The big .30-06 was doing damage, much more than his 9mm rounds had. He saw some of them fall, but they got back up. She was doing body shots. Couldn't blame her for that, head shots were difficult at the best of times, but she was definitely slowing them down.

He heard the sound of smaller caliber rounds being sent into the crowd from the men at the front door of the truck stop, and the rapid fire from the M-4 that Scratch had. He spun gravel, fast shifting, trying to get some speed out of the rig. It was loaded heavy and he had to wind each gear before he could grab the next.

The creatures heard him, the sound of the air horn blasting and some of them changed course, heading right for him. But some had seen the patrons standing in the windows of the diner, hands to mouths, looks of shock and disbelief written all over their faces. They charged, scream-ing, howling and keening, full force toward the fresh food.

Gunny jumped the curb and plowed down the shrub-bery between the truck parking lot and the automobile gas pumps. He grabbed another gear, foot to the floor, the big diesel roaring in protest at the abuse and speed shifted again, hitting sixth and pegging the tach all the way over to its governed limit.

He blew past the front of the building, angling in over the handicap parking spots, bouncing the red Ferrari off of the Kenworth's unforgiving bumper. It went sliding into Billy Travaho's cruiser, knocking it out of the way, too. He was trying to get close to the building, trying to park the semi in front of the windows, to stop them from being shat-tered and the people inside overrun.

He scraped along a few other cars, up over the sidewalk, tearing up Martha's flowerbeds that were directly under the windows. The closest sprinter was ignoring the noisy diesel, seeing only the people standing there, ripe for the taking. He sprung, hands extended, reaching for the woman in the blue shirt, ready to sink his teeth into the flesh, to tear, to rend, to feel her blood in his throat...

He impacted with the grill of the truck, bouncing off toward the windows in a bone broken spin. The woman in the window screamed a high piercing shriek and fell back, away from the monstrosity, and then the truck's tires were there, crushing it to pulp and blocking the view of all inside.

Gunny swung the nose of the tractor out, knocking some foreign car out of the way... or maybe it was American, they all looked the same nowadays, to him. He jammed the Kenworth into reverse and slipped the clutch, maneuvering the trailer tight against the building and up against the main hut. That would keep anything out.

The windows ran the length of the smaller Quonset hut and were set about four feet up off the ground. The seventy feet of this tractor and trailer covered them up nicely, except for the catwalk between the truck and its trailer, but that area was small. Even if they did manage to get up there, they wouldn't have any force to break the window. It would do for now.

He heard Wire Bender on the radio hollering for someone else to do the same to the Driver's Alley windows and the front of the store. Gunny shut the motor off and leaned back in the seat. He looked into the side mirror, saw a truck slipping in close to the double doors at the main entrance. It tore off the rest of the awning that he had broken when he came flying in.

There were a few of the creatures left, still trying to get to him, but they were pretty busted up. Kim had really done some damage with the big gun, but they were still crawling or dragging themselves toward the sounds of humans. There were maybe a half-dozen of them, all coming in from the direction of Reno. The two bikers had come in from the other way, so these things must be everywhere.

The bikers...

That one had been bitten pretty badly. So had the deputy.

He grabbed the mic for the CB and keyed it. "Wire Bender! Kick it back stat!" he yelled,

"Yeah, c'mon Gunny."

"You've got to isolate anyone that's been bitten!" he said urgently. "They'll turn into those mindless things! It's contagious!" He couldn't bring himself to say zombies, although he knew that's what they were. What else could they be? But he didn't want to be laughed at, thought of as an idiot.

"I'll be in in a minute. I think I can get to the roof from the top of the trailer," he added, thinking it would be easier to explain, maybe convince them in person, rather than over the radio.

"You mean zombies?" Wire Bender came back, laconically. "They're in Doc's office and we got it under control."

Gunny harrumphed. "*Should have known*," he thought. "*Biggest conspiracy nut I know. He probably heard about this a month ago.*"

Wire Bender was an odd duck. Old Cobb had rented him space in the Driver's Alley and let him plug in his little RV and park it out in the junkyard. He was supposed to be the night watchman, some of those old truck parts had gotten valuable lately. With eBay, you could find a guy who would pay fifty bucks for an original Diamond Reo fuel gauge.

But he stayed on a cot in the back of his radio shop half the time. The internet was better and the bathroom was closer. He had been a radio man back in 'Nam. Had probably smoked too much, or seen too much. No one really knew, he didn't talk about his time in-country.

Somehow he had landed here in Cobb's strange little Truck Stop with the other misfits who didn't quite fit into polite society, and had been fixing CBs and Ham radios for as long as anyone could remember. His name was known far and wide. Everybody knew if you wanted a Big Radio, Wire Bender from the Three Flags was one of the best. He could tweak things and didn't give a tinker's dam if the FCC frowned on some of his modifications.

Gunny ejected the mag from his Glock 19 and counted the rounds. There were five in the mag and one in the pipe. He shoved it back in the well and slid it into his holster. He wanted to put bullets in the brainpans of every crawling thing left out there, he knew they were a threat. But they weren't an immediate threat, and his life might depend on those six rounds. He had another box in his truck and it was safely tucked away in the shop. He wanted to get to it before he started wasting ammo on half blasted creatures.

Zombies, he corrected himself. They're zombies. Real, live, honest to God, zombies. Well, maybe real DEAD, honest to God, zombies. He didn't know how it could possibly be, how science fiction and Haitian horror stories could be real, but he knew what he saw. He thought he knew what he saw.

And good Lord, if he was wrong, if they were really just crazy or drugged up, he was going to be facing a very long prison sentence. He closed his eyes, got his breathing under control, played it all out in his mind again. Not second guessing. He'd learned long ago not to do that. He replayed details, trying to see if there was something he had misread, some clue he'd missed. He was writing an after operations report in his mind. Looking for the flaw in his logic where some POG lieutenant would try to bring him up on a court martial.

He sighed. Plenty, he concluded. It didn't matter if there was a clear and present danger. In the end, he'd gunned down unarmed people. He knew fear caused hesitation and hesitation would get you killed. But prosecuting attorneys didn't think like that. If this wasn't a freaking apocalypse, he was going to need a lawyer.

He pulled his phone out of his pocket, dialed his wife Lacy again. Nothing. All circuits are busy. Please try again later.

He looked at the creatures outside his window. A couple had seen him. One was fairly lively, jumping and clawing at the side of the truck. The other was trying to pull itself up on the steps with a crooked arm and was getting repeatedly stepped on by the jumper. He didn't sense any real danger, though. He was safe for the moment.

He felt weak, drained. The adrenaline had fled his body and now he just wanted to crawl back in the bunk and sleep for a minute. But there wasn't time for that right now. He hopped out of the driver's seat, over into the passenger's side, and rolled down the window.

He climbed out and onto the long Kenworth hood, glad this wasn't a new Volvo or Freight Shaker with all the sloping aerodynamics that would have been all too easy to slide off of. These old Kenny's were just blocks and squares, all flat surfaces. Like driving a brick wall.

He hopped up on the roof of the sleeper and then took a quick run and jumped the short distance to the top of the trailer. Kim was still on the catwalk of the main building, holding the old World War Two rifle down at her side in a one-handed grip. She was talking to the other driver that had blocked the windows on the Driver's Alley side.

They were trying to figure out how to get over to the catwalk. It wasn't far, the problem was that the Quonset hut was rounded, and the catwalk was a good fifteen feet higher than the top of the trailer. You could jump, the building's incline wasn't too steep this high up, but if you slipped...Well, it was a long slide down to the ground.

As Gunny made his way back to the end of the trailer, Kim turned and said, "I'm going to get some rope or something, I'll be back in a minute." Then she was off, jogging toward the other end of the building, and the roof access panel.

The driver who had blocked the main entrance came over to the end of his trailer and hailed Gunny. "What the hell is going on?" he asked. "I woke up to guns and horns and screaming, and Wire Bender yelling at me to block the doors!"

Gunny recognized Pack Rat, the old gray-haired geezer who definitely lived up to his name. He was the guy who opened his truck door and, more often than not, empty coffee cups or fast food wrappers would fall out.

"Dunno, Pack Rat. I think the riots that have been hitting all the cities just hit Three Flags."

"Who the hell would wanna riot here?" he asked querulously. "I thought Wire Bender done lost his mind. I wasn't about to pull up in here till I saw you busting everything up like you was on a Hollywood movie set. Reckoned something boocoo dinky dau must be going on."

He spat a stream of tobacco over the edge of his truck and into the face of one of the women that had been attracted to their voices. It was clawing at his trailer, trying to get at the bearded old codger. Her sun dress was hanging off of one shoulder, exposing a bra and a big hole in her breast, and a bigger one in her back. There were bits of broken bone sticking out of it where Kim-Li's .30-06 had punched through. She had a bloody chunk of one of her arms missing and a piece of her neck was gone. Probably bite marks. He watched her for a minute then said, "Looks like we got us a zombie problem."

# LACY

## ATLANTA

## Day 1

Lacy walked into the office, already pissed off. She had caught their sixteen year old trying to hide the fact that he was making a lunch for school. "Why are you doing that?" she had asked. "Only broccoli on the menu today?"

He was surlier than his usual grumpy, morning self and she finally drug the story out of him in monosyllabic grunts and aggravated gestures. He had in-school detention again. Confined all day, in an unused classroom, with the rest of the trouble makers.

They were supervised only by the camera which fed directly into the secretary's office. They were given their assignments that had to be turned in at the end of the day, then left alone. It was a private school and they took discipline very seriously.

It had been a lunchroom fight over something stupid. This was the second time this year and it was only

September. If it happened again, they would be looking for another school.

"Text your dad." She had told him. "Try to explain it to him." Johnny had been threatening him with military academy, but it was an idle threat because they couldn't afford it. Jessie didn't know that, though.

"He's in California today, but he's got a load back home, so you'll be having words with him by the weekend."

That really put a darker cloud over his mood. She hated the whole "wait till your father gets home" routine, but it was the one thing that would set him on the straight and narrow. For a little while anyway.

What annoyed her the most is that he still couldn't admit he had been wrong. Too much of his dad in him. Punch first, punch second, then punch some more. That's why they hadn't been getting along very well this past year or so.

They were too much alike. She sighed heavily as she slammed her purse down on her desk. He wasn't a bad kid, he usually made good grades, and he wasn't on drugs or getting his girlfriend knocked up, but damn if he didn't have his father's temper. If he wasn't careful, he would wind up making some of the same stupid mistakes Johnny had.

She grabbed the coffee cup off of her desk and walked down the hall to the break area to start the pot brewing. Lacy was the first in this morning, she had dropped some friends off at the airport for an early flight and came on into work. She had to catch up on some of the environmental reports she had been saddled with.

It wasn't her job, she was human resources, but with budget cuts, everyone was doing the work of two people. But that damn kid. If he didn't get his temper under control, he would find himself in a situation like the one that had eventually landed them here in Atlanta. It wasn't a bad life, but certainly not the one they had planned.

Johnny wouldn't be out driving a truck, and gone for weeks at a time, they wouldn't have spent all of their savings and a lot of her 401k, if his temper hadn't gotten the best of him over in Afghanistan. Or at the tire store back in high school, for that matter. She sighed again. Water under the bridge. Ancient history. Can't change the past.

She didn't dwell on it, but life was strange like that. No matter what you planned, it never seemed to work out the way you wanted. They had hoped for a house full of kids and a place in the country near their hometown, but their only child came late in life after they had almost given up.

And they sure hadn't planned on him being a little hell raiser. Well, she hadn't, anyway. Johnny laughed it off as "just being a kid." He was probably secretly proud of him. Men!

She busied herself firing up her computer and digging out the files she needed as the pot brewed, filling the little kitchenette and lunch room with the aroma of mountain grown. When it had finished its cycle, she poured herself a cup and walked over to the windows looking out over Atlanta. It was a beautiful view from twenty-eight stories up, the urban landscape of the early morning stretching out as far as she could see.

She watched the ribbons of headlights and taillights on the intersecting freeways in constant motion, and the ever changing lights of the digital billboards. She was probably lucky she didn't have a window in her office, she'd never get any work done. With another sigh, she refilled her cup. Her mind was clear enough from this morning's argument to get down to doing what she got paid to do and went back to her office, shutting the door behind her.

She looked up when she heard the scream. Had she actually heard it? It was faint, coming from far away. The music from her computer speakers was playing at a low volume, but she had definitely heard something. She glanced up at the clock. Nine fifteen. She did a double take. She should have heard the noise of all of the rest of the office crew coming in a half hour ago.

She stood, grabbing her cup, going after a refill, and to see why it was so quiet. It was usually barely subdued chaos around this time of the morning, with everyone coming in and getting ready to start the day. No phones were ringing, no printers running, no chatter about last night's game or who was eliminated in the latest talent show.

Had she missed some mandatory meeting? She googled her brain as she walked to the break area. Was today the awards ceremony? No way. That was always held in December. She walked in to see one of the I.T. guys standing at the window, looking out over the city. It was Eric. Nice enough guy.

She walked up to stand beside him. "Where is every-body?" she asked, but trailed off when she saw what he was looking at out of the window. "What the hell?" was all she could say as she took in the cityscape.

The first thing she noticed were the fires. There were dozens of them, spread out everywhere she looked, the flames reaching into the sky and the black smoke billowing.

"What the hell is going on?" she asked dumbly, noticing more the longer she looked. Eric said nothing, just continued to stare as she took it all in. The freeways were at a complete standstill. Pileups and wrecks everywhere. The secondary streets were jammed, too. She thought she could see people running and attacking each other, but from this high up, it was hard to make out exactly what was going on.

"Are we at war?" she asked, but Eric just continued to stare out at the chaos, in some kind of shock. "Eric?!" she said, and shook him by the arm. He ignored her, just continued to stare. She looked back over the city, at the stalled and clogged roads, at the fires burning unchecked in the residential neighborhoods.

"Eric!" she yelled this time, but there was still no response. She needed information. She left him standing there and ran back to her office, the coffee refill forgotten. She logged on to the network, entered her password for outside access and started searching the web for anything on the local news channels.

There were no local channels. The live streams of the morning shows were down. All of them. And that was scarier than seeing all the fires. One search led to another, and all too quickly, she had a world view of what was happening. People coming back from the dead. Invincible to bullets.

Mad mobs of screaming, leaping, hordes killing every-thing in their path. She tried to call Johnny. All circuits busy. She tried to call Jessie. All circuits busy. She clasped her hands in front of her face as she watched live video feeds from different cameras around the state, then around the country and then around the globe. She tried to call Johnny again. She tried to call Jessie again. She needed to go get him. He was shut up in that room in detention. If the city was in chaos, the suburbs must be, too. Her mind raced. The roads were gridlocked, there was no way to even move along them. She needed a motorcycle.

Hell, she needed her gun that was in the glove box of her car down in the parking garage. She watched the live streaming cameras from different cities. She wanted to know what she was up against. She watched them tearing and biting, watched them leap inhuman distances and take people down with inhuman strength.

Her analytical mind went into overdrive, already discarding the simple explanations that didn't ring true. She wasn't being pranked. It wasn't rioting mobs of college kids celebrating a basketball game. It wasn't a political protest. It wasn't Black Lives Matter or the Ku Klux Klan. It wasn't aliens doing this. It was other people. People she saw with grievous injuries, people with arms completely ripped off, and still attacking.

She was watching a zombie uprising. She didn't know if the books and movies were true, that the only thing that could kill a zombie was a shot to the head, but she would take that as a truth for now. And definitely avoid being bitten. Had the government known something like this could happen? Is that why there were so many zombie TV shows and movies and books?

Is that why even the CDC had a "how to prepare for a zombie outbreak" booklet on their website? She was thinking too much like some of her Internet friends now. A conspiracy for everything, and everything a conspiracy. Wonder if there's any tin foil in the kitchen so I can make a hat? She slapped herself mentally. "Get it together, girl. This is real. Don't skiz out."

They had a sign hanging on a tree in their driveway. It had a picture of a gun and said, "We don't call 911" on it. She dialed anyway, not really expecting anything and got another "all circuits are busy."

She needed a weapon. And protective clothing. She couldn't get bit. Part of her mind was screaming at her, "*Are you retarded? A zombie apocalypse?*" but the other part was cold and analytical. Sorting the images and video she had seen, compiling it with what was outside the window. It was absolute civilization ending chaos.

No one was going to come rescue them. Maybe in a few days, when things settled down, but right now it was every man for himself. She was going into Mama Bear mode. Her baby needed her.

She was in her office, mind racing on what was the best course of action to get to the school to get her son. She had nixed the idea of stealing a motorcycle, too dangerous. She had seen the way those ghouls had leaped and run at anything that was still human on the traffic camera feeds around the city.

They would pull her off in a heartbeat. She needed something big. Something that could drive down sidewalks and knock the little cafe tables and chairs out of the way. Run over parking meters, if necessary. A Hummer. Maybe some urban cowboy's pickup truck that had a bull bar up front. The parking garage attendants had keys to a lot of the vehicles, the ones that were on the lower levels in valet and long term parking areas. Maybe there was a truck down there. She knew you couldn't hot wire one like they do on TV all the time.

Johnny was always quick to laugh at those situations every time one came up, talking to the television and asking, "What about the locked steering column? What about the chip in the key? How are you going to release the shifter?" until she would have to elbow him to get him to be quiet.

She was looking around, trying to see what could be used as a weapon before heading down to the garage when she heard a commotion in the lobby.

"Crap!" She should have locked the doors! Stupid, stupid, stupid! Her office was devoid of anything that could be used to hurt someone. No ball bats, no heavy art objects.

Not even an umbrella. Her eyes fell on the shelves along one wall. The office came with its own bookcases when she had moved up a notch on the corporate ladder a few years ago.

However, one of the first things she had done was add a few shelves to hold some of her photos and plants. Holding those shelves up were large L-shaped brackets picked up from Home Depot and screwed into the wall. She ran over, swiping everything off and onto the ground, the clatter of crashing planters and breaking picture glass loud in her ears. Louder than what she heard down the hall, shouts and sounds of furniture being tipped and drug around.

She ripped the shelves off the brackets easily enough, but had to struggle to work the screws out of the walls. They finally broke free and she bent them hurriedly into U shapes and gripped one in each hand. She had something now that could be shoved into the face of any attacker. It wasn't much, but it was better than the little key ring knuckle duster she had in her purse.

She went quickly to the door and inched it open, trying to see both ways down the hallway. The only noises she heard were still coming from the lobby, but she caught voices. It sounded like Mr. Sato, his English was good, but he still carried a distinct Japanese accent. She ran toward them to see if she could help, it sounded like they were blocking the doors. As she rounded the corner, somebody saw her and screamed, then she saw Phil turn and bring his gun up toward her.

"Whoa, Whoa, Whoa!" she yelled, holding her hands up, the brown shelf brackets wrapped around them looking like little spears. She could see where they had drug desks and filing cabinets over to the glass doors, blocking them. Outside in the corridor, she saw mangled people in business suits and dresses beating on the doors, trying to force their way through. There weren't many, maybe eight or ten, but seeing them up close for the first time drained the color from her face. It was worse than anything she could have imagined. The fury as they fought each other to get to the living was unreal and unrelenting. They were tearing each other apart out there. As she watched, a man in a shredded suit pulled a huge hank of hair out of a woman who was pressed against the glass, trying to force her way through. She was jerked backward and the suited man took her place, his bloodied hands and face against the door, smearing it with gore from the handful of bloody scalp he still clung to. The pounding was relentless, but the doors shouldn't break, they were tempered safety glass and they were in steel frames. They'll hold, she told herself. There were a half dozen people in the lobby and they quickly went back to stacking and dragging things in front of the door. She joined in, tipping over a bookcase and struggling with it, until Phil came over and helped her put it in place. After a few minutes, they had a substantial barrier that went all the way from the doors to the solid wood at the base of the receptionist's desk. There was no way for the doors to open now, but if the glass broke... well, that was a different story. Those things could probably force their way through the pile of office furniture if it did.

Lacy looked around at the frightened, sweaty faces. She recognized a few by sight, but the only ones she knew were her boss, Mr. Sato, Eric, and Phil. He was one of the security guards that manned the station on the ground floor. He was a burly black man, quick to laugh and smile, but also quick to run off anyone causing trouble or panhandling on the sidewalk out front. He had been the first person she had met years ago when she entered the building, slightly scared and slightly desperate, resume in hand. He had escorted her to the 28th story and on the way up in the long elevator ride that seemed to stop at every floor, they had struck up a friendship. It was him, more than her carefully prepared resume, that had gotten her the job. Plenty of qualified applicants had applied, but he had walked her right past reception and directly into the Human Resources office. Told the HR director this was the one, he had a feeling about her. Then he nodded and walked out, heading back to his post. She had really, really needed the job. Johnny had been kicked out of the Army over that incident in Afghanistan nearly two years before, and had been unable to find work. Their savings was gone, her 401k cashed in. She had gotten the job and she had thanked him profusely. Even bought him a new holster for his gun with her first paycheck, when she noticed his was looking a little threadbare.

"Everybody get away from the doors," Phil said. "If they don't see us, maybe they'll wander off."

"I've got coffee in the break room," Lacy said, "Every-body, this way," and led the unfamiliar people away from the receiving area and toward the lunch room. The coffee was still hot, but it was going on three hours old. No one seemed to care as they got their cups and either sat down looking exhausted, or wandered over to the window to stare out at the chaos. Anyone that had a phone was trying to dial numbers and then sharing with the ones that didn't. No one was getting through.

"What happened downstairs, Phil?" Lacy asked as he was the last to pour, doctoring his cup up with plenty of sugar and milk.

He didn't look over at her, just slowly stirred and

poured, methodically making his coffee just the way he liked it.

"It happened fast, Mizz Lacy," he said. "There was a disturbance outside and Jerry went over to see what was going on. We had both just come on duty and I was still running over the paperwork for shift change. One minute, the early birds was coming in like normal, the next...The next, everybody done gone crazy. I saw Jerry go down when he tried to break up a fight. I saw him fall, saw his head get ripped nearly clean off. Saw enough blood shoot out of him to kill any man. Before I could get to the door, I saw him get back up and start running after people. Biting them."

Lacy didn't say anything. Didn't know if there was anything *to* say to that. She dumped the remainder of the coffee out in the sink and started making another pot.

"They was a few people running for the doors and I let them in and locked up behind them. We was all just standing around, not believing what we was seeing. Then some guy came running at us from across the lobby, crazy like the ones outside. I put two bullets in him and he didn't even slow down. Jumped on old Mrs. Carlton from fourteenth floor. I ran up and put one in his head before he would stop chewing on her."

Lacy poured the water into the Brewmaster and dug the coffee and filters out of the cabinet, listening with dread and a feeling of sickness in her stomach.

"We tried to help her, stop the bleeding and such. They's a first aid kit at the security desk," he went on, almost in a monotone, his language slipping back to the way he used to talk on the streets before he had landed this job in the corporate world. He was remembering, but trying not to see it again in his mind's eye. "But she turned into one of them, too. By the time we had the bandages on, she was trying to bite me. Only took one bullet that time, though. I knew where to shoot."

He hadn't taken a sip of his coffee yet, still stirred the already thoroughly mixed contents.

Lacy hit the button on the machine to get the next pot started and laid a hand on his massive arm, stopping the stirring action. She squeezed, no words possible, no words needed. Phil seemed to shake himself internally, gave her a half smile and put the cup to his lips, blowing to cool it down a little.

"That's when Mr. Sato from twenty-eighth said he had a satellite phone in his office," he went on. "Everybody was trying to call and no one was getting anything other than busy signals, or not even that, just being disconnected before it would ring. So we started to head up here. But while we were waiting for the elevators, a bunch of those crazies came in through the mezzanine entrance. I didn't have enough bullets to take them all down, so we ran for the stairs. There were a lot more of us in the lobby when this all started, Mizz Lacy. I don't know if they split off and hid, or if they got taken down in the stairwell. I was first in, maybe I should have been last. I don't know. I was just trying to make us a path up here. We went up to the third floor and ran to the elevators there. We made it in, but when we got out here, there were a bunch of them in the hallway. The rest of the story you know. That's about when I almost shot you." He grinned a little. "Glad I didn't," he added.

"Me, too," Lacy said. "Is there any way to get down to the parking garage? Phil, I need to get out of here, I need to get to the school to get my kid."

He shook his head. "No way. The garage is open to the street, it's probably full of those things. Mizz Lacy, you haven't been out there among them. They are faster than us.

They are stronger than us. They're nearly invincible. You couldn't pay me any amount of money to go back down there. Not until the police or the Army get things cleaned up."

Mr. Sato, the CEO of the American division of Satoshiri Electronics, came bustling back into the room with his satellite phone in his hand and announced that he had made contact with someone in the Governor's office. They had assured him that the Army would be out soon to get things back under control. And yes, of course, they would be evacuating personnel from the rooftops with helicopters. There was a quiet cheer as the small crowd greeted the news.

"Did they say when?" someone asked.

"Do we need to get up there right now?" another added, fear evident in his quavering voice.

"How will we get past those things in the hall?"

Mr. Sato looked at a loss as all the questions came flying at him, the people talking over one another. As Lacy handed him a cup of coffee, Phil raised his hands and made shushing motions. "Settle down, people. I don't think we need to leave here just yet, we have a clear view of the city. When we see the Army or the National Guard clearing the streets, or we see the choppers start coming in, then we can head to the roof. The elevators will take us almost all the way. I have the keys to the access door, so we're only five minutes away when we need to be."

There was an audible sigh of relief from the harried office workers. Just ten minutes before they had been out in the hallways and stairwells and had seen half of their number killed or bitten, drug down and savagely attacked with claws and teeth. They had no desire to go back out there.

Just then, Lacy's phone sounded off with a toot toot of a big truck's air horn. The text tone from Johnny. It was like a minor miracle. A message had gotten through on the collapsing, overused, digital network. "I got a text!" she announced and reached for her phone. Everyone else caught on quickly and pulled theirs out and instead of trying to place voice calls, they started to text message, hoping theirs would make it through the overworked system.

6

As Gunny came down the ladder off the catwalk and into the back of the kitchen, Tiny was there, waiting to go up. He had the Garand slung over his shoulder, a box of shells in his jacket pocket, and a two-way radio clipped to his belt. Gunny raised his eyebrows, questioningly.

"Cobb wants a watch, can't see much out of any of the windows now," Tiny said.

Gunny nodded then asked, "Billy okay? Gumball and Ozzy make it in here?"

"Ozzy did. Ain't seen Gumball. He get bit in that scuffle?"

"Yeah. Him and a couple of other guys I don't know. They back at Doc's?" asked Gunny.

"Yeah," Tiny said. "This is some crazy shit, man. You ought to go see Cobb. He's down there with them." The big man was subdued. Saddened, as he turned toward the ladder.

Gunny laid a hand on his arm, "You get a hold of Tanya?" he asked. Tiny just shook his head and mounted the ladder, heading up to take first watch. Gunny cut through the back way into the kitchen, through the store rooms and out into the back of the main building.

He knew what Tiny was going through. Tanya, his wife, worked in downtown Birmingham. Gunny's wife worked in Atlanta. Both bad situations, if this were everywhere.

He needed to see Wire Bender, see if there was news from the internet, or any of the Ham operators near home. Gunny knew this route through the maze of store rooms because he had helped Cobb carry in some produce that had "fallen off a truck" more than once through these doors.

Many of the drivers would give Martha anything extra they had, and when dealing with fruits and vegetables, there was always something extra. Receivers would reject whole cases if there was even one bad orange spotted. Melons, if they were a day late arriving at the docks. Boxes of steaks if the thermometer readings weren't right on just one sample.

Martha passed the savings on to her customers. She and Cookie would always whip up something from whatever she was given, and it was the daily special. Many of the tourists couldn't believe they could get a slice of peach cobbler for fifty cents, or a five dollar steak.

Gunny had to pass Doc's little office before he got to the CB shop and looked in as he walked by. Wire Bender seemed to know what they were facing, and had said everything was under control, so he wasn't worried about anyone else turning. He figured they had been isolated or something.

What he saw stopped him in his tracks. Apparently, no one else DID know what they were facing. The biker girl was grim-faced and stoic, finished with crying, putting the finishing wraps on Deputy Travaho's arm as he sat gray-faced in one of the waiting room chairs.

Doc's assistant, Stacy, was there. She was a night school nursing student who worked for him during the week. She had Ozzy laying on the reception counter, his pants cut off to above the knee, and was trying to clean and flush the nasty looking bite wound on his leg. Billy held his radio with his free hand, but there was no chatter on it.

He looked for any of the other men who had been bitten from the brawl in the parking lot. The guy who had been scratched was sitting in one of the other chairs, holding a towel across his chest. He glanced around for the other biker or the painter. They both got it pretty bad. These guys all seemed okay. They weren't going to die or anything.

"Where's the other biker?" he asked. "Gumball?"

"Gumball took off. So did a bunch of other guys," Ozzy grimaced through the pain.

"The biker is on the table in the back," Stacy replied. "We did what we could with what we have. He needs to get to town, to the hospital."

"Not sure if that's going to happen anytime soon," Gunny said. "If it's as bad in Reno as here, there won't be any ambulances free to run up this way."

He walked past the desk and into the examination room. The biker was laying on his stomach, a big gauze pad that was starting to seep red taped to the back of his neck. His face was a mess from where he had it crammed into the asphalt. He had his eyes closed. There was a long strip of his scalp and hair missing that they also bandaged.

Gunny shook him a little then stepped back. "Hey, you awake?' he asked, one hand firmly on his gun.

"Hmmm?" the guy said.

"Just hang on, buddy. I'm going to wheel you to the other room," he said. He didn't like this. He had seen how fast the guy in the parking lot had turned. Moaning in pain one minute, ripping out throats the next.

This guy was barely coherent, and he knew he wasn't doped up because Doc didn't keep meds in here. This was just a place where truckers could pay their sixty bucks and get their medical card stamped for another two years. Or pay a little more, if there was a little something wrong with them, and still get it stamped for two years. He was kind of surprised they even had bandages, but he supposed the board of health checked up on these places from time to time, so they had to at least look official.

He released the locking wheels of the exam table and started to roll him out into the waiting room, and the corridor beyond.

Stacy looked up from Ozzy's leg she was irrigating. "Are you taking him to the hospital?" she asked.

"To the weight room," Gunny replied, "It'll be safer in there."

"Wait!" she cried out. "It's filthy in there. There's infection to think about."

*Yes, there is...*" Gunny thought. He looked at Ozzy and the shirtless man. The only other two people who had seen someone go from human to dead to monster, in a matter of seconds.

They looked at the biker, lying face down and unresponsive. He had lost a lot of blood.

"Does that thing have straps? Strap him down," Ozzy said, with a little bit of panic in his eyes.

"I'll help," the shirtless man jumped up and hurried across the room, holding open the door.

"Where's the other guy, the painter that kid brought in?" Gunny asked as he wheeled him out into the corridor.

"He didn't make it," Stacy said. "He didn't have a pulse or anything, so we laid him in the freezer."

Gunny stopped and looked at her, disbelief evident on his face.

"He was dead," she said defensively. "I didn't know what to do and that was the only option I had for now."

"It's all good," Gunny said. "I'll check on him." He turned a hard left out of the office and started to run, pushing the heavy examination table in front of him.

"Go down to the shop!" he yelled at the man running beside him and helping to steer the table. "Grab some ratchet straps, there's a bunch in the side box of my wagon. It's there in the 2$^{nd}$ bay!"

The man took off at a dead sprint. Gunny was a little impressed, the guy seemed unflappable. He had a good build. The muscles in his dark skin defined as he sprinted. Either he hadn't been trucking very long, or he kept up an exercise regime. No stupid questions. No hesitation. He pegged him as a Marine. Maybe Infantry. Definitely military of some kind.

He stopped just short of the door to the gym and pulled it open, then quickly got the front of the table in before it could close. He chose this place because it was as far away from the central area as possible, and the doors had big handles that could be chained shut. He thought he could tie him to one of the machines, but if they strapped him down, that probably wouldn't be necessary.

The man came hustling back in by the time Gunny had the biker in the back of the room and they quickly wrapped the poor bastard in 3-inch-wide heavy-duty straps and tightened them down. Not too snug. But enough he wouldn't be slipping out of them if he turned.

They looked at each other over the table, both still

breathing a little hard. Gunny glanced down at the scratches on the man's chest. They had started bleeding again, but it wasn't bad, mostly from his nearly missing nipple.

"Yeah," he said in acknowledgment of Gunny's look at his chest. "I've got a very serious vested interest on how this all turns out."

Gunny nodded. Stuck out his hand. "They call me Gunny," he said as they headed out of the room.

"I've heard," the man said. "I'm Hot Rod."

"Vet?" Gunny asked.

"No," he said and knew what Gunny was really asking. How are you so cool under pressure, not freaking out like most civilians would? "I race dirt track and stock cars. Wheel to wheel at a buck fifty. Done it for years."

He smiled and held up his arm for Gunny to see. "Or at least I used to." There was a long, wide scar going from the inside of his bicep all the way down to his wrist, ragged looking on his coffee brown skin. "Reflexes aren't what they used to be. Now I truck."

"I'm headed to check the freezer, you sterilize those scratches yet?"

"Raw alcohol," Hot Rod replied.

Gunny grimaced.

"Yeah, it stung a bit," he deadpanned. "I'm going to smear some antibacterial in these, now that they've mostly stopped bleeding."

"Keep an eye on Billy," Gunny said. "Ozzy, too. You saw how fast they turn if they die." Then he took off at a jog to the big walk-in freezer. As he passed back by the Radio Shop, he saw a dozen drivers in there, crowded around Wire Bender's counter and his computer, Scratch and Cobb among them. He opened the door and yelled for Scratch, who still had the M-4. Cobb came, too, seeing more than ordinary concern on Gunny's face.

"Sit Rep," he barked.

Gunny spit it out as fast as he could, "If the wounded in Doc's office die, they'll turn into one of those things. I saw it happen in the parking lot. Twice." Before he could say anything else, Cobb had already pointed Scratch in that direction. "Make sure no one else gets mangled," he told him and Scratch was double timing instantly. Gunny barely believed it. Ol' Cobb hadn't even batted an eye. Just took it for gospel.

"Next."

Gunny was caught up short for a second, he had intended to send Scratch down there himself because he had the M-4, and now had to get his train of thought back. So much was happening all at once.

"Next," Cobb said a little louder.

"Um, the biker is strapped down in the weight room. He's bad off and he'll probably turn."

"Secure?" Cobb asked.

"Yeah," Gunny said. "Ratchet straps off my truck."

"Next " Cobb barked again.

"Stacy put that painter guy from the gas pumps in the freezer, said he was dead."

"That's bad," he said, and started running. Gunny had to hustle to keep up. They went the back way into the kitchen area, and both breathed a sigh of relief to see the freezer door still closed. There was no way to lock someone in. It was a safety feature that all you had to do was push against the big release bar inside to spring the door wide open.

Cookie was still at the grill on the other side of the

room. "Really?" he said over his shoulder. "You're putting bodies in my freezer?"

"It might not be a body," Gunny replied and drew his gun as he approached the door. He looked at Cobb. "Where's your pea-shooter?" he asked.

"Gave it to Tommy, got a few of 'em checking the fence behind the shop, make sure there ain't no holes in it. That's the weak side of the building. I must've been down there when she told them to put the body in here," he sighed. "I'm getting too old for this."

"But you guys did good out front," he continued. "It's about as secure as it can be. That was some fast thinking, son. You woulda made a good Marine."

Gunny nodded, not knowing what to say. He'd never heard Cobb give out a compliment before. Maybe Hell had frozen over.

Cobb looked around the kitchen for a weapon he could use, then opened the oven and grabbed one of the oversized racks out of it.

Gunny gave him a quizzical look. "I wasn't planning on cooking him," he said.

"If it's come back from the dead, I don't want you splattering brains all over the freezer," Cobb growled. "I'll push him against the back wall and you can plug him. Don't go shooting like some Air Force puke, either. One shot. Don't fill my freezer full of holes."

"They're kind of strong," Gunny said, looking at the old man out of the corner of his eye as he reached for the handle to open the door.

"You saying I'm not?" Cobb said, a menace in his growl as he held the oversize rack up in front of him like a shield.

"Nope. But they're really freaking fast, too."

"Open the door, ya panty wearing girl," Cobb spat out

and readied his heavy rack to slam into the creature if it came snarling out.

Gunny jerked the door wide and brought the Glock up in a two-handed grip to steady his aim as Cobb took half a step forward then stopped. It was there. Standing upright, but moving in slow motion, frost and ice already hanging off of it in the sub-zero walk-in. It heard them and growled deep in its chest and they could see it straining to reach them. It overbalanced and toppled face first to the floor.

Gunny shut the door. "Well, that's interesting," he said. "At least we know they won't be a problem in the winter."

"That bastard was frozen solid," Cobb said.

"We should still kill it," Gunny said. "It's still dangerous if it thaws out."

"Of course we should," Cobb rasped out. "But now we don't have to make a mess. We can wrap it in a tarp so we don't blow its brains all over the ice cream."

"Right," Gunny said. "I'll grab one from the store. But there's no rush, I've got to get with Wire Bender. See if he's heard anything from the Hams back home."

Cobb nodded, told Cookie to watch his step if he went in there and said, "Go on. I'll get Pack Rat or one of the others to give me a hand. Prolly just shove a Ka-Bar through its melon. Quieter that way. I need to talk to the folks in the diner. Pass on what little info Billy could get from the radio."

"What did he say? They sending some more deputies over here, try to figure this mess out? He tell them we needed an ambulance?"

Cobb looked at him for a minute, realizing that Gunny had just come in off the roof, hadn't heard any of the radio chatter from Billy's two-way. "No," he said quietly, pulling a Lucky Strike from his pack and inhaling on it, unlit. "There ain't nobody coming. Billy was in contact with the office, they had heard from Reno. Total FUBAR. Sheriff's office sounded panicked. They quit responding after there was some gunfire heard over the channel. Most of Billy's deputies either weren't answering, or were screaming for backup themselves. Last thing he heard from 'em was a couple was holed up in the office making their way to the jail cells. Then nothing. Sounded like there was a scuffle. Don't know if they made it or not, they aren't answering the radio."

Gunny was stunned. That fast? How did it all go from a few isolated fights or riots...or incidences... To complete meltdown, so quickly?

"Is this shit airborne?" he asked, panic starting to sound in his voice. "How did it spread so fast? It's got to be some kind of attack. Is it all over, or just here? Is there some sort of government chemical lab around here?"

"You gonna lose it on me, too?" Cobb barked at him. His hard eyes fixed on Gunny's. "Buckle up, Snowflake. We got work to do."

Gunny stared at him for a minute, breathing quickly, processing what Cobb had just said, then closed his eyes, taking it all in.

Cities have fallen in a matter of hours.

No way.

It's impossible.

So are Zombies.

You just killed two of them.

Cities have fallen.

Thousands... no MILLIONS of these things were out there.

Right now.

Zombies.

What are you going to do?

What is most important right here, right now?

Prioritize.

Gunny reached his hand up to his forehead, stretched out his thumb to form a C with his fingers and in a slow, measured, fluid motion, he raked his hand down his body. He closed his chakras. All of them. Completely. He would deal with all this later.

It was a trick he had learned in his mandatory counseling sessions to determine his mental stability before he was quietly handed his walking papers. He was told never to darken the door of any government institution again. Army, Navy, Air Force, Marines, Coast Guard, National Guard, Reserves... All ties severed.

*Don't call us, we'll call you.* He had asked if that included the IRS. They were not amused. He didn't know if he really had chakras to close, or if it was all just a mumbo jumbo new age calming device, but either way, it worked. The one good thing that came out of those hour-long sessions twice a week was a way to close off his mind, to slow down the nightmares, to contain his rage before it got out of control. To shut off emotions for a while. To get his headspace and timing back in order.

He opened his eyes to Cobb still staring at him. "I'm good," he said, breathing evenly. Calm again. "I'm going to go talk to Wire Bender, then I'll grab a tarp and take care of this. But I don't have a good knife. You have keys to Switchblade's shop?"

Cobb unhooked a big ring of keys from his belt loop, handing them to Gunny. "It's marked. Switchblade doesn't open till nine. I don't think he's gonna make it." Gunny took them and started to turn away

"Get a good one," Cobb said. "He keeps those in the

glass cases. Ain't got a key for them, you'll have to snap the lock. Now I gotta go tell these people it ain't just the Three Flags. The whole damn world is melting down." Cobb sighed, seemed to sag, and looked older than ever.

Gunny felt a bit sorry for him. It wasn't a job he would have wanted. He looked out past Cookie, at a diner half full of people who didn't have the experiences with hardship and death that most of the drivers here had been through. Most of them weren't going to take it very well. He looked back at the haggard old man.

"Semper Fi, Top," he said softly.

Cobb seemed to shake himself, harrumphed and spat out his Lucky. "Don't you got some business to be attending to?" he growled, but Gunny saw his shoulders straighten and his back became stiff again as he turned and stomped out of the kitchen.

Switchblade's knife shop, The Cutting Edge, was near the main hall and carried a vast assortment of knives and swords and other less than lethal weapons. He had paper weights cleverly disguised as brass knuckles. He had props from every movie that ever had a sword or fancy knife in it, tons of cheap Chinese knives and, like Cobb had said, a small selection of quality knives locked away in display cases.

These weren't his best sellers, why buy a two hundred dollar knife if you didn't need it? You could buy a whole handful of twenty-dollar knives that looked cool and came in garish colors for the same money.

After he had let himself in, Gunny grabbed a sweet looking dagger with a stack of skulls for a handle and stuck it in the little lock to snap it off the showcase. It snapped at the hilt. So he grabbed a bright green knife that looked like a snake was curling around the grip.

It didn't do much better, although the blade lasted longer than the plastic handle. Sighing, he looked behind the counter and saw a screwdriver. It snapped the little lock right off. Switchblade didn't have many high-quality knives, only a few dozen, but they really were top shelf.

Genuine Ka-Bars, Gerbers, a few SOG Seal Team knives and H&Ks, among others. Gunny just grabbed a Gerber because the sheath was right there with it, and it looked as sturdy as any of the others. He slid it onto his belt, then finally headed down to the CB shop to see if there was any news from the Atlanta area.

As he passed Doc's office, he could see Scratch standing near the entrance door, talking to Hot Rod, but he was a good distance from the others.

Gunny smiled to himself, remembering a quote from General "Mad Dog" Mattis, "Be polite, be professional, but have a plan to kill everybody you meet."

It looked like Scratch was doing just that. As he opened the door to the cluttered Radio Shop, he could hear the sound of a dozen different voices over the CBs and Ham and shortwaves. They were vying to be heard over the televisions and internet feeds from around the world on all the monitors he had rigged up.

A visit to his den was always a headache-inducing endeavor if you didn't like the sound of background static and roger beeps and distant voices over loudspeakers, but now he had really cranked it up a few notches. Some of the guys noticed him as he came in and gave him nods.

"Cobb said those things are all over the place. That true?" he asked, raising his voice to be heard over the pandemonium coming from the speakers. He looked around at the multiple monitors and screens and saw the answer on their faces without being told.

Wire Bender finished talking to someone on one of the Ham radios, noticed Gunny, then hit a switch quieting the cacophony down so he wouldn't have to yell to be heard.

"Saw what you did out there, man," he said in his somewhat reedy voice, nodding toward the closed circuit video monitors on the back wall. The whole five minutes was on replay on one of the screens. It looped from the time the couple on the bikes left, to him and Pack Rat climbing up out of view toward the catwalk.

He watched it for a minute, saw himself shoot the little Mexican kid in the face, then turned away to see the rest of the men staring at him.

Hard men with hard faces.

Were they judging?

Did they think they could have done it better?

Were they Monday morning quarterbacking what he had to do?

Griz finally spoke up, said, "I don't know if I coulda done it, bro. That was some pipe hittin' shit." Then held his massive fist up for Gunny to bump. The tension broke and there were a few pats on his back, and "it had to be done" and "Thank God you didn't get your ass bit" comments. Then truckers, being who they were, somebody had to crack wise about Gunny's bow legged run. Then they were chuckling over the Ferrari he had plowed into.

Gunny went to the counter and Wire Bender was sitting there surrounded by his electronics, like an all-knowing oracle, like he had been waiting for this ever since Gunny had walked in the door.

"Atlanta?" he asked.

"Not good," Wire Bender said. "I got on the horn with some guys I know in that area about the time you were introducing Mr. Kenworth to Mr. Ferrari."

He tucked a length of long gray hair behind his ear. "Only one of 'em answered. He's way out in the sticks. He hadn't seen anything. As far as Atlanta proper.... Man, it's the same as everywhere else. All hell broke loose about seven or eight o'clock, their time. I've been up since way early, watching this develop. It's not just here, Gunny. While we were sleeping, most of Europe went through this. It's like it's following the path of the sun, or something. People wake up and turn zombie. I didn't think it could happen here, though."

Gunny watched the televisions, the internet channels. It was the same all over. Fire, mayhem, zombies, police in full riot gear.

"Some of the East Coast TV stations aren't even broadcasting. Half of the sites I go to for real news in Germany and France and England, aren't there anymore. I scan the radio dials and you don't hear voices, just music. Playlists on repeat, probably."

"But if it's been going on around the world, maybe following the sun as you say, why haven't we been warned? You know the military, the government has been watching all this!" one of the drivers said.

"Maybe it was all too fast," another opined. "If it comes with the sun, by the time Washington realized it was happening here, it already had."

"How can the sun make people turn into zombies?" Gunny asked, "there's no way unless...." He thought for a minute. "Unless we're already infected with something and the sun is the catalyst that sets it off?"

It was a stupid idea, but no one could come up with anything else that was even remotely more plausible. It was getting hot in the overcrowded room, and Gunny started edging his way out. He still needed to get rid of the thing in the freezer and watching all the footage and the news reports had left him utterly resolute. He now had no qualms whatsoever about putting one of those things....zombies.... down.

There was no shred of human left in them, as far as he was concerned. As he slipped through the door, he pulled his phone out to check for any texts that may have been missed in the noise and confusion, and saw that there were. Two of them!

He breathed a heavy sigh of relief and hurriedly swiped the screen to read the rest of the messages. They were both from his wife. The first must have been sent much earlier, but they both came through at the same time.

It read: *Dropping Terry and Linda off at the airport this morning. He said you can use his boat, but don't drink all his beer this time. LOL. Your boy has been fighting again. I'm out of oranges, can you pick some up at one of those roadside stands? Avocados, too. XOXO*

The other one read: *Been trying to call you for hours. Can't get through. Thank God you are OK. If you're reading this, then you know what is happening. Haven't heard from Jessie, but he had in-school detention. If he stays put, he will be OK. I am at work, but a group of us have barricaded ourselves on the 28th floor. We have Phil with us. He has killed 2 of them so far. We are OK for now, going to get to the roof. Mr. Sato said the Army would rescue people off rooftops. Once I'm off, I'll get Jessie. I love you, Honey. Please be safe. We will probably be in an Army camp when you get back. XOXOXO*

Gunny leaned against the wall, almost weak with relief. Lacy was okay. She was at work. That sucked, would have been better if she wasn't, but she was safe. They had 30 more stories to go to get to the roof. He wondered why they just didn't hop in the elevator and go.

Phil was the security guard and Gunny had seen that he carried a pistol when he'd met him on a few of the occasions he had taken her out to lunch. Her boss, Mr. Sato, was there with them. That was good. He was the CEO and if he said the Army was rescuing people, he must have a connection somewhere. They were setting up refugee camps. He hadn't heard or seen that on any of the news feeds they'd been watching, but that didn't mean anything.

Things weren't as bad as all that if the Army had birds out pulling people from rooftops. And Jessie was in detention. But that was good too. He knew from hearing him describe how isolated, unfair, and horrible it was the last time he wound up in there.

Locked up in a dungeon was how he put it. No cafeteria lunch, had to bring one from home, or go hungry. Had to beg for bathroom breaks. No phone. No iPod. A camera watching your every move. Just a notebook, paper, and one book.

Oh, the unfairness of it all. He'd told him to take his fights off the school grounds next time. Lacy had told him to walk away and not resort to violence. Whatever. He wasn't raising a Nancy Boy. His family was safe. That was good. Now all he had to do was drive 2400 miles through zombie infested country, find the right refugee camp, and collect them.

Piece of cake.

# JESSIE

## DETENTION

## Day 1

Jessie was taking care not to bob his head to the beat of the music, the ear buds ran carefully up his sleeve, out the top of his shirt, and hidden under his collar-length hair. Of course, the iPod was strictly forbidden in detention, and that was why everyone had one. Or their phone.

It was going on ten o'clock and the essay he had to have finished by the end of the day was nearly done. The old man always said if you had a job to do, just buckle down and get it over with. Not that he'd follow any advice the old man gave, but he didn't want to spend another day in this hell-hole of boredom, so he'd knock out the assignment and then knock out Kyle Farson's teeth after school, and off school property.

He's the bastard that got him in this mess. Then when the old man got home, he'd have to deal with him being pissed off and going on about military school if he screwed up "one more time". Kyle would pay for that, too. Busted nose. Maybe black both his eyes. Or not. He knew he would just let it go, but it felt good to dream of revenge.

Jessie didn't think of himself as a badass or anything, it's just that these private school kids were all a bunch of pansies. He'd been raised up on the military bases and even after his dad got out, he still went to the daycare and school on base because his mom worked there as a civilian. Military kids were pretty rough and tumble, they played hard and weren't mollycoddled when it came to scrapes and cuts. More than once he'd heard, "What are you crying about? I don't see a bone sticking out."

When they moved to Atlanta, he kept up with his karate classes and when he got in his teens, the old man had started showing him some really devious fighting moves. Stuff they didn't teach at the dojo. Stuff that he had to swear never to use unless he was prepared to be arrested and maybe sent to jail. Stuff only to be employed in a life or death situation. Brutal moves his old man said he'd been trained in while he was in the Army.

Things like eye gouging, elbow breaking, and neck snapping. Moves designed to kill or permanently maim. With the knowledge that he could crush anyone that came up against him, he had walked away from a lot of fights, had let them push him and call him a pussy or whatever. Because in his mind's eye, he could see the outcome, could see the jerk laying on the ground screaming in agony in about 2 seconds, and that was enough, just knowing he would win.

But Mr. "My Dad Is A Lawyer" Kyle Farson the Third had caught him off guard with a blow to the back of his head, had knocked his lunch tray out of his hands and sent it flying across the floor.

True, he'd called him a cock gobbling douche nozzle,

but that wasn't enough reason to sucker punch him. Jessie had kicked out on instinct and followed up with a few punches before he stopped himself. By then it was too late.

All the teachers saw was him pummeling on the richest kid in the school, it didn't matter that Kyle had started the whole thing. Poor little Kyle was laying on the floor with the wind knocked out of him and bleeding from a split lip, and Jessie didn't even have his hair messed up. So unfair.

Jessie looked up from his writing. He thought he'd heard something. Sheila was staring at him with an exasperated look, obviously trying to get his attention. Had he been singing along with the music?

He moved his hand to his pocket and hit the pause button, then nodded his head in a "what?" gesture. They never knew when someone from the office would be looking at the monitor, or when they would turn the sound up to listen in to ensure there was no talking in the room.

But he heard it now, heard what she must have been trying to get his attention about. He could hear screaming. Faint, but definitely there. They were in the basement of the school, in the mostly unused section, now that the new wing had been added a dozen years back.

The only classrooms down here that were still used on a regular basis were the practice rooms. Band, cheerleaders, the Glee Club. Basically, anybody that was loud. And, of course, detention.

Jessie glanced around the room. Everyone was listening now, nobody was pretending to do their work while playing on their phones, or zoning out to music. Definitely screams. He stood up and went to the door, trying to see out of the frosted window. Nothing. The door was locked, but he tried it anyway, jiggling the knob. Sheila had walked up to the camera and was waving her arms at it, saying, "Hello! Hello! What's going on?"

Gary rolled over in his wheelchair and cupped his hands against the door's window, trying to see out, but it was useless. The glass was too opaque to make out anything definite, just a single running figure that darted by.

"Fire drill?" Doug asked, standing behind the wheel-chair, looking over his head, also trying to see out of the frosted glass.

"We would have heard the alarm," Gary said.

Another shadowy shape ran by and he started pounding on the door, yelling for them to open it.

Whoever it was kept on going.

"This is so weird," Sheila said, giving up waving at the camera. "I heard if you even get out of your chair, someone is on the speaker telling you to sit down." This was her first time in detention, a result of getting caught texting for the third time during class.

"True enough," Gary said. He had been here a few times before, his "poor attitude" and angry outbursts always seeming to land him in hot water. He had only been para-lyzed for a few years, was still trying to adjust to it. The dirt bike wreck that had broken his back hadn't even been that bad. He had just landed a small jump wrong and woke up in the hospital, paralyzed from the waist down. He couldn't even remember how it happened.

He was one of those popular kids who got along with everybody: the jocks, the stoners, and the nerds. It didn't matter to him, he was usually an upbeat and friendly guy, and the teachers had let him slide on a lot of things.

Sometimes he went too far and found himself in the dungeon, paying for his outburst with a day of monotony and boredom. His black moods and depression, which had plagued him since the accident, seemed to be finally lifting a little and his competitive spirit was coming back. He had recently taken up wheelchair racing and was concentrating on more of the computer science classes, finding he had a knack for it.

Doug walked over to the call box and pushed the button. It was supposed to be used to call the office if there was an emergency, or if someone needed a bathroom pass. He pressed it repeatedly, but no one answered. He was the jokester of the group, one of his pranks went a little too far and he wound up down in the basement with the rest of the miscreants.

Jessie rattled the door again, jerking on the knob, trying to get it to force open. "This is a load of bull," he said. "Isn't there laws against locking people in? What if there really is a fire or something?"

"The Woodland Academy of Higher Learning for the Woefully Inadequate does not have to abide by such pedestrian rules, old chap," Doug intoned in his best British snobbery voice.

Jessie grinned, despite himself. "Well, I guess if there is a reason for us to bust out, we just throw a chair through the window." But he was concerned, and getting more so. They heard another scream, somewhere far away.

Sheila had her phone out and had been trying to call the front office, but wasn't getting anything, just an all circuits busy recording. Everyone else brought theirs out and tried various numbers, all with the same results.

"Try text," Gary said. "It may get through, the data packet for messages is tiny."

Jessie's first text was to his mom and was tongue in cheek. "*Something going on. Trapped in the dungeon. Office isn't answering the buzzer. May have to make a jail break!*"

The guys finished a few texts apiece and then watched Sheila as she typed away on her phone, her fingers moving at incredible speed.

"You writing a book?" Doug asked.

She looked up and saw them all staring at her and was getting ready to answer with something snarky when they heard a group of people running by the door with ragged breaths, and a guttural howling thing fly by the window after them.

They stared at each other, all humor gone, and edged back over to the door, trying to see anything through the opaque glass. There was more running, more howling things, and the sounds of doors slamming and breaking windows, then screams of terror and pain at the end of the corridor.

Jessie looked down at the doorknob, now very glad it was locked.

"Was that..." Gary started, but couldn't find the words and trailed off. Not a fire drill. Not a joke of some kind, the screams were real. They were the 'terrified and filled with pain' kind of screams that couldn't be faked. "School shooter?" he finally asked a little lamely.

No one had an answer. Things had just gotten real. Joke time was over. They had just heard people die, they were sure of it. Whatever was going on out there was really happening. As teenagers raised on a steady diet of horror movies, video games, and comic books, they probably accepted the unexplainable faster and more readily than the grownups.

"Werewolves?" Gary asked in a half whisper, not really believing it could be.

"It's daytime. No moon," Jessie whispered without thinking. They could still hear the sounds of the dying.

"Vampires?" Sheila asked.

"Not unless they're the sparkly kind," Doug said in a hushed tone.

"God, I wish I had those legs!" Gary whispered vehemently, slamming his fists down on his useless ones in frustration.

They all knew what he was talking about. They'd heard him mention them often enough. Where he went to do his rehabilitation therapy, there were a set of mechanical legs that he could strap on and operate with hand controls. He couldn't actually run in them, but he was able to move around a lot better than he could in the chair.

The only problem was the cost. Insurance didn't cover them and his parents didn't have an extra hundred grand laying around. They all glanced at his chair. At his limited mobility. What had been an incredible inconvenience before, might now be a death sentence.

A shadowy figure lurched by the door and Sheila gave a short little involuntary gasp. It stopped, as if listening. Everyone froze in place, eyes wide, Jessie making a shushing motion at her. She covered her mouth with both hands, her eyes huge and full of terror.

A hand slapped against the window, leaving a trail of dark liquid in its wake and she jumped, squeaked out a stifled cry. It heard and the door rattled violently as it threw itself against it, hands trying to reach through the opaque glass. It started howling and keening, and soon it was joined by more.

They could see the outlines of a half dozen bodies through the frosted glass, all of them clawing at it. It was only a matter of time before one of them swung a fist hard enough to break through, and then it would be all over. They backed away, Jessie and Gary both looking for something to use as a weapon, then they heard a chilling high-pitched scream out in the hall.

It sounded like it was coming from the boiler room at the end of the corridor. The things outside abandoned the door they were trying to get through and ran, howling, toward the sounds of sheer panic. The screaming didn't last long.

## 7

Gunny left the CB shop and walked up to Doc's to check on the deputy, Ozzy, and Hot Rod. He stepped over to Scratch as he walked in, quietly asking, "Everything okay?"

Scratch nodded to the affirmative, but he was well away from the rest of them, near the door, trying to act nonchalant about being in the doctor's office with a rifle in his arms. His finger was off the trigger, but right there near it.

Ozzy was pale now and lying flat on the countertop, his leg bandaged and elevated on a pillow. Billy Travaho had both girls hovering over him and he was completely sprawled out on the couch, breathing shallowly. Hot Rod found a shirt somewhere and had put it on, and although he had an apprehensive look about him, he seemed no worse than before.

"I think we should at least tie their feet," Gunny said to Scratch when he saw they were getting worse. "You saw how fast they moved."

"Yeah," he said. "But Cobb told me to stay here. Can you grab some rope?"

"I'm on it," Gunny said and left, heading toward the mechanic's bays. He noticed Pack Rat and a couple of the drivers in the weight room, but kept going toward the garage. He didn't have any rope on his truck, but he was sure Tommy had some in the shop somewhere. When he walked in, there was a flurry of activity going on, all of the mechanics, and a few of the drivers were busy barricading the windows at the back of the shop.

Out of the front windows, there was another rig parked lengthwise, effectively blocking them from any flailing zombie attack. The back windows were within the perimeter fencing, but Gunny knew that fence was old. It had probably been there for twenty years.

He jogged over to his truck, found his box of ammo and reloaded the nearly empty magazine in his Glock, then dumped the rest in his jacket pocket. He spotted Cobb's son, Tommy, helping hold a piece of angle iron over a window while one of his mechanics welded it to the steel wall of the Quonset hut.

He saw that they were doing this for all of the windows, basically making bars close enough together that no human-sized forms could get through. "Hey Tommy," Gunny yelled over the noise of the welders arcing and the hissing of the cutting torches.

Tommy looked up, made sure the angle iron had enough of a weld on it to hold in place, then headed over to meet Gunny in the middle of the shop.

"Got any rope?" he asked. "Some people have been bitten. It's probably best to restrain them in case they turn."

"Yeah," Tommy said. "Over in the parts room. There's some on a spool."

"Got it. And if you need any of that wood off of my trailer, take whatever you want," Gunny said, indicating his

106

flatbed that was in the second bay, loaded with fine New England lumber. '

"Thanks," Tommy said with a half-smile. "But we're using steel for now. A little stronger."

Gunny watched him head over to another flatbed a few bays over, loaded with angle iron and rebar, and grab another long piece to drag over to the man with the cutting torch. Tommy was a Marine, too.

*Once a Marine, always a Marine,* as they say. But he did his four years and got out. Served honorably, but it just wasn't his thing. Tommy was Cobb's only son and he probably joined just to keep up the family tradition and keep Cobb off his back. His heart was in turning wrenches and building things.

He had grown up in the Three Flags with his mother and grandparents whenever Cobb was off on another of his, seemingly endless, deployments. Occasionally they would go live with him when he was stationed in the States for a few years at a time, but it always seemed temporary. The truck stop was home.

Tommy's kids, Kim-Li and Daniel, had played and worked there ever since they were born. Kimmy helping in the kitchen, Danny washing trucks and following the mechanics around. Daniel was in the Marines now, still in his training rotations. Unlike his dad, he'd eagerly jumped in with both feet and had been selected for Force Recon. Fourth generation Marine, and an officer to boot.

Gunny bet ol' Cobb couldn't wait to hang his honor box up on the wall behind the Missing Man table. He was just waiting for him to get some more ribbons or medals so there would be something to display.

He cut a few lengths of rope off of the spool with the Gerber strapped to his leg, then headed back to the Doc's office. There was quite a commotion going on in the weight room as he passed, all of the drivers were standing near the middle of the room, staring at the thrashing man strapped to the examination table.

Gunny sighed. He knew that biker was going to turn. He hurried on down to Doc's, the thing on the table wasn't going anywhere, and maybe someone would take care of it, put it out of its misery. He rushed in and without preamble, just started tying Ozzy's feet in a tight hobble. He would still be able to walk, albeit short steps, but if he tried to run he would fall on his face.

"Toss him one of those," Scratch said, indicating Hot Rod.

Gunny did and Hot Rod started to hobble his own feet, leaving a little more room to walk than Gunny had given Ozzy. "I want to be able to get away from these guys," he said in his defense, when he noticed Scratch giving him a hard look. "They look like shit, man. I'm scared, but I ain't feeling anything. Nothing like them."

"He has a point," Gunny said, and Scratch relented. A little.

The girls weren't paying much attention to them, they were fussing over Billy with cold cloths, trying to get his fever down. Ozzy had a wet towel over his forehead also. The biker girl kept glancing back at Ozzy, and then looked up to Gunny from where she was kneeling by the couch. "Maybe you should tie his hands, too," she said as she held hers out for a piece of the rope to secure Billy's legs. "They're both fading fast. That must be some seriously virulent saliva."

Hot Rod looked scared, his brown skin was ashen as he sat there in the borrowed shirt, texting on his phone. Maybe his last goodbye to someone back home. He caught Gunny staring at him and kind of half grimaced, half smiled. "I wanted to apologize for running out on you out there in the parking lot, man. I lost it. I was scared to death. When that dude came at you..." he trailed off. "I shoulda stayed to help," he finished quietly.

Gunny shook his head. Poor guy. Making his peace with the world.

"I probably would have ran, too. Don't worry about it. You getting the fever yet?"

"No.," he said. "I didn't get bit, just scratched. I'm feeling okay, all things considered."

"He's not showing any of the signs these two did," the biker girl said, finishing the knots on Billy's hands and feet. Stacy stood up from the deputy and walked over to Hot Rod, placing the back of her hand against his forehead. She wasn't quite a nurse yet, but she had started her last year of school so she was the closest thing they had to a medical professional. Working at Doc's little clinic allowed her the time she needed to study during the day because business was usually pretty slow. "A little warm, but not bad," she declared. "I'm starting to think that only the saliva is the carrier for this virus, or bacteria, or whatever it is."

"You don't think it's airborne?" Gunny asked.

"I kind of doubt it. No one seems to have any symptoms other than bite victims. I'm getting a clearer picture now of what we're dealing with after talking to these guys and seeing the reactions. Have you checked the other biker out lately?" Stacy asked.

"His name is Brian," the leather clad girl said. She looked at Gunny, waiting for an answer.

"I'm sorry," he said to her. "He's, umm...changed. He's like the ones in the parking lot."

She nodded. "These two are going to change also," she

said, matter of factly. "Normally I would say we need to secure them somewhere until help arrives, but let's face it. Help isn't coming. I heard that policeman's radio. They were screaming and crying and dying. All of them. I've accepted it, and now someone has a job to do. I guess it's just like in the movies, right? It has to be a headshot?"

Gunny was again caught off guard. He had seen it up close and personal, had fought and killed those things, and this gal, just from hearing a radio transmission, was having an easier time accepting it than he did. "Yeah," he said after a moment. "That rapper guy shot one at least 12 times and it kept coming. I put a bullet in its head, and it dropped instantly."

"So the one we put in the freezer, has anyone checked on him?" she asked.

"It's back alive but frozen solid. I need to take care of him. Just haven't yet," Gunny said.

This chick must have ice water running through her veins, he was thinking.

"Sara is an EMT in Reno," Scratch chimed in, seeing the questioning look on Gunny's face. "She's probably used to blood and guts and stuff."

The girl half smiled. "Yep. But we didn't usually have people reanimating after they've expired."

8

Gunny grabbed a couple of blue tarps and a roll of duct tape off of the shelf in the main C-store. He could hear voices raised in the diner, the sounds of arguments. Cobb must have told them what was happening. He headed back to the weight room that was really just a hodgepodge of home-built lifting contrivances.

Cobb wasn't about to pay for professional gym equipment, and the truckers that worked out didn't need fancy spa machines, just steel bars in blocks of concrete to lift, old engine blocks hooked on pulleys to lift, heavy cranks cleaned up and used as dumbbells to lift... really just anything heavy to work with. The small group of truckers was still gathered around the thrashing form of the biker, strapped firmly to the exam table.

He was still face down, but his head was turned and he was gnashing at the men who were staying well out of his reach. His eyes were solid black, the pupils fully dilated. His whole body was spasming and straining, trying to sink teeth into anyone or anything.

The vinyl of the table was ripped and some of the

stuffing was falling out. They looked at Gunny, standing there with the tarp and tape, and knew what had to be done. He looked at them. Pack Rat, Griz, Squeak, Shakey and a few others. "Any takers?" he asked, holding out the knife to them.

"Be easier to just shoot it," Pack Rat said. "But I guess I see your point. Do it quiet-like."

"I've never killed a man with a knife," Griz said. "We used bullets in the sandbox. If it came down to a knife fight, you already screwed up." He paused, then added, "But if you can't, I will."

Gunny saw that no one wanted to do what had to be done so he set the tarps down and walked over to the keening, thrashing, form. Before he could think about it too long and lose his nerve, he grabbed a handful of hair to hold it still and swung the knife down to drive it into the back of its head.

The blade slid off the hard bone and down the side of the creature's face, leaving a deep furrow and ripping its ear off as a large piece of scalp flapped over, revealing the yellowish bone of the skull.

"Oh, that's sick," someone said as the snarling, flailing thing snapped at Gunny's wrist. He hurriedly slammed the knife down a second time, and again it careened off of the skull, not driving in like it was supposed to, but grooving down the other side of its head.

Gunny was trying to hold the head still with his hand, gripping a shank of hair, but the way it was jerking around, it was scalping itself. The hair ripped free from the skull and Gunny let go, jumping back with a look of disgust. The flap of hair was over its face and it was biting and chewing on it, pulling more off, more of its bloody, yellow skull being exposed.

One of the drivers ran out of the door, they could hear him retching in the hallway. Gunny stood back, watching in horror as the thing ate itself, ripping its own face off in a frenzy with its incessantly biting teeth. "Fuck this," he said, pulled out his Glock and fired once, sending brain splatter all over the back wall. There was silence as they all stared, grossed out, but unable to look away.

"You should have rammed it up into the skull at the base of the spine, it's softer there than..." Pack Rat trailed off as Gunny turned and glared at him, a hard look on his face, nostrils flared and a twitch under his right eye.

The smoking gun was still in his hand, and Griz and Shakey stepped away from the old know-it-all. "But a shot with the pistol, now that was good. Yes, sir, sure was. Here, let me help you with those tarps," he said, hurriedly reaching for them before Gunny decided to shoot him too.

"Gunny," Griz intoned. "You are one hard son of a bitch." Then he grabbed the other tarp to help the old man wrap the corpse.

*"Three more..."* he thought, heading back to the Doc's office. Three more, and I'm done. I'm going to get a long, hot shower, get in my truck, and get the hell out of here. He went through the door quickly, still reeling from the botched mercy euthanasia he had tried. Man, that was disgusting.

*"The old man was right, though,"* he thought. Base of the skull, right at the spine. No bone there. How had he forgotten that? He wanted to tie Ozzy and Billy up TIGHT! Just hobbled, he realized now, they were still dangerous, and there would be no way to take them out with a knife without getting chewed up in the process. Maybe gags, he thought.

The biker girl was just standing up from the couch,

using a paper towel to wipe off a long metal letter opener in her hand. Billy looked at peace now.

"Why did you shoot?" she asked, staring straight at Gunny. "I thought you were going to do it quietly."

"I tried," he said. "The knife kept bouncing off."

She gave him a look that made him feel like an idiot. "Come here," she said. "Watch." She walked over to Ozzy, whose breathing was shallow and quick. She turned his head to one side and placed the letter opener right at the base of his neck, where the cervical vertebra was held to the skull with only a thin layer of muscle and skin.

"You're not going to wait until he's dead?" Scratch asked.

"He's already dead," she said. "He was dead the second the bacteria from the bite was carried to his brain. There is nothing I can do. There is probably nothing anyone can do, or they would already be doing it, not dying by the millions to these things. You want to wait until he starts thrashing around, maybe bites you while you try to hold him still?" she asked, holding the letter opener out to him.

Scratch looked at her, at Ozzy struggling for each shallow, hitching, breath that he took, and shook his head.

Stacy took it from her outstretched hand. "You did Billy. I got this." She moved fast, just a quick thrust and wiggle, and she was pulling it back out, wiping it off on the paper towel, then composing Ozzy's hands on his chest.

She looked over at Hot Rod.

He held his hands up to start to protest.

"I think you're good," she said. "You aren't showing any signs. Sara, you concur?"

She did, but they all agreed that Hot Rod needed to remain visible, stay in the dining room, and everyone was going to be keeping an eye on him. He wasn't out of the woods, yet, maybe scratches were slow acting, whereas bites were a much faster way to death.

Hot Rod agreed quickly, eyeing the cold-blooded women. One in a doctor's lab coat and one in leather, thinking he had just dodged a bullet.

Scratch went after more tarps and tape, and Gunny went to talk to Tommy. After a quick discussion, they decided to bury the wrapped bodies at the back of the junk-yard. The soil would be soft, and no one really wanted them stacked up in the freezer. Griz grabbed a tire cart and easily stacked all three corpses on it, and took off toward the back with a handful of drivers carrying shovels. Pack Rat followed along, telling them all the best way to dig a grave. "We'll have one more in a minute," Gunny called after them

"I'll be back," Griz said in his best Terminator voice.

Gunny chuffed and shook his head. Even in the middle of a zombie apocalypse, these guys still hadn't lost their sense of humor. Probably because as bad as this was, most of them had seen worse. War is an ugly and brutal business, and something about it pulls the survivors together in an unexplainable way.

There are no bonds of brotherhood that are stronger than those of men who have fought together, killed together, and watched friends die together. All were glad when it was over, and hated it when it was happening. But there was a small part of them that craved the intensity of battle. After you had experienced it, every other sensation in life paled when compared to it.

They were almost like junkies, dreading the war, but thriving on the adrenaline rush. Hello Darkness, my old friend.

As Gunny was headed toward the C-store to get yet another tarp, hopefully the last one he would have to use, the biker girl and Stacy came out of the little clinic and fell in beside him.

"I'm Sara," the leather-clad girl said. "The fellow with the prosthetic, you call him Scratch? He told you I'm an EMT, right?"

"Yeah," Gunny said. Not sure where this was going.

"Before you euthanize this guy in the freezer, we want to run a few tests."

Stacy picked up the conversation at Gunny's puzzled look, "If he's frozen, he won't be able to move around much. We need to find out a few things. Like check for heartbeat and blood pressure, see if his pupils react to light."

She held up a little medical flashlight and indicated her stethoscope. "When Billy died, when he stopped breathing, I had my 'scope to his chest when he opened his eyes. I didn't detect a heartbeat, but Sara had the letter opener up into his brain almost instantly, so I really couldn't tell."

Gunny didn't see what it mattered, but he didn't understand doctor things. Above his pay grade. But they were right, if the guy was frozen, they could check those things in relative safety. "Sure," he said, grabbing a roll of tape, along with one of the last blue tarps. "I'll drag him out into the kitchen and you can test away."

As they entered the kitchen through the back corridor, the argument in the dining room sounded even worse than before. A bunch of people were all shouting over each other, trying to be heard. Gunny ignored them and laid out the tarp, opened the freezer door, and dragged the frozen man out.

He set him on the plastic and then stepped back, letting the girls do whatever it was they wanted to do. They talked quietly, Sara jotting notes as Stacy quickly ran through a battery of tests she wanted to get done. Gunny waited while they poked and prodded and tested things, and looked out over the order counter into the dining room.

The driver's area was nearly empty, only a few guys still in there watching the argument in the main diner area. The black kid that had helped carry in the man the girls were running their tests on was sitting by himself, staring out of the window through the gap between the tractor and trailer. He was ignoring everyone, and Gunny could see tear tracks on his face. He said he had known these guys.

They must have been close. A corpulent man in a salmon colored polo shirt was waving his finger at Cobb, who was doing his best to be diplomatic and treat his guests with respect. Gunny figured that wouldn't last much longer when he heard Martha's voice jump into the mix. This was surprising because he didn't think she was the type to get fired up and start yelling at customers. Cobb, sure. Cookie, all the time. But she was always polite to her guests. He was paying attention now, trying to follow her angry, broken English as she waved a spoon in the fat man's face.

"You scare 'cause you hear gunshot? You mad?" she yelled at him. "You think truck driver crazy with gun? What you think happen here we no have gun? You think zombie peoples not eat you?"

"They're not zombies!" the man roared. "They are just sick people! How many times do I have to tell you, there are no such things as zombies!" He had a woman half his age by his side. She was drop dead gorgeous and she just nodded her head at everything he said, agreeing sycophantically.

Martha was right back in his face, wagging the spoon, "You think you know better than soldier? All these men who save you life, they soldier! They almost die to save all you and you want call cop to take them to jail for hitting you car?"

"It wasn't just a car! It was a Ferrari!" he yelled right back.

Cobb reached up to take Martha's arm, to calm her down, but she whirled on him. "You no say me calm down!" she yelled, her broken English getting worse in her anger. Cobb backed off. The petite little Asian grandmother was fired up, and she wasn't about to take any more of this man talking bad about her boys, her soldiers, her truck drivers.

The men whose fast thinking and quick actions had saved all their lives, and she didn't understand how this fat fool couldn't see that. How most of them in the dining room couldn't see that. She went right back to telling him how lucky he was that he was here and not somewhere else where he would already be dead, half in English and half in her native tongue when she couldn't find the right word.

"Damn," Gunny said to Stacy as she stood, finished with what she came to do. "I've never seen Martha so pissed. Even Cobb looks a little scared of her."

"He should be," she replied. "You never heard the story about when she almost killed him?"

Gunny looked at her. "No. Really? How did that happen?"

Stacy pulled an antiseptic wipe out of her pocket and started cleaning her stethoscope and other tools she had.

"Well," she said. "The way I heard it was that it wasn't long after they first got married, Cobb came home drinking with loving on his mind. They got into an argument and he hit her. Gave her a pretty good shiner, Kim said. After he passed out, she sewed him up in the bed sheets good and tight. A couple of layers, so he wouldn't be able to break out.

"You can imagine how mad he must have been when he woke up the next morning. She just whacked him with a frying pan, told him to shut up. Every time he started to

118

raise his voice, she would hit him again. She beat the tar out of him. Ever notice Cobb's crooked nose? That didn't happen in some bar fight. She broke it with a frying pan. She wasn't playing. Kim said she smacked on him for days with that pan. When he finally learned not to shout, he started telling her what he was going to do to her when he got out. How he was going to teach her a lesson she would never forget. He struggled for a long time before he finally gave up and realized there was no way he could get free. She left him there.

"He pissed himself, he crapped himself. After a few days, he was begging. She didn't feed him, or give him water. She told him he was going to stay there until her face was completely healed. If he died before it was, then the Gods had willed it. Cobb knew he wouldn't be able to last much longer without water. He begged and promised. Anything to get out. She had broken him. Something the toughest Marines, or the wars he was in, couldn't do.

"You know Cobb doesn't drink, right?" she asked. "He hasn't touched booze since then. She finally cut him loose when he was too weak to stand. More dead than alive. She bathed him, gave him soup, told him she loved him more than any woman could love a man, and would until she was old and gray. But if he ever hit her again, or hit one of their children in anger, she would sew him in the sheets and take the children and go back home to her people. He believed her."

"Good for her," Sara said.

Gunny didn't know what to say to that. Wondered how much was true, and how much was family legend. Best not to say anything when women were telling women stories. He watched Martha over the counter, unafraid of the big man, not letting him say anything disparaging about her drivers, her soldiers. Her friends. But other customers, and the blonde in the skin tight skirt at his side, were siding with the man, shouting their own opinions in when they got a chance and he knew this wasn't going to end well. Cobb was going to blow a gasket and punch the guy any minute.

Cadillac Jack stood by Cobb with an angry scowl on his face, but he was seventy if he was a day. There were only a few drivers in there, mostly guys that had come in for a quick break. The rest were out doing what needed to be done.

Digging holes in the ground and burying dead bodies. Reinforcing the windows and walls. Standing guard on the roof, or patching the fence. Establishing communications with other pockets of people and trying to figure out what was going on. Trying to save the wounded and running tests on dead bodies to try to determine some way to help.

And these spoiled, lazy bastards, sitting in the air-conditioned diner this whole time sipping coffee, were giving Martha and Cobb hell for doing what had to be done to save their sorry asses. He kept hearing the same mantra over and over from the people out there. You are delusional, there are no such thing as zombies, this isn't a Hollywood movie set, and that truck driver had killed two people. He had smashed up a bunch of cars, and as soon as the phones were working, he would be arrested for murder.

Gunny was getting pissed. They were all experiencing cognitive dissonance. They were refusing to believe what was plainly self-evident, but it was too much for them to grasp. It would shatter their little world of make believe they had created for themselves over the past few hours. They weren't helping do anything because then they would have to face the truth. They would just sit in here, reassuring everyone and themselves that it would all be just fine.

Things would sort themselves out. The police, or the government, would get things under control shortly and things can get back to normal. Help would be here soon. He heard a moan from the blinded painter who had half of his face missing. He was thawing out. Gunny didn't think in his anger, just grabbed the edges of the tarp, wrapped it around the thawing corpse and started dragging it through the kitchen and into the dining room.

When they saw him coming through the doors a few of them pointed at him. "There he is," he heard. The man in the pink polo shirt wasn't shy, he yelled right at him, "You killed two people! We saw you and none of your trashy trucker friends can cover that up! Where's that police officer that was here? What did you people do to him? And you destroyed my car! It cost more than you can ever earn! I hope you have insurance, I'm going to sue you for every dime you have, and every dime you will ever make!"

The blonde had her hand on his shoulder and bobbed her head up and down like an idiot bobble-head doll.

There were other comments and shouts at him, but he ignored them all, just drug his struggling load wrapped in the tarp to the middle of the room near the man, where they all could see then, dropped the ends he was holding.

The room got quiet as the blinded thing inside pushed away the ends of the plastic and struggled to sit up, still half frozen.

"He's been in a sub-zero freezer for the past couple of hours," Gunny said quietly. "That should have killed him."

There were gasps, and the scraping of chairs, as everyone moved back a few steps when they realized what it was. Mr. Ferrari grabbed his girlfriend and pushed her in front of him as he backpedaled away.

"He was bitten in the neck, his jugular vein ripped wide open. That should have killed him."

They all looked on in horror as it tried to stand. Gunny kicked him back down, then pulled out his gun and shot it in the chest. The people screamed and there were shouts of protest.

"That was a nine-millimeter hollow point bullet aimed right into his heart from two feet away. That should have killed him." The thing had bounced off the floor and continued to try to sit up. Gunny shot it thirteen more times in rapid succession, pulling the trigger as fast as he could, riddling its body, shattering bone, blowing big holes in its chest and bigger ones out of its back.

The roar of the gun and the screams of the people were deafening in the confined space as the bullets went through it, the linoleum, and into the hardwood floor. The last shot's echo faded away, the cordite smell filled the room, and with gun smoke still curling from the barrel, the blinded thing struggled to sit up again. It couldn't, its spine was shattered.

It pulled itself over and started crawling toward the blonde woman, who was still screaming. Its forward progress was slow, still half frozen, but relentless. Gunny paced it, just watching as the horror clawed toward the human sounds it heard. Its ruined face half missing, its eye sockets hollow, and the remains of its squished orbs dangling on grizzly stalks.

"Do you still think he's just sick?" he asked the crowd, who was backing away, their eyes glued to the crawling wreck of a human being. "Do you think he's still alive?" he asked, looking at them, trying to catch their eyes. "Anyone want to check for a pulse?" He looked around at the crowd, at the looks of fear on their faces as they kept pushing away from it. "Anyone?" he said, barely above a whisper.

There were no takers.

It dragged itself along the floor, trailing blood and slime from its blown open chest, chunks of broken ribs and spine jutting out of its back. "If he bites you, within a few hours, you will become just like him," Gunny said, walking softly beside it. He didn't have to raise his voice, the room was deathly silent, except for a quietly crying blonde woman with her hands over her mouth, desperately trying to silence herself.

"He can hear you," Gunny whispered and the gurgling sound coming from the crawling man's throat, the rasp of fingers and skin on the floor as it pulled itself along, seemed uncannily amplified. "It can't be bargained with," he murmured.

"It can't be reasoned with. It doesn't feel pity or remorse or fear. And it absolutely will not stop, EVER, until you are dead."

The crowd had moved away from the woman, who couldn't manage to stop her hitching, crying, sobs. She was against the wall and couldn't retreat any further. She was alone. Her boyfriend wasn't helping her. The people she had befriended these past few hours weren't helping her. The thing on the floor pulled itself toward her, its useless legs trailing behind in a smear of blood and intestinal juices, its teeth starting to gnash in anticipation of food.

"The world has fallen, people," he said. "I don't know how, or why, or who did it, but the world we woke up to is gone. The sooner you realize that, the longer you will survive."

"Please..." the woman sobbed, tearing her eyes away from the crawling thing only a few feet away from her,

DAVID A. SIMPSON

looking at Gunny. Her mascara was streaked and running down her cheeks, her tears flowing freely. "Please don't," she whimpered, still unable to move away, or stop her crying.

"Stop it," someone in the crowd cried. "Just stop it!"

Gunny grabbed the scrabbling thing by the hair, drug it back to the tarp and placed the gun against its forehead. He used the last bullet to stop its struggles, then wrapped it back up in the tarp. He dragged it out toward the shop to be buried with the rest, feeling like an asshole for scaring the woman so badly. He wasn't going to let it bite anyone. He just wanted them to understand what they were dealing with, but it probably went too far.

Especially that Terminator quote.

## 9

"Prone to theatrics much," Kim asked when Gunny, Tiny, and most of the rest of the drivers and mechanics came back into the diner an hour or so later, finished with their tasks of burying the dead, repairing the fence, and securing the building as best they could.

"It got the point across," he said, a little defensively.

"You're right about that," she replied. "Nobody wants you arrested anymore. Except maybe the Ferrari guy. He's probably still upset. But his girlfriend hates him now. Called him a coward for pushing her in front of him. Kind of funny, actually. You want some lunch? Cookie made up a bunch of stuff, just grab a plate and head to the buffet."

There seemed to be more people than there were this morning and Gunny mentioned this as they got in line behind Scratch, waiting to load their plates.

"There are," Tiny said. "After everything quieted down, when you guys were all out back digging the graves, a bunch of guys that had stayed in their trucks made a run for the front doors. There's enough room to squeeze past Pack Rat's trailer and get inside. But Cobb's blocked that now, there are too many of those dead things out there."

Gunny hadn't been up on the roof again, and the view from the windows was blocked by the trucks. "Really?" he said. "They're coming in off the road?"

"Yeah," Tiny replied. "They're trickling in by ones and twos. Sometimes a half dozen. But they just keep coming. There is probably sixty or seventy out there, now, just milling around. I was up on the roof for about an hour till Peanut Butter relieved me. I guess the noise, or maybe the smell of people, is attracting them."

"Crap," Gunny said. "I was planning on leaving after I ate and said my goodbyes."

"Might want to wait till Wire Bender has his say," Scratch said. "He's gathered all the information he has so far, and him and Cobb are planning on giving a little brief to everyone. Kind of let everybody know everything that they've been able to figure out, I guess."

Gunny nodded and added an extra slice of meatloaf to his plate. Cookie had been a Mess Sergeant in the Army and his food was never very fancy, but it was always good and filling. He found a booth by the window and the three of them sat in the same configuration they had just a few hours ago, watching the firm backside of the leather clad girl on the motorcycle, ignorant to the death and destruction that was only a few minutes in their future.

"Déjà vu," Scratch said. Voicing what all of them felt.

The TV was off now. None of the cable channels worked, and the local stations only had test patterns. Some of the radio stations were still playing music, but they hadn't heard a live voice over the air in hours.

Cobb clomped in a few minutes later with Wire Bender and The Preacher following close behind, both of them carrying papers in their arms. "Preacher made it in. Cool," Scratch said. "I was wondering if he was out in the chapel."

"Yeah," Gunny said. "He was out back with us while Cobb had you on cleanup detail. He said some words over the ones we buried."

"Right," Scratch groused at him "Thanks for that. Next time do you have to let it leave a blood trail a mile long?"

"At ease!" Cobb barked and the truckers quieted down instantly, the others in the dining room soon realized the strange command meant 'shut up' and stopped talking to pay attention. He was standing near the entry doors and Wire Bender was helping Preacher unfurl a map of the world and pin it to the bulletin board, covering up the 'trucks for sale' and 'drivers needed' posts that were on it.

"Since Gunny's little display of marksmanship, and the proper way to ruin a perfectly good floor," Cobb started in without preamble, his drill sergeant voice carrying easily to the back reaches of the diner. "Everyone knows what we are up against. Right now there are about seventy of those things outside, wanting inside."

There were gasps from some of the people, and a murmur started up. Cobb didn't get louder, or acknowledge the interruption, just carried on in his command voice and the people talking quickly hushed.

"Wire Bender has been in communication with people all over these United States and between that, and monitoring the internet, he's put together a pretty good picture of what we are dealing with. These two girls have some medical experience and have a little something they want to say about what they've been able to figure out."

He pointed his chin at Sara and Stacy to indicate them. "The Padre here is going to say a little prayer, and then Wire Bender will brief you on what we know." He moved aside and Preacher stepped up and asked for the people to bow their heads. If there were any atheists in the room, they didn't voice any complaints.

Preacher was succinct in his prayer, mentioned the bible passages that talked about the dead rising, asked for guidance, and when he finished, there was a hearty Amen.

Wire Bender stepped up then, looking a little nervous at all the eyes on him. He started out hesitantly, with many "um's" and "er's", but once he got going, the facts and figures and numbers came fast and hard. He referenced the map, pointing out all of the cities he knew for certain were in utter chaos. He had highlighted them in red.

They were all red. Paris, Berlin, Moscow, Tokyo, London, Seoul, Beijing, New Delhi, New York, Mexico City, Washington D.C., Los Angeles, Atlanta.... All of them. This contagion had spread so fast, no one could figure out the trigger that had caused it. From gleaning through all the news reports, he had determined that it started two days ago in limited areas, but today it had exploded worldwide.

Everywhere at once. There was something instigating it, some release mechanism no one had figured out yet, and it was following the path of the sun. The CDC scientists in Atlanta and the Military had been frantically working all night, trying to determine the cause, but when the sun came up in America, our cities had gone the way of the rest of the world. As near as anyone could determine, it had started in Japan, spread to China and Russia, devastated Europe in a matter of hours and started in North America around 6 am, Eastern Standard Time.

Reports from South America were spotty, but from everything he had heard, they weren't spared either. As far as he knew, Hawaii, Australia, and the islands in the Pacific hadn't been affected, maybe some of the Caribbean Islands, but he didn't know for sure. There was stunned silence when he wound up his report, nearly every city on the world map was red.

Overrun.

Dead.

Except for one glaring exception.

"What about the Middle East?" Gunny asked. "Tehran? Cairo? Damascus? Riyadh? I don't see any red marks in any of those countries. Anything from Israel?"

Wire Bender looked back at the map like he was seeing it for the first time, seeing it clearly. He tilted his head, hand to chin, looking like he was deep in thought. "I never noticed..." he started then took off out of the diner, heading back to his shop.

"He probably doesn't have any communications with them. He doesn't speak Muslim does he?" someone asked.

Most of the former soldiers snorted or laughed. Muslim wasn't a language, and every nation over in the Middle East had their own tongue. But they were right in their assumption. Wire Bender probably didn't speak any of the languages from those countries.

Stacy stepped up and gave a brief rundown of what happened to the deputy, Brian and Ozzy. How fast it attacked their respiratory system, how the fever spiked, then they died. And came back. All from one bite, all within a matter of hours. But based on what the drivers told her, if you die from blood loss, or any other reason, after being bitten, you came back almost instantly.

Like a shot of heroin in the veins, the saliva was in your system as soon as it broke skin and got into your bloodstream. She told Hot Rod to stand up and explained about his scratches, and how he was showing no symptoms, then briefly told about the few tests she could run on the painter that had been in the freezer.

No pulse, no heartbeat. No change in pupils with white light stimulation. No blood pressure. The only way to kill them is to destroy the brain. It was alive, somehow, and controlling the rest of the body. Kill the brain, kill the body. She stressed how important it was that if anyone was bitten, that they be isolated. Even the smallest bite.

Cobb came back up to squint at the map for a moment then started in again with his drill instructor's voice, "People, we've made this place as secure as we can, and everyone here is welcome to stay as long as you want. By the same token, you're welcome to leave if you want to try to get back home. If any of you drivers have loads of food and you're planning on staying here, then plan on unloading the truck. Tommy is working on a way to safely get them in the bays."

"I'm planning on heading out," Squeak said, "but we can unload a bunch of cookies and crackers if you want."

A few other drivers voiced the same, offering some of their freight, from fruits and vegetables to refrigerated beef and ham.

"Fine, fine," Cobb barked. "Get with Cookie and let him know what you can spare! Now 'as-you-were' and let me finish." He continued, "If your car got smashed up in the parking lot melee, we'll figure something out." He eyed the man who had been so vocal about his dented up Ferrari. He wisely said nothing.

"If it's too damaged to drive, just come back inside when we open the doors. If you're leaving, the sooner the better. Those things are steadily piling up out there. They seem to be pretty calm unless they see a person, then all hell breaks loose."

"How are we going to get to the parking lot, then, if they

are already outside?" a woman with a couple of children at her side asked.

"We'll create a diversion," Cobb replied. "Speaking of which, Gunny, I need you and Griz for a powwow with me and Tommy after this. You two got the most sandbox experience. We need to figure out the best way to get these folks to their cars in one piece, if they're leaving."

Gunny nodded and Griz gave a "Roger that."

"I don't suppose anybody's hauling ammo?" he asked, without much hope.

No one was.

Cobb went on a few more minutes about some other things and Gunny scanned the room from the back, where he was standing. He knew the drivers would be paying attention and that Cobb had their respect. He wondered how the tourists, the civilians as he thought of them, were taking his words now that they realized he had acted in their best interest when he was barking orders and guns started blasting a few hours ago.

All of them were attentive. There were a few sour looks about some of the things Cobb had said. But as they listened and heard the interactions between this grizzled old codger and those younger and stronger than him, they were starting to realize he was much more than just a grumpy, scarred up old man.

Gunny tried to get into their heads, to get a feel for what they were thinking, tried to read them through their facial expressions and body language. Tried to see if there were any potential problems. He was falling back into old military habits without even realizing it.

Carl and his girlfriend, Tina, had stopped in to check this truck stop out after reading about it on one of the travel blogs they subscribed to. They liked it, very quaint and unique. Now he couldn't decide if they were lucky they happened to be here when the Zombie Apocalypse happened, or if they would have been better off to have skipped it and had breakfast at home. If they hadn't stopped, they would still be in their car and then been able to drive back to their apartment. Their Prius was one of the cars that truck driver, the one everybody called Gunny, had smashed into. It bounced off the front bumper of that big rig and he didn't know how much damage it had sustained, it all happened so fast he couldn't tell. It looked okay from what he could see out of the window, just the plastic bumper cover was hanging askew.

At first he and Tina had thought these uncouth drivers were a bunch of redneck jerks. They had heard them make fun of that poor boy with the missing arm. But as they watched them, they heard them joking with him and treating him the same as anyone else.

Cobb hadn't even batted an eye when he told him to grab a mop and clean up the mess in the dining room left by that crawling monstrosity. He had no consideration for his handicap. The young man did it. No excuses, no complaints. There was respect and deference when they talked to the old man, when they called him Top. It seemed to be a military rank or something.

He must have been somebody important at one time. That guy was kind of a nutjob, with all those loaded guns just lying around where the kids could have gotten to them. But he had been fast to realize what they were up against. He supposed he really had saved everyone's lives. Him, and that one they called Gunny.

Now he was a scary one. Cold-blooded killer. He was the first one to react, the first one to run out in the parking lot and shoot that little kid in the face. And he had let that thing just crawl within a few feet of that poor frightened woman. Then he blew its head half off and drug it off like they were going for a Sunday stroll. Wouldn't want to get on his bad side.

The old man had said something about him, and that huge guy called Griz, having a bunch of time in the sandbox. He knew that meant Afghanistan. Or Iraq. Or anywhere over there, he supposed. He wasn't even sure which countries they were fighting in anymore. It had been going on for nearly his whole life, and no one on campus cared about such things.

He looked around the room, at the men in the diner and then at the men over in the "Professional Drivers Only" section. Wow. What a difference. He felt a little awkward about his and Tina's matching Salvation Army outfits now. He had quietly untied the hand-dyed scarf that he'd been wearing as an ascot.

They had thought it so jaunty, but now he thought it was ridiculous. The guys on this side all looked a little soft, he had to admit. Slacks and polo shirts. Loafers and Dockers. Those guys over there looked like hard cases. Blue jeans and flannel. Canvas jackets and T-shirts with $2^{nd}$ Amendment phrases on them.

It looked like the world was reverting to survival of the fittest, and those guys had a pretty good head start on everyone else. No wonder most of them were packing pistols. He would have to get one. Learn how to shoot it. He was pretty good at Call of Duty, it shouldn't be too hard.

Well, at least he wasn't wearing pink, like that fat guy who kept screaming about his stupid Ferrari. Or Li'l Wayne over there with all his ghetto gangsta clothes and tattoos, and that big chrome grill in his mouth. That guy hadn't said a word since he came in and sat down in the booth. Just kept staring out the window at the gap between the truck and its trailer. He had even been crying.

He had helped bring in that poor guy that died and turned into a zombie that Gunny had shot to pieces. Wonder if he knew him? They had pulled up together. Even he had a gun. And probably a criminal record as long as your arm. But that was racist. Profiling. Shouldn't think like that.

He and Tina went to Berkeley and they prided themselves on not being judgmental. He was better than that and felt a little ashamed for even thinking such a thing. She was in electrical engineering and he was studying philosophy, still undecided on a "real" major, as his dad kept cajoling him to declare. It was almost laughable.

Last week... hell, yesterday, he would have told anyone there was no reason to own a firearm. But today he was thinking he needed to get a gun, learn how to use it. He was looking at the differences in the people, their clothes, their hair, and their attitudes. What separated 'them' from 'us.' It had to be more than the fact that they all looked uneducated, maybe barely graduating high school.

The people on his side of the diner looked more refined, definitely. Better clothes that didn't come from Wal-Mart, expensive watches, good haircuts. Maybe it was because most of them seemed to have military experience. Poor people joined the army. Maybe that was it, being raised in deprived conditions. He noticed the one called Gunny staring at him and rapidly turned back to pay attention to what Cobb was saying, feeling like he was back in school and had just been caught doing something wrong.

10

After they had wolfed down their chow, Gunny and Griz headed to the shop with Tommy and Cobb. The rest of the drivers were making their plans to either leave or stay, still trying to call and text and find out any information they could from the internet.

It was the only news source that still worked, although more and more websites, especially those housed overseas or on the east coast, were failing to load. Many of the tourists pitched in to help with the kitchen and dining room cleanup, waiting until they could safely get to their cars.

They had appreciated Cobb's offer of a safe place to stay, but most didn't even consider it. They needed to get home. They had loved ones waiting for them. Once the families were back together, then they could make plans, then maybe come back here if things were really that bad out there.

As they walked into the shop, Tommy grabbed a paper floor mat they put in all the customer's trucks when they worked on them, to keep the mechanic's dirty boots off of the carpets. He laid it on the counter and flipped it over to the blank side, then quickly sketched out the layout of the Three Flags.

"All of the people in the diner are parked here," he said, indicating the automobile parking area in front of the store. "So, how do we get seventy zombies away from there long enough for them to slip out and get to their cars?"

"How much ammo do we have?" Griz asked. "Not pistol, the M-1 or the .223."

"Not enough for what you're thinking," Cobb said. "I've got about a hundred rounds, total."

"I'm thinking we need a diversion, something to draw them away," Gunny said, looking at the quickly drawn map. "Someone on the roof can see if it's clear, and radio down when it is. We open up the front doors, they slide out under the trailers and run for their cars."

"What diversion, though?" Tommy asked.

Cobb drew on his Lucky Strike and added a few more lines to the makeshift map. "If we take the tow truck out of the back gate," he indicated the seldom-used junkyard gate behind the shop, "we could bring it around to the front, hit the lights and air horns, and then drive off. They should chase it."

"Right," Gunny said. "Once they are all away from the store, floor it, get turned around, and then come back and run over 'em. That big-ass push bumper should do some serious zombie bowling damage."

Griz smiled. "I like the way you think," he said.

## 11

"Whaddayamean, I'm riding shotgun?" Gunny asked, when Cobb tried to hand him the AR-15. "I plan on heading out, too."

"We didn't finish the service on your truck," Tommy said. "All we did was get the oil drained. It'll be a while. I'll get the boys on it right now, by the time you and Tiny get back, it should be done."

Gunny grimaced and took the AR. It was a perfect replica of the M-16 used during the 'Nam conflict. Aside from the full auto selector, of course. "Fine," he grumbled.

The shiny, black Peterbilt heavy wrecker rumbled quietly at the back of the shop. It was an old 359 model from the 80s, but well maintained, and gleamed in the early afternoon sun. Tommy kept it waxed and all the chrome polished to mirror finishes.

Griz and Hot Rod were standing by the back gate, ready to pull it open as soon as they got the signal from Scratch. He was on the roof with the M-1, with a clear line of sight along the road and fence.

DAVID A. SIMPSON

"You're good," he said into the handheld CB. "The nearest one is at least a quarter-mile away."

Tiny heard him over the radio in the Pete and released the air brakes, grabbed 5$^{th}$ gear, and nailed the throttle. The big Cat under the hood roared and like the torque monster it was, never even hiccuped at taking off in the higher gear. By the time they were around the little bend in the junk-yard and headed for the gate, the two men had it open and were standing by to hurriedly shut it behind them as soon as they cleared it. Cobb was there with the M-4, waving them on. Tiny turned toward the front of the truck stop and, as they had planned, flipped on the flashers and the emergency lights, then got on the air horn.

He circled into the parking lot, and just as they expected, they had the full attention of every single walking cadaver. Gunny had seen their speed and ferocity, but even he was taken aback at the brutal single-mindedness as they came screaming across the lot, straight at them.

This was the first time Tiny got to see them up close and he started cursing a blue streak when the first of them slammed into the push bumper and bounded up and over the heavy iron grill guard. He spun the wheel and hit the throttle hard and the flailing man went flying off the hood as the main body of them plowed into the truck, screeching and leaping at the faces they saw in the windows.

They didn't seem to be coordinated enough, or have enough foresight, to actually hold on to a grab bar or chicken light cluster. They just kept reaching and running at them. Tiny hadn't seen combat on the warship he was on during his stint in the Navy, but he'd trained just as hard as anyone else and that training kicked in, overriding the natural instinct to panic.

But he'd never seen anything like this. Those things had

138

absolutely no sense of self- preservation. They were running headlong into twenty tons of accelerating steel, and it was pulverizing them under its wheels as they bounced over, and through, the crowd of zombies. As they crushed their way through and got out in front of them, leading them away from the store front, they heard Scratch over the radio giving the people that wanted to leave the all clear signal.

Tiny slowed down a little, glancing down at the speedometer. "I'm going twenty miles an hour and they're gaining," he said, and gave a little more gas.

"Well, the ones you didn't bust up are," Gunny said. "See how long they can keep it up."

Tiny held the truck at a little over twenty, staying just ahead of the lead runner. They were both watching the mirrors, enthralled, as the zombies didn't slow or seem to tire out. The path behind them was strewn with the running dead in various states of damage.

# 12

Long Dawg was standing by with the rest of the people that wanted to leave, to get back to family and loved ones. He wanted his coke. He'd been in a daze these last few hours. He lost both his cousins, and best friends, here and he wanted to get away. He'd heard what those truckers said about how bad it was out there, but he didn't really believe it.

Those cowboys in their big bus said they were going to wait. The fat guy with no Ferrari was going to have to wait. A bunch of the truckers said they were just going to stay here and see what happens. All of the mechanics that worked here were going to get their families and bring them back. But most of the people that were lined up and ready to run out the doors were headed back down toward Reno, back to their homes.

This shit wasn't that bad. Couldn't be. People were overreacting. He needed to get the van and get it away before some government officials started poking around. They would be here soon, when they came to do their investigations of The North Reno Truck Stop Mayhem. Or whatever the news reporters were going to call it.

They all waited, tense and ready to go and once they heard the all clear over the radio, they pushed open the doors and everyone scrambled to be the first out. He was through like a shot, and crawling on his hands and knees under the trailer as fast as he could. The trick with the lights and horn had worked, they had led all of those screaming dead things away. He ran past his 300, still sitting at the pumps, straight for the van and jumped in, went to turn the keys...No keys.

*No! No! No!* Had Mario put them in his pocket? Fool. This wasn't the hood. Nobody was going to jack your car here in the middle of nowhere. If he had, they'd been buried with him. Maybe Jimmy had them. He jumped out of the van and nearly got run down as all the cars were screeching out of the parking lot, fishtailing and squealing tires.

He dodged the remaining ones and joined the sprint to the big truck parking area, falling in behind the few truckers who opted to leave. He saw Jimmy's body and ran up to it, nearly tripping over him as he slid in the gravel, dropping to his knees and frantically patting the pants pockets.

*"Don't look at him, don't look at him,"* he kept telling himself, trying to feel the keys.

*"Bingo! Was his name-o!"* he thought insanely, digging his hand in deep and pulling them out. He looked up as one of the semis dodged around him, spitting gravel and dust plumes from its tires. There was an old school bus sitting there that had been tucked in between the trucks. It was painted black and had writing on the side, probably some crappy band on tour, he thought.

What tripped him out was that some ratty-haired guy

was sitting in the driver's seat, eating a bowl of cereal and watching him rifle through a dead man's pockets. He didn't have time for this. He started to run back toward the fuel pumps, his head on a swivel, looking for more of the zoms. And the big rigs who weren't obeying the "5 mph in Parking Lot" sign. He saw the couple that owned the Prius pulling on the plastic front bumper and tossing it aside, then climbing in.

The fat guy's Ferrari was a total loss, he could see that from here. The whole front end was caved in and one of the wheels was sitting askew. He jumped back into the van and started trying keys until he found the right one.

The big wrecker had turned around and came flying by with a few of the zombies chasing after it before he could get the van out of the parking lot. He let them go, better to be behind that crowd than in front of it, he reasoned.

Tiny and Gunny were looking out of the mirrors and saw a line of cars screeching out of the parking lot, all of them heading back toward Reno, a couple nearly colliding as no one yielded and everyone floored it toward the exits.

"Idiots," Gunny said. "Somebody's going to have a wreck, driving like that."

"Yep," Tiny agreed.

"I guess we ought to follow them a little ways, make sure they at least get down to Reno. I'd like to see the road conditions, anyway. That's the way I'm going as soon as they get some oil back in my truck."

"Roger that," Tiny said. "I'll wait till you're ready to go and roll with you. I need to get back to Birmingham." Then he sped up toward a crossover so he could get turned around.

"Sounds good," Gunny said. "Safety in numbers. Have

to see if anyone else is rolling that way. Get us a little convoy going."

Tiny spun it around and headed back toward town, pointing the nose of the truck at all the runners and stragglers still in pursuit. It wasn't hard, they all aimed themselves right at them. They passed a few of the big rigs headed to California by the back roads and tooted their horns.

*"Probably a smart move,"* Gunny thought. Less traffic, less people, less trouble. By the time they went past the truck stop again, they had killed or seriously maimed most of the horde that had been chasing them. Gunny got on the radio, told them they were going to do a quick recon run down toward Reno, see how bad the freeway was.

The road was wide open, zero traffic. Up ahead, they could see some cars crashed on the highway and a smattering of gimps struggling along the road, all heading in the same direction they were. Tiny grabbed another gear and started bouncing them off the front bumper, sending them flying off into the desert in mangled heaps. The big truck barely felt the shudder of impact while he dodged around the scattered cars that had been abandoned.

"It's amazing how it happened so fast," Tiny said, still trying to take it all in. "I guess it only took one to run out into traffic and everybody stops, or wrecks, trying to avoid him."

"Yeah," Gunny agreed. "Probably the same thing out in the subdivisions, too. It spreads like wildfire."

They continued on for another few miles before the crowds on the road began to get thick. They weren't exactly starting to bog down, but the undead were attacking them now, turning and charging toward the sound of the big diesel.

"I don't see how those cars made it through here," Tiny said. "They must've got off somewhere."

"Or all these things started chasing after them when they drove by," Gunny replied, bouncing in the seat as Tiny plowed over a pile that had fallen under the wheels.

"There's no way this many were on the road before." Tiny's door shuddered as a particularly fast one crashed into it at full speed, vaulting over the already fallen bodies. He flinched away instinctively, and dropped a gear as he slowed the truck, still hurtling through the masses of undead.

Gunny fired up the CB and gave them a quick report. "Crowds are getting heavy down here, Wire Bender. They're climbing all over the truck and no sign of any of the cars that left."

"Man, this ain't good," Tiny said, fighting the wheel as he started trying to avoid the bigger clusters. "We run into a thick enough pile of them, and we could get stuck."

"Yeah," Gunny said. "Can you get turned around? Those poor bastards are on their own. They must have drawn this crowd as they drove by, or maybe they turned off, they sure as hell didn't drive through this."

"I'm looking, man, I'm looking," Tiny said. "I don't want to slow down too much, they'll dog pile us. This thing will push down a building, but only if it has traction. I get in a pile of blood and guts and we'll be spinning in place."

"Did you make it down to the interstate?" Wire Bender came back.

As Tiny man-handled the steering wheel, aiming for openings in the teeming masses and around the more frequent abandoned cars, he was scanning for a wide area to get turned around.

Gunny reached over and flipped in the interaxle lock,

giving power to both rear axles. There was an emergency vehicle turnaround spot coming up. It was a place where the local smokies would usually sit, shooting radar at unsuspecting motorists. It was full of the infected streaming over from the other side of the divided highway, running toward the noise of the screaming undead. Gunny keyed the mike and replied, "No way to get down that far, Wire Bender, it's too..."

"There's too many of them!" Tiny yelled. "Take this one or try the next off ramp?"

"Take it! Take it!" Gunny yelled right back, forgetting to let go of the talk button in the urgency of the situation. He could see an upcoming exit and it was jammed with abandoned and wrecked cars. The mobs were getting thicker, more and more joining the hunt as they heard the sound of the motor revving. Tiny tried to keep the speed up as he downshifted, black diesel smoke rolling from the twin stacks.

The turnaround wasn't very wide, a little over two car widths. He swung into it hard and fast, knocking screeching men and women out of the way like bowling pins, the steering wheel fighting him as he bounced over cadavers and fought the big truck into a 180-degree turn. He was sliding in the dirt, slowing down fast, and the horde of undead just kept piling on them, no concern for their own bodies being battered and bounced off of the rig. They were screaming and leaping, launching themselves relentlessly and repeatedly careening away, knocking others down in their wake to be ground under the tires.

Tiny hadn't even gotten the truck straightened back out again and he was grabbing another gear, trying to get a little speed back up. The nose of the truck was buried under the tidal wave of bodies who were now scrambling over the tumbling, rolling mass of flesh in front of the bumper.

Their vigor was renewed when they could actually see the frightened faces of fresh meat only a few feet away. A woman with bloody matted hair and a pastel jogging outfit made it over the top of the push bar and radiator grill first, but others were soon following. She dove straight for Gunny, hands reaching, not understanding the concept of glass. Or maybe she did, somewhere deep in her reptilian brain, and just didn't care.

Her face slammed into the windshield and it spider webbed. It didn't shatter, but she wasn't the only one. The pile of bodies built up against the front of the truck was making a rolling, seething, ramp and they were scrabbling up and over the fallen in their blood lust for flesh. Tiny was doing his best, he had the rig floored, motor screaming, and was jagging the wheel from side to side in an effort to sling them off. There were thousands of them, they were burying the truck.

He couldn't see out of the windshield anymore from all the bodies piling up against it, and was only able to keep on the road by judging where he was out of the side windows. He flipped the air splitter on the shifter to high range and double clutched into 6th gear.

He kept slinging the steering wheel from side to side and the bodies were starting to fly off now that he was building up speed and the whipping movements were getting more effective. The truck shuddered and bounced as the last of the piled up bodies in front of the push bumper were finally either drug under the rig, or slung to the side, and the screaming masses were starting to fall behind.

"I think we got this!" Tiny grinned when the last man

trying to bite the glass in front of his face slid off the hood as he whipped the wheel one last time.

"Watch out!" was all Gunny had time to shout before there was a bone-jarring crash. The big truck slammed into the concrete barrier that had been placed in the hammer lane, along with the 'left lane ends merge right' sign.

Tiny's big body went flying through the windshield that had withstood so much these last few minutes, but couldn't withstand 300 pounds at 40 miles an hour. Gunny bounced back against the seatbelt, the CB mic flying out of his hand. The big truck came to a complete stop when it hit the barrier, wrapping itself around the angled concrete. It drove the solid mass into the rest of the barricades that protected the workers who would ordinarily be going about their business patching up the road.

Normally, they probably would have just bounced off of it, but Tiny had the truck at a bad angle, trying to sling the zombies off of the hood. Normally he would have seen the solid wall of concrete, with their bright orange stripes, and all of the signs warning him of the upcoming lane closure. But today was anything but normal.

Clouds of steam hissed and billowed up from the punctured radiator as the engine ground to a shuddering silence. A dazed Tiny tried to push himself backward, over the steering wheel and back into the cab. His big bald dome was split open and blood was running down his face in sheets. Gunny had his seatbelt off and grabbed the big man's belt and started pulling him back in as fast as he could, but the screaming, clawing mass had caught up.

The ones in front could do nothing more than stretch for them, not tall enough to reach the top of the hood. The shuddering impacts of more and more bodies slamming into the dinner table started the pileup. Within a few seconds, the fastest of them were up and over the press of bodies and reaching for the freshly laid out main course.

Gunny had him almost in, Tiny was pushing frantically with his hands when a teenage face clamped jaws down on his wrist. He bellowed in pain and rage and fear and slammed the meaty fist of his other arm against the side of the young man's head, but more reaching hands and biting mouths were there.

Inertia was against them.

Physics was against them.

Gravity was against them.

But they had raw strength and numbers, and they were pulling him back out of the window opening. Gunny couldn't hold him in and Tiny couldn't fight them off. He was crushing faces with his mighty free hand, twisting in anger, trying to pull his other arm loose.

Gunny let go and grabbed the AR, shooting directly into the crowd, hoping he didn't hit Tiny's flailing arm by mistake, but pulling the trigger anyway. He was splattering heads, blowing holes in chests, sending bullets tumbling through bones and dead flesh. Tiny still raged, still fought, but dozens of hands had him now and were pulling him over the edge of the hood, down into the feeding frenzy.

He went over the side, bounced off the fender and landed on his feet, still screaming in pain and fury. Gunny leaned out of the empty windshield frame and ran the magazine dry then grabbed for his nine. As he cleared the holster, he noticed the painter's van up the road, beyond the masses. He must have taken the previous exit.

The black kid was there, his pistol in his hand and the door of the van open. He looked like he wanted to help, but there was no help. Gunny saw that now. Saw it on the kid's face. Heard it in the screams of Tiny, and the thousands of undead rushing toward the feast. They were already four and five deep, surrounding the wrecker, with more on the way. Rocking it, pushing toward the warm blood. He couldn't help Tiny. He couldn't jump down and run. He couldn't drive away. He couldn't keep them out of the truck with only fifteen bullets. He waved to the young man. An acknowledgment of his willingness to help. A thank you. A "you better save yourself" goodbye salute.

He turned back to Tiny. He was still on his feet, but no longer fighting, too many of the undead had his arms, were taking great chunks of warm meat out of them. The only reason he didn't fall was the press of the bodies against him, battering and pulling him this way and that. Gunny put a bullet into the top of his head, then ducked back into the cab.

He had fourteen more rounds.

Thirteen dead made permanently dead, and then one for himself.

Easy math.

He was calm now.

Panic mode had subsided.

Fearless.

He knew the future.

Knew how it would end.

Knew he had a minute, maybe two.

He wished things had turned out a little different, but they were what they were. He grieved for Tiny, but knew he did the right thing. Knew Tiny would have wanted him to. This wasn't the first time he had danced with Lady Death. Not the first time he had looked her square in the face and smiled, fully expecting to be in her cold embrace within the next few heartbeats.

He slipped back into the tiny little sleeper and waited

for them to make their way through the windshield. As soon as they were finished with Tiny, they would be coming for him. They were still screaming and keening in a high frenzy, like a school of piranhas, and he knew he couldn't hear the sounds of flesh being ripped and chewed.

He knew it was only his imagination that heard the crack of bones being broken and warm marrow sucked out. He couldn't hear those things. Only in his mind. He thought about closing the privacy curtain, maybe they would forget about him if they couldn't see him, but he didn't want to be taken by surprise.

He would just sit here on this bunk and wait for them. Wait for that uncaring, cold embrace of the Lady he had danced with in the past. There was only one easy way in, through the broken windshield, and he wanted thirteen head shots. A flimsy vinyl curtain wouldn't stop them anyway, not even for a second. They'd be here, any minute. They'd finish their grisly meal and then start tearing the truck apart to get to him.

*Or would they?*

At the truck stop, they just milled around aimlessly, like they had forgotten why they were there, that there were people inside. Like they had pretty short attention spans and if they didn't see or hear a meal...

Suddenly Gunny felt fear. His heart started racing again. He wasn't calm and cool any longer. He thought he just might cheat the Old Girl one more time. He quietly slid off the bunk and reached under it to grab the latch. He lifted the bed and hoped the storage area under it wasn't completely full of heavy chains and bulky tie downs, but it was nearly empty. Tommy only kept the safety triangles, a stash of rags, and some cleaning supplies in it.

"Thank God for guys who like to spend time polishing

chrome," he thought as he silently slipped into the little alcove, not much bigger than a coffin. As he pulled the hinged bed back down on top of him, he could hear them scrabbling up the hood and clumsily making their way into the cab.

# 13

Long Dawg knew now. Knew there wasn't going to be any investigation by any government officials of the North Reno Truck Stop Mayhem. Wasn't going to be any reporters. Wasn't going to be anything. He had seen the mob of the undead and knew this van wouldn't plow through them, so he had exited the highway.

It would be like driving into the ocean. You would be surrounded, stopped, and covered. There were thousands of them. Thousands upon thousands. How had a whole city turned into zombies in only a matter of hours? It boggled his mind. Chemical spraying from the air?

No. Couldn't have been. The medics at the truck stop were pretty sure it wasn't some airborne virus, and that made sense because no one there had caught it, except the ones that were bit.

He wracked his brain on the way back to the truck stop, trying to think of what it could be, what caused it, what to do next. Where to go next. Home was out of the question. Hell, if this little wide spot on the road was completely infected and overrun by those things, LA was worse. If that was possible. Those maps must have been accurate, all those cities.... All those countries were lost.

He drove slow, feeling bad about the truckers he couldn't help back there. That Gunny guy had probably saved his life when all this started. He'd been living the gangster lifestyle for a few years now, but he hadn't forgotten the creed that had been ingrained in him during his stint in the Army. It was deeper and stronger than the so-called street creed.

Nigga's in the hood would rat you out just so they wouldn't have to do a few months in County. All the Rangers he'd tagged along with in South America would take a bullet for you. They would never leave a man behind. He had, just now. But that was a hopeless situation, and if he had tried anything, it would have been three dead instead of two.

That Gunny guy knew it, too. He saw. He had waved for him to leave. Still didn't sit right with him, though. He needed to get back to the truck stop. Let them know what he saw. Let them know how bad it really is out here. He doubted if anyone that had left the safety of the Three Flags was still alive. He had to get out of his hood attitude, get back into a military mindset.

That's what had kept everyone back there alive, and if he wanted anything, it was to stay alive. They were the best chance, joining up with them. He wouldn't last no time at all out here on his own. Besides, where would he go? No. He'd throw in with them.

That truck stop was plenty safe, had plenty of food and water, and a lot of vets who knew a thing or two about defenses. And killing. They'd figure it out. But he wanted to bring something to the table, also. He'd just watched two of them get eaten, and they seemed like they were pretty well known to everyone at the Three Flags. Pretty well liked. He could just say he hadn't seen them, but that would be hard to pull off. He'd pulled out of the truck stop after they went by, and that one armed guy on the roof had seen that.

No. He'd tell the truth. Be brutally honest. Tell them what he saw. Give an accurate situation report. And to give an accurate sit rep, he needed more information. His mind made up, Long Dawg took the next exit to do a little scouting. To get a feel for the extent of the spread of this infection. Travel a few miles off the main roads, see if there were survivors or zombies. He was careful, he had a few hours of daylight left and a full tank of gas.

If he saw a group of them, he would get turned around ASAP. He just needed to bring a little something to the table if he were going to join this group as an equal, and not as a civilian they would think they had to take care of. It was an ugly truth, but it was a truth nonetheless that civilians saw the color of your skin and, more often than not, judged you for it.

Soldiers didn't. Everybody that wore a uniform was green. They judged you on your abilities. Although he'd joined Uncle Sam's Army to do the least amount of work, in the easiest job possible, he'd learned a lot under the tutelage of the Rangers and Delta Force and the CIA guys he had been assigned to translate for.

He was a fast learner and an extra gun in the field, who knew what he was doing, was better than one that didn't. There was a lot of downtime at the base and they had taken it upon themselves to make sure he was competent in the field.

By the end of his tour, they were all encouraging him to

re-up, to go to Ranger school. The LT said he would make sure he got a slot, but Long Dawg had other plans.

Plans to get rich, not hump a pack and get shot at. Plans that led him to right here. Right now. Scanning the road ahead of him for escape and evasion routes.

# 14

It had been hours. The clock was ticking closer and closer to midnight. The atmosphere in the diner was tense as everyone was waiting. Anticipating the big wrecker to radio, to tell them to open the gate, they were coming in.

They were trying to hold on to hope, but it was fading with each passing minute. They had heard Gunny's and Tiny's frantic yells as the mic in the wrecker had been keyed and held open. They heard the screaming of the zombies, the roar of the motor, Gunny yelling, "Watch out!" a sound of impact, and then nothing.

The kitchen radio, the one Kim got on sometimes to advertise to the truckers the daily specials when business was slow, had been turned up loud, but there was only static over the airwaves. Nearly everyone that was left at the truck stop sat around at the tables talking quietly, waiting for the radio to speak, and sipping coffee or tea.

The cowboys and some of the others had brought in a few beers from the cooler in the C-store. Cobb had refused payment for anything. He and Martha knew the score better than anyone in here. She'd lived through the collapse of everything she knew. Lived through utter lawlessness in her home country until Cobb had come back and spirited her away.

She'd helped him when he was injured, when half of his face had been ripped off. She hadn't saved his life, she couldn't claim that, the doctors had done that. But she'd been there for everything else. She was one of the local orphan girls who was hired by the Americans to run errands, change bedpans, and do laundry.

She picked up enough English and was soon helping with in-country rehabilitation for injuries that didn't warrant a long trip back to the States. She helped him learn how to walk again on his crutches, speak again with a growl, and accept the fact that his face was no longer handsome.

When Saigon was falling and she was sure to be killed because she had helped the 'enemy', Cobb had gotten to her, met her among the chaos and bombs and fires. He had taken her back to the last military outpost and had the chaplain marry them right there. She barely understood what was happening, only had the clothes on her back. The next thing she knew, she was on an airplane bound for America with the rest of the civilians and dependents being evacuated.

They eyed each other over their mugs of tea, both reliving those dark days when a country fell into ruin and death and destruction. That was bad. This was worse. The whole world had fallen into ruin. And death. And destruction.

He gently squeezed her hand and stood up. He wasn't one to sit around, and there were things to do. Things really were as bad as bad can be. He needed to start figuring out a long term plan. Not just a week or month long plan. A years long plan.

He stomped into Wire Bender's shop, shoved between Griz and Hot Rod leaning on the counter, and dropped an armful of USB sticks he had gathered out of the store. "Still got internet?" he growled.

"Yeah, but only from the satellite feeds, and it's going fast. Local access is down," said Wire Bender.

"Start downloading everything you can about survival stuff," Cobb said. "Blacksmithing, seed saving, repair manuals, solar and wind power stuff... I don't know. Anything you can think of before it's all gone. Save it. Make back-ups."

Wire Bender's eyes went big and his mouth dropped open a little.

"Close your gob," Cobb grumbled as he clomped out of the room. "You look dumber than you normally do."

Cobb made his rounds, checking on security, talking to the men that had been posted around different areas. There wasn't much happening. Just the occasional infected showing up now and then.

"They seem to know we're in here, but as long as they don't see us, they're pretty calm. Just kind of wander around and bump into things, but always stay nearby," Scratch said when Cobb joined him on the catwalk. Kim was up there with him, watching the glow of the lights of Reno that was visible over the horizon.

"Hard to believe it's only been less than a day, Paw Paw," she said.

He grunted noncommittally. Then he told her and Scratch what he had Wire Bender doing, and if they thought of anything he needed to download, make sure he radioed him to let him know.

"They aren't interested in the cattle that Peanut Butter is hauling," Scratch noted, watching the undead meander around the parking lot. "I think they only want to eat human."

Cobb grunted again.

Kim-Li turned back to watch the distant city lights, her hand resting over Scratch's on the railing. Cobb glinted at Scratch, who suddenly felt nervous and self-conscious, almost like ol' Cobb had caught him doing something he wasn't supposed to.

He held Cobb's gaze with what he hoped was an innocent look on his face till the old man looked over at the back of his grand-daughter. He turned his hard stare back at Scratch and Scratch wasn't sure, it could have been a trick of the flickering light, but he thought he saw the old man's lip curl a little, the hint of a smile, as he turned around and clomped back toward the trap door.

When Cobb announced to the dining area what he was having Wire Bender do with the internet before they lost it completely, he hadn't expected much of a response. What could a bunch of truckers think of that wasn't already being downloaded? But Sara and Stacy both jumped up, nearly spilling their herbal teas with a chorus of, "Oh my God!" and they both ran for the door rattling things off to each other as they went. "Surgery" "Pediatrics" "Dentistry" "Alternative Medicines" "Herbal Remedies" until they were out of earshot.

Cookie mentioned something about preserving foods without refrigeration, and canning, and some other stuff as he headed out of the back of the kitchen.

Cobb looked at the rest of the group still sitting at their tables.

"Sure you don't need to know how to drive a space shuttle or something?" he asked, a bit of menace in his voice.

"It really is the end of the world?" Buttercup asked. She was only in her 20s and Cobb could tell she'd been crying, but seemed to have it under control now.

"I think so," he said. Softening his growl a little.

"Well, we better get some things on livestock care and animal husbandry, then."

Peanut Butter nodded and they both stood to leave. "We know horses, but cattle and sheep are something else, entirely."

"And we need to either set the cattle free that we have in the trailer, or start butchering them tomorrow," Buttercup said. "They can't last another day without water."

"We have incoming! It looks like the painter van is coming back," Scratch blasted over the kitchen CB from the handheld he had on the roof. "And some guy from the parking lot is making a run for it, too! Get the front doors open!"

Cobb and most of the truckers were on their feet and running for the C-store. They had guns drawn and were ready to lend fire support, if needed. Griz came charging up the aisle from the CB shop, where he'd been hanging out, his Colt .45 at the ready.

They could hear the sounds of bodies thumping against metal and the screams of the undead starting to chase after the fresh meat. As soon as they got the doors open, they crouched to look under the trailer blocking the entrance and could see the van leading the zombies away from the store front again. He had made a quick pass in, ran into a few of them, and was leading the rest back out after him on a merry chase.

"Smart," said Griz, and all agreed.

The van lead them out onto the main road, then did a quick U-turn and came flying back in, plowing into as many as he could, sending them flying in all directions. There had only been about a dozen milling around and he had effectively cut their numbers in half. The broken and maimed ones were still a danger, but a gimping, limping, broken down zombie was nowhere near as dangerous as a screaming runner who could leap twenty feet and had two good arms to shred you with.

The one headlight that still worked picked up a running figure as he made his way toward the doors, coming out of the truck parking lot. But he really didn't look like any trucker they had ever seen. His hair was vivid black, and in a Mohawk. He was wearing leather pants and a biker leather jacket, but the most striking thing of all was the Hannibal Lecter Mask. Or maybe the Wolverine style armbands he wore, with the jutting blades glinting in the sodium light.

A few of the runners had seen the man hurtling for the safety of the truck stop, and changed their path to intercept him. Griz leveled his .45, but it was already too late to get a clear shot, the masked man was behind the targets. The van slid in quick and the doors on both sides flew open, even before it came to a complete stop. The black kid was back and Gunny was with him, already taking shots at the faster ones heading toward them and the weirded up guy in the mask. The first of the runners leaped at the mohawked man running toward them and he picked up his pace and crouched lower.

Not a full out sprint, just enough so the infected's leap was a little too long, and he brought up the Wolverine claws and drove them in, raking his belly wide open. They dug in a little too deep as the zombie flew over his head, its guts starting to spill out of the deep furrows in its belly.

The blades hooked on the pelvis bone and snapped off, sending them both crashing to the ground. The zombie head first into asphalt with a face-breaking crunch, and the leather clad man flat on his back, his feet flying out from under him. His arm was stuck wrist deep in the dead man's abdomen, the broken blades protruding out of his rump.

He was quick to rebound though, wiggling his arm out and on his feet, punching powerfully at the screaming woman, with her arms outstretched, reaching for him. He caught her square in the eyes, right where he had been aiming for, and the blades punched out of the back of her skull.

He shook her off, using a booted foot to her mouth to help her along, the blades twisting his arm at an awkward angle as he finally jerked them free. He heard the reports of gunfire and jumped over a falling body as he continued his run for the doors. He went into full sprint mode, dropped to his knees to let the plastic pads slide him under the trailer, right past the two guys from the van who were scrambling for the door.

He slid gracefully through the entrance and popped back up on his feet, like he had been practicing this move for months. Actually he had. Not the whole sliding under the trailer thing, but sliding across the slippery stage, slapping outstretched hands as he whizzed by, and popping up on the other side.

He made a show out of slicing things up with the claws onstage when the band went into a screaming guitar, or thundering drum solo. The singer had to do something so he didn't look like a tool just standing there when there wasn't anything to be sung. He'd slice up watermelons, political posters of hated candidates, piñatas filled with little bottles of whiskey to sling out into the crowd, or beach balls that had been bouncing around. Anything that was messy and made a spectacle.

By the time he did the stage slide hi-fives to the fans in the front row, he had quietly changed the razor sharp claws out for a dulled and blunted pair. The bouncing, brawling fans didn't know that though and part of the whole shtick was you may lose your fingers at a Brutal Retort concert.

As helping hands pulled the others to safety, and the doors were barred shut again, the air was filled with questions.

"Where's Tiny?" "How bad is it out there?" "Where are the others?" "Did you make it to Reno?" and "Who the hell are you?"

Cobb was there, telling everyone to shut the hell up, let them breathe for a minute, and the crowd quieted down. Nearly everyone in the truck stop was there, trying to get a look at them, all with questions.

"Tiny?" Cobb asked.

Gunny just shook his head, still trying to get his breath. He had been running at a pretty hard jog when the van had come off the exit ramp just a few miles up the road and had stopped for him. He was covered in dried gore, his shirt soaked through with drying blood and brain matter and sweat. The biker, or punk rocker or early Halloween guy or whatever he was, looked even worse. He was covered with foul-smelling nastiness from the gutting and head splattering of the two he had killed.

Long Dawg looked none the worse for wear, never having tangled with the undead up close and personal. He let his Beretta do his talking. His gold chains and chrome grill still intact and spotless.

163

Cobb pointed at Gunny. "You, hit the showers. You're stinking up the place," he growled, then pointed toward the truckers' hallway. "You, too, Stabby McStabsalot. You're dripping all over my floors."

"I'm Jody," the masked man said in a thick British accent, by way of introduction.

"Sure you are," Cobb rasped and made shooing motions toward the showers.

The gathered crowd started sending questions at them again as they started to move off.

"There will be plenty of time to tell stories after they've been checked out and when they ain't stinking up the place," Cobb raised his voice to be heard over the crowd again.

Gunny looked at the newcomer, who had slipped the mask up on his head. "Come on, Stabby," he said, and the crowd parted quickly to let them by, not wanting to come in contact with anything that was dripping off of them. Sara and Stacy were on their heels. "Where are you going?" Gunny asked when he realized they were being followed.

"Anybody that comes in looking like you two gets checked for bites," Stacy replied.

"That's right," Cobb said. "We've come up with a few rules while you were out goofing off. That's the main one. Nobody comes back inside if they've had contact, unless they are checked out. Nobody. If you don't like it, there's the door." He jerked his thumb behind him.

"Soooo...you want me to get naked?" Gunny asked, a half grin on his face.

"I had your junk in my hands for the hernia check last time you came in for a physical," Stacy retorted. "If I remember right, I won't be getting too excited."

There were hoots of laughter from the drivers and he

was saved from trying to come up with a witty one-liner by the British guy.

"You come with me then, Luv. Maybe I got something you can get excited about."

She just rolled her eyes as they started for the shower area again.

15

Gunny didn't dawdle in the shower, just cranked the water up as hot as he could stand it and stepped in, fully clothed, except for his boots. He didn't have to get naked for Stacy after all. She made him pull his shirt off, but there were no tears in his pants, no seeping blood stains, so she pronounced him good.

She left, clucking to herself at the criss-crossing of old battle wounds scarring his back and chest. He scrubbed mercilessly at the crusted gore, watching the drain water circle red as he stripped off, cleaning the worst of it out of his clothes as he went.

While in the shower, he reflected back on the past several hours. He had waited in the cramped area under the bunk, hoping the milling horde would forget about him and leave. A few of them had managed to climb or fall into the cab, and couldn't figure out how to get back out. He was afraid they would smell him, or hear his pounding heart, but they never reacted, never suspected there was a 200-pound dinner just for them only a foot away.

They just kept bumping into each other and half falling

over the shifter, from the sounds of it. The horde outside of the truck calmed down after their meal was finished and just bumped around, milling about from what he could make out. They stayed for a long time. Hours.

Gunny kept waiting for something to draw them away, hoping there would be a noise somewhere, but knew if there was, that meant this mob would be chasing down some other poor soul. He was afraid to sleep, to even doze for a second. He was prone to snore, and if he did, even once...He kept going over what he knew about his wife and son. She was probably safe with the group in the building she was in, but for how long?

His son was at school. Maybe he was safe locked away in detention. Maybe he had been one of the ones that were infected. What had caused the infection anyway? What could turn the whole world into mindless killing machines in a single day? It followed the path of the sun, that he knew, but what was the trigger? Chemtrails? A passing comet full of deadly bacteria from the other side of the universe? Aliens clearing the planet so they could have it? The Illuminati? He was getting ridiculous and he knew it.

All those things had been in movies he'd seen over the years. That wasn't it, though. It was something a little closer to home, he thought. Some man-made bug. He wracked his brain, trying to remember, just what was the trigger in all the zombie movies he had seen? This was life imitating art.

Or had the governments of the world had this particularly nasty virus, and art had been imitating life? The movies and books usually blamed it on the CDC having a security breach, or the Russians or the Chinese. They would blame an infected vaccine, or a cabal of the super-rich wanting to eliminate all the useless eaters, or some mad genocidal maniac deciding the planet would be better off without humans.

The whole world fell in a day.

Except possibly some islands.

And the Middle East, if Wire Bender was right. Could the Muslims have done this? They had the desire, the crazy ones did anyway, but that was as farfetched as the aliens doing it. He had known a lot of decent people he met during his time in-country. Muslims that hated the extremists even more than he did.

They would have never let something like this happen. Anyway, how could they? They didn't have the means. They couldn't spray that many chemicals in the air, or dump tens of thousands of gallons into every water supply, all over the world, without being caught and stopped.

It wasn't airborne. No one in the truck stop had caught it and people from north and south of them had. It wasn't in the water. They had the same city water as everyone else. The sun wasn't causing it, plenty of them had been out in it, but it was a trigger. Sun came up, people went mad. All around them, but not them.

No one there had been infected, except by being bitten from someone who hadn't been at the Three Flags. Divine Intervention? Gunny believed in God, but didn't think He would destroy the world except for a slightly rundown truck stop in an out of the way part of Nevada. Maybe the Globalists.

He'd been to the Georgia Guide Stones since they moved to Atlanta. It said right there on the stones that world population should be reduced to five hundred million. But how? That was the question that was more important than who. If they knew how, maybe they could stop it. Or at least make sure they avoided whatever was causing it. He listened intently for a few moments, quietly trying to stretch the aching muscles in his back. They were still milling around outside, just inches away. Still bumbling around in the cab of the truck, occasionally falling onto the bunk, then clumsily getting back up.

Weird how they could be so dumb and slow now, but if they see prey, they are like a finely tuned killing machine. He went back to his exercise in futility, trying to figure out something the best and brightest in Washington hadn't been able to do with all their NSA databases and spy satellites and war colleges and whatever else his tax dollars paid for.

The sun came up, the world went mad. Not just the States. The whole world. What did we all have in common when the sun came up?

We woke up.

Nope. Nothing there.

We took a shower.

Nope. Not in the water.

Maybe the soap?

No. Some soap was months old, some new. Wasn't that.

We had breakfast. How could that be it?

Breakfast in Japan was rice and soup, fish and sausage. Breakfast in Europe was cheese and rolls, maybe some salami or something. Italians have spaghetti or pizza for breakfast? What did Russians eat? Bear? Africans? Didn't they eat bugs and stuff? Lions and tigers? Maybe that was the Asians. Or maybe they ate cats. What about the Brits? Blood Pudding and Spam? He knew he was being ridiculous again. His mind kept wandering off on crazy tangents. He didn't know what other cultures typically had for breakfast. He knew an American breakfast was anything from biscuits and gravy to sausage and eggs, bacon and eggs, ham and eggs. Green eggs and ham...

Common denominator?

There was none. Maybe eggs, those are eaten all over the world. Somebody spike all the chickens with zombie virus? Meat. That was pretty universal, he thought. More so in America, but most countries usually had some type of meat available. The Indians, dot not feather, didn't eat beef, but they ate pork and goat and chicken. Zombies ate long pork. He groaned to himself. Geez, you are one sick bastard. The Middle Eastern countries certainly didn't eat pig.

Probably a death by stoning if they caught you eating a ham sandwich. But none of the Middle Eastern countries were infected, if Wire Bender's map was right. And they didn't eat pork. The rest of the world did. Haji bacon, Scratch had called it. "You think Paw Paw would serve that here?" Kim had asked.

Gunny's heart seemed to stop in his chest. His mind reeled at the implications. The Muslim countries had formed a coalition, and had used massive amounts of their oil money to buy up meat packing plants, it had been all over the news. They were starting a new era of peacefulness. They were going to show the world they could adapt and blend into the modern age, no longer holding to century's old customs. They had begun producing all manner of pork products and shipping them all over the world. Today was the first day they were supposed to be used, although all had been delivered and were selling in stores yesterday evening.

The day before the attacks had started happening sporadically around the world. Today there had been all kinds of breakfast festivities of friendship planned, with free products, and everything on the store shelves had been reduced to costs so low the company was losing billions. The CEO had said they would make up the difference in sales later. They had given every school, every military post, every government cafeteria free samples in hopes they would consider buying their products in the future.

He couldn't believe it.

Wouldn't believe it.

It was too monstrous, too evil. No one would do that, he told himself. But now that he had thought it, he couldn't unthink it. He needed more information. That little bit he had heard when he was listening to the traffic reports in the different cities wasn't enough. The news had been playing while he was waiting for Helicopter Bob or Janie at the traffic desk, but he hadn't been paying attention, just waiting to hear which way was the best way to go. But it all came back now, the news he had been ignoring. The president praising an end to hostilities soon. The helicopters flying in fresh Salaam products to the Navy ships at sea. The thankful clips of city officials telling the reporters how many homeless and low-income families they would be able to feed with the generous gifts from the New Muslim Alliance of Nations. Peace and goodwill to men. The world without conflict by Christmas. He had to be wrong. Had to be. But the pieces all fit. Of course there would be no more war. They had won. He felt sick. Were there really Army safe zones for refugees like his wife had said they were going to? From what he'd seen and heard today, he doubted it. He bet the military got hit the hardest, they were the earliest to rise and they always had bacon and sausage for breakfast.

He understood now why the government didn't have some kind of warnings out, to shoot on sight anyone acting strangely. They had seen Europe fall, knew it would be here when the sun came up over the Eastern Seaboard. They were probably scrambling everybody that drew a government check to try to find a way to stop it; hunched over keyboards, testing air and water samples, measuring gamma radiation, or whatever NASA did.

As they ate their bacon and egg biscuit.

The military had surely been on red alert, all soldiers report for duty, calling trees initiated, all passes denied, all leave canceled, all hands on deck.

"Now have a hearty breakfast while we wait for orders."

Gunny had been so lost in his thoughts, the sudden screaming of the horde as they sensed some new prey made him start, bumping his head against the bottom of the bunk lid above him. He heard the two, or was it three, inside the cab of the wrecker keening and scrambling to get out, heard them bashing themselves against the windows and clawing at one another. *"Now or never,"* he thought, while they were distracted and making too much noise to hear him. He didn't want them to stay trapped in the cab and then go back to their aimless bumping around. He gave it a few seconds, until he heard the last of the horde outside disappearing down the road, and slowly opened the lid just enough to see out.

They were at the driver's window, trying to go through it, but one of them had climbed up on the dash and seemed to realize he could just go back out the way he came in. There were only two and he had the Gerber pulled out of his leg sheath and in his hand. Hopefully this time he could hit the soft part of the skull, through an eye or ear, if not at the base of the spine. It hadn't gone as planned. They had heard or sensed him and both came at him, forcing him back into the sleeper and just stabbing frantically at faces and chests and arms, barely keeping their teeth off of him using the pillow on the bed as a shield. It was nasty, gruesome work, with blood and guts and all manner of disgusting body fluids splattering everywhere. By the time he finally killed them with lucky stabs, they both had been cut wide open and must have had 50 gaping wounds in them. It had been simple after that, he had opened the door and started running toward the truck stop, the horde having disappeared in the other direction.

The water running off of him and his clothes on the tile floor of the shower was clean finally. The gray matter and black blood all washed away.

## 16

Gunny came out of the shower wrapped in a towel and carrying his wet clothes and boots. He walked down to his truck that was still in the shop and grabbed a fresh pair of jeans and t-shirt, draping his wet ones over the mirrors to dry. He wanted to get with Wire Bender, run his theory of how all this happened by him, see if he could dig anything up to either corroborate it, or to let him know he was way off base.

As he neared the shop, he heard raised voices coming from the diner again. He was going to ignore them, wasn't his problem, but he heard someone say, "Your fault, boy." He couldn't place the voice, but he knew they had to be talking to the ghetto kid.

None of the black drivers he knew would let that slide if it were said in anger, and he didn't hear the sound of someone's nose breaking. He didn't even know the kid's name, but he knew he had tried to help him at the wreck, and he'd been out scouting the rural areas. He'd picked him up on the road when he was pretty much done in from all the running he had been doing.

He dressed like some rapper gangster from the 'hood, but he had a calmness about him. A good head on his shoulders. He was more than he seemed to be.

Gunny didn't hesitate. He opened the door to the CB shop and yelled in, "The Muslims did it. They spiked all the meat they were selling, they sent it out with the zombie virus. See if that checks out."

He didn't wait for an answer, he just lengthened his stride, heading straight for the commotion. When he came through the doors, he stopped and just watched the little drama play out for a moment. Shakey was in the kid's face, red-faced and angry about something. He looked sweaty, even though the air conditioning was working fine. He was pointing his finger, poking it in the kid's chest, punctuating each word.

Shakey was a big man. But big as in he'd let himself go over the years. Too many buffets, too many bags of chips and sodas driving down the road, and not enough exercise. He had been in the military, but he was always a little vague on specifics. Gunny had seen him around over the years, but only had a passing acquaintance with him.

He held his tongue for the moment. He didn't want to fight another man's fight, but if push came to shove, he'd be there. The kid had more balls than Shakey did. Ol' Shakey hadn't been outside the safety of the truck stop all day, and that kid had been scouting alternative escape routes if they needed them.

"If you hadn't been playing that jungle music at full volume, they wouldn't have come in the parking lot in the first place! It's your fault Gumball and Ozzy got bit, and it's your fault the deputy is dead, boy!" Shakey repeated himself, his face nearly purple with rage, using his 280 pounds to intimidate.

Long Dawg just stood there and took it, the red-faced man and his poking finger. He had planned on shedding his whole ghetto persona, had planned on quietly slipping out to the bathroom and scrubbing off the Henna neck tattoos, stripping off this costume he was wearing, because that's exactly what it was. A costume.

He mentally kicked himself for not getting rid of it when he had been driving around, but it hadn't occurred to him, he was too busy trying to stay alert and alive, scratching out notes of different routes by the dashboard light. But the old man had drug him in here, "where the light was better" and had him roll up his sleeves as he scrutinized him for bites.

Then the argument started. He had been playing the part of some cheap Nigga from the hood to draw any police attention away from the van, but all they saw was what he wanted them to see. The hood rat. His plan was working too well. He had decided to get back to his normal self but this cracker had got in his face before he had a chance. Blaming him for everything. Said he ran off and left the rest to die, didn't believe for one instant that he was scouting routes. Probably got lost and just now found his way back. Long Dawg sighed. When all else fails, show 'em what you've got. At this point, talking was useless. He'd been talking and it hadn't done a bit of good. They weren't hearing him. Weren't listening. Words were cheap. If he wanted to throw in with this group, and most of them seemed okay, he had to show them he wasn't a liability. He had to show them that he could be an asset. Had to show them he wasn't going to take any shit from some redneck peckerwood.

He was snake fast and moved like lightning, pulling his Beretta out of its holster, grabbing the fat man's finger with his left hand and violently twisting it up and around his back. He bent him over the table, his face against the wood, the cold steel of the 9mm against the back of his head.

It happened so fast, was so quick and savage, even everyone watching didn't quite know how it happened. The silence in the room was deafening. "My name is Lawrence. Not Boy," he said. "But only my mom calls me that. My friends call me Lars."

A quick glance around the room reaffirmed to him that no one else had pulled their iron, this was just between the two of them.

With his arm nearly dislocated and twisted up behind his back, Shakey was helpless to do anything about the steel pressed against his head. He closed his eyes against the pain and tried to wrap his mind around how the tables could be turned so fast. He waited for a shot, but the kid stepped back quickly and holstered the weapon.

Then to everyone's amazement, he snapped to attention in a posture any marine would have acknowledged as perfect. He pulled out his Beretta again, the same model he had used for years in the Army, this time bringing it up to port arms, then expertly dropping the magazine, catching it one handed and slapping it down on the table in front of Shakey's face.

His movements were precise, measured, and with full military discipline. Quick and smooth, robotically perfect. He executed a one-handed slide lock, catching the ejected round cat quick and slapping it on the table, nose up, beside the perfectly placed magazine. He held the weapon out in an inspection arms gesture, as if to an officer who wasn't there for a few seconds, then with a quick twist brought it back to his chest.

Shakey had pulled himself up off the table, and along with everyone else, was just staring at this kid executing a perfect military small arms inspection process. He had even done the one handed slide lock, a very difficult maneuver. The snaps and clicks, the pops and slaps sounded loud in the silence. As he smacked the magazine back in and let the slide go home chambering a round, he twisted the Beretta in the robotic way formal military actions take and slid it firmly back into its holster.

He immediately went to a parade rest position and addressed Shakey.

"In the Army, I was called Sergeant Brown," he said. He let the quick and jerky military actions go and hitched up his pants, tightening the belt so they rode around his waist, not his ass. He removed the sideways hat and pulled the chrome grill out of his mouth, revealing perfect white teeth. He tossed them on the table and snapped the fake gold chains around his neck and they joined the rest.

"Back on the block, they called me Long Dawg," he said. "But that nigga is dead. You know why I was dressed like that? You know why I was driving that hooptie and blasting Tupac? You ever see Smokey and the Bandit, shithead?"

He waited for an answer.

Shakey nodded his head. Like everyone else, a little dumbfounded at this strange turn of events.

"Then you know what I was doing. I was Burt."

He poked himself in the chest, enunciating it.

"I was The Bandit. I was running interference for any cops we happened to cross. Make them eyeball me, not the van. And my cousins in the van, they were the Snowmen. Except we weren't smuggling Coors to a party. We had the real snow. Millions of dollars worth, right there in the back.

Not worth much now, and there ain't no more law that's worried about a bucket full of powder.

"So there you have it, Bubba. I told you the roads are full of them things just wandering around, looking for somebody to eat. I didn't draw those zombies, they were coming in here whether they heard my music, or not."

He reached out and picked up the single round from the table and held it up in front of Shakey's eyes. "And if you call me boy one more time, I'll put this bullet through your cracker ass face."

The tension was ratcheting up again, but Shakey wasn't so sure of himself anymore. This kid wasn't who he thought he was. Wasn't afraid of him. But he wasn't going to back down, not in front of everybody. How come nobody in the crowd was helping him? If Gunny had the kid's back...Maybe he was telling the truth, had tried to help. Maybe he had been out scouting roads, and not running around lost.

They eyed each other, almost nose to nose, each waiting for the other to make that first move. The tension was building, nearly crackling the air as jaws tightened, eyes narrowed, and fists clenched.

"You owe two dollars to the cuss jar, Lars," Kim said, walking over and standing between them, shaking the jar with the big hand printed label on it. "No swearing in here, or you have to pay." She smiled sweetly. "A dollar for every dirty word." She held out her hand for payment.

There was a collective sigh and nervous laughter in the room as people let out a breath they hadn't realized they were holding.

"Them's the rules," Shakey said, and laughed with the rest of them. Partly out of relief and partly because he thought he had just avoided an ass whoopin'.

"Better pay up quick, she'll be adding interest if you don't," somebody hollered.

Lars couldn't help but grin and shake his head as he reached for his wallet. What kind of people had he thrown in with?

17

Gunny went up to the counter, caught Martha's eye, and asked if there was anything left to eat.

"You say what you want, I make myself," she said. He knew she wanted to stay busy, wanted something to do, and he was the only one left who hadn't eaten. So he ordered up a bacon and peanut butter cheeseburger and asked the cowboys if he could snag one of their beers.

"Come on over here," Cobb barked at him. He was at the biggest table with Griz, Stacy, Sara, Cadillac Jack and his son Tommy. They had some papers spread out in front of them, and it looked like they had been making plans.

Gunny slid into the oversized booth as the girls scrunched up a little to make room.

"Tell us what it's like out there," Cobb said without preamble. "How far did you get?"

He told them. He told them about the hordes that numbered in the thousands, about the main arteries being completely gridlocked with abandoned cars. About their pack mentality and the feeding frenzy. Their inhuman strength and speed. The fact that they felt no pain, had no fear, but were pretty dumb and docile if they weren't on the chase.

Stacy quizzed him relentlessly about everything he heard and saw when he was under the bunk, then she and Sara were speculating why they didn't go after him. They must hunt by sight, maybe sound. Couldn't be smell. He wasn't sure if he was being insulted or not. Gunny noticed they had quite a crowd gathered at the other tables, everyone listening in intently. He told them his theory, his idea that he had yelled out to Wire Bender. Yesterday he would have been called an Islamophobe or racist for even thinking such a thing, but today there was contemplation, even though most people couldn't believe such a thing could happen.

"Wire Bender made contact with some brass at Cheyenne Mountain," Griz said "They got hit pretty hard, too. Some of the guys coming off night shift managed to lock down the areas they were in, but most of it is lost."

"Are they in communication with anyone else?" Gunny asked.

"A few dozen countries have been on the Ham, but it's just guys like us. Some survivalist type groups. Some remote hunting lodges. Quite a few up in Idaho and Canada. The Russians up in Yamantau Mountain claim to be unaffected, but they're scared. They watched the whole world fall, Moscow included. They had been in contact with Washington before it fell. They hoped we would be able to stop it. Man, there ain't no Commies and Yanks anymore. Just people wanting to survive."

"They're cut off up there, without resupply infrastructure," Cadillac Jack chimed in, drawing on his years of service in Military Intelligence. "The Road of Bones doesn't even go near them, and it's the only road through that whole area. They've probably got their winter supplies laid in, but they won't last forever."

"The boys under the mountain in Colorado Springs aren't any better off," he continued. "They're not allowed to have weapons in there, so they're stuck in a big hole in the ground. Unless they have access to the mess area and all the food, they're screwed. Probably only have what little bit is in the office refrigerators. They don't even have snack machines down there."

One of the tourists raised a hand and timidly asked, "We still have military operating?"

"Not really," Cobb answered. "We've talked to NORAD and that's it."

He saw the uncomprehending look on her face and elaborated.

"NORAD is who launches the nukes. They're outside of Colorado Springs, underneath Cheyenne Mountain. They are in the most secure bunker in the world, but only a handful survived the initial outbreak ,as far as we know."

"So a bunch of Military Intelligence eggheads would have to battle their way out of there with improvised weapons. I don't give them much of a chance," Gunny sighed. The news that Wire Bender had been able to glean was catastrophically bad. No word from Washington, or anyone claiming to be in charge. No word from the President.

"He probably ate the first Hajji bacon this morning for the cameras. You know politicians," Griz said, and they all had to agree. Everyone Wire Bender had either talked to directly, or anyone the boys in Cheyenne Mountain had told him about, were all in the same situation. Isolated and cut off. Acting autonomously because there simply was no more government. No one was in charge. The soldiers in assigned nuclear bunkers and fortified bases around the world, that hadn't been overrun, were just people wanting to understand and live. They no longer had politicians pointing at another country and telling them they were the enemy. Every survivor he had been able to contact had lost nearly everything.

Martha brought Gunny's burger out with a heaping supply of seasoned fries and he dove in, offering the fries to anyone that wanted some.

"Shakey, go relieve Scratch. Tell him I need him here," Cobb barked out and went back to his list he'd been looking at. "Anybody know how long the electricity will last?" he looked up and asked the room in general.

After a moment a hesitant voice spoke up. "It depends. But if no one is there to replenish the coal supply, two or three days. Four on the outside," she said. "Reno gets its power from coal-fired plants, not hydro. So probably about four days."

It was the girl in the matching clothes with her boyfriend, Gunny noted. He thought they had left with the rest. They all just looked at her, eyebrows raised.

"I was studying to be an electrical engineer," she said shyly. "We toured some of the local plants. They have huge automated conveyor systems to feed the furnaces directly from the rail lines."

Cobb grunted and nodded and scribbled something on the paper. "Our biggest concern is going to be water," he said. "We've got generators that will run the place, and the fuel tanks were filled up a couple of days ago. They're three-quarters full still. Guess I won't be paying that bill. But we're on city water and as soon as the electric goes out, we'll be out of water. There's an old well out back that the old man had before they piped water in, but it ain't been used in years. We'll have to get a few guys on that tomorrow." He made a few more notes and one of the women from the surrounding tables asked if there was any place to sleep, glancing at the little girl nodding off in her lap.

The truck stop used to have a bunk house for drivers when most trucks didn't have sleepers on them, but it was long gone, the space converted to the various shops in trucker's alley.

"We're going to have to rough it tonight," Cobb told her. "The most comfortable spots will be here in the diner, at the booths. There's plenty of Mexican blankets in the store, help yourselves to them. We'll clear out some areas in Driver's Alley tomorrow, make something a little more private."

"I've got a pallet of moving blankets in my wagon," Hot Rod said. "They'll make good mattresses piled up a few thick."

"Them doors ain't being opened up at night," Cobb growled with finality. "We can fix things up tomorrow when there's light to see."

Gunny looked around as he finished his burger and asked, "Where's the Stabby guy? I have got to hear his story. Why was he all dressed up like Halloween?"

Griz chuckled. "Seems like we got us a rock star in our midst. He said they had a show tonight in Reno. The rest of the band took off to go party, but he stayed behind in their tour bus to play Xbox. They never came back."

"He is fried out of his gourd on something," Stacy said. "He's strung tight. I'd say Meth, but his teeth are still good. Skin, too. So probably cocaine."

"Probably coked up," Sara agreed. "We see it a lot."

"Well, it's not booze," Gunny said. "You see the way he took those two out? Like watching a blood ballet. Even

185

when he got knocked on his ass, he bounced up like it was a Michael Jackson dance move."

"It does have that going for it, but unless you've been using it for a while, you would likely just get stoned," Stacy said. "It builds up, affects dopamine levels, which affect your muscle and reaction times. Quickens them in some people. Messes up the frontal cortex in your brain, so you don't feel fear, or worry about things. Like being eaten by zombies. So he could be a great zombie fighter when stoned, and a huge incompetent blob when straight."

"He's still in the shower?" Gunny asked, not seeing him in the diner.

"No," Tommy said. "Pops turned all the arcade machines to free play. He's down there with the rest of the kids."

Scratch came up to the table, overhearing the last of their conversation. "Dude, he's always on something! Don't you know who he is? That's Jody Blades! The front man for Brutal Retort!" he said excitedly. "He's all over the net, he posts pictures of himself snorting cocaine off of hookers asses! He lives the rock 'n roll life, man. Destroys hotel rooms and everything. I caught one of their shows last year in L.A. It was unreal. The whole stage was trashed with all the stuff he was chopping up, I heard one dude lost half his hand during one of his stage slides, the mosh pit was soaked..." He trailed off when he saw all of them just looking at him with those old people looks of, 'We couldn't possibly care less'.

"Uh, anyway. Yeah. He's kind of famous for being a coke head," he finished lamely. "You needed me, Top?"

Cobb went on to quiz him about the behavior of the infected. How long they stayed agitated, what he thought was drawing them to cluster around the truck stop. Scratch had been on duty on the roof most of the night, hadn't wanted to be relieved. He kept watching for Tiny and Gunny.

Kim would take him a sandwich and cool drinks from time to time and keep him company. Cobb already knew most of the answers, but since everyone was listening in to his little meeting, he wanted to get everything they knew out on the table so everyone had as much information as they could.

There were some hard decisions coming up tomorrow, and he wanted people to sleep on their choices. They were life and death choices. Stay here or try to leave again. Scratch reiterated what he'd already told Cobb for the benefit of everyone else and when he was finished, Cobb looked around the room and spotted who he was looking for. "Hey, Bob Marley, show us on this map the roads you scouted again."

Lars was near the back, talking quietly with a few of the other people, his long beaded braids quietly clinking back and forth as he shook his head 'no' again as he was asked about getting through Reno. He chuffed. He knew the old man wasn't being hateful. That's just how old First Sergeants talked to everyone.

He'd heard the guys call him Top. and judging from his demeanor and scars, it had been earned, not given. He spun the map toward him and scanned it for a moment then, pointing out the different roads he had taken, how far he had traveled down them before turning, and the infected situation. It was pretty simple and straightforward.

The dead had all day to find and infect everyone. If there were people, there were zombies. He hadn't seen anyone alive, but it wasn't out of the realm of possibilities, if someone had burglar bars on their windows and doors and had been inside.

Cobb went back to scribbling notes and Gunny took the opportunity to ask Tommy about his truck. He still wanted to leave, still had to try to make it home to his family.

"I've got some ideas," he said. "After that fiasco with Tiny," then paused, remembering the screaming, clawing, gnashing masses...Tiny being drug off of the hood. The unbridled fury and raw strength of those... Those.... Those monsters. The fear he had felt, the nearly incapacitating fear...

He realized he had stopped and everyone was looking at him. He gave his head a half shake and took the last swill of his beer. "Right, I need to armor up my truck, build a cowcatcher, and reinforce the windows," he continued. "I don't care how much truck you've got, if you run into a horde, they will overwhelm it. You need to be able to shunt them aside, not let them pile up and over the hood. That's how we lost Tiny. They were up and over and smashing through the windshield, breaking their way in."

"Like a snow plow," Tommy said and flipped over a paper placemat and started sketching. Between them, with Tommy knowing what was practical with the iron pieces he had on hand, and Gunny having just been through a horde of zombies and gridlocked cars abandoned on the road, they came up with a pretty good design.

The weakest point was the front tires. If one of them blew from debris on the road, or from bouncing a car out of the way, the truck was stopped. No way around it.

"We've got some industrial tires we keep on hand for the local construction trucks, and there are plenty of old dump trucks out back with the oversized wheels on them," one of his mechanics chimed in. "It wouldn't handle very well at high speed, but they're just about bullet proof."

Tommy quickly added the oversized extreme duty tires to the drawing and erased part of the fenders so they would have clearance.

"Looks like Mad Max," Scratch said. "How many can you build?"

"None tonight," Tommy replied, "I'm going to bed. It's going on two o'clock."

18

Gunny was asleep in his bunk. Just by the sheer dumb luck of pulling his rig in for a service, it was safe in the mechanic's bay and he got all the comforts his truck had to offer. He'd told Cobb and Martha they were welcome to use it, but they'd refused. Scratch said he would use it, as a matter of fact he needed it, because of his arm and all.

Gunny just gave him the finger as he had walked toward his truck, and his comfortable bed. There was a knocking on the side of the sleeper. He was awake instantly, listening. It wasn't a lot lizard, that much he knew. Not here inside the bay.

"Gunny," he heard. It sounded like the British guy.

"What's up?" he said. No drowsiness or confusion in his voice.

"That Wire Bender bloke needs you, mate."

Geez. Doesn't he ever sleep? "Tell him I'm on the way."

When Gunny walked into the shop a few minutes later, fully dressed, armed and alert, Cobb and Griz were there, also. Wire Bender was the only one looking frazzled and red-eyed. Stabby was on one of the computers, loading up USB sticks.

"He's here, Sir. Transferring the coms now," Wire Bender said and slid the big silver table top Ham radio microphone over the counter toward Gunny.

He just looked at it and held his hands palms up in a "What?" gesture.

"It's General Carson at NORAD," Cobb said around his unlit Lucky Strike.

"Who? What's he want with me?"

Cobb gestured to the mic. "Just answer the radio, Gunny," he said.

Looking a little frustrated at the lack of answers, he hit the push to talk button and said, "This is Gunny. Go ahead."

"Is this Sergeant First Class Meadows formerly of the 1st Special Forces Operational Detachment?" the voice came back through the mike.

*"What did these guys want?"* Gunny thought. The old anger in him rose up to the surface, faster than he thought possible. He went from frosty to insta-pissed in half a second. These officers and political appointees had ruined his life for a while, and being called by his old unit and rank brought it all back.

He and his wife had a long-term plan worked out, that included him retiring after 20 years, drawing a nice pension, and finding a quiet little town to live in. A place where he could get a job as a deputy or patrolman, and she could find work at the school.

There they would reap the benefits of a comfortable life after the grueling years of active duty. The long separations, all of the missed birthdays and Christmas' and Thanksgivings. The constant danger he found himself in, obeying orders and doing ops all around the world.

It would have all been worth it with a small town life, where all he had to do was break up a few bar fights on the weekends, maybe catch a speeder every once in a while, and get in plenty of fishing. Hang out at the local café with the rest of the town folk. Maybe build himself an old school hot rod. But Uncle Sam was finished with him after he gave them fifteen years.

No benefits. No retirement. No Medical. Just Dishonorable walking papers. They had very little savings, and it went quickly. Lacy had finally landed a good job in Atlanta, while he floundered. He couldn't go to the police academy with a dishonorable discharge. Hell, he couldn't even find work driving a forklift in a warehouse once the background check was run on him.

He didn't have the stomach to join up with some of the contractor outfits like Griz had done. He just wanted peace and quiet, and to be left alone. That's when he stumbled on the idea of driving a truck. Money was good.

You were your own boss so there were no embarrassing questions about your past and the inevitable, "I'm sorry, sir, but our policy....." He and his wife were used to separations, and at least it would only be for a few weeks at a time, not months. And most important, nobody was shooting at him. Now they were calling him by his old rank, the one they had stripped from him.

"No, Sir. That would be Private Meadows. But I'm not even that. I'm sure you have the paperwork right there in front of you, General. If you need a military man, may I suggest First Sergeant Cobb or Sergeant First Class Grizzwold. Both fine men."

The General wouldn't be deterred that easily. "Funny

thing, Sergeant. I'm looking right at your file. I have page after page of glowing performance reports, awards, medals, a few purple hearts, bronze stars, a silver star.... Hell, son. You've got a Distinguished Service Cross. I don't even know anyone that has one of those. Then I have a one page DD214 where it shows your rank as private, with a dishonorable discharge and that's it. No reason given. Everything redacted. Can you clarify?"

Everyone else was staring at him now. Griz stroking his beard and looking quite impressed. Stabby asking, "Is that good, all those stars and thingies? Are you like a hero or something?"

Gunny didn't like to talk about his military life. None of these men knew much about his former career except what little they had gleaned over the years. They knew he had been a grunt and had seen some action. A lot of guys who had seen too much over there were like that. Quiet. Observant. Rarely talked about their tours. They knew not to pry. Everyone had secrets, some darker than others.

"I punched a General," Gunny said and released the button. *"That ought to shut him up,"* he thought.

There was laughter in the background when the microphone came back to life, "Well, if you did, I'm sure he deserved it," General Carson said. He knew Gunny wasn't being honest. There would have been a court martial in there for that, and some jail time, but it didn't matter. Everything else in his jacket told him this was the man he wanted. And he had a strong hunch this was the man he needed. "But I didn't wake you up to talk about that. Sergeant, I'm going to put you on speaker here. My counterparts in Russia, China, and Germany will be listening to us. Unfortunately, these are the only governments that any of us have been able to raise. We've contacted a number of ships at sea and most of the submarines, but as far as friendly governments, we four are it."

The General paused for a second where they assumed he was patching in the others, then finally got to his point, "Tell us how you came to the determination that the Muslim extremists were behind this attack through infected meat products."

Gunny was taken aback. "I... I don't know if it was," he said, trying to adjust to the change in the direction of the questions, and suddenly aware there were a lot of people listening to him. "It was just a logical conclusion I came to and asked Sergeant Kowalski to see if there was anything on the news about it, to see if it was even within the realm of possibility."

"You hadn't had any inside information, something leaked to you by any of your former military associates?" The General asked

"No, sir. Just a deduction with the few facts that I had," Gunny replied. "I was guessing." Did they think he had something to do with this? That he was discharged because he had terrorist ties? That he was still pissed and had decided to kill the whole world because of it?

"If I may..." came an Asian accented voice over the microphone.

"Of course, go ahead General Feng," Carson said.

"We were not affected as severely as much of the rest of the civilized world," he said, his English spoken slowly and very clearly. "Our military bases did not partake in the gifts from our Islamic neighbors. When we learned of this theory from Sergeant Kowalski, we immediately began to investigate the possibility of such an act. We sent entire companies of soldiers into the town to bring back a sampling of the Salaam meats. Many of my men died, but the packages they returned with, that were not labeled halal, were very much infected with a most disturbing contagion."

*"Those bastards!"* Gunny thought. It was one thing to think you knew something, something else entirely to KNOW you knew something. "Is it reversible?" he asked.

The Chinese general came back to answer. "No, we do not think it is. The reanimates are truly dead as near as we can determine, in the short time we have had. No heartbeat. They do not breathe. It seems that the very essence that makes one alive, makes one human, is gone. Their spirit. Their soul, if you understand. This appears to be a virulent mutation of a serum many nations have been trying to perfect over the years. A super soldier injection, if you will, that would help a wounded soldier heal quickly, ignore his pain, and continue to battle in a hyper-aggressive manner. Apparently, the Islamic scientists gained a sample to alter, or perhaps even created their own."

"Now what?" Gunny said. "They won. They kept it out of their countries. Now all they have to do is defend their borders until these things die off, and they own the whole world."

"This will not be happening," a Slavic voice said, heavy with menace and barely controlled rage. "They will not take the world as easy as that. They have released the zohmbee on us, we will be releasing Mother Russia's fury on them."

The conversation went on until near dawn, when everyone finally signed off. Gunny made his way back to his bunk, hoping to get a few hours of sleep, bone tired and weary from all of the things he had learned. It all seemed hopeless. Worse than he could have imagined.

The conversation replaying in his head. Iran had nuked Israel and was already in a mopping up extermination campaign. From the satellite images, it was wholesale slaughter. Door to door murder. The Israelis had used the Samson option and had sent their own nukes flying, but there were a billion Muslims and even the moderates were caught up in the frenzy.

This year's trip to Mecca was the largest ever recorded. It seemed nearly every Muslim that was able had made the trip to Saudi Arabia. Did most of them even know what their leaders had done? Had they known what was coming and went to a safe area, or was it just a general demand from Imams this year that all believers must go?

Were they afraid not to rejoice and celebrate, and do victory dances in the streets, even if they secretly didn't agree? Afraid of being targeted, themselves, by the extreme religious fanatics that had taken control of their religion, while they had sat back and done nothing? Too late now. The Russians had control of their nukes and they were pragmatic about it. They couldn't maintain them. If they didn't fire them off, they would eventually be a danger to everyone in the vicinity. They could have shot them off into space, or the ocean, Gunny and a number of other voices had argued, but General Carson had told all Hams to maintain silence, or they would be shut out of the one-sided conversation completely.

He, or one of the other commanders, would occasionally ask a specific question to various individuals around the world, but that was the only input allowed. So the last living representatives of humanity had to shut up and listen while four men discussed and decided the fate of millions.

It seemed that a lot of conversation had happened before the Hams were privy to it because the Generals were uncannily honest with each other. No posturing for position. No ambiguity about how much firepower they could bring to bear. They all knew there were no more backdoor channels to negotiate through. No months of waiting for answers to questions. They all laid their cards on the table.

China and Russia had control of their ships, nukes, and subs. America had no access to nukes at the moment, but it was a possibility within a few weeks. They still had the military fiber optic networks, links to the NSA databases, and control of their satellites. Germany only had contact with their Navy. No one else. Russia was pushing for full nuclear annihilation of the entire Middle Eastern region. Scorched earth. Glass parking lot.

Gunny got the feeling they were going to do it whether anyone agreed with them or not, but they were at least going through the motions of trying to have a consensus. By next week, another billion people would be dead. They hoped to completely destroy all things Middle East, eradicate everyone who practiced the "religion of peace." By their reasoning, then the rest of the world would have a chance to rebuild, without being slaughtered as infidels or forcibly converted.

The deciding factor for all of them, aside from the Russian General who seemed pissed off the entire time they were in on the conference, was the latest satellite imagery. It showed barriers along the borders of the peninsula of northern Turkey, completely sealing it off from Europe. By going back through the previous satellite photos, they could see the materials for it being amassed months in advance.

The Turkish Government had known it was coming and were prepared. In Egypt, the Suez Canal was heavily guarded and all crossings of it were thoroughly blocked. To the east, massive fortifications had gone up overnight in a well-planned action that sacrificed some Muslim territories, but protected most of them.

There had been unprecedented movements of people

into the guarded areas. Basically, the entire Middle East, and all of the Muslim countries, had been walled off. The people responsible for noticing these things in the various governments throughout the world must have chalked it up to the annual pilgrimage to Mecca. It was a strange few hours, discussing killing that many people.

It left Gunny with an empty feeling, knowing there were good people over there and he found it hard to believe that they didn't try to warn anyone, that an operation with so many involved, didn't have anyone who disagreed. That their Caliphate was so important to them, they would write off everyone who didn't believe as they did.

The remaining governments had all agreed to wait at least another week before retaliating, so the Americans could gather as much information as possible from their eyes in the sky. Even though there was irrefutable proof which nations had either done it, or been privy to the infor- mation and let it go forward, there were still millions and millions who had nothing to do with it.

They would all die for what a handful of their leaders had done. Guilty by association. Gunny guessed all wars were like that, though. It just seemed so BIG now. Push some buttons, a billion people die. But those same nations had banded together to send out deliberately contaminated food, and it worked perfectly. They didn't deserve mercy or leniency. Four or five billion people were dead because of their actions. Still walking around, but dead, nonetheless.

After the other command centers had signed off, General Carson asked if anyone in the Ham radio audi- ences had ever held elected office in America. No one had. He tried to get everyone's names and most gave willingly, although a few of the survivalist groups were hesitant at first. They gave the number of people in their group after some cajoling and being reminded that a census was Constitutional, so Cheyenne Mountain could try to guess how many people remained.

Did we still have a nation if there were only a few thousand survivors left? The General offered them the only help he could. He said if they would give him their addresses, he would give them the latest satellite information of their areas when they spoke again. They still had access to NSA computers and all of the imagery, as it updated, but he didn't know how long that would last.

He would let them know what the areas around them looked like, if there were any huge hordes moving in their direction. Cobb had given the address of the truck stop and Gunny gave his wife's work address, specifically the rooftop, and his son's high school. That's where he was heading as soon as he got his truck welded up the way he wanted. It took a while to get the information from everyone, but the General pointed out that it was his job to keep the American people safe.

That usually meant big things, but if it were down to individuals now, his men would do everything they could to help. They weren't going to abandon their post in this time of need.

Gunny tossed and turned. Dead tired, but not sleepy. His mind still racing with the horror of what he had learned. What had happened and what was going to happen. The Chinese had the most complete labs and personnel, and they hoped to know more about the infected by tomorrow... today.... when they would once again have a virtual meet up. There seemed to be more the General wasn't saying. But that was military men. He just hoped it wasn't more bad news. And he hoped Jessie would stay at the school and not try to make his way home.

## Day 2

Jessie was trying to pee as quietly as possible, but it was still embarrassing. They had decided to hunker down for the night, hoping the infected in the building would wander off if they kept quiet. They had moved the trash can over to one corner of the room, and put the white board in front of it to act as a simple barrier for privacy, but it didn't cover the splashing noises.

Whatever. At least he didn't have to take a big stinky poo. Yet. Wouldn't be so bad if it was just the guys, but he wasn't in the habit of going to the bathroom in front of a girl.

It was morning, the hazy sun filtering through the quarter windows set high up along the walls. They barricaded the door as quietly as they could yesterday, and then waited. They never did get through to anyone on their phones, and the longed for police sirens coming to rescue them never came.

Late in the evening, as fewer and fewer people were

trying to use overburdened cell towers, they started to get internet access, although it was spotty. They learned enough, though. It was zombies that had been prowling the hallways, and it wasn't just their school.

They had surfed the net, looking for information until, one by one, their phone batteries were nearly dead. By then, they knew it was over, that the world was lost and no one would be coming to save them. The game servers were empty, only NPC's populated them. Nobody was updating their Facebook status. Instagram had nothing new. Snapchat was dead and there were no tweets on Twitter.

The news reports and updates they found on websites that still worked were all hours old. No new stories were being reported and in the end, they could only log onto traffic and city camera feeds, but there were enough of those from around the world for them to know the outbreak wasn't isolated. It was global. Sheila had cried quietly and the guys would never admit it, but they had, too.

Their world was dead. It had happened so fast, was so complete, it took them a while to wrap their heads around it. They whispered long into the night about how it could have happened, and why they hadn't been affected. It must have been an airborne virus, they reasoned. And they were all immune.

Gary said that was mathematically impossible, but it was the only thing they could come up with. They had slept fitfully on the tiled floor with only books as pillows. When they awoke to the gray light of morning, they had all accepted the end of the world and were pragmatic about it.

They had watched thousands of zombie movies, apocalypse films, and dystopian futures, played out on the small screen. They had spent hundreds of hours in the wastelands with various video games. They understood it like no adult ever could. Sure, they were worried about family and friends, but hadn't they come through it unscathed? They were smart enough not to panic and break out of the room yesterday, and lucky enough to be where they were. No one would come out and say it, but they all felt like they were the chosen ones, the heroes of the movie and they would battle their way through and come out victorious in the end.

They were teenagers and each felt invincible, to a degree. They had nibbled on their lunches, making them last through dinner. The problem was water. Sheila had brought an apple juice, the boys figured they would get a drink from the fountain if they were thirsty. Now they were all craving something to quench their dry throats.

Jessie was shading his eyes, trying to see out of the door, trying to spot any movement, but was having no luck. The glass was just too opaque, like a shower door. They had tried to pick the lock like they'd seen done on hundreds of TV shows and movies, but it was futile. They knew they couldn't break the glass, it would bring the undead running.

Late last night, after the phones were nearly dead, they went over plans to escape and had decided to slip through the quarter windows. Their first idea had been to hotwire a car, then drive to each of their homes to look for family. That was quickly shelved after the frustrating and useless try at picking the door lock.

They came to the conclusion that stealing a car wouldn't be as easy as the movies made it seem and they didn't want to be exposed in the parking lot for an hour trying to figure out how to do it. The plan they finally came up with was to sneak into the woods behind the football field and cut through them toward Jessie's house. It wasn't the closest by roads, but out of all of their homes, they could get to it without having to go through any neighborhoods.

Jessie's place wasn't exactly rural, but it was on a lake and the lots were huge, so it wasn't built up too much. When they had first moved, he thought they were kind of rich, having their own dock and living on the water. But in Georgia, there were so many lakes the homes on them didn't cost much more than ones that weren't.

The lake was between the school and his house and by bus, it was a thirty-minute ride to go all the way around. If they could steal a boat and paddle across, it wasn't far as the crow flies. Most of the houses had kayaks or canoes on their back porches and Jon boats or pontoons tied to their docks. They only had to go on land for maybe a half mile or so.

With the last of the battery life on his phone, he texted both his mom and dad to let them know he was fine and would be heading home. He would wait for them there. He put the phone in one of the Ziploc baggies he had brought sandwiches in and offered the other bag to Sheila. She had a Lunchable yesterday. Just cardboard to throw away.

Jessie ran his dry tongue over his dry lips and tried to clear his dry throat. He was so thirsty. They all were. They had to do this today, they would be crazy with dehydration if they waited any longer. "We ready?" he whispered, and they all nodded in the affirmative. The one good piece of luck they had was that the detention room was at the back of the school, with only the outdoor lunch area, the football field, and the soccer practice fields between them and the woods. And the lake.

And then home.

Doug pulled on the window slowly, anticipating a screech of rusty hinges, but it came open smoothly and quietly. It was hinged at the bottom, opening from the top, and Gary had the armrest of his chair already off, handing it to him to use as a pry bar to pop the retaining arms off so they could remove the window completely.

Doug did so as quietly as he could and in seconds had it off and handed it down to Jessie. He cautiously stuck his head out and looked both directions, then quickly pulled back. He motioned frantically for the window and Jessie gave it back to him. He slipped the bottom hinges back into place and closed it, hurriedly twisting the lock shut, then climbed down.

"How bad is it?" Sheila asked.

"There's four or five of them just wandering around in the patio area, kind of aimless like," he said in a hushed voice. "I think one of them was Mr. Prater."

"That sucks," Jessie said. "I liked him."

"What sucks worse," Gary said. "Is that he's between us and freedom."

"We need a decoy, something to distract them," Sheila said. "Who's the fastest runner?"

"That would be you," Gary said dryly. "I'm not so quick anymore."

"It WOULD be you," Doug said quietly. "You run track. We don't. You volunteering?"

Sheila realized they were right and quickly backtracked. "You saw how fast they were in the hallway yesterday," she said in a loud whisper. "I can't outrun that, they're like super human, or something."

"We don't need to sacrifice anyone," Jessie said. "We just need a distraction, something to make them take off in the opposite direction so we can sneak in behind the bleachers. From there, it's a straight shot to the woods and we're kind of hidden the whole way."

They looked helplessly around the room for anything they could use. "I could throw a stapler or something, but I don't think I can get any distance from the angle down here," Doug said. "It would have to go around the corner of the building to draw them away."

"Right," Jessie said, still glancing around the room, unconsciously running his hands around his belt line, tucking his thumbs in his underwear. Then his eyes lit up.

"Sheila, give me your bra," he said, eying her chest. She had a pretty good set of hooters, although he couldn't begin to guess what size they were.

"What!!" she whispered, so loudly it was nearly a normal tone, looking at him in shock and crossing her arms across her breasts.

"Nobody wants to see your boobs," Jessie half laughed, raising his hands in a placating manner. "We can use it as a slingshot."

"Speak for yourself," Doug said. "I wouldn't mind seeing them."

"Yeah, that will work! I made an improvised grenade launcher out of a bra in Battle of the Wastelands 3," Gary jumped in with a little excitement in his voice as he worked the arm loose from his wheelchair again. "We can tie the ends to this." He held it upside down and it was just about perfect. Sheila saw what they were talking about, but was still too busy giving Doug her dirtiest look to acknowledge them at the moment. He wilted under her stare and mumbled something about looking for that stapler as he headed over to the teacher's desk.

It only took her a few seconds to slip out of the bra, with all of them watching. It was like a magic trick. One moment she's wearing it, the next she was sliding it out from the bottom of her shirt and handing it to Gary. All three of the boys looked a little perplexed at what just happened, but quickly tied either end of the sturdy bra to the ends of the armrest. "Glad you weren't wearing some frilly, dainty thing," Gary said, using teeth to pull the knot tight.

"Speak for yourself..." Doug started to quip, but it quickly died on his lips at the glare from Sheila He busied himself looking for anything else that might be slung out of their improvised slingshot and make noise as it clattered on the concrete.

Jessie opened another window quietly and removed the stops holding it in place so it could be taken out quickly when they needed it. They moved a student desk under it so it would be easier to climb out, and placed the teacher's big desk under the slingshot window. Jessie helped Gary onto the desk and took his chair and folded it up. It was a lightweight modern wheelchair and collapsed in on itself, so it was no bigger than the wheels when he was finished. Last night Gary had told them to just leave him behind, come back and get him later, but they wouldn't hear of it. There was no guarantee any of them would make it, and even less of a chance they would be able to sneak back over here with a car.

The school had hundreds of students and they were probably all over the front of the building. If he didn't go with them now, he would die a slow, painful death by thirst, locked in the dungeon. It would be like never getting off the first level of Dungeon Crawl. Besides, now he could get those bionic legs from the rehab center, make some modifications and be like Ripley from Aliens. Become a badass zombie killing machine.

They were ready. Or as ready as they were going to be. They quietly removed the windows and Jessie prepared to slide the chair through the opening as soon as the milling crowd was drawn away by the slingshot distraction. Sheila stood by, ready to help boost Gary through.

Doug stretched the bra back, bracing the armrest against the block wall with his feet. He aimed the best he could, shooting for the metal umbrella that was half visible over the picnic table at the edge of the building. They all held their breath as he let it go, the air filled with flying pens, staplers, and the empty glass apple juice jar. Some of the closer zombies started to turn at the twang from the bra being released, but their attention was soon diverted by the clatter of breaking glass and the cacophony of metal pelting metal.

There was a roar from the front of the school and an answering one from those few in the back, as they started running toward the noise. Jessie had the chair out of the opening and followed in seconds. As he was unfolding it, Doug and Sheila had Gary through the other window.

Jessie ran the few feet over to them and held the chair steady as Gary grabbed it and threw himself in, Doug placing his feet in the stirrups like they had practiced. It only took seconds, and then they were running toward the bleachers, hoping their movements wouldn't be noticed.

But they were.

Halfway across the end zone, a keening howl went up from under the bleachers. Someone had been bitten and crawled in there to escape, but only managed to die and come back, trapped by the crisscrossing bars, unable to figure out how to get over or under them. They glanced over at her as they ran past, it was Carly from Jessie's biology class.

She ran at them, ignoring the bars and supports she kept slamming into. They were smashing her face and body, but with the sheer intensity that she was slamming into them, she was bouncing over or under the bars. They ran. They had to get to the lake.

Behind them they could hear her crashing into the steel supports, her howls never ceasing, and with them, she brought the rest of the pack. If they came at them through the bleachers, that would slow them down. Hopefully enough so they could make it to the woods, maybe they could lose them in there.

Jessie ran flat out, pushing Gary's chair, with him helping as much as he could, pumping the wheels, his hands flying, urging them faster. Sheila was leading, she was past the bleachers and running in a sprint across the soccer practice field, aiming for the trees. Jessie chanced a look behind and his blood seemed to freeze.

There were hundreds of them streaming around the end of the school, and the fastest ones were already at the other side of the end zone, screaming with outstretched arms. There were a lot of them getting tangled up in the maze under the bleachers, but not enough. He couldn't go any faster, he was already at 110%. Had it cranked up to 11.

Sheila was at the edge of the woods, disappearing into the gloom, with Doug only twenty yards behind her. Jessie was halfway across the soccer field and already scanning the wood line, looking for the best entrance. His breathing was ragged, his thirst nearly unbearable, his lungs aching and the stitch in his side was screaming at him.

He wasn't used to running flat out and rarely ever did, unless he was late for the bus. He hoped the woods weren't wall to wall kudzu, like a lot of places in Georgia were. There was no way he could get a wheelchair through it if it were. Hell, you could barely walk through it. But they couldn't plan for everything.

Sometimes you had to trust fate. He pumped his burning legs, one of his old man's stupid sayings popping into his head, "Pain is just weakness leaving the body." He spotted where Doug and Sheila had gone into the gloom and aimed for the same path, it looked clear from what he could see, not too much undergrowth. He couldn't see much past the shadows a few feet in, and silently cursed them for leaving him behind. He shot a look over his shoulder as he entered the dimness, the mass of keening undead were clearing the end of the bleachers and charging out onto the soccer field.

"Watch out!" Gary yelled and Jessie turned around just barely in time to stop, before he plowed headlong into a fence. Sheila and Doug were there, arms outstretched to pull Gary over.

"Hurry," they said, as Jessie could do little more than try to get his breath, taking in huge, gulping lungs full of air. He got the chair against the fence and Gary was over in a heart-beat, Doug dragging the chair over next and getting him in it. It only took a few seconds, and they were off, Jessie still panting, holding onto the fence.

"Come on!" Sheila said, and she was chasing after them.

Jessie didn't have to be told twice. This fence was a godsend. He took one last deep breath then sprung over, hitting the ground running. He was sure the horde would get through it, but it looked fairly sturdy, it should hold them back for a few minutes. Maybe long enough for them to get to the lake.

Jessie quickly caught up with them, the chair was diffi-cult to maneuver through the underbrush and around the trees. Gary was helping to steer and still pumping the wheels as hard as he could, but they had slowed a lot. Doug was already breathing in short ragged breaths when they heard the mass of zombies hit the fence. It held the first ones in place, their desiccated brains unable to figure out what was stopping them, their legs continuing to try to propel themselves forward.

They kept piling on, kept slamming into the simple wire fence. Within seconds, it seemed, they had enough weight pushing against it and it went over easily, the unfortunate ones in the front being trampled underfoot of the rampaging, howling, horde.

Jessie and Sheila had taken each side of the chair and were pulling frantically toward the water as Doug still pushed and Gary tirelessly spun the wheels with his hands. The undergrowth was getting thicker, the ground muddier and they could hear the horde crashing through the fence.

"Not much farther!" they panted to each other. "Almost there!" But then they were faced with a massive fallen pine between them and the water. They wasted precious seconds, each trying to go in a different direction to get around it, with the sounds of the undead crashing through the trees getting louder.

They saw them coming. Screaming, keening, gnashing classmates, arms outstretched and heedless of the branches slapping their faces and whipping across their bodies. "Leave me!" Gary cried out to them in despair. "Just go!"

"Not a chance," Jessie gasped. "Forget the chair, Doug, grab his other arm!"

"The water is just ahead!" Sheila panted. "Come on, come on, come on!"

They draped Gary's arms over their shoulders and quickly climbed over the fallen tree, his feet dragging uselessly behind them. They could hear the crashing of the undead behind them, close now, right at the downed pine. A few of the sprinters in front found themselves impaled on the branches, but that didn't slow their raging lust, their number one priority, their need to replicate their numbers, to infect the uninfected, to spread as fast as possible to as many as possible, in any way possible.

The water was tantalizingly close, so close they could see startled turtles slipping back into the depths from downed trees they had been sunning themselves on. They could see the ripples of surfacing fish. They could see the ducks flap their wings in an effort to speed their flight away from the shores and into deeper water, to get away from the screaming and crashing coming from the woods.

And they could see they would never make it in time. The horde was flowing over the downed pine just a few dozen yards behind them, and the safety of the lake was a hundred yards in front of them.

"Climb!" Jessie bellowed, all his tortured lungs could get out, but they all caught the meaning and aimed for the nearest trees.

"We throw, you go," Doug said in jagged breaths and Gary nodded. They barely slowed as they came up to an Oak with low hanging branches, just shifted their position on Gary's arms and tossed him up as high as they could toward the lower limbs.

There wouldn't be a second chance if he didn't manage to grasp it and pull himself up. He would fall and be fell upon. But he didn't miss, his outstretched arms found the branch and like the ladder bars and climbing wall in the gym that he worked out on, he swung his body this way and that, pulling, reaching every time for a branch a little higher.

Sheila was scrambling up a pine covered in old climbing vines ahead of them, and Jessie was springing for a low hanging branch on some tree he didn't recognize. A Maple, probably. It didn't matter. It only mattered that it was there and he was up it and pulling his feet away from the flailing and grasping arms of his former classmates.

They slammed into the tree as he climbed, screeching and keening, jumping and grabbing, but too late. Seconds too late as the winded, scraped, bruised, and thirsty quartet climbed farther out of range. The mob howled in fury, their rage-filled faces upturned, seeing their prey so close, yet so unattainable.

Jessie found a fork in the tree some thirty feet off of the ground that made for a somewhat decent place to sit, and leaned his head back. He spotted the others, they had all found similar wide spots in their trees and were catching their breath. He let his heartbeat and breathing slowly return to normal.

It didn't take but a few minutes for the rough bark to get uncomfortable and before long, he was squirming, trying to find a position that hurt a little less than the one he was in. Where was an illegal deer stand when you needed one? He was so thirsty, his lips were chapped and starting to crack. The water in the lake only made it worse.

He could see it sparkling in the sunlight, less than a football field away. He closed his eyes and pulled some leaves from the tree and put them in his mouth, trying to suck any moisture he could out of them. How long would that mob stay down below? Could they out-wait them? He didn't know. It was up to luck now.

If something didn't distract them, draw them away, they could mill around down there indefinitely. The zombies sure hadn't been in any hurry to leave the school once they had everyone infected. Just meandered around in aimless circles, bumping into things. They would wait. Stay quiet and hope.

Maybe pray.

# 19

## DAY 2

By nine a.m., everyone that wasn't patrolling the perimeter fence or on the roof was in the diner, settling in to eat. Martha and Cookie had whipped up another buffet style breakfast and as everyone found their seats, Cobb started talking. He filled them in on everything the General had said, that their worst fears were true and the outbreak was global, except for the Middle East.

He reiterated that they were in a safe place, they could last here for months with what they had on hand, and that there are a few trucks that were loaded with food still out in the parking lot. They may get tired of Winter Squash, but Scratch had twenty thousand pounds of it. There are a few other trucks loaded with food, but no restaurant deliveries, unfortunately. That would have given them a diverse menu, but the drivers that had volunteered their loads all had bulk items.

Anyone that still wanted to leave was welcome to do so, but the diner customers that remained were afraid to try. If a semi-truck got overwhelmed by the hordes, what chance did they have in their cars? They hadn't heard from the rigs that left yesterday heading up into the mountains. It was anybody's guess if they made it or not.

Gunny and a half dozen other drivers were leaving, all of them wanting Tommy to reinforce their trucks first. There was talk of a supply run, especially more ammunition, and of course more guns. Everyone needed to be armed, they all agreed to that. Even the hesitant ones who just a week ago would have said guns should be outlawed, and had no clue how to operate one.

Now they saw the need and Griz, Pack Rat, and a few others said they could set up a target and training range at the back of the junkyard to teach them. Shakey wasn't looking too good this morning, was adamant about getting to his truck to get some medicine, but that wouldn't be a problem. He could go with the guys heading out to the parking lot later on.

Cobb drummed up some volunteers who were planning on staying to get busy repairing the old well, see if it could be made operational again. He organized a cleaning crew to empty out a few of the stores and set up sleeping areas. It was easiest to just have separate quarters, male and female, with the kids staying with their moms for now.

They would fix up something like small apartments later, when they had time. Gunny had volunteered any of the lumber he was carrying for the task. They made plans to get Hot Rod's truck in one of the mechanic's bays so they could unload it of all the moving blankets to make field expedient mattresses.

They'd bring in the rest of the trucks, one at a time, to be unloaded of any food stores they had. After that, the rigs of the few drivers that were planning on staying because they either lived in a big city, or had nowhere to go. They all wanted to drop their trailers and move the tractors in behind the fence so they could sleep in them. Everyone had given the General their addresses so he could look at the latest satellite passes in those areas to let them know how it looked, but most held no illusions of hope.

All of the people in cars had come from the cities. They were either just passing through, or had been out on a day trip to the mountains. They were trying to accept that they no longer had a home to go to, that this was the new reality of things. Peanut Butter said she'd let all the cattle she had in her bull hauler run loose in the junkyard, then volunteered it to be cut up to make the blades for the trucks that were leaving.

Aluminum was the perfect material. It was lightweight, strong, and already with plenty of holes for airflow. After some discussion, they decided to take Gunny's truck on a supply run, after Tommy had welded everything in place. Use it as a test truck, try out the improvements in the real world. They would try to get more guns, and as much ammunition as possible, with their first stop at the police station.

They hoped some of Billy Travaho's deputies were still safely in the cells they had locked themselves into yesterday.

Gunny had noticed the different cliques starting to form as he and Scratch ate in silence, from the corner booth. The Ferrari guy had a small group around him, the Prius couple and some of the guys from Jimmy Winchell's band. Even though he was a lot less caustic now that reality had finally set in, he just seemed like a pain in the ass. Cobb would have to watch him, he seemed like the kind of man who would just naturally try to undermine him. A 'glass half empty' kind of guy.

His pretty little blond girlfriend was smarter than she

looked, he mused. She hadn't gone back to him after that little incident where he tried to sacrifice her, just to save himself. She sat by herself in one of the corners. He really needed to go apologize to her for frightening her so badly.

He tried to remember her name, he was sure he'd heard it in passing. Cassandra? Tiffany, maybe? Some starlet name. One of the drivers would be hitting on her soon, she was easily the prettiest girl in the room, even without her makeup. She wouldn't have a problem finding a protector, and she might need one in this brave new world.

She seemed more of a shopping and nail salon type of girl, than one who could handle things on her own. Hot Rod had sat with the gal with the children and he actually had them giggling at some joke he was telling. That was good, Gunny thought. He was a standup guy, and he didn't know that woman's story, but she would need someone to watch out for her and the kids.

Lars had volunteered to help with the well, said he'd had a little experience with them in South America. He was sitting with Pack Rat and Cadillac Jack, listening intently to whatever Jack was saying. The old man had been in military intelligence in the 70s and 80s. A lot of his knowledge base was pretty outdated, but he always had a good tale to tell about the Cold War and the Russians, and the antics they got up to.

Cobb had a good setup here. About the best you could ask for, if they got the water flowing. The ground wasn't any good for crops, but with raised-bed gardens and hydroponics, they would flourish. Too bad it was so far away.

Maybe after he got his wife and son they would come back. The path would be clear, if they wanted to. He figured it might take him a week to get there, avoiding the big cities and having to probably plow his way through the smaller towns. But the trip back would be fairly quick. A couple of days.

Hot Rod had been telling stories of the Cannonball Run. Apparently, it was a real thing, and he had been in one. Some kind of illegal underground race. He said those guys raced cross country and could get from coast to coast in about 30 hours. The fastest guy had done it in less than twenty-nine hours.

Gunny knew he wouldn't be making those times in his mad dash across the country, but he was going to hammer on it as hard as he could.

The blonde girl started when Gunny stopped at her table and asked if he could sit. She looked a little rough up close, like she'd been awake all night.

"I just wanted to apologize for yesterday," he said. "I kind of let that go too far. And I'm sorry. I shouldn't have let it get so close." He trailed off, not knowing what else he could say.

She stared at him for a minute before she replied. "I'm not," she said. "I'm glad you did. It showed me something. It showed me that no one will help, no one cares, and you're on your own in this world."

Gunny shifted uncomfortably in the booth. That wasn't exactly why he'd done it, although it rang of truth.

"Well," he said, feeling embarrassed and having a hard time meeting her eyes, "you weren't really in any danger, I wouldn't of let it get to you."

"I know that, now," she said. "But I didn't yesterday, and no one else did, either. We thought you were a killer."

Gunny grimaced.

She glanced around the room then continued, "None of them would lift a finger to help, and I was too afraid to help

218

myself. I don't blame you, or them. I blame me." She pointed a slim, manicured finger at her chest.

"I want to learn how to do what you did. How not to be afraid of them. If you come back with guns today, I want one."

Cobb came in and started barking orders and assignments, getting everyone busy doing their various tasks, threatening the last one out of the diner with trailer decoupling duty in the parking lot.

# 20

It was late afternoon when Tommy flipped up his welding helmet and called it done. The Old Pete wound up looking like something out of a post-apocalypse B movie. It started the morning off as a head turner. A 359 Peterbilt, painted rosewood, with black fenders and striping, gleaming chrome Texas bumper and six inch straight stacks to roll coal. It had enough chicken lights to make it pop rolling down the highway at night, and polished aluminum steps and fuel tanks.

A real Rooster Cruiser. She had been a gleaming truck barreling through the night, with dozens of amber running lights all lit up... a beautiful sight. Now the steps had been torched off, the shining front wheels replaced with butt ugly steel rims and tires from an off-road dump truck, and the fenders cut out to make room for them. The big Texas bumper was gone.

A rude angled blade made from the cattle trailer was now attached to the front of the truck, acting as radiator guard and zombie shovel. A mesh of rebar had been welded over the windows and windshield, and Gunny had used every strap and chain he had to secure the remaining lumber, after they had unloaded enough for a dozen partitions to be built as small apartments.

He was going to drop the trailer in the junkyard and bobtail into town on the supply run, but when he left in the morning, he wanted his wagon. He might need the weight because big rigs were notoriously easy to get stuck if they were running empty. He'd seen guys get hung up and spinning in a gravel parking lot before.

Cobb was there with nearly everyone else, after he dropped the trailer and pulled up to the gate. Gunny hopped out to see who was going with him. Griz had volunteered, but Cobb said he wanted a full squad. At least five guys had to go so they would have a fighting chance if things got dicey outside the truck.

"Who's the ranking man?" Cobb barked as he walked up, eyeballing them both.

"He is," Gunny and Griz said at the same time, each pointing at the other.

"Figure it out quick, Cupcakes. We don't need two different people giving orders out there and getting everybody killed in the confusion," Cobb said, crossing his arms and staring at them, refusing to take sides.

"I was a private," Gunny said.

"Bullshit," Griz replied. "Look, I've got a lot of trigger time under my belt, but I was never the boss. I didn't make the plans, I just carried them out. I followed orders, I didn't give them. Hell, Gunny, I was never even a platoon sergeant. I'm good at killing, not so much anything else. You take it."

Gunny hid a sigh and nodded, held his free hand up for a fist bump and it was settled. They didn't have much ammo between them, and when Stabby came through the crowd with a new set of claws strapped to his arms, Gunny was glad. He'd seen the kid in action and he was definitely a good man to have on your side. Lars was right behind him, his Beretta and extra magazine with him. Scratch rounded out the quintet with an odd attachment in place of the usual hooks he had at the end of his prosthetic arm. It looked like a slim dagger, but when Gunny reached out to help boost him into the truck, the missing steps making it difficult to climb in, he noticed it was sharpened rebar.

"Nice one," he said. "Just be careful picking your nose with that thing."

Scratch tried to take the passenger seat, but Griz gave him a shove toward the sleeper, as he climbed in with the M-4. "Piss off ya skinny bastard," he said. "I make two of you, I'm riding shotgun."

So he squeezed in between the others who were already sitting on the bunk, grumbling about old beardy ass fat guys picking on the handicapped. Scratch never played the handicap card around normal people. In his mind, that's how he saw everyone who wasn't his friend.

People who would go out of their way to try to help, or give him sympathetic looks, or just look away, unable to even acknowledge him. With them, he would die before he admitted any weakness of any kind. Among his brothers though, he would do his best to get over on them. Of course, it never worked. They didn't see him as a man with a missing arm. They just saw him as a man.

They got an all clear from Hot Rod on the roof and the guys on the gate opened it quickly, shutting it almost before they were clear.

"Might as well take out the ones in front first," Gunny said and swung wide to meet the crowd that had been milling around the entrance of the building. As soon as they saw the Pete coming around the corner of the diner, they all turned and started running toward it, arms outstretched, the strange keening scream forming on their lips.

They didn't stand a chance. The sharpened blade was about 8 inches off the ground, and when he hit them, most of them left their feet bouncing around under the truck as the rest of their bodies skittered off of the plow and flew into broken piles on the side of the road. They weren't dead. Again. But missing your feet sure could slow a body down. They went from a "Danger, Will Robinson!", to a "Watch where you step", type of threat.

Gunny downshifted and turned the Pete toward town, following the directions on the GPS. He didn't know how long they would remain functional, none of the cell phone apps worked. Because it ran directly off of satellites, he supposed it would work until they quit orbiting.

He had no clue if they were self-sufficient, or if they needed occasional nudges from computers on earth. If that were the case, they wouldn't be up there for long. He'd have to remember to ask the General about that.

The sheriff's substation was south of them, near Silver Lake. Well before the gridlock and massive hordes of Reno. Since they couldn't Google "gun stores near me", they only had some vague directions from Cobb and Tommy. The "there's a pawn shop on the main drag, near the drug store" type of directions.

The roads weren't too bad pulling into the small town. There were cars stopped haphazardly, many with doors open. They could envision what happened, see it all too clearly in the dried blood, the crunched fenders, and the few bodies on the ground that had been savaged too badly to reanimate. It only took one infected to run out into the morning traffic.

Brakes would slam on, traffic would come to a complete stop, and people would open their doors and get out to see what the trouble was. They would see rampaging mobs attacking everyone. Biting and ripping, then leaping to the next fresh victim, leaving a mass of bleeding, frightened, and angry people in their wake.

Some who panicked and tried to crash their way through, some with arterial wounds which bled out and changed within minutes, many times with someone trying to help them. A whole town dying within hours of the first fried bacon sandwich being eaten.

Once they got off the exit, Gunny dropped the transmission into low range and started testing the strength of Tommy's blade. It slid the cars away effortlessly, the old Pete not straining at all, neatly shunting them to the side of the road.

"Awww, not that one," Scratch said as Gunny crunched into a beautiful ZR1 Corvette, cracking the fiberglass and large pieces broke off as he pushed it out of the way. "Dude, I would have totally drove that back to the truck stop."

"I just thought about it, but he's right," Griz said. "We can have any car we want. Hell, any THING we want. It's all there for the taking."

"Hells, yeah!" Scratch said, "Where's the nearest Ferrari dealer?"

"Monster Truck for me," Stabby threw in as Gunny negotiated around the last of the pile-up at the intersection and hit a stretch of clear road.

"1971 Eldorado, just like in Super Fly," Lars said.

They all looked at him.

"What? Brutha can't have a Cadillac?" he asked. "Man, I grew up watching old movies. Moms wouldn't let me out of the house in our neighborhood. I loved that pimpmobile."

"Can you dig it?" Gunny asked in the best Youngblood Priest voice he could manage.

"Give it up, Homie," Lars laughed.

"What about you, Griz?" Scratch asked. "What's on your bucket list of cars?"

Griz smiled as he answered, his shining teeth showing through his beard. "I'm getting a 1969 Hemi Charger with a 4 speed. Man, I've always loved those cars."

Amid the chorus of "Ooooh, nice one" and "Good choice", Stabby directed his question to Gunny, "What about you, mate? What's your driving pleasure?"

"I'm going to get the Batmobile," he replied. There was an eruption of laughter and questions of which one, which started an argument of which one was the best. The Tumbler won, hands down, as most practical, but there was a good debate on which was the coolest. The original from the TV show, the Michael Keaton or the Val Kilmer?

The George Clooney Batmobile was cool, but was there even a working version of it? Griz and Gunny let the kids battle that one out and went back to concentrating on their primary mission. The substation was only another half mile and they started looking for it, and the pawn shop that was supposed to have a large selection of guns and ammunition.

They had only seen a few zombies moving around, but every one of them had started following the noise of the truck, letting out those eerie, breathless screams to alert others of the promise of fresh meat. Gunny slowed as they approached the police station. It was on their left and there wasn't a big crowd around it, but there were a few milling about until they heard or felt the big truck coming. They turned to attack it, running at full speed directly toward them, keening and clawing the air.

"I'm going to make a pass, maybe two, there's a bunch

following us now. I'll try to get far enough ahead of them, then flip around and whittle their numbers down." It was go time now and everyone got serious and quiet as Gunny started working his way up through the gears, cutting a few down, leaving the rest of the screaming horde behind. He got about a quarter mile up the road, swung into a gas station to get turned around, then headed straight for the mob of at least a hundred, running up Main Street.

"Where did they all come from?" Lars asked to no one in particular. "They're like a swarm. Like ants...."

They didn't hear the rest of his thought because the first of them had started being cut down with the plow. The sheer numbers of them caused the big Cat under the hood to strain and he split a gear and hammered down, slicing through the middle of the pack. He was snapping bones like toothpicks, severing feet and hands and arms, and anything else that came in contact with the sharpened lower blade.

The rest of their bodies were breaking and being tossed aside at 45 miles an hour. The truck shuddered and jounced when the big front tires rolled over one of the infected who had missed the blade, but was crushed by the rolling rubber.

"Gonna have to build a deflector so they don't roll under the tires!" Griz yelled over the noise of the screams and impact of flesh. A few more bodies were crushed under the tires and the truck bounced the three men sitting on the bunk back and forth, as they tried not to stab each other with the assorted weapons strapped to their arms.

They finally cleared the small horde and Gunny went another half mile, taking out stragglers who had been too slow to participate in the mass slaughter. When he turned the truck around, gore and blood splatter covering the front half of his hood and fenders, they could see the full impact of what just one pass through a horde of them had done.

There were body parts everywhere. There were no standing zombies left, just a wreck of crawling bodies, all with missing feet or shattered lower legs. Most with more broken and mangled bones sticking out at unnatural angles. Gunny drove slowly over them, the big front tires turning them into bloody paste as they were ground under the blade. He stopped in front of the doors of the substation, and before they climbed out, he and Griz turned to check on the younger members of their group.

It wasn't meant as disrespect in any way, just a habit ingrained by years of service. Check your troop's gear, then check your own.

Scratch and Stabby looked similar in their appearance, both clad in leather shirts and pants they liberated from the costumes on the Brutal Retort bus. All of them wore gloves. The new blades they had made were intimidating.

Gunny realized now why he hadn't seen either one of them all day, they had been creating the stabbing arsenal they now wore. Scratch noticed him staring at his leather pants. "Got 'em from him." He cocked his head toward his new British pal, "And he helped me design my blade."

"Oi," Stabby said. "I learned last night that thick blades just get stuck in the bones and snap off when you poke those wankers. You need slender, sharp, and strong. Like this rebar. It won't break like my blades did."

Gunny nodded. They looked wicked. Deadly. No beauty in them, just total function.

Scratch had a single long piece of sharpened rebar attached to his metal arm and they had welded a small hook, right about where his forearm should be.

It took Gunny a second, but then realized it was a crude

barrel lock for the AR. It would hold the gun steady and alleviate muzzle rise. His other arm had an aluminum and steel fingerless gauntlet of sorts, with short spikes sticking a few inches beyond his knuckles. It left his shooting hand free to operate his rifle, and the spikes were short enough not to interfere with reloading.

Stabby had both forearms wrapped in thick leather, with three sharpened rods sticking out like Wolverine claws on each. He also had a clunky looking pair of knuckle dusters that had short bits of sharpened rebar welded to them. Backup weapon. Scratch showed him his pair. "This is still a work in progress, but we should see how well they work today, make some improvements if we need to."

Gunny was impressed. Griz, too. "I might need a pair of those. So don't go getting yourselves killed," he said.

"Tryin' not to, mate."

The crawlers were getting close to them, still intent on sinking their teeth into human flesh.

As he and Griz opened the doors to hop out, the other three were right behind them. Ammo was in short supply, so they didn't waste any as they ran for the doors that were propped open by a bullet-riddled body.

He and Griz entered first, breaking left and right, scanning the room, looking for any of the undead. It was an open floor plan, typical of a quiet sheriff's substation. Some desks, a few glassed in offices in the back. A hallway leading toward the restrooms and the back entrance. A stairway and elevator leading to the basement and the other two stories above them.

"Clear," said Gunny.

"Clear," Griz said a second later. Lars kicked the body down the stone stairs outside the building and pulled the doors shut behind them.

"Lars, hold here. Scratch and Stabby, find us another exit. Clear as you go. Griz, with me," Gunny said and headed toward the entrance to the lower level. The cells below were well marked with a sign over the stout metal door that led down the stairs.

He stood to one side and nodded to Griz, who quickly opened it and stepped back, pulling the M4 tight to his shoulder. He covered the high area and Gunny swung around the door in a crouch, covering the low. They could see the stairs leading down into the darkness, but not much else. "Electricity is already out?" he wondered out loud. "I thought it took a few days."

"Judging from all the bullet holes, I'd say somebody hit the breaker box," Griz said.

Gunny yelled out, "Hey, anybody home down there?"

Instantly they heard a snarl of the undead and the sounds of running feet, but also the cries of a few people yelling back up at them.

"Yes! We're here! Watch out, they're coming for you!"

"Get ready on the door, I'll take them out," Gunny said, and stood up and stepped far enough away so Griz could slam it shut if there were too many of them for him to shoot. Griz let the M4 dangle on its sling and grabbed the heavy door with both hands, his shoulder against it, ready to slam it as soon as he started to hear Gunny utter the words.

They could hear them coming out of the dark, snarling and keening, scrabbling on the steps, tripping over each other in their haste.

"How many?" Gunny yelled down into the blackness of the basement.

"There's four of them!" came the reply and he readied himself.

He needed four headshots.

On moving targets.

Coming up at an angle.

Out of the dark.

Fifteen rounds.

No problem.

As soon as he saw the first one coming up the stairs using its hands and feet, bounding as fast as it could, he started double tapping.

Boom boom.

It hesitated, bounced off the handrail, rocked by at least one of the bullets.

Boom boom.

The second set exploded its skull. It dropped instantly and started bouncing back down the stairs, tripping up the others as they clawed and scrambled over the now lifeless form.

Boom boom.

Another fell.

Gunny waited for the others to pick themselves up from being tumbled. They didn't sound like they were moving so fast. Maybe they busted a leg or something in the fall. He could only hope.

His eyes were getting used to staring into the inky blackness of the basement and he saw one coming, hopping in a broken way from step to step.

Boom boom.

Both in the head. Gore and bone splattered against the face of the fourth, who didn't slow down at all as she leaped over the falling body.

Boom boom.

Blood exploded out of the side of her neck and shoulder.

Boom boom.

Her head snapped back at a vicious angle and she crumpled to the stairs, finally dead.

"Twelve shots for four stiffs?" he heard Scratch call out. "Weak sauce."

Gunny swapped magazines for a fully loaded one and re-holstered his Glock. "Get out of the women's bathroom and find us an exit!" Gunny yelled back.

"Lars?" he asked, "How's it looking?"

"Half dozen crawlers at the door, a few more runners making their way up the stairs."

"Anybody have a flashlight?" Gunny asked.

But when he turned to look back down the stairs, he noticed a single light beam dancing across the stairwell wall, heard the sound of hurrying footsteps and a chorus of, "Don't shoot! It's us!"

"Are we glad to see you!" the female deputy said as she came through the door, but stopped short when she saw they weren't police officers, just a couple of hard-looking men with beards and guns. "Who are you?" she asked, her hand automatically dropping to the butt of the gun she still wore in its holster. Gunny and Griz just looked at her.

It was empty. They knew it was empty, and she knew they knew it was empty, so she let her hand fall away.

"Billy sent us," Gunny said. "We need guns and ammo. You have access to the arms room?"

"There's no arms room here, just a cabinet."

The other two from the cells stood behind her, one young man in a sheriff's deputy uniform, the other a tattooed woman in dirty jeans and tangled hair.

"Billy didn't send you," she said and started edging toward the desks. Probably where she kept a spare gun, or at least a loaded magazine.

"The back's clear!" yelled Scratch. "But it's the only

other way out, so let's not dick around till it gets jammed up!"

The runners had reached the top of the steps and were throwing themselves at the doors, shuddering them in their frames. The quiet screaming of all of the infected ratcheted up a notch as they came closer to their prey.

Gunny saw the look of fear and determination flit across the deputy's face when she heard Scratch's voice. He realized she had been out of contact with everyone since they had fled into the cell, that none of them had a walkie-talkie, and she had no idea how bad things really were. In her eyes, they looked like some wild desperados waving guns around in her police station. He made a snap decision to level with her. They didn't have time to mess around.

"You're right," he said. "Billy didn't send us. He's dead. But we heard your last transmissions on his radio and we came to try to get you out. We need guns and we need ammunition. I don't have time to explain everything right now, so we're leaving. Come with us or stay here, doesn't matter. But we've got to go. If you want to join us later, we're at the Three Flags." With that, he said, "Let's roll," and him, Griz, and Lars took off for the back doors.

"Wait for me!" the woman with the dirty clothes said and ran after them.

The two cops didn't have to consider the situation for long and yelled for them to wait, come help carry the guns and ammo.

There wasn't a lot, it wasn't like this sleepy little outpost had a swat team with a bunch of exotic hardware, but there were a dozen pump shotguns and another half dozen hand-guns that hadn't been assigned. All of them Glock 17s. As the two deputies quickly reloaded their service weapons,

Griz and Gunny stuffed everything into the duffels that were at the bottom of the locker.

They split the boxes of ammunition between the bags so they wouldn't be so heavy, then ran for the back exit. The sturdy front entrance doors were still holding, but the onslaught was relentless and they wouldn't last much longer.

"Runners coming in," Scratch said as he flung open the doors and they hurried down the steps. Griz stopped halfway down, aimed and dropped both of them before hustling to catch up, keeping the group tight, the two cops carrying the duffels and the other woman in the center.

"What are you driving?" the deputy yelled, a little breathlessly, as they rounded the corner, but could have saved his breath. The blood and gore splattered semi-truck, with the vicious looking plow welded to the front ,was in the middle of the street. It stood as a bloody testament to its efficiency. There were hundreds of crawling zombies slowly trying to make their way toward the police station on broken and shattered limbs.

It was pretty obvious what they were driving.

"Stabby, Scratch. Clear us a path to the truck," Gunny said.

The two took off at a sprint toward the semi, not really clearing, but certainly killing a path to it. The feetless and broken zombies were moaning and reaching for them with outstretched arms, teeth gnashing. They found themselves with puss oozing holes in their heads as the boys ran through them hacking and stabbing.

Brutal, sharp points were poking little holes of death nearly as fast as they ran, both arms swinging and slashing. They made short work of the crawlers until soon every dead thing between them and the truck was truly dead.

Griz stood guard, M4 occasionally barking out a death warrant, as they all clambered inside and found room for the bags of guns under the bunk.

"Go," Gunny said, and he and Griz jumped in and slammed the doors, elbows reaching back to hit the locks without thinking.

"Which way was the pawn shop?" Gunny asked, firing up the big Kitty and aiming for as many deaders as he could manage as he took off, bumping and crushing over them.

"Back the other way, on the left. Right across from the KFC," the woman said, that Gunny figured was probably a prisoner in one of the cells before all this started happening.

"Got it!" he yelled back over the noise of the winding engine. "I'm Gunny, that's Griz." He pointed to the big, bearded man between shifting gears. "Back there with you is Lars, Scratch, and Stabby."

Stabby stuck out his hand to shake and nearly impaled the deputy.

"Whoops. Sorry," he said, as Scratch and Lars laughed.

"It's fine," the lady deputy said as she checked her arm, making sure there were no cuts on it. "I'm Deputy Collins, this is Deputy McBride, and this young lady is Ms. Cruz."

"Everybody just calls me Bunny," the little Hispanic woman chimed in, happy to be out of her cage and away from the infected that had kept them trapped.

Gunny gave them a very condensed version of what they knew about the world, and what was happening, as he swung the truck around again and headed back toward the pawn shop. Scratch and Stabby jumped in occasionally to add a tidbit of depressing information. Again, he plowed into as many of the infected as he could, the blade flinging them off into mangled heaps.

He spotted the Colonel's House of Deep Fried Chicken

and then saw the pawn shop across the street. Wide sidewalk, no telephone or lamp posts in front of it. No cars parked there. Canvas awning about 8 feet high over the entrance. Burglar bars on the windows and door.

He swung wide and bounced up on the sidewalk, the oversized tires taking it all in stride, to a chorus of, "What are you doing?" and "Oh shit!" and Stabby yelling out, "WOOOOOHOOOOO!" like a cowboy at a rodeo. He drove the blade into the gated doors and they crumbled and tore loose like balsa wood.

Deputy Collins was yelling something about "Illegal" and "Can't do that" and "Destroying property", but Gunny just threw it in reverse and backed out onto the road, a snarling, clawing undead thing coming out of the destroyed door after him. Maybe the quick version of world events these past two days that he had given her hadn't sunk in yet.

"Scratch, you got this?" he asked, and Scratch leaned over to the sleeper door and opened it. "Here, zombie, zombie, zombie," he said, and when the thing saw him and came running up, it got a six-inch long spike to its forehead.

"Ewww. That's nasty," Bunny said. But she didn't look like she was going to be sick like Deputy McBride did.

Gunny and Griz were already out of their doors by the time the thing collapsed on the ground, and were hustling for the now wide open front of the store. Griz stood guard near the entrance, scanning both ways, M4 ready at his shoulder. They were lucky, the zombie Scratch had just killed was the proprietor and he had already opened the safe and was setting out his merchandise. He had a lot of guns, most of them hunting rifles and junky off brands, but there were a few nice ones. They made a fireman's chain and started handing them off, filling up the area beneath the bunk with all manner of firearms, pistols, and any ammunition they could find, Griz urging them to hurry.

As they grabbed the last of the hardware and Griz was giving them warning that the crawlers were getting close, Lars smashed a glass case with the butt of his Beretta and grabbed a pair of fancy sunglasses.

"Need another gun out here," Griz yelled and popped off a few shots, taking out the closest of the crawlers. "We ain't got time for fashion accessories!"

"These are genuine Persols, man!" Lars yelled back, putting them on as he slipped outside and took up a defensive position across the door from Griz.

"Steve McQueen wore these."

He dropped to a knee and took out a runner, but there were more coming and they were starting their keening screams. He started popping off shots, his pistol barking an answer.

The rest all ran for the entrance with the last of the guns and started jumping back up into the truck. The runners were getting close as the last of them finally climbed aboard and slammed the doors. In his rush to get back inside the cab, Gunny slipped on the battery box and barked his shin on the serrated metal step on top of it, letting out a roar of pain and a blue streak of obscenities that would have made a merchant marine with Tourette's blush.

When he finally finished cussing Tommy for torching off his lower step and got it in gear and rolling again, he heard Lars and Scratch quibbling over money.

"Eighty-seven dollars," Scratch insisted.

"No, definitely eighty-four," Lars came right back.

Gunny was rocking in his seat, grimacing and white knuckling the steering wheel, his shin still screaming in pain at him. He could feel the blood soaking his sock from the shredded skin. He had really flayed it up good.

"What the fuck are they bitching about?" he grunted to Griz, his face contorted, tears still rolling down his cheeks, finally getting his breath back.

Griz didn't answer, he was breathing hard, sounded like he was choking and Gunny looked over, thinking maybe he was hurt, too, but it was obvious from the look on his reddening face. He was trying his best not to burst out laughing, trying to hold it in, one hand covering his mouth.

"How much money you owe Kim," Scratch brayed, barely getting the words out before he fell into a heap of helpless laughter.

"Fuck all y'all," Gunny muttered back, to still more sniggers and giggles, the pent up tensions and fear fell away in the boys' contagious laughter as everyone joined in.

# 21

The sun was just setting when Griz radioed they were coming in and the gate was opened as they approached. Gunny pulled the rig in, aiming for the bay doors.

He wanted Tommy to make a few improvements. Like putting his steps back on. If a zombie had enough coordination to climb up on it, he'd just have to shoot it in the face. It was too much hassle to try to climb up into the cab without something to stand on. Sara and Stacy were there with orders for everyone to start stripping down to their skivvies, modesty be damned.

Bunny didn't seem to mind, but Deputy Collins insisted on a modicum of privacy and they relented, taking her and Bunny inside to the ladies room when they had finished checking out the guys for bites.

Cobb was pleased with the haul they made and got a crew carrying everything in to be inventoried, cleaned, tested, and divvied up to anyone needing a weapon. Gunny laid claim to a nice short barrel M-4 that was equipped with a couple of tasteful add-ons, and a few boxes of ammo for it and his Glock, before it all got carted away.

He got dressed again and checked with Tommy to let him know how the battlements held up, and what things needed to be improved upon. There were a half dozen trucks in the rear yard already being up-armored and looking ready for anything.

"They're going quick once we knew what to do. Got an assembly line started," Tommy said, by way of explanation when Gunny expressed a bit of amazement on how fast he churned them out.

He still wanted to leave at first light. Hopefully, the General would have some information about Atlanta from his satellites. They were all supposed to be on the channel at twenty-two hundred hours. He had time to get a deflector for his left fender welded up, a step put back on, and grab a shower. Maybe see if Martha or Cookie had any leftovers that were still warm.

He also needed to find out who all was planning on running with him. He hoped it wouldn't be a bunch, too many guys just slowed things down. But three or four trucks headed east would be nice. He still needed to stop by an RV dealer, or find an RV on the side of the road to snag the water pump from.

They all had little 12-volt pumps to operate the water for the sink and toilet. He figured he could use it to refuel along the way. Maybe use three or four at the same time. It might take a while, but it was better than a mouthful of diesel every time, with a siphon hose.

By the time he and Tommy had welded up a deflector for his front tires and he'd gotten a shower, it was going on nine o'clock. Another hour till the General came on, so he headed to the diner to find some food. Nearly everyone was there and Stabby was regaling them with tales of horror and glory of their afternoon's experience.

He was exaggerating quite a bit, with Scratch and Lars jumping in from time to time when Stabby wasn't eloquent enough in describing the wastelands beyond the gates of the truck stop.

Gunny stepped up beside Griz, Hot Rod and a few of the others, listening for a moment. It was quite entertaining to watch them. Stabby was a natural showman, with Scratch and Lars acting it all out with exaggerated motions, sound effects, and facial expressions.

"Got us some real Shakespeare's here," Griz said with a grin.

"Apparently I took out a whole horde with just my K-bar."

"More like the three stooges," Deputy Collins opined sourly. Her role in this impromptu three-man show had been only that of a damsel in distress. She had been rescued by the dashing heroes who risked life and limb, cutting through countless zombies to save the ladies.

As the story finished with the gallant Gunny driving over a mostly destroyed bridge with exploding cars sending up great walls of flame, all the while shooting zombies off of the hood one handed, the small crowd applauded and Ms. Bunny Cruz ran up and kissed them all, proclaiming, "My heroes!"

Griz and Gunny were laughing out loud and applauding with the rest.

"Nobody is going to believe all that tripe," Deputy Collins grumbled, but she, too, had a smile on her face and clapped along with everyone else.

"I didn't say it before, but thank you for pulling us out of there," she said, looking each of them in the eye.

"No worries, ma'am. Just doing our job," Griz grinned at her.

She almost smiled back.

Gunny headed over to the buffet area to see what was left, but hollered before it got too loud, "I'm rolling east at first light. You guys that wanna convoy, come see me and let's figure out a route."

## 22

Wire Bender had run some coms wire along the toy train tracks and through the walls so he could put a speaker in the dining room. Everyone couldn't fit in his CB shop and he was really uncomfortable having so many people hanging out there all the time now, hoping to hear a snippet of news. As everyone in the diner quieted down in anticipation of when the first of the Ham's around the world started checking in, Gunny headed over to the CB shop.

He needed to ask the General about Atlanta, and he figured they owed him something, he had given them the answer to what had caused this whole pandemic of death. He heard the Germans confirm they were on the air as he walked in and nodded to Wire Bender, Griz, and Cobb.

"They had us go up to a different frequency," Wire Bender was telling Cobb. "They say this one is secure, unauthorized radios can't listen in."

"I didn't know you could do that with open air coms," Gunny said.

"I can't," Wire Bender replied. "They're the 'Gummint. They can do a lot of things with military grade transceivers.

There's a bunch of Hams from all over the world listening in and I guess they are using narrow band and repeaters, maybe even satellite bounce."

Gunny didn't ask what any of that meant. He was just happy to hear there were more groups of people being found.

It was an unusual symbiotic relationship between the remaining powers. The Russians had little more than nukes and secure video feeds into most locations within their borders and satellite countries. The Chinese had the best medical and scientific laboratories still operational, the Germans had a pretty good overview of Europe and still had control of their drones.

The Americans had full satellite imaging capabilities and access to the massive NSA databases. With mutual cooperation, they had a pretty good picture of the world, and had been in communication with each other on secure channels continuously these past 24 hours. They had all tried every broadcast option available, that was still operable, to reach the civilian populations about the cause of the disease and how to take precautions, but it was too little, too late.

They each, in turn, gave a quick synopsis of what they had learned and in the end, it was far worse than anybody had even imagined.

The German captain was the highest ranking officer on land, although the ships at sea had officers well above his grade. He reiterated what everyone already knew. They had sent drones over most of the major cities and most of them were on fire. There were survivors on rooftops and enclaves of people that had barricaded themselves in at various locations, surrounded by thousands of undead trying to get to them.

All they could do was watch and report. They had no way of rescuing them, although every ship they had at sea was heading back toward land. There was a chance of using helicopters to aid some. But that was just a drop in the bucket.

General Feng broke down what his scientists had been able to determine, and what it boiled down to was the infected were indeed dead, no cure possible. The super soldier serum, which removed all inhibitions and fear and had clotting agents powerful enough to stop arterial bleed-ing, had been radically altered with experimental nanotech and crossed with animal DNA, for a more predatory and aggressive disease.

They believed the nanotech, with its molecular self-assembly, is what kept the dead from lying down and being dead. Chemical components of PCP had been added for inhuman strength, and apparently so had a virus-like molec-ular level command to reproduce. To make more of them. To replicate, duplicate, populate. To bite and infect as many humans as they could.

They didn't seem to need food, and they didn't particu-larly try to kill, just bite and move on to the next victim. But given enough of them attacking someone, all of them wired to reproduce the only way possible, through saliva, people caught up in mobs of them usually were damaged too badly to reanimate.

The blood was dead, contact with it didn't spread conta-gion, it passed from the host only from bites, or saliva conta-mination. The head and brain were essentially the only things still alive, the rest the body dead and decaying, although at a much slower rate than normal. This was due to the introduction of the nanotech assemblies. They would continually repair the flesh and bones, but at an ever increasing degraded rate as there was less and less "clean" material to work with.

From all of this, the conclusion was that the zombies were not indestructible or immortal. They wouldn't last forever. In their best estimates, an undamaged infected would deteriorate to the point of being nonviable in about five years, maybe longer if it wasn't exposed to extreme temperatures and harsh conditions. But these were just guesses, the tests they had thus far been able to run had widely varying results.

The Russians reiterated what the Germans had said about Europe. They didn't have drones available, but through the extensive fiber optic networks and redundant solar powered battery backups, they had eyes through most of the governmental cameras throughout the Eastern European countries. Their traffic and surveillance cameras told the same story in every city. Some that had minimal infestation yesterday had been overrun 24 hours later.

They finished up with pronouncing that they, in target coordination with the Chinese, were ready to destroy every major and minor city in every territory that the satellite imagery had shown to be prepared before the outbreak started. Scorched earth. Nuclear and conventional weapons would be deployed, pounding any survivors back into the stone-age in a radiated wasteland.

The world was a bleeding, broken, zombie infested mess, with an estimated four billion dead in just 48 hours.

Then came General Carson's turn to share all the bad news they had managed to uncover over the past 24 hours. They determined Hawaii was overrun like the rest of the States, hard to know about the smaller islands, although logic would suggest they shouldn't have been infected.

The few Navy ships that had managed to contain the

outbreak had orders to check out some of the smaller sustainable islands and were in route. But all it took was one person to annihilate a city in a matter of hours, with the rate the disease spread. The Designated Survivor from the President's cabinet hadn't been found. There was always supposed to be one person who was eligible to take over in a worst case scenario, but whoever it had been on the day of the outbreak hadn't made contact.

Gunny rolled his eyes. Who cares who's in charge? There's nobody left to rule.

They only had sporadic contact with a few Ham radio operators in South America, most of them were in remote areas at weather stations, or logging operations, in the jungles. From the satellite photos, though, they could see clouds of smoke billowing from the cities during the days and blackness where there used to be lights at night.

They hadn't had a lot of time to dig through the NSA's files pertaining to meat packaging business acquisitions, but once they knew what to look for, the evidence piled up fast. The Salaam Company had either purchased outright, or made hostile takeovers of, nearly every meat packing plant in the world. The expense was staggering, but most of it hadn't even been paid, the funds promised but never delivered. The lawyers had already been fighting it in the courts as an unjust monopoly, but the Muslims didn't care about that. They knew it would never get past the posturing and filing of papers before all of the infidels were dead.

The shortage of meat of all kinds last week had been intentional, so there would be a run on the supermarkets when they started deliveries again with the tainted products. There had been a lot of FDA inspectors killed this past week, but everything happened so quickly, the FBI hadn't picked up on the significance of it from all of the scattered reports from the different police departments.

No one had connected the dots. The General didn't have direct knowledge of the same thing happening in other countries, but surmised it was much the same way everywhere. He told everyone listening that most of the following information he had was only a known factor in the United States, but it stood to reason the same plan had been followed worldwide.

It had been a huge operation, involving thousands of people, and nothing could have enticed so many to keep such a terrible secret. Nothing except religion. A belief that they were doing the right thing, they were heroes, ushering in a World Islamic Caliphate.

There was a pause, a rattling of papers, a brief exchange between the General and someone else there with him, and then he started again.

"There's no sugar coating this," he said. "Most of our techs here have been working a theory from a pattern we noticed, and we think we have conclusive evidence now with the latest thermal pass from our birds. We've convinced our counterparts not to lay waste to the Middle East just yet, waiting on the confirmation I just received."

He paused for another moment, probably speed reading whatever had been given to him. "We have known about the nuclear power plants being in danger of melting down as soon as the electricity goes off completely," he continued. "A scenario like this was never envisioned or planned for, and there is nothing we can do except tell the survivors where the safest places are to go.

"We've taken into consideration the expected runtime left, with the reserve fuel supplies and automatic generators kicking in as soon as grid power goes down. There are some hydro-electric powered stations, but most run on coal. We've been working on computer models of prevailing winds, shifting jet streams, amount of rainfall...In short, we've been working diligently to determine the safest place for everyone to go, and how long you have to get there, in a worst case scenario."

Gunny could hear groans and angry words from the dining room.

Cobb just grimaced. "Hadn't even thought about that," he said.

"Wonder how long the dams will last?" Gunny asked. "I'd hate to be below the Hoover when it goes."

General Carson started speaking again, probably mindful of the uproar he had just caused, but plowing on anyway. "Right now, our greatest concern is the reactors melting down when the generators run out of fuel. When this happens, there will no longer be any water flowing over the nuclear rods to cool them. They will boil off the water in their tanks and start melting through the concrete floors. There are 100 active reactors in the United States and 185 in Europe, so there will be nearly 300 Fukushima type meltdowns spreading radioactivity everywhere the wind blows."

At every radio listening in around the world, there was quiet. Translators quickly explained what the American General had said. Everyone was speechless as it sunk in. It didn't matter if they survived the zombies. They would all die of radiation poisoning. An unseen enemy that you couldn't fight. Hair would start to fall out. Your teeth. Bleeding gums. Open sores. Death.

Gunny waited for him to continue, his mind racing. He said there were safe areas where the winds wouldn't carry the radiation. He had to find out where and then get on the road to get his family. They were smart. He knew his wife was alive, and if she had survived the initial onslaught of the dead, she would stay alive.

That's what killed everyone so quickly, the speed of it happening, the surprise of trying to render aid and then being attacked. Not knowing your enemy. But she had lived long enough to figure it out. She was a tough one. She'd shrugged off the difficulty of all those years of military separations, raising their son by herself.

She camped and hiked and shot a gun as well as anybody. She was fit and she was savvy. Once a person lived through the first hour of the outbreak, they knew what they were up against, knew not to run in to try to help a coworker who was having their face ripped off if you were unarmed. Knew not to get bit ,and knew if someone you were with did have a bite mark, that they would become one of the undead.

She had survived. He knew it. If he went in with enough firepower, he could blast his way all the way up to the roof and get them out. He was rolling at first light. Grab a bag of coffee to dip like tobacco, and hammer down until he got there. Maybe see if any of the drivers had a few California Turnarounds they could spare. That would keep him awake for however long it took. Remember to grab a pack of smokes, too.

Not that he liked smoking store bought cigarettes, he hadn't had any in years. But they made a great alarm clock if your body absolutely had to take a nap. A lit cigarette, stuck between your ring and pinky fingers, would burn for about 10 minutes and then wake you up when the cherry started burning your skin.

You simply did not sleep through that alarm, no matter how tired you were. Too late now, but he should have stopped at an auto parts store while they were out and grabbed a bunch of off road lights to add to his rig. Maybe tomorrow. Then it would be easier to drive at night. Light up the road for a mile with some super bright halogens.

He stopped his rambling thoughts as the General came back on. "That is the worst case scenario," he repeated. "It isn't necessarily that dire. With this newest set of prints from the last flyover that happened just minutes ago, we have confirmed a silver lining in this disaster. I'll lay this out briefly, so you understand how important it is for any of you out there not to take matters into your own hands and attack any mosques.

"We know this plan of theirs has been in the making for years. The purchase of the meat packing plants, the defenses in place to throw up overnight in the Middle East, the placing of many Muslims in high ranking positions in the Governments all around the world, the call for ALL Muslims to go to Mecca this year, and the list goes on.

"The data was there, no one saw it. By going through the NSA data of visas issued, there has been an inordinate amount of nuclear scientists and students flooding into the States over the past month. By checking shipping and purchase records, every Mosque in America has been quietly fortifying itself with massive amounts of food.

"People, we confirmed tonight that those same Mosques are all up and running. None have been overrun by the dead, and in their parking lots, they have similar heavy duty equipment that some of you near Reno have built. Except the trailers they are pulling appear to be modified tankers with external refrigeration units attached to them. We have no records indicating they are heavily armed, but our guess would be yes.

"They have been gearing up for this for a while, and

from what we can determine, they are planning on removing the radioactive rods from the power plants. We don't know what they are going to do with them, but if they planned this far in advance, I'm pretty sure they have a safe disposal site picked out. So that's the good news. Our conquerors plan on saving the land for themselves, not leaving it uninhabitable for a thousand years."

Cobb spat on the floor. Gunny felt the same. That word 'conquerors' didn't sit well.

"This is why there has been no retaliation," the General continued. "We must let them think they have won, that we are powerless. We must let them finish their plan of shutting down all of the nuclear power plants before we engage, because frankly gentlemen, if they don't do it, it won't get done. We can't determine if any of the European Mosques have laid up supplies, but our guess is yes. We can see large tanker trucks near all of them so we would assume the same plan is being carried out there."

"Don't know if I can do it," Griz said, his fists clenched. "I'd be hard pressed to drive by a hajji and not put a few rounds in him."

The General went on for a few more minutes, detailing more of what they knew, but it basically boiled down to leave any Muslims you may see alone, do not interfere. Let them decommission the power plants first, then we would do our best to annihilate them. After the big news, the General told the rest of the world they should go to the European, the Russian, or the Chinese channel, whichever one was the closest to them. They had all been working on computer simulations for their areas and would share any more information they had about safe locations.

He was going to spend some time with the North American groups he was in contact with, relay what little bit of information he had that affected them directly. When he finally got around to answering questions from the Three Flags group, making them wait until last, Gunny found out that the satellites hadn't picked up anything from the roof of the Hartwell Tower, or any sign of live people at the high school.

The General said the GPS units would work for another five to ten years, as those satellites were in high orbit, but the spy satellites would all be down in 18 to 24 months. That's how long they had an eye in the sky. By then, if the Chinese guys were right, most of the zombies wouldn't be so agile and fast, and they could start rebuilding instead of hiding out and surviving.

He'd rather fight some shambling thing any day, over a raging monster twice as strong and fast as him. He'd also learned that, just going by rough estimates, there were a lot more people in the world than just the handful on the ham radios. For the few hundred or so they had been in communication with, they figured there were at least another ten thousand the computers had spotted from the flyovers, once they started them searching for certain parameters.

As the last of them at the Three Flags that had given Cheyenne Mountain an address to check on finished their questions and headed back to the dining room, Wire Bender said, "That's the last, Sir."

When Gunny got ready to leave, Cobb told him to wait. There was more. Gunny looked at him quizzically, but the old man's gnarled face gave nothing away.

"Take it down to the secondary channel, Sergeant Kowalski," came the General's curt reply.

As he adjusted the dials with his left hand, he slid the microphone over the counter toward Gunny.

"Sergeant Meadows, do you copy?" his voice came back.

Gunny sighed. Now what? Still wanting to know why I got kicked out? Still think I know more about the Muslim's plan?

"Private Meadows here, Sir," he replied.

"Is the room secure?" came the General's query.

What? Gunny glanced around. Just Cobb and Wire Bender were left.

"First Sergeant Cobb and Sergeant Kowalski are present," he replied, unintentionally dropping his smart-ass attitude and falling back into his military bearing at the unusual question.

He heard the tail end of a heavy sigh as the General came back on. When he started talking again, he didn't sound like his professional, unflappable self, didn't sound like a General in the Army who was always in control, who always knew the answers.

He sounded like an exhausted man who had watched his country, and the world, fall apart in the last two days. He sounded like a man who had been run ragged trying to gather all of the information he had just spent the last few hours disseminating. A man utterly worn out from trying to help the only survivors in the world they were in contact with. Gunny wondered if he had slept at all in the last 48 hours, then felt like an ass for giving him a hard time. He needed to lighten up. This guy wasn't the enemy, and was going above and beyond to help everyone.

"Sergeant Meadows," he began. "I don't even know where to start so I'm going to just ask you a few questions so we can ascertain a few things. It may not make much sense at first, but it is important, so I ask you to bear with me. I would appreciate sincerity in your answers."

Well, that was a polite way of telling him to stop being a smartass. Gunny looked up at the clock. It was going on midnight. He wanted to leave in a few hours and needed to get some sleep.

"Yes, Sir. I'll do my best." Here it comes, he thought. Why did you get booted from the service? What the hell did it matter now to this guy, he wondered? If he thought he was going to draft him back into active duty, have him running around doing rescue missions of VIP's or something, he had another thing coming. He was still trying to figure out what his angle was when the General asked, "Are you familiar with the order of presidential succession?"

Well, that came out of left field.

"Um, sort of," he replied, wracking his brain, trying to recall high school Government classes. "It goes to the Vice President, then the Speaker of the House, then to senior cabinet members. I think."

"Right," the General said. "And if all cabinet members are presumed dead, including the Designated Survivor?"

What was all this about? What did his opinion on anything matter? He was a disgraced soldier, and now just a truck driver.

"I don't know, Sir. I guess the highest ranking military officer." Was this guy making a play at becoming president? Was he actually campaigning for votes? And really, what did it matter? Who cares who the president is? President of what? Three hundred million dead people?

Cobb and Wire Bender both had big grins plastered all over their mugs and Gunny knew the joke was on him, but hadn't figured out what it was yet.

"No, son," the General replied. "It has to go to an elected official. A person that holds, or has held, public office. The Constitution is clear on the separation of powers, and the Commander in Chief has to be a duly elected civilian. If a military man just decides to take over because there is an absence of power, that would make this country no better than some third world banana republic.

"The succession of power starts at the Vice President and then goes all the way down to the lowliest dog catcher in the smallest municipality. The one requirement, other than being of age and a natural born citizen, is that they are a public official, chosen to hold office, and elected to that office by their peers."

Gunny waited for more, not knowing what to say. He'd never held public office, so the General wasn't hinting at him to be a president. That was laughable.

When he didn't reply, the General went on.

"Out of every name I have, of every known, living citizen in the United States, you are the only one that has ever held public office. You, by the best guesses of everyone here at NORAD, are the only person left alive who is legally qualified to be President."

"Um," Gunny said. "I appreciate the offer, but I've never held any kind of office. I think you have the wrong guy."

"It's not an offer, Sergeant. It's your duty. You swore an oath to the Constitution when you raised your right hand to join the service. That oath didn't end when you got out. Weren't you on the Greater Woodland School District Board?" he asked.

Gunny wracked his brain for a minute before remembering. "Yeah, but that was just a fluke. One of the board members moved out of state and they needed a fill-in until the next election. My wife was there for a PTA meeting and volunteered me as a joke. Since I was the only name presented, they told her I was it. Nobody wanted that job. I never even went to a single meeting!"

"That doesn't matter," General Carson came back. "It is

DAVID A. SIMPSON

an elected position, you were duly assigned a role in local politics. As near as we can determine, you are the next in line for the presidency."

"Is this a fucking joke?" Gunny asked, incredulously.

Cobb and Wire Bender both were quietly laughing, knowing what had been coming as they had discussed this with NORAD earlier in the day.

"No, Sergeant, it is not," came the reply, starting to sound annoyed. "You do, of course, have the right to refuse. But keep in mind, you are the only eligible person for the job that we have been able to find.

"Anybody could take over, claim to be President, but it wouldn't be lawful, and that would make the United States, as we have known her for over two hundred and forty years, null and void.

"Someone is going to be in charge, and as we start to recover from this, there needs to be a clear and undisputed lawful leader. If not, any jumped up warlord can claim he's the president, the king, the emperor, or the Grand Poobah!"

The General was starting to get worked up and was becoming more forceful.

"Essentially, this country will no longer exist and we will become another defeated state that has passed on into history. They will have won. The Continuity of Government is important, Sergeant! The longest America has ever been without a president before this was when JFK was killed. It took 99 minutes before Vice President Johnson could be sworn in aboard Airforce One. We haven't had word of the President, or any Cabinet members, for almost 42 hours and we know they were all at the Friendship breakfast the Salaam Corporation had sponsored. This country does not exist without a government, without a president!"

The General was really getting passionate, starting to sound more like a pissed off First Sergeant. "So if you refuse the job, this nation as we have known it is over. Admiral Harris will assume the position as Commander in Chief, but the old America is defeated and we will be starting a new one."

Gunny didn't know what to say. This wasn't right, dumping this on him and then throwing a guilt trip on top of it. It all seemed so pedantic, so unnecessary. He wasn't a politician. He didn't want the job. He didn't know jack squat about how to be the leader of a nation.

Hell, he could barely take care of himself. Besides, what did it matter? There were only a few thousand survivors left. It would be a hundred years before there were enough people to care about electing someone for office. It seemed like a waste of energy to even think about it. There were much more important things to be worried about.

Cobb was serious all of a sudden. "Gunny," he said. "You've got to do it. It's just for show, it's only on paper. It keeps this country a country, not just a bunch of enclaves trying to do what's best for themselves. If you don't, them goat-humping bastards won the war."

"He's right," Wire Bender said. "It doesn't change anything, man. Just name General Carson as your Vice and let him do all the heavy lifting."

"I can do that?" Gunny asked, his mind racing, trying to find a way out of a bunch of responsibility he didn't want to shoulder. The last time he had people depending on him, they all wound up dead.

"You can do anything, man. You're the Prez," Wire Bender replied. "You can find out what's in Area 51, or if we really landed on the moon. You can even order them to help you save your old lady and your kid."

"It's only for a year, election is next November. Besides, if they do find someone else, a mayor or something," Cobb said. "You can resign, let him take over."

"Sergeant Meadows?" General Carson said.

"Yes," Gunny replied almost instantly, hitting the press to talk button, grasping at Wire Bender's last words before he could come to his senses and change his mind. Before he could tell them to keep looking, surely they had missed somebody. "I'll take the job. And I'm naming you as Vice President."

Carson balked, then started rattling off names of various people who would be a much better choice. Gunny had never heard of any of them and he already knew the General was a tireless man, with a good head on his shoulders.

"I think you'd make a great number two. You're it. In addition to your current position. Um, Sir," Gunny said.

"Now let's get this whole swearing in stuff over with, I'm tired and I've got to get up at zero dark thirty. And please keep looking for somebody that's actually qualified for this job."

# LACY

## Day 3

They waited.

And waited.

One day turned into two.

Two into three.

They never saw a single airplane or helicopter out of the windows. They never saw the Army or the National Guard come, the streets never changed. The jammed roads were never cleared, the freeways remained impassable.

The fires raged and consumed whole neighborhoods, entire swaths of town. They had eventually burned themselves out, with the help of the thunderstorms, on the third day.

They watched everything they could on the Internet as, one by one, websites and servers went down. They found a police scanner site and listened to the chaos of "officer down" and calls for backup on the first day. After that, nothing.

By the end of the second day they had lost electricity,

and with it, the water pressure. Among the stores of supplies they had searched the floor for, they had discovered the maintenance closet with some five-gallon jugs of water for the two water coolers they had. The food supply was critically low, however. There weren't many leftovers in the break room refrigerator, and the only food they had were snacks scavenged from desk drawers.

Lacy had tried to text different people a few more times, but most of the time they wouldn't send and on the rare occasion they did, she didn't know if anyone received them. She never got anything back. The message from Johnny was the only one that came through. He was fine, he had said. He was at a truck stop near Reno and was going to wait till things settled down a little and then head back to Atlanta. He'd do it, too. This she knew.

She was sitting at her desk, thinking back to years gone by. He was an obstinate ass sometimes, but he was as tough as they came. Had some hard bark on him, as they say back home. He'd been blown up, shot twice, had shrapnel from grenades in him, went down in a helicopter once, had been gassed... she couldn't recall all the times he'd been hurt, and he always went back.

Always seemed to be the guy who escaped with only a minor injury, while others had legs and arms blown off. All that from a boy who had only wanted to turn wrenches at a local car dealership, maybe do a few odd jobs on the side for extra money. Then that incident at the tire shop and him having to join the Army.

Of course, Johnny couldn't just be a cook or something, do his four years and get out. He had to go all gung-ho and join the infantry. Then he went airborne. Then the Rangers because all his buddies were. After that, he had to be a Green Beret. Be the best of the best he said. Special Forces.

Might as well, he said. The rest of his friends he'd been training with were signing up. And you got hazard pay. Then he got recruited into Delta, and again, he didn't say no.

So more training, more missions he didn't talk about, more deployments around the world, doing who knew what to God knows who. She was proud of him, he had turned the old proverbial lemon into lemonade. He was taking out terrorists and doing his part to keep the world safe. All he had to do was keep himself alive and whole for another five years and it would have all been worth it.

They were already planning the 'retirement at thirty-eight' party. But then that incident in Afghanistan happened. She didn't think she knew the whole story, but she knew enough to know that the military didn't want the world to know what had happened. They had kept him out of jail, out of a trial. They just wanted the whole thing to be forgotten, so they got rid of him and told him if he ever went public, they would press charges. Murder didn't have a statute of limitations.

If he ever said anything, he'd be facing life in prison. She couldn't even be mad at him for what he did. She probably would have done the same thing if she had walked into a room with a bunch of men raping a group of crying, bleeding, boys.

It didn't matter that they were the local religious leaders and the police captain they had been training to fight the insurgents. It didn't matter that in the eyes of local Islamic law, they weren't doing anything wrong. He had killed them all. It hadn't mattered to him, either. He had his regrets, though. Whether from that, or other things, she didn't know. He wouldn't tell her everything, but she knew he had nightmares for years. He had lost his whole team shortly after, and he didn't talk about that either. He came from the Solitary Meadows part of the family. They kept themselves to themselves where he grew up, way up in a holler. Getting him to talk about his feelings was damn near impossible.

The creatures in the hallway had stopped their pounding after a while, and as long as everyone stayed quiet, they seemed to have forgotten there were people inside the offices.

On the third day, the city was eerily silent.

The city was dead.

The only life they saw was the occasional flicker of candlelight from the windows of nearby buildings.

They heard no more screams, no matter how faint or distant. No sirens wailing. No horns honking. Mr. Sato's satellite phone hadn't been able to reach anyone since yesterday, no matter how many numbers he tried. If they peeked carefully around the curtains and stacked up office furniture, through the glass doors, they could see the cease-less wanderings of the creatures in the hallway. They just seemed to shuffle around aimlessly, bumping into each other or the walls.

Eric, and one of the ladies that had come in with ,Phil had put a bit of effort into making everyone dinner that evening, with the last of what they had scrounged. Lacy was pretty sure a few of them were holding out, had hidden power bars or peppermints from everyone else, but it didn't matter. A few more bites of granola wouldn't have made a difference. They needed to get out of here. This was their last meal and in a week, they would be as good as dead if they didn't move out.

As they ate the last of the beef jerky and protein bars with the juice concoction the "cooks" had whipped up from the liquor cabinet in Mr. Sato's office, Lacy brought up leaving. She was trying to get a feel for where everyone stood. In the end, it didn't matter because she was going whether anyone else was or not. She just wanted to know if she was going alone, or with a group.

"We've got to get out of here," she said abruptly, loud enough so all of the other people could hear her. "Has anyone given it any thought? How do we make it down to the bottom?"

"We can't go!" the plump lady from the architectural firm nearly squealed. "The Army will be here soon. We just have to wait. They won't leave us like this."

Lacy had dealt with these types of people before, as a military wife. She had rammed her shopping cart right through protesters during a rally at a mall once, had tried to debate people at the opposite end of the political spectrum online, but in the end their philosophical differences were so far apart, there was no middle ground. She was from the backwoods of Kentucky, where everyone had a strong independent streak and disdain for people who wouldn't help themselves.

"No one is coming," she said, and turned her back to the woman, who probably had a whole stockpile of diet bars hidden away somewhere, she thought to herself. She had dismissed Eric as any kind of help, he had completely frozen up and shut down the first day. He would be useless. She knew she was being cynical, but she didn't want everyone to go. Most of them would just slow her down.

But a few of them would be an asset. Phil, for one. He had the only gun. Carla. She was pretty fit, young, and into hiking and biking. Alex, from the accounting firm twelve stories above. He looked to be in pretty good shape. Robert... Maybe. Middle-aged and withdrawn, but not too flabby.

Mr. Sato was pretty spry for an old guy, they had talked about how he had beat one of those things off with his briefcase in the stairwell, smashing in its head.

"Phil?" she asked. "You have any ideas? Mr. Sato?"

"Sure, try to get the only man with a gun to go with you," the annoying woman chimed in.

Lacy was starting to think she knew how Johnny felt now, when he would just haul off and punch someone for talking shit. She ignored her and kept her gaze on the two men.

As it turned out, they did have some ideas. For some strange man-logic notion of chivalry, or some such nonsense, the men had been going over plans for the past day or so, running ideas past each other and trying to formulate something solid to get them down to the parking garage.

Their plan was pretty simple. Open the doors just wide enough to let one monster in at a time and kill it with one of Mr. Sato's golf clubs. They do that until all are dead, and then make their way down thirty flights of stairs to the sub-basement. The emergency lights should still be on. No one knew how long they would stay that way, but Phil said they had all been upgraded to LED lights a few years back, so the emergency batteries should last a long time. Once down the stairs, they could determine the next best plan of action, depending on what they found.

It was a pretty good plan and now that it was out in the open, the rest started to bring up ideas the men hadn't thought of. They decided to break the ends off of some of the putters and make stabbing objects out of them, so they wouldn't have to depend entirely on swinging a heavy driver in the confined quarters of the stairwell.

They were going to use both the head gripped in their fists as a stabber, and the shaft as a short lance. Lacy found her fist spikes she had made from the shelf brackets and worked on them some more, so they fit her hands better, using a lot of duct tape until they felt comfortable.

Phil went through the secretaries' drawers until he found a half dozen letter openers and taped the handles to make some pretty lethal daggers. In the end, they had hashed out something they all thought was workable, even the annoying woman whose name Lacy could never seem to remember. They were sure they would find some heavy duty SUVs in the valet parking.

Once they decided which vehicles they wanted, it would be easy to grab the keys from the office.

# 23

## THE THREE FLAGS TRUCK STOP

The President. What a joke, Gunny thought as he woke up to the alarm clock on his phone. His one, and probably only, presidential order that he had given was a good one. He had made General Carson Vice President. It was all legal and constitutional, so if he got killed on his trek back home, or even if he decided to disappear with his family, there was an established hierarchy again. Or chain of command. Or whatever it was called.

Carson would make a good president, if he ever got out of the bunker. He was sure the General would pick all kinds of cabinet members from different areas, so the "government" would carry on. It was on the bottom of his worry list, he had done what they asked. It was all official and if he made it back here, he'd worry about acting presidential or something. Meanwhile, he had a long way to go and he'd already wasted too much time.

He glanced at his phone again, checking for messages out of habit. None of the apps he had downloaded worked except solitaire. He switched it back over to airplane mode so it wouldn't search for a signal all day and run the battery down.

The sun was just below the eastern horizon as he threw on some clothes and headed towards the diner. He had told the guys he was convoying with that he was rolling at seven. Be there or be left behind.

The little apartments they were planning on building weren't finished yet, but most of the people had bedded down in the empty broker's offices, so the diner was nearly empty. Martha was up and poured him a cup of coffee as he approached the counter. Gunny could smell biscuits baking in the oven and nodded his 'good morning' to Cookie, who was at his griddle.

Cobb came out of the back and stomped over to where Gunny was sitting and took a stool beside him at the counter.

"We've got a problem," he said. Typical Cobb. No pussyfooting around.

"What's that?" Gunny asked.

"That General said we're in a fallout zone if the reactor in Washington goes up."

"Yeah," Gunny said. "But didn't he say there were teams that were going to take care of it? Remove all the rods?"

"Yup, but the nearest muzzie mosque is 150 miles away from it. I can't risk staying. Besides, there's no future here. We couldn't get the well to work yesterday. It's bone dry, so in a couple of days we won't have any water."

Gunny looked around at the truck stop, at all they had, and all Cobb's family had built over the last half century.

"That sucks," he said. "Your family has had this place for what? Fifty years?"

"Just because all the good land was taken," Cobb said.

"This ain't nothing but desert scrub nobody wanted. Now there's plenty of land available. And it's all free."

"What are you planning on doing?"

"There's a big reservoir near Latoka, Oklahoma according to the General," he said. "It's in a safe area if everything goes wrong and the Hajji's can't get all the rods out everywhere. Good water, good land, good hunting, good fishing, and not in the wind path of any reactors. We need to get there."

"Who's we?" Gunny asked.

"Everyone," Cobb replied. "After you took off to your truck to crash out last night, we had a little powwow in here. Wire Bender had flipped the coms on in the diner once you said you'd take the job as President, and everyone heard you do the swear in thing with the General. Everybody knows we have to leave, and everybody agreed the best way was to convoy down with you and the rest who were taking off this morning."

Gunny grimaced. He wanted to leave soon and didn't want to be responsible for a bunch of drag-ass civilians.

Cobb saw the turmoil on his face, guessed at what he was thinking. "You have a bigger responsibility, now, than just yourself," he said. "Like it or not, all of us are going to depend on you."

Gunny sighed and rubbed his hand across his eyes. "Okay," he said. "You're right. It's smart to leave anyway, even if you did have water. If they screw up with getting the rods out, you wouldn't know it until it was too late. How soon till we can roll?"

"Realistically?" Cobb asked. "Tomorrow morning. Griz and that deputy you brought back are going to run a refresher course for the vets this morning, make sure everyone is up to speed on communications and tactics and road procedures. Going to be a big convoy. We don't want to lose anyone. We've got a lot of packing to do."

He continued in his rusty voice, "We're never coming back and we need to take as much as possible with us. I wish we still had the internet, I could see what kind of businesses were down there so we wouldn't have to pack generators or welders if there were a bunch already there. But we're going in blind, so we need to take everything."

"Right," Gunny said. "I'll grab my maps and start planning a route, avoiding the cities. But seriously, Cobb. I need to be on the road tomorrow morning. My wife is trapped in a high rise and my kid is stuck in a room at his high school." I hope...he added to himself.

"Yeah, about that. I got to thinking and had Wire Bender get a hold of Cheyenne Mountain this morning. You being the president and all, I told him to see if they can pull your wife's phone records from NSA. She may have emailed or texted you some more, and it didn't deliver. If it uploaded though, they should be able to find it. I told them to check your kid's, too."

"But they don't know their numbers," Gunny said.

Cobb just laughed cynically. "They know everything," he said.

Gunny gave a sideways grin. "You're pretty savvy for an old timer," he said. "Thanks, Cobb. I didn't even think about something like that. You should be the president, not me. I don't have the brains for it and you know it. Hell, everybody knows it."

"Feeling sorry for yourself?" Cobb rasped, glaring at him.

"No," Gunny replied. "But you know you'd do a better job of it."

"Probably," Cobb said. "But it ain't me. It's you. And I

don't reckon you'll screw it up too bad. Just don't get so big for your britches you forget to take advice from people who are smarter than you."

Gunny nodded and the old man grunted, grabbed his coffee cup, and clomped off.

24

The morning started out slowly, with the night shift guards coming off duty and the people sleeping in the temporary apartments waking up and wandering in for coffee. Of course, when Scratch, Lars and Stabby came in and noticed Gunny sitting at a table going over his maps, they immediately ran over. They started bowing and scraping, calling him your Royal Highnessness, offering to shine his shoes and "Shall I comb your eminence's golden hair" and "Shall I wipe your royal butt, your most esteemed one".

Gunny's 'Piss off' only brought more bowing and scraping, with profuse apologies for being so inadequate for his Majesty's most magnanimous Royal Greatness and the world was blessed because they were impotent and wouldn't curse the planet with their inferior offspring. Each was trying to out-bow and out-grovel the other. The gathered people were much amused.

Cobb clomped in and put an end to it with a list of everything that needed to be done. Gunny wondered if he ever slept. He started assigning tasks to everyone, including the kids, and told them to all hurry up and eat, no time to sit around jack-jawing.

Gunny had an idea and stood up to ask if anyone could fly a plane? A helicopter? It would make things so much easier. But no one could. The closest was Carl of the Prius, and he only had experience on a computer flight sim. He and his girl had seen the mayhem when they left and managed to get turned around and made it back to the safety of the Three Flags.

Later in the evening, when most of the tasks had been completed, when all the materials they had on hand was used to up-armor the trucks and they were loaded and were ready to roll, everyone was called in from their jobs for a hot supper. They were having the last full course meal for the next week or so, and Preacher wanted it to be a little something special.

This may be their final supper, they were facing the unknown in the morning. He said a prayer over their meal and everyone dug in. Cookie and Martha and Kim had outdone themselves, making a dinner to remember. Forty people ate with gusto, with the only ones not able to join being the unfortunate few who had guard duty.

Scratch, Stabby, and Lars had worked on improving the designs of the stabbing weapons they had used the previous day and made as many as they could for everyone; the wicked, spiked knuckle dusters being a favorite because they left the hands free to handle guns easily.

Stacy had commandeered much of Lars's cocaine stash, saying it was originally used as medicine and it was going to be used as medicine again. She left him a small bucket of it and gave them very stern warnings that if she ever suspected their use of it endangered anyone's lives, there would be swift and serious old west style justice coming at them from the end of a rope.

It was a free country, but by God, they better not abuse it. Sara was there giving them the evil eye, clicking her nails on the handle of the 9-inch blade she had strapped to her thigh. They didn't know if she was kidding or not, but decided to take her at her word. She was kind of scary when she was pissed and Scratch told them how cool and calm she was about shoving letter openers into the brains of people still alive.

"Damn," Lars said as they walked off with a few million dollars worth of powder. "They could teach Tony Montana a thing or two."

"Yeah," sniffed Stabby. "Stacy and Sara. The S.S. sisters."

A couple of the trucks had PTO pumps on them and they had been modified to be able to pump fuel out of the ground of any gas station or truck stop they came to. That covered resupply for the trucks ,and the 12-volt pump idea Gunny had was still a good one for Sara's motorcycle. Until they found one, though, they had filled up a handful of five-gallon cans and strapped them on the catwalk of Griz's truck.

She had gotten her Fireblade around to the shop and Tommy had stripped some of the plastics and built a light-weight exoskeleton frame for her, to protect the most vulnerable parts of the bike if she went down. She wanted to ride point a few miles ahead of the main group and let them know if anything bad was coming up. She had shot down everyone who tried to talk her out of it. It was her bike, her life, and she was riding. So piss off, as Gunny liked to say.

Wire Bender had been working all day rigging up

radios. He built a hands-free mic for Sara's helmet and mounted a peaked and tuned CB, with a small amplifier and its antenna, to the back of her bike. He put a better set of antennas, an extra CB, and a Ham radio in Gunny's truck, so he could talk to Cheyenne Mountain if needed.

General Carson had tried to speak with Gunny about a few organizational things, but his reply had been the same every time. "Take care of it. You're in charge of that. Any luck with my wife's phone?" And pretty soon, the General had quit bugging him.

After dinner, Gunny and Cobb walked around all of the vehicles lined up in the junkyard, checking each for any problems or deficiencies that may have been missed. It was most of the trucks that had been there, modified big rigs, and their trailers full of food or supplies. When Tommy cut up the livestock trailer to build the plows, they had let the cattle out to graze what they could from the weeds growing up around the rusting hulks. It wasn't much, but they would leave the gates open when they left and the cattle could fend for themselves.

There would be plenty more to round up once they got to where they were going. The cowboys had their tour bus fully fueled and it was to be loaded with the people in the truck stop, and the few surviving family members of Tommy's mechanics. No one wanted to drive their car, they all felt safer in the armored bus. And it had a bathroom. Besides, once they got to where they were going, they could go to the nearest dealer and pick out any car they wanted.

They walked on past the last truck, past the impromptu gun range where Griz had been drilling everyone, and to

274

the small graveyard near the back fence. Gunny noticed a cross for Tiny had been erected.

"Preacher do that?" he asked.

"Yeah," Cobb replied. "We lost some good men that first day."

Gunny stayed quiet. He had nothing to add to that. They stood in silence for a moment, remembering, and he noticed a small, hand-carved sign hanging on the fence above the graves. It read: John 3:16 has conquered Zechariah 14:12.

"What's that all about?" he asked Cobb. "I know the John verse, 'God so loved the world he gave his only begotten son', but what's the other one?"

Cobb looked at it through the haze of his Lucky Strike. "Preacher said this whole zombie uprising was written about by the Old Prophets. He said there's a bunch of passages about the dead rising. Like most of the weird stuff in there, everyone just thought it was an allegory or something. Guess it wasn't."

"I've read the Book a few times," Gunny said. "But I don't remember anything about zombies."

"It's in there," Cobb said. "I just didn't think it meant what it said."

"I was thinking," Gunny started, wanting to change the subject. "Maybe we should go by Cheyenne Mountain, try to get the General and his men out, or at least clear out the zeds for them. They're just a bunch of egg heads and we've got a pretty hard crew here."

"Already discussed that with him," Cobb said. "They may be POGs, but they ain't dumb. They made a kind of maze out of the cubicle dividers in their area. They'll open the door and one or two zeds will rush in and they'll close it behind them and then stab them to death with sharpened

275

chair legs from behind the maze walls. They set up trip wires, all kinds of things to slow them up so they can kill 'em."

"Pretty smart," Gunny said. "So they are whittling the numbers down?"

"Yeah. They've killed about thirty so far. Haven't lost any of theirs. The biggest problem is the smell."

"I can imagine," Gunny said. "Thirty bodies piled up in a corner, rotting away. How are they set for food and water?"

"It's a problem. They've got water, as long as the place keeps ticking along. He said they need to get out to service the generators, but Jack said the electricity is powered by turbines from an underground river. So I don't know. Maybe they've changed since he was in M.I. The place is supposed to be fully self-sustaining. They hope to have all of them killed, out of the immediate area, over the next day or so. The mess area is only a few hallways away, once they clear the communications block they are in now. He said they should get there soon. Then they can go on indefinitely."

"So they don't need our help?"

"We couldn't get in the front doors, even if we went there," Cobb said. "It would take a dozen tanks a dozen reloads to blow the barriers. Besides, General Carson said our priority is to get these people to safety, and pick up anyone we find along the way."

Gunny had been busy all day, hustling to help everyone get their trucks loaded and ready, checking and rechecking weapons, and making final improvements on his own rig. There was Griz's mandatory training class, dropping trailers they had no use for, and reloading wagons with supplies they thought they might need. There had been zombie killing duties, and he had pulled a shift atop the roof to take them out before they got close to anyone working outside.

He hadn't had much time to think beyond the immediate. Hadn't had time to think of his "presidential" duties, but Cobb had been on top of things. It was weird having Top defer to him, instead of telling him he needed to shave or something. To treat him like a superior when Gunny was just Gunny. Just Johnny Joe Meadows from Backwater, Kentucky. Same old truck driver he was yesterday.

Except now he didn't have a house payment.

Or any more credit card bills.

And he could get himself a new $60,000, fully loaded pickup truck just by walking into the dealership and looking for the keys.

Hell, he could find the fanciest mansion in town and claim it, if he wanted. Well, if the owner was dead, that is.

But all of these things were the last of their kind. There wouldn't be a next year's model. Once the shelves were empty at the mall, they wouldn't be refilled. Once they ran out of your shoe size, it would be back to hand-cobbled. How would you get a replacement if you broke a window? None of that seemed important at the moment, as he looked down at the wooden cross where Preacher had carved Tiny's name. Death was very close now.

He sighed. He didn't even know Tiny's real name. He'd just always been Tiny, all the years he'd known him. Didn't know where his wife lived. He had gone through his truck, hoping to find something with his home address on it. His wallet must have been on him when he went down, and he didn't find anything else in his search. His phone was missing, too. Probably also in his pocket.

"General asked if you would check in around ten o'clock, our time," Cobb said.

Even that was weird. 'The General asked if you would.' Gunny had been used to taking orders from officers, not giving them. Not being ASKED to do something by a General.

"Right," he said, glancing at his watch. "I'll be along in a few minutes."

Cobb just grunted and walked off in his limping gait, knowing the man needed a moment to himself.

He stared at the crosses with the names carved into them, at the mounds of sandy soil. Guys he had known only in passing, and guys he had known for years. Pure dumb luck he wasn't one of them, buried six feet under or worse, one of the screaming undead. He was lucky he hadn't been caught outside and taken down in the first few minutes, like so many others had. He was lucky he had fifteen years of military training to snap him into the reality of what was happening, almost instantly.

But even that was a fluke. Wasn't part of his plan of years ago. He had been senior, getting ready to graduate from the Tri-cities vocational school, with a degree in auto mechanics. He was working part time at the tire store in town and had his applications in at all of the big car dealerships, hoping to land a job as a service tech. Life looked good for him.

He was a great mechanic, with a wonderful girl who was going to community college that Fall to study to be a teacher. He had plans to put a ring on her finger in a few years, when he was making good money. But life got in the way of his plans. Big Billy Wilson and his crew of guffawing idiot jocks came in to get the oil changed in the new Camaro his daddy had bought him. He could put up with their bullying and being an asshole to everybody that didn't play football, love football, or love them because they

278

played football. Their snide comments rolled right off of him.

But when Lacy came in after her shift at the McDonald's to wait for him to finish up, things got ugly. He hadn't meant to break Billy's jaw, he honestly didn't realize he had the ratchet wrench in his hand when he swung on him after he had grabbed her ass. The only way the judge wouldn't charge him with felonious assault as an adult, was for him to join the military.

The judge made it clear he was going to be leaving, one way or another. He wasn't going to have a small town feud between two hotheads causing more violence or bloodshed. He was leaving as a recruit in boot camp, or as a new fish in prison. Not much of a choice, really, so he decided to join the Army as a mechanic. Repair their trucks and tanks. Good work experience and enhance his resume.

The recruiter said there weren't any slots available for any mechanic jobs. If he could wait until next quarter, there would be some opening up. But he couldn't wait. Judge needed his early enlistment papers at the next court hearing in a week, or he was looking at jail time. Air Force or Navy didn't want him with the charge pending, and he didn't know if he could cut it as a Marine.

So he went back to the Army recruiter and went over his list of available positions. Supply Clerk, clerical assistant, ammo specialist, trumpet player. A whole list of dreadful options in his opinion. But infantryman was always open, the recruiter had said. And there's even a ten thousand dollar sign on bonus.

Gunny sighed, coming back to the present. He reached out to touch the cross, to say goodbye, then turned and headed to the CB shop.

There was a new voice on the radio. He introduced

himself as Captain Barnett and called Gunny "Mr. President" when he addressed him.

"Yeah, no need for all that, Sir," he said. "Where's the General, is he all right?"

"Yes, Mr. President," he said. "He is sleeping and asked me to relay this information to you when you checked in. Shall I wake him?"

"No, of course not," Gunny said. "What's the good news?" He crossed his fingers, hoping it WAS good news.

"We were able to pull messages from your wife and son's phones. They were uploaded from the Atlanta towers, but that's as far as they got, they were never delivered."

"*No shit,*" Gunny thought, but said, "Can you read them to me?"

# JESSIE

## IN THE WOODS

## Day 3

They were miserable. Utterly exhausted.

Parched beyond belief, and ate up by mosquito and ant bites. Jessie didn't even care if the whole world watched him take a morning leak on the zombies still milling around down below. Not that he had anything left to pee, he was so wrung out. The crowd below knew they were still up in the trees.

They had settled down, stopped their screaming and frantic jumping after a few hours, but they weren't giving up. Some had wandered off, but there were still dozens gathered around each of the trees they were in. It was like they knew all they had to do was wait them out, the meat would be falling from the sky soon enough. It didn't matter if it took a day or a week, they would blunder around and wait. They had nothing better to do, no pressing engagements to attend.

Jessie, Doug, and Gary had been able to lick a little

moisture from the bottom of the leaves that had accumulated during the night, it wasn't much, but he supposed it helped. Sheila had it worse than all of them. She had climbed a pine and the needles didn't have any place for the dew to form. And she was covered in the tacky pine sap.

They had spent a dangerous night trying to be as quiet as possible, tying themselves to the trunk of the tree with their clothes, belts, or vines so they wouldn't nod off and fall out. It was really a sign of how bad things were for them when Sheila, bare to her jeans, didn't try very hard to hide herself as she struggled back into her sticky shirt, and Doug barely noticed.

"No more!" Gary shouted, struggling around on the branch he was perched on, to face them. That got the undead gathered around his tree animated again and they started their keening and jumping.

"Listen, they aren't going anywhere, they can outlast us and I'm freaking ate up with mosquito bites. I'm tired of this shit. I'm gonna get them all over here and then you guys make a break for it."

"How you going to do that?" Doug asked. "Jump?"

"Yep," he replied. "You guys would have made it if I hadn't slowed you down. Thanks for trying, but this is the only way. You know we can't last another day up here. Sheila, can you show me your hooters before I go?" He was trying for nonchalance and bravado. He almost nailed it.

"Wait up a minute," Jessie said. "I've been trying to come up with some ideas. Let's figure something out."

"Maybe tomorrow," she teased, her voice cracking a little from the dryness. "For now, what are you thinking, Jessie?"

He grinned at that one. Good for her.

"When I was little and we would visit my grandparents in Kentucky, my dad showed me something he did as a kid. He used to climb saplings, up until they would bend over from his weight, and ride them back down to the ground. He'd let go and the tree would spring back, with him ready to find another. We called it the hillbilly roller coaster. I think we can do the same with these trees," he finished, cracking on the last words, trying to swallow with nothing left to moisten his throat with.

"These trees are way too big," Doug said. "There's no way."

"Only gotta bend to the next tree, closer to the water," Gary said, seeing where this was going. "Do a Tarzan kind of thing, tree to tree."

Jessie could only nod. His voice was shot. He grabbed a few of the fattest leaves he could find and tried to suck anything damp out of them.

"And if you miss? Wind up out in an open area?" asked Sheila.

"Better than staying here for another night," Gary said, and laboriously started to make his way to the thin branches at the top of his tree.

Doug shrugged to the rest of them as if to say, 'there isn't a better plan, why not?' and started to climb. They were all exhausted from the miserable night they had spent slapping mosquitoes and trying to find a position that was comfortable for a few minutes. It could have been worse, Jessie guessed. At least he didn't pick a tree that was ate up with ants.

He looked up, trying to determine the best way to climb, wishing now he hadn't picked such a huge tree. It went a long way up before it looked like it was thin enough to bend with his weight. He followed the path it would go, determining which tree he would need to land in. It was the pine that Sheila was in.

He watched her climb for a minute, then got started himself, the milling horde of undead getting agitated at their movement and starting to keen and claw skyward toward them again. Gary had the farthest to go out of the four, he was the first one they tossed up into the gnarled old oak. He was managing, though, using only his upper body, swinging and scrabbling, steadily moving upward.

They all climbed until the branches were too thin to stand on, and the tops of the trees swayed back and forth dangerously with them. They could see each other clearly now, three figures with arms wrapped tightly around the narrow tops of their trees, each nearly a hundred feet off the ground. Gary was far below them, resting. He didn't have the strength to go on, his arms were shaking from the exertion.

From this vantage point, Jessie could see he didn't have a chance. Even with a good set of legs, the old Oak towered a long way above him, and he doubted if Gary could get it to bend in the right direction.

"Forget it, Gary," he yelled hoarsely over to him. "Your tree tapers off the wrong way, you'll never get it to swing toward the lake."

"Just hang on, dude," Doug added. "When we get down, we'll figure out a distraction to draw them away."

Gary just nodded, too tired to disagree, or even answer. Jessie looked over at Sheila who was frozen, arms wrapped tightly around the gently tilting pine. It was going the right way, if it bent far enough it would take her all the way to the lake, but he knew it wouldn't. It would snap before it went that far down. But there was a decent sized something... Oak? Maple? Poplar? He didn't know, but it was there, right in the path of the Pine and it had branches that stretched out over the water. All she had to do was go a little bit higher and ride it over.

"You good?" Doug yelled over at her. "Ready to do this?"

She nodded her head, but didn't move, her eyes were tightly shut and they could see she was breathing in short little gasps.

*"Crap,"* Jessie thought. *"She's afraid of heights."*

They tried to talk her over it, to get her to move, but she was stuck in place, couldn't commit to another step higher, and the irreversible bending of the tree that it would bring.

"I need that tree," Jessie croaked out, his voice nearly gone. They'd only had a few sips of apple juice each in the last couple of days. "Go back down," he whispered as loud as he could, and she nodded again, slowly inching her foot back toward the thicker branches.

Doug's voice was no better and he finally just reverted to hand signals, pointing to himself then the lake. He was going to go first. He had at least one tree to get to, maybe two, before he was close enough to ride a branch down into the water and he started his final ascent to the upper level of his tree.

The water. So close, but so far away. *"Water, water everywhere, but not a drop to drink,"* Jessie thought, wondering where he'd heard that from. If he hadn't under-stood what it meant before, he did now. They were dying of dehydration, tongues starting to swell, lips cracked and chapped, and just a hundred feet away was millions of gallons of cool, crisp, life-giving water.

Sheila was halfway down the tree, the thicker the branches got, the faster she climbed and Jessie decided he wasn't going to wait to see if Doug made it or not. He would die today if he didn't get to the water. Either from sheer exhaustion causing him to fall out of the tree and into the waiting arms of those things below, or simply from dehydration.

If Doug didn't make it and he had to listen to him crashing through the branches, then being torn apart, he might lose his nerve, might just belt himself to the trunk, fall asleep, and never wake up. It was go time and he drew on his inner strength, hoping it was enough, and climbed another ten feet, the top of the tree leaning slowly at first, then picking up speed.

His back was toward the pine and he let his legs dangle, holding on only with his hands, a hundred feet from the ground and swooping quickly now. The tree top was tender and green and had a lot of bend in it, more than was needed, he hoped, before it would snap. He looked over his shoulder and saw he needed more distance and reached hand over hand a few more feet toward the top of the tree.

Gravity had taken over and there was no turning back, it would bend until it broke and it was a long, long way to the ground. His stomach was in his throat and he knew why it was called a rollercoaster now. He heard a snapping, not a complete break, like old dead wood, but the slow letting go of fresh growth and he fell toward the pine tree's branches.

He let go of the maple and it whipped back as he used his entire body to fall across the pine's prickly limbs, grabbing for a handhold wherever he could. He crashed down through a few layers, hearing Sheila's scream below him, before he got a good grip and jangled to an abrupt halt, splayed out over two different branches, bending precariously with his weight.

He held on tightly, not caring about the myriad of cuts and scrapes. Not feeling anything except his heart thudding against his ribcage. He opened his eyes and looked to see if Doug had made it. To see if he was sprawled out in a tree, hanging on for dear life, or if he had missed and fallen. Neither. He was standing on a branch laughing and giving Jessie the thumbs up.

"Show off," Jessie croaked out, flipped him the bird, and started pulling himself to the trunk of the tree so he could do this all over again. One more time, then he would be trying to drink up the whole lake.

# JESSIE

## THE LAKE

## Day 3

He and Doug had both made it to the trees closest to the water, the undead howlers screaming up, below them. This particular section of the lakefront was undeveloped because it was a low-lying area. It was prone to flooding during the rainy season, mosquito infested and swampy the rest of the year.

There were no boats or private docks nearby, and neither boy wanted to continue to risk tree swinging down the shoreline until they came to one. Both had come danger-ously close to plummeting all the way to the ground, in their barely controlled falls between trees. There was a swim-mer's dock a few hundred yards out and down-shore, maybe a quarter of a mile.

"Let's just hope Zed don't swim," Doug had said, judging the distance to the platform.

"What if they can?" Sheila had asked, far down below them, in the thicker branches of the pine.

Jessie didn't answer, just looked at the distance he had to cover and started making his way out on the branch that hung the farthest over the water. There wasn't a choice. Staying here equaled one hundred percent chance of death. Risking the water equaled a fifty-fifty percent chance, as far as he figured.

As fast as they were on land, he was sure he couldn't outswim them if they did have the ability to tread water. If they didn't, if they could only try to run underwater in the muck and mud, he was pretty sure he could outdistance them. Maybe they would get lucky and those things wouldn't even go in the lake.

But they did.

They followed him out on the branch, staying underneath and waiting for him to fall. They kept their blackened eyes on him, arms outstretched, as the branch got thinner and thinner and he started dipping toward the surface. This wasn't going to work. They were only chest deep and he couldn't get out past them.

They were still moving around even though the muck was sucking at their feet. Slower than normal, sure, but if he jumped in now, he was fairly certain they could move well enough to get to him before he put the ten or twenty feet between them and deep water. He started scooting back toward the base of the tree. He would have to come up with a different plan.

Doug had been watching from his vantage point near the top of the poplar tree he was in. He was going to ride his tree down like he had the others, getting over to it. Another hillbilly rollercoaster ride. The height and closeness to the shore would put him way out in deep water. Jessie didn't have that option. He was in a huge old tree, but the top wasn't bending in the right direction, it was leaning back the way he came. That made it easy to get to it, but impossible to make it take him to the lake.

"Can you get a run on the branch, just dive off the end past them?" Doug rasped at him.

Jessie had made his way back to the trunk of the tree and was leaning against it, trying to figure something else out.

"I'm not that coordinated," he managed to croak out. "It's small and I'd be bouncing it every step. I'd just slip and wrack my nuts."

He was so thirsty. The water was only a few feet away. He'd drink anything right now, even the murky bug-filled swill pooled here and there on the ground.

"Maybe when Doug goes in, they'll chase after him," Gary said from his tree.

"It looks like they've zeroed in on each one of us," Sheila said. "You notice the ones from your tree followed you over and these on my tree haven't left, they stay right with me?"

Jessie looked down, really looking at who was below him for the first time. He hadn't wanted to identify them, it was easier when he was high up and they were just figures far below, just "them," not actual people. Now he looked and saw who they were. These had been his classmates. There was Tyreese, still in his letterman's jacket, one of the starters on the football team.

Sharon, the mousy girl who never said anything, now snarling and reaching for him. Porsche, the light skinned girl whom he'd had a bit of a crush on for months now. He didn't know all of them by name, but he recognized them. Every one of them. Even one of the ladies that worked in the office, missing a lot of her hair and nearly topless, her blue-veined skin dully shining on her exposed breasts.

Jessie looked away, closed his eyes. There were at least

twenty down below him. People he had known, joked with, been annoyed with, teamed up on class projects with, ate lunch with, and cheered on at the pep rallies.

Now all of them were screaming for his blood. Something his old man had said during one of their sparring practices came back to him. He was explaining how people got themselves beat up or killed. How women got raped, or used as punching bags. He had said it wasn't because they were helpless, it was because they didn't have the killer instinct in them, anymore. It had been forced out by years of civility. Jessie had argued that a hundred pound woman didn't have a chance if some big bruiser came after her. His dad had disagreed and then had started showing him ways to kill people with anything.

An ink pen. Car keys. An empty soda can. Your fingers. He had said even though someone was hurting you, maybe even killing you, most people wouldn't fight back. It was almost as if they were afraid of injuring their attackers. They were victims with a victim's mindset. They were sheep, he had said dismissively. They wouldn't stick their fingers knuckle deep in someone's eye. They wouldn't go for an artery with their teeth and rip it open.

Just look at all those videos of ISIS chopping people's heads off, or the Germans executing the Jews. The people just sit there and take it. Instantaneous Stockholm Syndrome or something, he had said.

Jessie had never hurt anyone. About the worst he'd ever done was bloody Kyle's lip. He daydreamed about kicking his ass, but he knew he'd never actually do it. He needed to be more like his old man, wished they would have kept up with the sparring. They hadn't been getting along very well the past few years and he really didn't know why. They just seemed to get on each other's nerves so easily now.

He knew his dad had killed people. He wasn't supposed to know about it, not any of the specifics, anyway, but sometimes Army guys would come over and hang out. His old man was in some group that was supposed to help vets, but mostly it seemed they would just come over and barbecue, then go in the garage. They would drink beer and mess around with that old Mercury he'd been working on for years.

They lived in a bi-level and the garage was adjacent to his room. If they didn't have the classic rock station cranked up too loud, he could hear them talking. Late at night when he should have been asleep long ago and he knew they were a whole bunch of beers into it, he would hear them telling stories. About shooting people, about getting shot. About friends who had died. When they didn't think anyone but themselves could hear, they talked about some really horrible stuff. Jessie had heard them talk about killing women. About a guy who got killed by a little kid asking for candy. About killing people you thought were going to kill you, and then finding out they were just farmers carrying shovels.

Sometimes he had heard men crying, apologizing to long dead people for the things they'd done, or things they hadn't done, but should have. Once he thought it was his dad sobbing, talking about getting everyone on his team killed, but he'd been half dozing. It must've been one of the other guys because his dad didn't cry. It was a little ironic, these guys riding Harleys and wearing leathers and looking like they'd kill your mamma for a quarter were some of the nicest guys he'd met.

Even when he was little and was probably pestering them to death, they never yelled at him to go play and leave them alone. Those guys were serious badasses. It was almost like they had done so much violence in their lives, they went out of their way to avoid it now.

But they weren't sheep. They hid their inner monster well, but it was there, just below the surface, ready to come back out if it was ever needed. Now he had to decide if he was like them and would do whatever it took to survive. If he had a monster inside. A lot of them had nightmares and regrets later, but they were alive to have them. He glanced down over the branch, at the mass below him. There was no second guessing required.

He wouldn't be mistakenly killing someone who just happened to get in the way. Every one of them was trying to kill him. To rip him limb from limb with their bare hands. Did he have it in him? Could he kill them?

Yes, he thought he could. No problem.

Would it give him nightmares?

Maybe. But at least he'd be alive to have them.

He had an idea.

When he looked up again, Sheila was hissing at him, "Hello! Hey! Did you fall asleep? Doug's getting ready to go!"

He shook his head and watched Doug as he started his final climb to the top, leaned over toward the lake and held on. Gary and Sheila tried yelling the best they could, maybe distract the creatures around his tree, but they only had eyes for him. When he started on the downward rush, picking up speed as he plummeted toward the water, they splashed into the lake after him, ignoring everything else.

Doug had been near the very top of the tree, swaying dangerously on the tiny branches that far up. He had hoped to ride it gracefully to the water, but when he was still a good thirty feet in the air, it snapped off and he flailed the rest of the way down, trying not to land on his back and hoping the water was deep enough he didn't bury himself in the mud.

Aside from the drawn out, "Ohhhhh shiiiiiiiiiiiiiiiiiiiit," that was cut off abruptly when he hit the surface with a resounding splash, it was an uneventful fall from the top of a giant tree. They waited anxiously for him to pop back up, not knowing if he'd been grabbed underwater. The dozens of undead that ran out after the meal falling from the sky were gone from view, none of them floating, but they could see dark swirls of muddy water bubbling to the surface that made their path clear.

When he came back up, sucking air, he was a long way from where he went in, and stroking furiously toward the floating dock.

He made it. It took him two tries to pull himself onto it and once he did, he just lay there panting, one arm raised with a thumb up in the air.

They all cheered. The prospects of surviving this had just gotten better. Jessie looked up his tree until he saw what he needed, then started climbing. He would do what it took. He would be a survivor. He would not be one of the sheep. Even if Doug came back with a boat, he'd never get near enough to shore without being swamped by those things. He should have thought of this two days ago, he chastised himself. Maybe he wasn't ready then. His inner monster had still been sleeping.

Maybe he wasn't desperate enough then, and his mind just wouldn't even allow the thoughts to form. But he was now. He was tired, thirsty, ate up with mosquitoes, and getting pissed off. He let the anger build as he snapped off a half dozen dead branches a little smaller than his forearm and five or six feet long. He tried to get them to snap to a point, like a spear. They wanted to play? He was going to teach them a new game. Poke a hole in the zombie's head until it was dead. Step right up, Ladies and Gentlemen. Everyone can play. Winner gets to live, loser gets to die.

He made his way back down to a big branch, just a few feet out of their reach and lay out on it, making sure his feet could curl around something solid to help hold him in place. He wove the extra spears into leafy branches so they wouldn't fall, then readied himself, still feeding the anger to get into a killing frame of mind.

He heard Sheila and Gary hoarsely yelling at him, asking him what he was doing, but he ignored them. Gary couldn't. Sheila wouldn't. It was up to him. He looked down, straight into Porsche's black eyes. She was three days dead, her skin gone grayish, old blood around her mouth and chin, her hair matted and tangled. She was wearing that Hello Kitty shirt he liked, the one that was about three sizes too small and showed off her lovely assets. It was torn and dirty. Blood stained. Her assets were sagging, looking empty, somehow, and not so lovely anymore.

She was a mess, gnashing her teeth and jumping for him, broken fingernails clawing just feet below where he lay. He wondered if there was any of HER left inside of the monster trying to kill him. Did she know what she was doing and couldn't help herself? Did she care that it was him? Did she remember those stolen kisses and all the times they'd shared lunch? If he tried, could he bring her back from what she is, to what she was?

He closed his eyes, another one of his old man's stupid sayings coming into his head, "A wolf doesn't concern himself with the opinions of the sheep."

When he opened his eyes, it wasn't to see friends and acquaintances. He wasn't looking through the glass, darkly. He was seeing clearly, through the eyes of a wolf. His inner monster was awake and angry. The wolf in his head was pacing, wanting to be freed. He drove the spear down hard, through her eye and directly into her squirming brain. She fell in a heap and was quickly replaced by his $4^{th}$-period teacher.

He used her fallen body to get another foot closer, leaping and clawing for flesh. Jessie shoved the spear into his open mouth and through his spine, then jerked it back to drive it into the next screaming zombie to reach for him. He plunged it in and out, blood and brains making it slick. They kept coming and he kept stabbing. The bodies piled higher. He thrust his homemade spear into eyes, hearing them squelch.

Through soft noses, hearing the cartilage break as he drove it deep into their brain. When the stick snapped, he reached for the next one and kept on killing. When it was so coated with his classmate's blood that it pulled out of his hands, he grabbed a third. He was a machine. Thrust. Kill. Repeat. Thrust. Kill. Repeat. Thrust. Kill. Repeat.

It became a mantra and the monster inside screamed at the monsters below. His arms were covered in blood. Gore splattered his face. He raged at them with uncontained fury. Punished them for making him become something less than human. He climbed a branch higher as they got closer, standing on the scores of dead.

He didn't think beyond the immediate, didn't see the piles of corpses stacking up, and the undead faces looming ever closer to his. Didn't see the horrified looks of Sheila and Gary as he lay waste to the undead. Didn't hear his own snarls and guttural curses. Didn't feel his seared and parched throat, the blood trickling down his face from cracked and bleeding lips.

This had to be done. They died, or he died. He couldn't

spend another day trapped in a tree. He stabbed and swung until his arms were exhausted and trembling, then stabbed and swung some more. He cursed and spat at them. He let the bodies pile up and the things get closer, so he wouldn't have to reach so far to kill them. He hated them with every fiber of his being.

Every time he thought he was nearly done with the butchery, more would run over from Gary or Sheila's tree. How many had he killed? Forty? Fifty? He couldn't keep it up. If he only had something to drink, his mind kept telling him. Then he could carry on for a few more minutes. His throat was raw from sucking in air through the dry passageway to his lungs, and he kept spitting out blood.

It felt like his tongue was so swollen it would cut off his windpipe, but he kept swinging and stabbing. Always the face. Sometimes clean thrusts into the brain, sometimes glancing blows that shattered teeth and ripped off cheeks or lips. The pile of bodies got so high they were using it to scrabble up into his tree and leap for him. They didn't have the coordination to hang on to a branch, or watch where they were stepping, and as soon as they managed to get near him, he would swing and they would slip and tumble back down. Sometimes not moving again as they landed on their heads, sometimes never being able to climb again with their broken legs and arms.

Jessie kept stabbing. A berserker frenzy driving him beyond caring about exhaustion and pain. A Crusader swinging his sword at unending masses of heathens. A Viking striking ceaselessly with his battle axe.

A Knight slaying his way through the armies of his enemy. His hands were raw and blistered and bleeding, from the constant shoving motions on the rough spears. His face was on fire from a deep gash, spouting blood. He had to stop, to climb a little farther up and rest, but they wouldn't let him. They kept coming and the pyre kept getting higher. Their screams never stopped and he answered them with a hoarse roar, blood spraying from his raw throat. They thought they were so close to having him, they could taste his blood as it splashed from his snarling mouth and down on their faces.

He stabbed and stabbed and stabbed, the pointed end of his stick brutal in its simplicity. Impale. Withdraw. Find another face. Impale. Withdraw. Find another face. He continued until he couldn't anymore, then continued anyway. They threw themselves at him and he stacked their bodies on a gory altar of death.

When the horde finally stopped coming at him, he was surprised and disappointed that there was nothing left to kill. He let his last stick be pulled out of his bleeding hands and it fell to the ground some twenty feet below, stuck in the eye socket of Cody from 3$^{rd}$ period. He was done. His chest heaved. His heart raced. Sweat poured from him and blood dripped from his flayed-open cheek. He stared list-lessly at the few that remained, as they tried to climb the pile of bodies and get to him.

They were all broken. All had made multiple attempts to lunge at him and had fallen, flailing, to the ground. Legs were dragging at odd angles, shattered arms refused to pull them up the pyramid of dead.

Jessie leaned back against the trunk, balanced on a wide branch. The monster in him was retreating, its taste for destruction had been sated. If one of them made it up to him now, he didn't think he would even have the strength to open his eyes, let alone try to fight it off. He was through. Maybe if he could get his arms to stop shaking, get a little feeling back in his legs, he might try to run down the mound and into the water.

But then what? He knew he didn't have enough left in him to make it to the swimming dock. It was too far. He wasn't thinking clearly, his brain in a fog. He needed to take a short breather.

He rested. His ravaged hands throbbed with every heartbeat. His face hurt from where it had been torn open. He didn't even know how it happened. One of them rake him with their claws? Caught it on a branch? Stabbed himself in the frenzy? He was too weary to care. Too weary to move.

# JESSIE

## HOME AT LAST

## Day 3

Jessie awoke with a start. Had he really dozed off? He looked down toward the ground, at the thunking sound he was hearing and was surprised to see Doug with a baseball bat, crushing the heads of the all the broken zombies that were clawing their way toward him. He couldn't believe it. Doug was back and he had a Jon boat pulled up on the shore. He was cleaning up the mess that Jessie had started. When had all this happened? He thought he'd only closed his eyes for a few seconds.

Jessie half tumbled, half climbed, down the tree and slid down the bloody pile of his classmates and headed directly into the water, splashing out a few feet, then diving in head first, trying to drink the whole lake. He drank until he came up for air and then vomited it all back out again. He didn't care, he dove back under, swam a few yards and started drinking again. Dirty pond water never tasted so good.

Then he remembered the zeds that had followed Doug

into the lake and disappeared under its murky surface. Crap. Did something just brush his ankle? He sprinted for shore as fast as he could in the waist deep water, only to meet Doug and Sheila settling Gary in the boat and staring at him. They all had bottles of water and were drinking greedily from them.

Doug had blood splatters on his face from the gruesome task he had just finished. They all looked a little freaked out at what had just happened. And they wouldn't stop staring at him. Jessie's ripped cheek and hands were still bleeding, dripping on the churned up earth. He reached over to the water and tried to rinse them off, but they remained bloody and dripping.

"We need to go," Gary said, finally looking away from Jessie and at the huge pyramid of undead that towered ten or fifteen feet tall.

They started pushing the boat back out into deeper water.

Jessie hustled over and climbed in, grabbing one of the paddles and getting some distance between them and the shoreline. When they were far enough away, he grabbed one of the bottles of mountain spring water from the half dozen still floating in the warm water of the cooler. He chugged it down, still trying to hydrate himself, not caring that it smelled of fish. Everyone was quiet, still sneaking glances at him and each other. Doug lowered the trolling motor down into the water and flipped it on. "Which house is yours?" he asked, spinning the little boat away from the bloody carnage of what used to be their friends and teachers and classmates.

Jessie pointed across the lake at a bi-level house about a half mile away, set a few hundred yards up a hillside from the lakeshore.

As they got closer, the problems defending the house against a horde of the undead became apparent. The whole top floor was all glass fronted, affording a view of the lake. The deck was easily accessible, with the wide stairs leading up to it from the dock area.

"I don't know, Jester," Gary said, finally breaking the uncomfortable silence. "If those things get up on the deck, not much stopping them from busting through the windows."

"Yeah, but if we knock the deck down, they can't get up to them," Jessie said. "And on the other side of the house, it's all garage, and there's only one window in the kitchen. We can nail some plywood or something up over it. The entry door is pretty stout, so it should hold if we brace it."

"You have any wood there?" Sheila asked. She was also trying to forget what she had just seen. For a minute, she had been more afraid of Jessie than she had of the zombies. He had been a complete maniac. Screaming and hurtling ugly curses like a man possessed. Coated in blood and brains, and he just kept stabbing and killing and snarling like a rabid animal. He had killed about a hundred people, just now. Not people. Zombies, she corrected herself.

"I know there are some sheets of plywood in the garage, up in the rafters," Jessie said, joining in with the chatter and trying to put the last three days behind him. "The old man had me help him put some up there a while back so he could store car parts. Fenders and stuff for that old rust bucket he's working on."

"I am soooo hungry," Sheila said, rubbing her stomach and bringing all their minds back around to their bellies. They were already forgetting the nightmare, or at least pretending to. "I hope there's loads of food that hasn't gone bad."

Jessie finished his water and started scanning the shore for danger.

"No worries there," he said. "There's a ton of canned stuff in the basement. My parents weren't exactly survivalist types, but the old man would always go to Sam's Club and buy everything by the case."

As they neared the dock, Jessie told them all to wait while he went up the hill and got the house unlocked. He grabbed the baseball bat with his bleeding hands, wincing a little, but ignoring it. He patted his pocket, making sure the keyring was still there.

It was.

"I'll give you an all clear if I don't run into any trouble."

He didn't.

Within five minutes, they were all locked inside the house, raiding the cupboards and eating everything from peanut butter and jelly sandwiches, to cold cans of soup. Jessie wrapped his hands in dishtowels so he would quit splattering blood everywhere and Sheila taped his cheek back together with duct tape. They would fix it better after they ate, they said.

They talked about proper ways to secure the house as they stuffed themselves and had every intention of doing it, but once they started washing days of sweat and blood and dirt off of themselves and sat down on the comfortable recliners and couches, they were through. Within minutes they were asleep, the last three days of panic, terror, and pain sliding off of them as they each dropped off into a heavy and much-needed slumber.

## Day 4

Morning found Lacy in her office, using the small paring knife from the kitchen to cut the carpet into strips. She brought a bunch of them into the break area as everyone was nervously drinking what may be their last cups of coffee.

"What are those for?" Phil asked.

"You ever been to the Medieval Dinner Theater?" she asked.

She got blank looks from everyone.

"You know, the knights do battle and all that while you eat with your hands?"

There were slow nods as they understood the question, but not why she asked.

"Knight's armor," she said proudly, indicating the carpet strips and roll of duct tape. "Those nasty things won't be able to bite through this!"

Suddenly they all got it and were excitedly trying it out,

wrapping it around their forearms, creating makeshift gauntlets.

"Good idea, Mizz Lacy," Phil grinned at her. "I'm starting to feel like one of those gladiators." He had wrapped both arms and was helping Mr. Sato wrap his.

"There's a place off Maple that sells costumes for the Renaissance Faire crowd," Carla said. "Quality stuff, real thick leather."

With the last of the coffee finished and everyone armored up, Phil stood and the room got quiet. "We all know the plan," he said. "It should be easy. Remember, we don't come back here to the 28th floor, no matter what. There's no food. We'd die of starvation if we get trapped here. If the stairs are jammed, we find another floor to get on, hopefully one with more food hoarders than these guys were. They can't get to us if we're in any of the offices, the doors open out into the stairwell and they don't seem to have enough sense in 'em to pull them open."

He looked around at the other men and women listening to him. At their makeshift armor and weapons. At the grim determination on most of their faces. He saw the ones who would fall. He knew the type. The weak ones. The ones still hoping to be saved by someone, not realizing that person would have to be themselves.

He'd never been in the military, but he'd been big all his life. He'd been a boxer for a while, then a bouncer, and finally worked his way into security. He knew a fighter when he saw one and Mr. Sato had grit. So did Mrs. Meadows. Some of that Army life had certainly rubbed off on her. The others, he wasn't so sure about, but he'd do his best to keep them all safe. It was his job. And they had become his friends.

"This is gonna get bloody," he said. "You ladies stay back and try not to faint."

There was a quiet titter of laughter from one of them and Lacy asked him, "You ever had a baby, Phil?"

He gave her a quizzical look. "No. Why you asking that?"

"You don't know blood like we know blood," she said and led the way to the pile of office furniture to start dismantling their blockade.

They left one door completely jammed and stacked the overturned desks and bookcases against the other one, leaving about a foot that could be opened once it was unlocked. By now, with the noise they had made, the slavering lunatics outside had resumed their attack on the doors, trying to get to the warm bodies only a few feet away. Lacy was going to unlock the door, but the sharpened claws she had taped to her hands were in the way and she was having a hard time turning the latch. "You do it," she finally said to Phil. "I'll take this first one."

They switched places and she drew her fist back, tightening her already white-knuckle grip on her untested battle blades. The screams in the hallway were getting more intense as they sensed their prey nearby. She heard the click of the lock and the door burst open the full foot they had allowed it, easily shoving Phil aside.

A keening, snarling, thing had forced itself halfway through the opening and was reaching for her. She plunged the makeshift blades deep into his eye sockets and felt the shudder as they stopped at the back of his skull. He fell instantly, and she was glad she had taped the blades to her hands. She would have lost them if she hadn't. The next one was clawing her way over the man as he fell, and Phil rammed a sharpened golf putter straight through the side of her head with a mighty grunt.

It came right out the other side and stuck deep into the wooden bookcase. She hung limp, like a lifeless doll, effectively blocking the doorway from any more of them being able to enter. "Don't let your end go!" Lacy shouted at Phil over the howls of the undead as he held the bloodied woman there like an oversized shish kabob. She had freed her spikes and was looking for another target when Mr. Sato politely yelled, "Allow me!" as he shunted her aside.

He swung a big driver over the dangling woman's corpse and smashed down into another woman's face, imploding her skull and sending blood and brains splattering for yards. She collapsed, taking the driver with her, still stuck in her head. Mr. Sato stepped back to get another club and Lacy thrust her fist into another gnashing face, aiming for the eyes. The natural shape of the skull guided her right into where she wanted to be. She was quick to pull out this time and already had her left fist flying for the face of the screeching woman missing a large portion of her hair.

The days had been rough on her, Lacy noticed. She must have been fighting with the others to get in, because she was horribly misshapen, one eye already gouged out in the frenzy to feast. She fell and that was the last of them, but there was still screaming. Lacy looked back. The annoying woman had her hands on the side of her face and was getting ready to suck in another breath when Alex slapped her. Not hard, but hard enough to get her attention.

She was hyperventilating. *"How the hell did she ever make it all the way up here?"* Lacy wondered.

"You're going to get us all killed," she said. "Maybe you should stay here. We'll send help up. How's that sound?"

The woman just nodded rapidly. Yes, yes. She would

stay. She couldn't go back out there. She had been on the third floor when she had heard the screaming. That's when she had been caught up in the mad flight to this level, pushed into the elevator as she stood in the hallway, trying to see what was happening. She didn't belong with these savage people. She couldn't. She wouldn't. She had enough food hidden away from them, she could last a while by herself, until help came.

"I don't think that's such a good idea, Mrs. Meadows," Mr. Sato said, but stopped from saying more when she turned to face him. Her arms were covered in gore and blood, brain matter dropping off of her spikes. Her face was hard and speckled with red drops.

"If she screams like that out there," she said, and pointed with a dripping hand toward the stairwell "We'll all die. She'll bring them running, if they already aren't."

"No, it's okay," the woman hurriedly said, before they tried to make her go back out there. "I want to stay. I'll be fine here."

"Block the door after we're gone," was all Lacy said as Phil pulled the spike out of the woman's head and she fell to the floor. Part of him didn't really want to leave Mrs. Dawson from third up here, he knew she would die if they didn't make it down, clear a path, and send help back up, but she would wind up bringing those things running with her shrieks.

She hadn't even been in danger, she had been behind a wall of furniture, and behind everyone else who had stood ready to jump in. Part of him had already written her off as one of the weak. Lacy climbed over the pile of bodies and squeezed herself through the opening. Phil needed to clear a few more feet out of the way before his big bulk made it through.

There were sets of stairs on either end of the building, and as they gathered in the hallway in front of the banks of elevators, it was a toss-up which way to go. There had been more of the creatures three days ago, so they had managed to push against the doors and wander out onto the stairs. Once in the stairwell they wouldn't be getting back in, though.

They all wondered how many had been trapped there, endlessly wandering up and down. What a nightmare. "If we had to have a zombie outbreak, why couldn't we have the slow-moving shamblers?" Lacy asked and noticed, with some satisfaction, that no one drug the bodies out of the doorway for the silly woman. She would have to get her hands dirty if she wanted to lock the doors leading into the tomb she was building for herself.

"Well," Phil said. "We know there are a bunch in that one." He pointed to the left. "So I guess we take a chance on the other."

As they headed to the right in the dim light filtering through the tinted windows, Lacy reached out and pushed the call button for the elevator. Nothing happened. No light ring lit up. No ding of an elevator arriving. No doors sliding open. She sighed and readjusted her spikes, making sure they were comfortable in her grip.

The stairs were empty. They slid in one by one, being as quiet as possible. Lacy had told them about what Johnny called Battle Rattle, and they had all made sure they didn't have anything clinking and clanging around on them. They didn't have weapons and gear they had to use black tape on, but they had each eliminated anything that could make unwanted noise.

They padded down the stairs quickly, the lights from the emergency signs weak after two days of being constantly on. By the time they hit the twelfth floor, they could smell the undead and by the time they got to the eighth, they could hear them. They hadn't run into any on the stairs, and it seemed the dead only went down, they didn't like to climb up unless they had a reason. Like six savory bodies to gnash on. They could hear them below, quietly milling around and making small noises.

Lacy held up a fist to indicate for the rest of them to stay put, and she slipped down a few more flights until she could see over the railing to the mob below. They were packed tight, shoulder to shoulder in the faint green glow of the lights, from about the fifth floor down. Hundreds. How did so many wind up in the stairwells? Had a bunch of people tried to hide in here and all of them turned? Had the stairwell doors been jammed closed by survivors? She had no idea why they wouldn't push open to the garage. She knew from fire codes they were supposed to open outward to the ground levels. This side was blocked, maybe the other was open.

She crept back up and motioned for them to climb. They went back up four more floors before they thought it was safe to whisper, and she told them what she'd seen. They agreed, they had to try the other side. They were all nervous now, sweating in the uncirculated heat of the building. The fire doors had no windows, so they didn't know what they would find when they were opened.

They couldn't risk tapping and bringing whatever was there screaming out at them and getting the horde from down below flying up the stairs. Their only choice was to chance it here on the twelfth floor, or climb so far up they could deal with any problem before the dead below could reach them. They decided to go up to the twentieth, that way there should be plenty of time to deal with any threats and get inside the hallway. They got to the sixteenth and said screw it.

This is good enough. They were all winded. Phil said this was the insurance agency's floor and none of them ever came in early. Better than even chance it would be deserted. They sat down to rest, all of them breathing heavy in the Georgia heat and from the long climb up they had just done. It wasn't just the climb, it was the tension, the humidity, the stale air that seemed thick and hard to breathe.

After a few minutes they were ready and as quietly as they could, opened the door just enough to see in. Clear. Phil pulled it a little wider. Still clear. They all slipped in and made sure it was latched behind them. Lacy hustled down the hallway to the big glass doors of the agency and tried them. Still locked. They were good, this floor was empty. They continued to the other stairwell and followed the same procedures, slipping down quietly until they ran into masses of them, packed in tight, around the fourth floor. Why didn't they push open the door and go out! It was frustrating. In a hurried conference, with barely audible whispers, they decided to return to the sixteenth floor. They would have to regroup and figure out something else.

Not all of the undead had wandered their way down. As the crew was silently making their way back up the stairs, they heard a snuffling keen above them. Then the sound of hurrying footsteps coming down. They all froze. Eric had been at the tail end of the procession going down, so he was at the front of the line going up. "Go!" Lacy stage whispered. "Get to the next floor!"

The creature above them heard the sudden sound of hurrying feet and let out a howling scream as it started racing toward them. It was running so fast its feet got tangled up and it started tumbling face-first down the stairs.

All they had to do was stay to one side as it bounced down in a series of arm flailing, bone-breaking falls.

The damage was done, though. From three stories below they heard the roar of a hundred voices scream up at them, and the trembling of the stairs as they pounded toward the warm blood they now sensed nearby. Eric made it to the landing on the ninth floor and ripped the door open, only to have a snarling she-demon attack him with out-stretched arms and gnashing teeth.

He fell backward as she landed on top of him, deaf to his screams of pain and horror, slashing deep gouges across his nose with her pretty white teeth. She bounded up again as soon as she had drawn blood, instantly searching for the next host to carry the seething viral nanobots. She took a sharpened golf club straight through her blackened eye and into her seething brain. More of the undead were starting to come out of the ninth-floor corridor, stumbling over the falling body of the woman and the screaming, kicking, bloody mess of Eric. Phil slammed into the door with his 260 pounds and forced it closed on them, snapping bones of the dead and the screaming Eric. He held it against the writhing creatures and bellowed at them to get to the next level.

He couldn't get the door to latch, too much flesh and broken bone poking out against the frame. Below, only two flights down and closing fast, the tumbling, racing mass of screaming undead were trampling each other in their haste to repopulate, to infect, to taste blood. As Lacy raced past him, the last of them, Phil let the door fly open from the undead pressing against it. He shoved the first three that came out as hard as he could down the stairs and into the path of the horde, before he turned and ran for his life. He could see them now, only one landing below.

He ran up the stairs three at a time, breathing like a great bellows, knowing he couldn't outpace them for more than one more flight, maybe not even that. He rounded the turn in the stairs, using the banister in his hand to propel him onto the landing and through the door Lacy was holding open.

She pulled it shut fast, but not fast enough that the lead zom didn't see her face as the door clicked closed. He slammed into it, raging and howling his fury, and was joined by the rest of the hundreds forcing their way up the stairs. "Other side," Phil gasped. "We need to get a few more floors up. Got to get above them."

As they neared the other door, though, they heard the screams of the undead coming from this stairwell also. The infected knew where they were. By the time they reached it, the mindless pounding had started. They all stared around at each other, panting hard, and eyes wide. They had lost Eric to the dead hunger, but everyone else seemed unscathed.

"The doors will hold," Phil panted. "Fire doors... Steel frames... They're too dumb to open them... and too many bodies crammed against them anyway."

Lacy leaned against the wall, hands on knees. She laughed humorlessly and shook her head. "We're in the same situation we were in before. Phil, who's on this floor? Couldn't get lucky and it's a freeze dried food company could we?"

"Tenth floor. This is the Williams & Williams floor. The law firm."

Robert started toward the doors that opened into the suites and offices of the attorneys. "Shall we see if they have better food than you guys did?" he asked pragmatically, a determined look on his face.

It turned out that the lawyers did have better food than the electronics firm. Their refrigerator was well stocked, but two days without electricity and some of it had gone bad. The few things in the freezer were thawed, but hadn't spoiled. They shared a half dozen frozen dinners, cooked over a fire built in the hallway in front of the elevator doors.

They had pried one set of them open and the smoke flowed upward in the pitch black cavern and out of the roof vents, thirty-eight stories above them. The pounding on the stairwell doors was muted, but still present. They didn't have much hope of them giving up and going away for a long time. Days maybe. And that's if they kept quiet and didn't get them riled up again.

Lacy stared out of the windows of the corner office that looked out over Centennial Park, the Ferris wheel, and water fountains built for the 1996 Olympics. Like most places in the South, Atlanta was a gun-friendly city. At the giant SkyView Ferris wheel, that was now a permanent downtown fixture, there is a sign that prohibits guns in the gondolas. However, they provide a storage locker for your weapon so you can ride legally. They discovered this when they took a ride one day when Gunny picked her up for lunch. With this in the back of her mind, Lacy started methodically going through every desk drawer, starting in the executive's offices. The others joined her and they tore the place apart, finding nothing. Maybe there were pistols in some of the safes, but no one had any idea how to open them.

Later, as they watched the moon rise over Atlanta in the conference room of Williams & Williams, Esquires, and sipping on some of their fine Louis XIII Cognac, the remaining survivors tried to come up with a plan that didn't entail them either being killed by the walking dead, or slowly starving to death.

"What about the roof?" Carla asked. "I've been zip lining before, maybe we can rig up something so we can slide over to the next building on the electric line or something."

"No lines up there," Phil said. "All the power and phone lines are underground, come up through the basement."

"Make a parachute?" Alex asked, but that was instantly shot down. Who would try it first?

"Perhaps we can strip enough cables out of the ceilings, make a strong rope and climb down, if we can get back to the lower floors," Mr. Sato suggested. They pondered that for a while, but with all the undead milling around on the streets, they would be hard pressed to get down, get off the rope, and get into the garage to find a suitable vehicle before they were overwhelmed. Those things were fast and no one present had a car even remotely rugged enough to go smashing through the city.

"Can we go through the heating vents to get to different floors?" Robert asked. "Maybe we can get down to the garage that way."

"Naw, too small," Phil answered. "But we can use the maintenance ladder in the elevator shafts."

There was a quiet uproar and everyone got excited. They hadn't even considered it, hadn't known there were ladders in the shafts. Phil smacked himself in the head, wondering why he hadn't thought of it before and Lacy reached over and lightly smacked him again, just for good measure.

"Okay," he said enthusiastically. "This is something we can work with. All the elevator cars are on the bottom floor, in the lower parking area. They automatically go down if there is a loss of power."

"Yes!" Lacy chimed in. "And they have access panels on the ceilings, right? We can climb down, open the panels, get in the elevator, then pry the doors open. Voilà! We're in the garage!" she beamed at them, the fine French Brandy already making her a little tipsy.

There were smiles and glasses held up in a toast all around the table.

"But what if the garage is still full of them?" Mr. Sato asked.

"We'll cross that bridge when we come to it," Alex from accounting said, and downed his snifter of 100-year-old spirits like it was bottom shelf, sour mash whiskey.

They slept comfortably that night. They had full bellies and a soft glow from the $3,000 dollar bottle of Cognac that most of them couldn't afford. The lawyer's offices had soft leather couches and there were plenty of spare golf clothes and tailored suits hanging in the closets to use as blankets or pillows.

They had a plan that held promise, and now they had a way to easily move between floors.

Tomorrow they would get out of here.

## 25

### Day 4

Everyone was up early the next morning, coffee and breakfast being served at six, people grabbing last minute items off of the mostly bare store shelves, the truckers making one final load check to ensure everything was tight and secure. They weren't sure what to expect, but no one was planning on smooth sailing.

Every vehicle had the best radios Wire Bender could tune for them, fuel tanks were filled to the brim. When breakfast was finished, Martha and Cookie washed the dishes and tidied up, much to the annoyance of Cobb, who wanted every hand to help with the final loading.

"I not leave this mess for people to see," she had told him. "What kind of pig you think I am?"

He knew not to argue, though, and stomped around in a mood, barking at everyone else to hurry up and get situated. "We're rolling at zero eight hundred," he kept snapping. "If you're not in the convoy, you're getting left behind."

The nervousness was in the air, some taking it better

318

than others. As it grew closer to departure time, Gunny noticed a few people make a hurried dash for the bathrooms, suddenly having to go in the worst way.

Some of the non-drivers were teaming up with the truckers to ride with them, and all of the ladies had been asked more than once. Most of the truckers that had seen real combat, had fired shots in anger, and were laughing the pre-trip jitters away. They were cracking jokes and doing their best to appear unconcerned.

Gunny had the paper maps spread out on the big table and was going over the route again with Sara, making sure their GPS's were all taking them on the same roads. Cobb had given her one of the big truck GPS units out of the store and Tommy had welded up a bracket for it on her handlebars.

The problem with them, though, is those units didn't like to route on the small roads and kept trying to direct them back to approved truck routes. That was part of Sara's job as scout. She was watching out for major road blockages from accidents, and making sure there were no low bridges they couldn't get under. They didn't need that kind of surprise along the way, and then have to back fourteen trucks and a tour bus down a little, windy road until they found a turnaround spot.

Firecracker and Jellybean were the only two drivers who wanted to head to their own houses to see if they could find family members. Firecracker had been lucky on the telephone when this all started and had actually gotten to speak to his wife. He had told her to stay inside, he would be coming to get her.

Everyone else was single or from a big city east of the Mississippi. Boston, Cincinnati, Orlando or the like. They didn't mention wanting to try to get home, and Gunny knew they had seen the videos and knew it was probably impossible. Maybe once they got to where they were going, they could get rescue parties together.

They had decided to take the northern route to Lakota, it wound through a part of the country that was much less populated. They were passing through Salt Lake City, so they could check on Firecracker's family. It was only five hundred miles, and once they wormed their way past Reno and Sparks on the back roads, they hoped the interstate would be passable all the way to the Salty.

"This just doesn't seem real," Scratch said. "I mean, it's supposed to be the end of the world and we're still eating home cooking, taking hot showers, playing video games' and watching movies. The kids are still bugging everybody for change for the vet's box."

Gunny glanced up at the train tracks with their semi-trucks making their never-ending rounds. He hadn't really noticed, they were part of the background noise, like the jukebox that never stopped since Cobb had put it on free play. He was gathering his road atlas and GPS, along with the other supplies he had on the table and before he could answer, the lights flickered once and went out. The Hank Williams that had been playing quietly in the background stopped mid-sentence.

"It just got real," he said. "Countdown starts now until the nukes start blowing, if the General is wrong and the Hajji's don't get them shut down."

The ambient light wasn't much with the trucks still blocking the windows, but it was enough to get everyone moving toward the junkyard area. Gunny's truck was lead, he'd been out in the new world twice now, and his Peterbilt was a little stouter than some of the rest. Griz had the only other heavy haul truck with a double frame, but he had a low boy trailer. Not so good for clearing a path because it was only a few inches off of the ground.

He'd had a single piece of huge steel pipe over nine feet tall on it, going to a construction site, but he'd simply unchained the load and turned the wheel sharply when he was bringing it around to the junkyard. The giant pipe rolled harmlessly out of the parking lot and stopped at the edge when it hit the soft sand, much to the disappointment of everyone who hoped he would crush zombies with it. They had discussed leaving the trailer, but decided if they came across a good bulldozer or earthmover, it would be nice to be able to take it with them. Might come in handy. Sara had pointed out that it was low enough so she could bounce her motorcycle up on it, if they had to plow through a big horde.

She could pass through the crowd without being stripped off of her bike. Most of the guys had reservations about riding a motorcycle into this brave new world, and had tried to talk her out of it, but she was adamant. She pointed out that it was infinitely more maneuverable than their trucks or a car, and fast enough to get away from any danger.

She readily agreed that if things got too hairy, she would load it up on Griz's low boy, but she wanted to ride. It was her decision, and they needed to back off and stop telling her what she could and couldn't do. They finally did.

Gunny climbed into the cab and started when he saw Bunny sitting in the passenger seat. She was smiling, wearing a T-shirt from the children's rack she had taken a pair of scissors to, looking good and drinking a beer. "Hi," she said, bubbly as ever. "Can I ride with you?"

"Um, yeah, if you want."

"The bus was getting crowded," she said and took a pull off of her Longneck.

He wasn't sure if he believed that. He was sure every unmarried driver there had asked her to ride with him.

It was eight o'clock in the morning and she was drinking a beer. She would want to stop to pee every half hour. He was trying to figure out a way to tell her he changed his mind, he didn't need some drunk bimbo flashing cleavage in the truck with him, and she needed to get out. But in a nice way.

Then the passenger door opened and he heard another woman's voice. "Ms. Cruz, I'm to be riding in this truck. That big man they call Griz is about five trucks back. He wanted me to ask you to ride with him."

As Bunny hopped down, happy to be away from the cop who had arrested her on numerous occasions, Deputy Collins climbed in. Still in her uniform. Hair pulled back tightly in a bun. "Do you mind?" she asked.

Gunny smiled. "Not at all. I think you saved me from a major headache. Griz really asked for her to ride with him?"

"Not exactly," she said, a slight smile on her lips.

Gunny nodded. Women's games. He wanted to stay out of that. He'd seen Griz giving the deputy an appreciative stare a couple of times and he was pretty sure she'd caught it, too. He bet the big teddy bear hadn't had the nerve to ask her to ride with him so this was her way of... what? Payback? Testing him? Who knew? They'd figure it out if it was meant to be.

"Cobb tell you to ride with me?"

"No," she said. "I was on the tour bus and saw her climb in. Thought I would do you a favor and get rid of her. I knew she wouldn't want to be in the same truck with me, we have a bit of history."

"Appreciate it."

"Besides," she added, "the president needs a bodyguard."

"Don't you start…" Gunny groaned. "I'm just a place-holder till they find the right guy."

She just nodded, thinking to herself, *"They may already have the right guy."* She was still grateful that he had gotten her out of the holding cells where they'd been trapped.

"Just help me negotiate through jams if we come to them. Watch for open areas, things like that," Gunny said. "Keep an eye out for big crowds of those things."

Cobb's voice came over the radio, which was surprisingly quiet. No static at all in the background and Gunny had the squelch all the way off.

"Take us out," he said, and Gunny dropped it in gear as Tommy opened the gate.

As soon as Sara zipped by on her bike and the trucks started rolling past the front of the Three Flags, the dozen or so zombies that had wandered in took off after them and the guys a few trucks back got to practice running them down.

For all of them except Lars, Scratch and Griz, it was a brand new experience, but no one faltered, they all did the grizzly job and none of the walking dead were walking when the last truck rolled by.

# 26

B y the time Gunny got up to speed, Sara was already out of sight, the tail light disappearing toward the cut off they wanted to use, a few miles up the road. Cobb was riding with Tommy, bringing up the rear of the convoy. After a few minutes, Sara came in on Channel 9 over the second CB Wire Bender had installed, asking for a radio check.

Most of the guys stayed on 19, Cobb had given very direct orders that channel 9 was for the lead and tail elements, if you wanted to blabber on about nothing, then stay on 19. Wire Bender had installed a second radio, along with the Hams and antennas in Gunny's and Tommy's trucks, to be dedicated to the emergency channel so Sara wouldn't have to worry about being talked over.

Before Gunny could reach the mic, the deputy had grabbed it and replied with a "Roger, Lead One. We read you Lima Charlie. What's your yardstick?" They went back and forth a few times, made sure Sara was within range and her radio was working fine. Sara knew most of the police radio protocols from riding around in her ambulance and picked up on the trucker terms the deputy threw in.

As they drove, they experimented with range and the radios seemed to work fine over a three to four mile area, anything over that and it got a little iffy.

"You've got the trucker lingo down pretty good," Gunny observed.

"Oh, we listen in when there's nothing else going on. How do you think we bust you guys dodging the scales?" she asked. Gunny couldn't tell if she was joking. Probably not.

"Making the first turn now," Sara came over the air.

"Now comes the fun part," Gunny said as he approached the turnoff a few minutes later and started downshifting.

"You got a name?" he asked "Something besides Deputy Collins?"

She looked at him sideways, hesitated before she answered.

Gunny picked up on it, quickly realized that she probably thought he was hitting on her. He flashed his wedding ring at her as he spun the steering wheel.

"It's Debbie," she finally said, a little grudgingly, her eyes going back to scanning for danger.

Gunny slowed at the bottom of the ramp and started nudging cars out of the way with the blade, swinging wide into the oncoming traffic lane to have the clearance for the trailer. He saw a few of them coming out of the strip mall parking lot, running toward them at full speed, the strange warbling screams that seemed to call to the others starting to come from their throats.

Sara was gone, having zigged and zagged through the stalled and crashed cars. Gunny's trailer caught the front of a Toyota that had been abandoned on the road and pushed it out of the way, the front plastic bumper tearing free as the headlights shattered. "Man, we should have thought of the wide swings," Gunny said. "Should have built some kind of deflector at the rear wheels of the trailer, hope I don't get a flat."

Collins was staring in the mirror as he knocked it the rest of the way aside. "Looks okay," she said. "You moved it cleanly."

The first of the dozens streaming toward them had made it through the maze of cars in the parking lot and started to fling themselves at the truck and its occupants, heedless of the danger. Gunny had the rig straight now, and grabbed another gear, trying to ignore them and the bouncing of the tandems crushing them under the tires.

"Save some for us!" Scratch yelled over the CB, still on the main road and seeing everything that was happening ahead of him.

Now that he was rolling in a straight line, the blade easily knocked the few cars he couldn't avoid out of the way and he kept the speed to an even twenty miles an hour. The jolts weren't too bad, and it was fast enough to keep most of the runners falling behind. Let the other guys cut them down, get in a little practice.

They wound through the secondary streets, staying on the bigger roads and avoiding ninety-degree turns where they could. The crowd of zombies kept getting bigger, more and more streaming out of the subdivisions, running at them as fast as they could. They were outpacing most of them, but the faster ones kept trying to leap and grab onto the trucks, most of them being ground to paste when they would miss and fall under the tires.

Cobb and Tommy had fallen back a little, letting the

rest of the convoy get ahead and then they hammered on it, running down the growing horde from the rear as they chased the trucks, slinging broken bodies yards into the air. They only had about fifteen miles of two-lane before they made their way back to the highway running east. Sara was at the top of the on-ramp with a clear view all around her, waiting for them to arrive. There were a couple of dead ones laying near her bike, bullet holes in their heads.

"Road is clear as far as I can see," she said over her helmet mic. "How fast can those big trucks roll?"

"Better keep it under sixty," Tommy cut in. "The over-sized tires we put on don't like speed too much."

"10-4," she came back, spun her bike around and pulled a small wheelie as she took off.

The day passed by in uneventful boredom. There weren't too many cars on this lonely stretch of highway. As they passed exits, sometimes there were some of the undead who would give chase, but they were either too slow and would be easily cut down by the blades, or chased Cobb and Tommy until they were out of sight. They stopped twice during the long day to refuel the bike and let Sara stretch her legs and drink.

She made for a good scout and had alerted them to a pileup under a bridge that blocked the road, and had them reroute over to the westbound side for a while. Martha and Cookie had been utilizing the little kitchen in the tour bus and when she called lunch break, everyone was pleasantly surprised at how good road food could be. Even out in the middle of nowhere, with no other vehicles in sight, Cobb had posted guards and they took turns eating.

Gunny, Griz, and Firecracker went over the maps for the umpteenth time, checking their speed averages for an accurate ETA. There was a good scenic overlook area before Skull Valley with enough room for all the trucks to make a sort of wagon train defensive perimeter on one side. With the steep cliffs on the other, it was as safe a spot as they were likely to find to spend the night. The trucks could stay there in an easily defensible position as a crew of them bob-tailed into town with Firecracker to check his family.

"We're making real good time," Griz said, tapping the overlook they were heading toward. "We'll make it there before nightfall if we can keep it up. I want to be able to scout the area before it gets dark."

"I could have made it in twenty minutes," Richard Bastille said quietly, but loud enough for them to hear. "If somebody hadn't smashed my car, that is." He had been making snide comments like this every chance he got, and not just about his Ferrari. He was a generally negative guy who was having a hard time adjusting to the new reality that his big shot days were over. He had been a movie producer and liked to name drop whenever he was talking to anyone.

Although he had been deferred to and treated with the respect he deserved during the first hours of this nightmare, all the people who had been his new friends had taken off in their cars the first day. The rest of these people didn't seem to care who he was. He had been rich, successful and a part of the 'in' crowd who went to all the right parties and knew all the right people. Now he was stuck with these truckers and mechanics, and his gal pal still wouldn't have anything to do with him. He just didn't want to believe the good life was over, and no one would jump and grovel to him like he'd been used to most of his adult life.

He wasn't a complete ingrate, he knew on some level that he was lucky to have fallen in with this crowd, but he just wasn't used to having to deal with these kinds of people. They had rough hands and rough manners. They didn't respect him at all. If he yelled at one of them that his coffee was too hot, they would probably toss it in his face.

He knew he should be trying to make friends, not alienate everyone, but he couldn't help himself sometimes. In his mind, he had lost so much more than all of them had. They hadn't lost a twelve bedroom house overlooking the ocean. They hadn't lost millions of dollars. They hadn't lost the ability to sleep with a different wannabe starlet every night.

Griz turned to look at him, but of course the guy wouldn't make eye contact and was busying himself acting like he was doing something important.

"Forget it," Gunny said, and they went back to the maps, determining the best route into and out of Firecracker's house on the western part of town.

They had been there about an hour and were making their final cleanup and checks to take off again when Shakey hollered out from the rear, where he had been standing guard. "We've got incoming! I can see some on the road!"

The people who had been riding in the tour bus dropped everything and ran for the doors to get back in, leaving Martha and Kim the only ones left packing away the dishes. Griz didn't even look up. "How many and how far?" he asked nonchalantly as the crowd at the bus tried not to push and shove, and were barely able to contain themselves.

"They're about a mile off," Shakey said. "But there are quite a few of them."

When they realized the danger wasn't imminent, a few of the men looked chagrined and stepped aside to let the ladies and the children go in first. Richard Bastille was already in his seat, looking out of the barred window. The vets continued to clean their plates, feigning extreme indifference. Scratch stretched and yawned loudly. Cadillac Jack pulled out his tobacco and slowly rolled himself a smoke. Lars pulled his hat down over his eyes and leaned back on the tire he was resting against. It was a little game they all played, had played their whole military careers.

We are not afraid.

We do not run.

We do not hide.

The Jarhead Marines were trying to outdo the Dogface Army guys in their uncaring attitudes. The Army guys going overboard to show the Jarheads they were even MORE unconcerned. But if you watched closely, you saw their eyes dart to their weapons, knowing exactly where they were and where their hands would fall on them, even if they were looking in the opposite direction. Saw them casually brush their pockets, double checking the number of magazines they had, mentally weighing the pull of each one, ensuring themselves each was fully loaded. Stabby watched all this unfold and sat back down, smiling to himself, feeling safe with these bunch of Yankee showoffs.

The mechanics from Tommy's shop had never seen G.I.s in action out in the field, and they were a little confused as they watched the guys just lay around when there were zombies coming. The rest of the people on the bus were as confused and concerned as they were. Peanut Butter just shook her head. She'd been around these kind of men long enough to know it was only an act. She winked at Buttercup, told her under her breath not to worry. Believe it or not, it was all under control.

Gunny wasn't immune to the game and he ambled slowly

to where Shakey was standing at the back of the convoy, stopping by Jack to bum a smoke. Shakey handed him the binoculars when he walked up. They were about a half mile off now, running at full speed, stretched out as far as he could see. He wondered where they had come from. Surely these weren't the same ones they had driven by miles ago. They couldn't still be coming after them. They had passed the last exit with any kind of zombie activity some twenty miles back.

"Scratch!" he yelled back to the soldiers. "Get your rig turned around and take these guys out!"

The three boys, who were all riding in the big Western Star, were on their feet and running toward Scratch's truck before he had even finished yelling. It was one of the few that didn't have a trailer. Scratch couldn't think of any reason to drag a whole load of squash with him. He was hoping to find a wagon full of exotic cars he could hook up to and take along. The zombies were untiring, running at full speed and a steady pace, whittling down the distance. They were mostly in single file so they would make easy targets for the big blade on the front of Scratch's truck, but they were disturbing in their single-minded intensity. Their unflagging efforts to get to fresh human flesh. This would be a serious problem, if every single zombie they passed started chasing them and never gave up. They would have to send a truck back every time they stopped to do cleanup, but that wouldn't always be an option. If they got bogged down in the front and after a half hour, hundreds came in from the rear....

He would worry about that later. The rest of the guys had come up to see, some of them grabbing the deer rifles from the pawn shop haul out of their trucks. They watched as Scratch aimed straight at them, slamming fifteen tons of heavy metal, fronted with a wicked sharp plow, into the line of undead at fifty miles an hour.

Bodies exploded and parts went flying. At those speeds, he didn't have to worry about anything getting tangled up under his truck. They watched him until he was around a bend and out of sight, the sound of the big Detroit Diesel engine finally fading from hearing also. After a few minutes and he wasn't coming back, Gunny walked up to Griz's truck.

He had a Big Radio with a linear and he grabbed the mic and hailed the boys. They came back faint, but he could make out that they were still on a killing spree, the line of stragglers went on as far as they could see. "That's enough," Gunny said. "Get back here ASAP. We're rolling out." He heard their acknowledgment and circled his hand in the air to everyone watching. "Mount up!" he hollered. "We're rolling as soon as they get back."

The General wanted a check-in every evening and Gunny thought this single-minded determination the infected exhibited would be worth mentioning to him. They needed all the survivors to know that, even if they think they escaped, the zombies will chase them for a long, long time.

Sara took off on her CBR again as soon as she saw the blood and gore splattered truck come up over the rise. The rest of the trucks pulled out and ran up through the gears as the convoy spread out over nearly a mile. The next few hours of the trip were uneventful, not even a wrecked car to skirt around. "I guess nobody had a Hajji Sausage sandwich through here," Gunny quipped when Deputy Collins had commented on it.

"There's a big Mosque in Salt Lake," she said, her hands

involuntarily clenching into fists. "I guess we're supposed to avoid it. No payback allowed?"

"Right," Gunny said. "Let them decommission all the nukes. After that, it's open season. Of course, if the survival numbers I've heard from Cheyenne Mountain are true, they outnumber us probably ten to one if all the Mosques are full of them."

"A lot of them will be women and children," she said. "They'll be easier to kill."

Gunny cut his eyes over to her, trying to see if she was joking. She was so intense, it was hard to tell, but he didn't think she was. As the sun went down behind them, the scenic turnout where they were going to camp out was coming up and Gunny grabbed the mic to let the rest of the convoy know. He was glad for the diversion because he didn't know what to say to the deputy.

He wanted to right the wrong the Jihadi's had done, but her cold logic was a little disturbing. He'd never killed a woman or a child. Not a living human one, anyway. Must be the Kentucky Gentleman in him coming out, never hit a woman or a kid. Or execute one. Her hatred ran deep and he wondered if there was more to it than just the death of most of the world, and the destruction of her country.

Nah. That was more than enough, he supposed.

Once they got set up, Scratch turned his truck around, waiting for the inevitable followers to start showing up. Some of the trucks were getting a little low on fuel, the bus critically so.

There was a truck stop on the outskirts of town, but it was agreed that it would be best to hit it in the morning, after they came back with Firecracker's family. Then they could take off and put another five hundred miles behind them, hopefully getting near Denver. There was no need to fight zombies all night coming at them from both ends and the run into town should only take an hour or so.

Griz and Cadillac Jack were prowling through the food provisions, examining different sized plastic bottles, much to the annoyance of Martha. As Gunny came back from getting rear guards set up, he noticed Martha with her hands on her hips giving them the evil eye. They were checking to see which bottles would fit snuggly on the end of the gun barrels. "Making suppressors?" Gunny asked.

"Yeah," Griz answered and the crowd that had been gathered around the small campfire, mostly ignoring them, perked up and started to pay attention.

"You can make a silencer with a mustard bottle?" Tina asked, somewhat aghast.

Deputy Collins followed the proceedings with a slight frown on her face, looking like she was trying to remember the exact code and subsection of the law that expressly forbade the manufacture, use, or possession of such items. But she was wise enough to know it no longer applied. Old habits die hard.

Gunny wondered if she knew about the buckets of cocaine Sara and Stacy had commandeered from Lars. Or that Stabby was slightly buzzing on it most of the time.

"I saw that on the telly," Stabby said. "It really works?"

"It'll work until we can raid a good gun store and find some real ones," Griz replied. "It's better than nothing for now, though." Then he threw the frowning deputy a wink, grinning at her in his boyish way.

Cobb came back into the group after setting up the forward outpost, saw what they were doing and told them to get the weapons out to the guards as soon as they finished cobbling them together. They didn't know if the infected would chase after a gunshot like they would a truck engine, but anything they could do to cut the chance of it, the better off they would be.

Later that evening, after dinner had been eaten and everything had been stowed away in case they needed to make an emergency departure, they gathered around a small fire and the talk turned to what they could expect when they reached the reservoir in Oklahoma. Other than the four on guard duty, this was the first time they had all sat around and discussed where they were going, and what could be expected.

The disaster and the days leading up to their departure had been chaotic and everyone had been busy. Now, bellies full of Martha and Cookie's spaghetti dinner, a relative feeling of safety with the guards keeping an eye on things, and the quiet night seeming to be void of danger, they finally talked about the future. Some of the drivers had been in the area, although no one could actually remember delivering to the little town itself. They described a rich land with streams and a huge, clear lake with plenty of fish and wildlife in the area.

According to General Carson, the soil was good and most crops would grow there. Bastille wanted to know what type of society it would be, comparing it to middle ages England, with peasants toiling the land while the high and mighty did nothing.

Cobb voiced an opinion that if you don't pull your weight and do your fair share, then you don't have any rights to take anything from the group.

"This we commanded you, that if any would not work, neither should he eat," Preacher Bible quoted, then said that if they raided the food warehouses from the cities, they would have more than enough canned and dry goods to last for years. Maybe even enough to last until the infected had finally withered away and died for good. Surely long enough for them to start growing their own crops again.

Shakey was worried about medical care and wondered if the hospital generators would still be up and running. Hot Rod said he knew a few tricks for gathering plenty of fish from the lake and he and Jack got into a discussion of the best bait. Griz and Gunny kicked around ideas for making the area defensible. Maybe even having their encampment on an island in one of the big lakes. Maybe build some cabins on it.

It was a good evening, a good first day on the road, and everyone was optimistic for the rest of the trip. Even their resident naysayer, Richard Bastille, had actually said a few things that weren't completely negative. The Cowboys had brought out their instruments and had a good laugh as Stabby updated their country songs in his death metal style. On his way back to his truck, Gunny was cornered by the SS sisters and in her usual blunt way, Stacy said quietly, "You know Shakey has diabetes?"

"No, he never mentioned it."

"Why would he? He'd lose his job. Why do you think he came to the Three Flags for his DOT exam?"

"Well, everybody knows Doc would let things slide. What's the big deal?"

They looked at each other, then looked back at him and he got the distinct impression he was being dense about something. She was looking at him like he was an idiot again. "He takes insulin shots, Gunny. Every day. Four times a day."

He was starting to see the picture now. "So we need to raid a drug store or something? To get him more? We can do that. We'll find one tomorrow."

Stacy looked exasperated. Sara asked, "You've never known anyone with Type 1 have you?"

"No," was his simple reply.

"It has to be kept refrigerated. You can't just walk into a drug store and grab some off the shelf. Once it gets hot, it starts to break down."

"There is a newer version available, but he's so damn stubborn, he wouldn't change to it. It's much better, but no matter what, it's going to be touchy unless we can get to the right testing equipment," Stacy said in frustration.

Gunny was starting to see why they were so concerned. This would explain some of Shakey's questions, asking about the hospital generators still running, and the general consensus had been most likely not. They only had a few hundred gallon fuel tank for them, at most.

"How much does he have left?" Gunny asked.

"Not much," Stacy said. "He was supposed to get his 'script from Doc when all this went down. He doesn't know I know, he's kept it hush-hush for years now. But I would guess what he has in the fridge of his truck is his last little bit."

"We can raid a pharmacy if we get a chance, the weather isn't too hateful," Sara said. "Even if it's gotten hot, it's better than nothing. It's still useful. So just keep that in mind, let's try to hit one up soon."

PREPARATION

# Day 5

Most of them woke up to the smell of coffee. Lacy and Carla had a small blaze going, using clients' files and remnants of the bookcase they had sacrificed for yesterday's fire. They had raided the cupboards in the lawyer's kitchen area and were boiling up a pot of cowboy coffee, using a sauce pan. As the rest of the crew gathered around, Phil and Robert pried open one of the other elevator doors and shined a flashlight into the gloom.

"There it is," Phil used his Mag Light to point at the metal rungs mounted in a channel along the back wall. "It runs from the top of the building all the way to the sub-basement."

"Wow," said Carla. "I thought it would be up front or maybe on the side. How do you even get to it?"

Phil shined the light down the shaft. Twelve stories to the basement. About a hundred and eighty feet. His light was strong and bright, but it didn't begin to cut into the darkness that far below.

The ladder was a good eight feet away. "You could probably jump and make it," Robert said. "Maybe."

Alex snorted, nearly shooting coffee through his nose.

"Yeah. If you were James Bond," Carla said dismissively. "Me, I'd probably pull my arms out of their sockets, even if I did make it past the cables running down the middle of the shaft."

Lacy walked back over to the coffee, giving it a stir, making sure it didn't burn. Nothing worse in the morning than burnt coffee. "We can make rope out of some cable, make a grappling hook or something," she said.

They had a fairly decent breakfast of oatmeal, granola, and coffee. The secretaries working for Williams and Williams must have had to pull some early morning shifts on occasion, from what they found in the kitchen. Afterward, they stacked up a few small bookcases on top of a secretary's desk and started pulling data cables out of the drop ceiling.

They were the easiest cables to get to, having been added by contractors after the building was finished, and held in place with just the occasional zip tie. As soon as the guys had enough pulled, Carla and Lacy set up a station on one of the desks and started stretching it all out, determining exactly what they had to work with. It took Lacy a few tries to remember how it went, but once she got started, the muscle memory in her fingers took over, and she showed Carla a new way to braid.

"I had to learn this when Johnny wanted a paracord sling for one his guns," Lacy said, and then demonstrated to her how to intertwine the six cables together into one that was extremely strong.

"I told him I would get him one for Christmas, not realizing how much those things cost," she continued as they worked the wires swiftly, making two ropes.

"Needless to say, I went to the Army-Navy store and bought some paracord and made it myself. What a major pain. Then he liked it so much, he wanted more for the rest of his guns."

Carla laughed softly, her fingers flying, now that she was in the groove. "What did you tell him?"

"Handed him the rest of the paracord and told him to have fun." She smiled. "One was enough. It probably took me seven or eight hours to learn how to do it and get it right."

"How many guns does he have?" Phil interrupted. "He's ex-army isn't he?"

Lacy looked up from her work and said, "Yes, he is, and I don't know exactly, Phil. He doesn't like to open the safe when I'm around and I leave it alone. I know of five or six that I've caught him trying to sneak in, telling me some nonsense about trading something for them, getting a good deal."

She smiled again and shook her head. "He thinks he's slick. I let him think he has secrets, but I'd bet my bottom dollar the gun safe is nearly full. He's been beating around the bush, saying it might be a good idea to pick up another one if we catch a good sale."

"How many does it hold?" asked Mr. Sato. "How big is the safe?"

"Biggest one they made," Lacy replied. "About as big as a side-by-side refrigerator freezer."

They all just looked at her in disbelief. "That many? Really?" Carla asked. "What does he do with them all?"

Lacy felt a little defensive. She knew Johnny didn't

need fifty guns, but they were something he enjoyed and he never let them go hungry or want for anything to feed his hobby, so she didn't see any harm in it.

"Shoots them. Some of them, anyway. He goes to the three gun competitions," She said. "But he's got all kinds, some of them are antiques and old western guns. You know, collector's stuff."

They nodded their heads in understanding. People collecting stuff, even guns, they could understand. Everybody collected something. Anything from Pokémon to ceramic frogs. It didn't get much more American than that.

They went back to their work, pulling and braiding and passing the morning away in quiet conversation, getting to know one another, bouncing ideas off of each other for their next step. Would they stay together or split up, once they got vehicles out of the parking garage? What would they do if the parking levels were full of the undead? Did any of their family members survive? Should they all stick together and try to rescue them? Where was a safe place to go?

By lunchtime, they were satisfied with what they had. Two long, and very strong ropes, with knotted hand holds every few feet. They planned on using one as a throw rope, grappling onto the ladder and the other as a safety, tied off to the person and something unmoving in the office, just in case. The plastic ropes were solid, but kind of slick. It would be easy to lose your grip if you weren't careful when swinging out across the abyss to the ladder.

Mr. Sato and Robert said they would figure out lunch while the rest of them went to search through the offices again, this time looking for anything that would make a good, strong, hook.

With the triple wrapped shelving brackets they modified

and bellies full of some spicy concoction from lunch, they gathered around the open elevator doors and started trying to throw the hook across the gulf to latch onto the ladder. After a few tries they got it to snag on, and despite Phil's hard tugs, it held.

They had drawn straws at lunch time to see who would go down first and Robert tied the safety rope around his waist as he sat on the edge of the drop-off. He wrapped the braided wire, that was hooked onto the ladder eight feet away, firmly around his arm and with a few quick breaths, slid out into the emptiness.

With Phil holding him back with the safety rope, he didn't slam into the far wall, but slowly slid over to it as the rope was let out. When his feet made contact with the rungs, there was a quiet cheer from those gathered at the open doors. He wrapped his arms around it once he made contact and stayed like that for a moment, getting his rapid breathing under control. They only had the one flashlight and he double checked that it was firmly in its holder, borrowed from Phil, then untied the safety rope and started down. They watched, heads leaning out over the darkness, as he disappeared.

They soon lost sight of him and then even the sound of his feet on the metal ladder. Every so often, they would see the light shine down in the blackness as he checked his progress, then finally saw it as a speck of white, moving around on the top of the elevator car.

They listened. Thought they could hear the sound of the roof access panel being removed, then the light disappeared completely. He must be inside the elevator, they all assured each other. Robert had a sturdy piece of flat railing they had pulled out of the ceiling, and used it to pry open the doors on the car. Using the flashlight, he could see the doors of the sub-basement, plainly marked B-2. He listened with his ear to them, but heard nothing.

Quietly as he could, he started to pry open the doors, just enough to see out.

Blackness.

Two stories below ground, with no electricity and the darkness was nearly as complete as it was in the elevator shaft.

He switched on the light and a snarling face was illumi-nated, a hand reaching for him through the gap. An inhuman screech echoed through the underground garage as it shoved its arms through the opening, forcing it wider.

Robert screamed and backpedaled, dropping the light, and jumping for the opening in the ceiling of the elevator. The undead thing squeezed through the doors and launched himself at the dangling legs illuminated in the rolling beam of the flashlight. Robert screamed again as he felt the hands tearing at him, pulling him back down.

They heard his screams from twelve stories up. First of fear, then of pain. Then nothing.

# 27

## Day 5

It was four a.m. when the gentle tapping came on Gunny's sleeper. He heard Deputy Collins come awake on the bunk above him, and told her it was okay. His turn for guard duty. Guess being president didn't get you off Cobb's guard roster, he thought sourly to himself. He dressed hurriedly, grabbed his AR, strapped on his Glock, and double checked his magazine load out.

He was relieving Bastille, and Bunny was coming on to relieve Griz. Cobb had made out the roster to have one civilian and a vet on duty each two-hour shift. It was up to the old hands to bring the civilians up to speed on what was expected of them, how everyone could die, including them, if they goofed off or nodded off. She stumbled up to the outpost, still half asleep, and sat down on a rock. Within a minute, her head was drooping.

Gunny poured out a cup full of cold water and threw it in her face. She spluttered and jumped to her feet, dropping the .22 rifle she had been cradling between her legs.

"What? What was that for?" she demanded.

"Sleeping," was Gunny's simple answer. "Don't do it on duty."

After she had calmed down, he went over her duties, explaining more than once that it didn't matter if she thought it was bullshit. For now, it had to be done. Once they got to Lakota, got things secured, things would be different. By the end of their shift at six, with the smells of breakfast in the air, she had a pretty good understanding of the basics of military life. She realized the importance of each person in the cog, and how they all made it work. Gunny knew a little more about her. She had been an exotic dancer and tended to drink too much. She and Collins had gone around and around a few times, and she always wound up spending the night in jail when they tangled. She supposed it was lucky she had this last time. Otherwise, she would have ended up like everybody else she knew. Dead and still walking around.

When Squeak and Preacher relieved them, they headed back to the trucks and got in line for chow, taking the cups of hot coffee gratefully.

By seven, everyone was fed and Gunny had gathered his crew to head into town with Firecracker, to see if his family was still alive. Cobb had tried to talk him out of it, said he was kind of too important to be running off on a dangerous mission.

Gunny had said that if I don't help them, then they won't help me when I go to Atlanta, and it's a hell of a lot more dangerous than Salt Lake. Stabby was already hopping from one foot to the other, anxious to get going. Scratch was cleaning his fingernails with the long shank he had on his prosthetic. Lars had snagged a pair of drop leg holsters from the pawn shop smash and grab, and had matching Berettas tucked into them, along with the two in Kydex holsters on his belt.

"You look like a Rastafarian Neo," Scratch said. "All you need is a leather trench coat."

"Nah," Lars said. "You can call me the four gun kid."

"You ladies get over here," Cobb growled out. "And what's with the sunglasses, Hollywood? You ain't got no fans around here."

Lars quickly took his shades off, not wanting to get on the rough side of Top's tongue this early in the morning.

"Hollywood," Scratch and Stabby snickered. "Fits you, man."

Firecracker was emotional when they all walked up to go over last minute plans. "Fellas, I can't thank you enough," he said. "I know you all volunteered, I know you don't know my wife or kids, but I sure thank you." He had a little more to say, but he was starting to get choked up and Scratch brushed him off, saying, "We're only going 'cause we wanna kill zombies. We've got some new weapons to try out!"

They could hear Bastille grumbling about the best killers they had going off on a fool's errand, leaving everyone unprotected, but no one was paying any attention to him. Preacher came over and said a prayer for their safe and quick return, then they were mounting up. Gunny had dropped his trailer and was taking his rig, and Firecracker was driving his Kenworth.

They waved their goodbyes and were soon out of sight of the encampment. Firecracker took the lead, zipping toward his house on the back roads. The plan was to go in fast and hard, get his family if they were still hiding at home, and get out before the inevitable followers caught up with them. The ride in was quick and Gunny took out the

few zombies they saw running after the lead truck whenever he could.

The suburbs weren't as bad as they had envisioned.
Either everyone had already left for work, or they had
turned inside their houses and were still trapped there,
unable to figure out how to operate a door. They hoped that
was the case. Firecracker hadn't been able to reach his wife
since the first day, but had sent her text messages, hoping
they would go through. He had told her he was coming and
here he was.

He laid on the air horn as he pulled up and jumped out,
sprinting for the door. Lars and Scratch both hopped out,
ran halfway up the drive and shouldered their M-4s as they
spread out to either side of it, ready to lay down covering
fire so the family could run out to the truck. Gunny and
Stabby flew by them and made the next right, circling the
block, planning to start taking down any followers with
the blade.

Firecracker hit the door at a dead run, pounding on it.
"Mary, open up!" he shouted. The door remained closed,
the curtains on the windows not moving. He pounded his
fists on it again as Scratch started taking head shots at some
of the runners coming toward them. "If they ain't answering, they ain't there!" Lars shouted, starting to take out
runners on his side.

"Maybe they're in the basement and can't hear us,"
Firecracker yelled back and fumbled the keys in his hand,
searching for the right one.

Scratch shook his head as he caught a glimpse of him
nearly dropping the keys, a little pissed off that he hadn't
even thought past yelling out her name.

Gunny rounded the last turn and floored it, trying to
take out as many of the mob that had started chasing them

as he could, before they got too close. Bodies bounced off of the blade and went splattering through the lawns, but he couldn't get the ones not on the road. Not the hundreds he saw streaming down the street, but peeling off into drive-ways and front lawns, chasing the sound of rifles over the sound of the big diesel.

As he plowed through a hundred on the road, fifty in the grass ran past him, heading directly for Lars and Scratch, who were still aiming for the heads as quickly as they could.

Where had they all come from! Where had they been hiding?

"I can't hold," Scratch yelled a few seconds later, and Lars saw they had made a fatal mistake. They were too far away from the truck to make it back before the horde of screaming, keening monsters would shred them to pieces. Lars took a fast glance over his shoulder and hollered, "To the house! To the house!" as Firecracker finally managed to get in, and they both ran for their lives across the lawn and into the open door, slamming it behind them.

Gunny spun around at the next intersection and banged gears as fast as he could, heading back to the house. There were already thirty or forty of them in the yard and on the porch, hammering at the door. He grimaced as he realized what they had done, taken cover inside.

He bounced up over the curb and slammed into the crowd, ripping bodies and sending them flying. He took out a dozen, and a few more started chasing him, but there were still too many attacking the house in a mad frenzy. It was only a matter of time before they smashed a window. Or the door caved under the relentless assault.

Firecracker ran through the house, yelling for his wife, screaming out his children's names. No one answered.

There were no notes on the table or the fridge as he ran through. The basement was empty. He pounded up the stairs three at a time.

Empty.

Nothing.

The mob outside were trying to throw themselves against the door, but with so many bunched up, it was an uncoordinated effort, at best. Gunny was plowing through the yard again, blasting the air horn, trying to get them to follow him and away from the house, but they were intent. They knew they had their prey cornered, and the madness of flesh so close was driving them into a frenzy of wanton abandon.

The door shuddered in its frame and Lars ran into the living room and started dragging the couch toward the entryway. Scratch joined in and they wedged it between the front door and the stairs, making a solid barrier that couldn't be breached.

Firecracker was near meltdown mode, they saw. "They're not here! I told them I was coming! I told them to stay here!" he said over and over, still searching the house.

Lars looked at Scratch. "You got the handheld?" he asked.

Scratch just shook his head. "Thought this was going to be an easy extraction, man. Should of known better. What a SNAFU." They could hear Gunny honking his horns and doing his best to kill those that he could on the lawn. They needed to get out and get out fast. With all the noise they were making, every zombie in Salt Lake City would be heading their way soon.

"Can we blast past them, get back to the truck?" Lars asked.

"Maybe if you had an M-60," Scratch said. "We don't

have time to pick them all off, and don't have the firepower to wade through them."

They heard a window break and both immediately ran for the stairs.

"Firecracker, come on!" Lars yelled and splattered the forehead of some brunette trying to paw her way through the window.

"They're not here! They're not here! I told them to be here!" he kept saying.

"He's losing it," Lars said. "I thought he spent time in the 'Stans."

"Probably never left the Green Zone, damn Fobbits," Scratch shot back.

They heard Gunny make another pass at the mob on the front yard, and knew their time was getting short when they heard another window break. They both yelled for Firecracker to come upstairs and they finally saw him climb over the couch and run up toward them. That's when they noticed he didn't have a gun. Nothing. Not even a club or a knife. They moved aside as he came up, then immediately went back to their positions at the top of the stairs, ready to shoot anything that came into view.

"We can hold here until they're all dead, or the ammo runs out," Scratch said. "How many of them you think there are?"

"More of them than bullets, probably," Lars said. "Fire-cracker, can Gunny get alongside the house? Can we jump out of a window onto his truck?"

"I don't know," he said and stood there behind them.

"Go check, mother fucker! I wasn't asking to pass the time!" Lars yelled at him, and Firecracker took off as he and Scratch started targeting the bloodied infected that had made their way through the shattered living room windows.

Gunny had been trying to raise them on the radio, but never got a reply as he cursed and swung around again, this time nearly tearing the porch off the house. He was trying to whittle their numbers down before they could crawl through the broken windows.

"Look." Stabby pointed with his wickedly sharp claws and Gunny followed with his eyes to see what he was supposed to be looking at. Firecracker was waving to them from a window at the end of the house. Pointing to the ground directly below.

Gunny got it as he roared through another half dozen and swung around again in the neighbor's yard, clipping the front of their Camaro with the blade. So much for those flower gardens, he thought. The turf was getting pretty churned up by now with the body parts, bloody guts, and spinning tires. He flipped the differential lock switch, essentially giving him four wheel drive, and aimed for the upstairs window. He slid up alongside it, getting as close to the house as he could. It wasn't much of a drop for them, only a few feet to the top of his sleeper, and he heard Firecracker yell, "He's here!" to the guys still firing. Gunny lowered his window and started blasting away at the surrounding mob trying to claw their way toward him with his Glock, listening anxiously to hear the team land on his roof.

"Go go go!" Lars yelled as they backed into the master bedroom. He had switched to his Berettas, letting the carbine dangle across his back on its single point sling. The onslaught had slowed some as the snarling horde struggled over the bodies on the stairs, and the narrow hallway made for a good killing field. When the first gun emptied, he started firing with his off-hand, but he wasn't getting head shots, the 9mm rounds only slowing them, making them stumble.

As soon as backed into the room, Scratch was there slamming the door behind him and grabbing the heavy king sized bed to drag it over. The door shuddered as a body slammed into it and Lars put two more through the thin wood at head level, then grabbed the other side of the bed and helped slide it against the door.

He saw Firecracker on the roof of the truck, waving at them to hurry and he told Scratch to go, telling him, "I'm right behind you." He quickly dropped the empty mag and sent a fresh one in, thumbing the catch to let the slide go home. He ran to the window and jumped the couple of feet over to the sleeper and crouched down, trying to find something to hold on to.

As soon as he heard the third body drop onto the top of his truck he heard them all start yelling for him to "Go, go, go!" No family had been passed through the window. No wife. No kids. No time to worry about that now. He eased out the clutch and accelerated slowly, trying not to throw them off, the rear tire tearing up sheets of vinyl siding as he rolled along the side of the house. The crowd of dead followed them, jumping and reaching, trying to get to the warm bodies. "Hold on!" Gunny yelled and bounced back onto the street, shifting gears and picking up speed.

Firecracker was halfway down the back of the sleeper, using the headache rack to hold on for dear life as the Pete tilted this way and that, through the yards and over the curb. Lars threw himself down flat, looking for anything to keep him from flying off, and Scratch simply reared back and stabbed a hole in the roof with his sharpened spike.

Lars grabbed on to him and they rode it out until the ride got smooth again on the black top. Gunny stopped about a half mile ahead to let them all slide off and pile back into the cab, but the horde kept increasing in size, every turn they made there seemed to be more running between the houses and taking up the chase.

"We need a long open stretch," he said. "Someplace we can outrun them far enough to get turned around and come back through them. We need to get back to your truck."

Firecracker knew a place and guided Gunny toward it. He had tears rolling down his face and Gunny didn't ask. He could only guess at what they had found inside the house. They were nearing the outskirts of suburbia and the roads were becoming rural, so he quickly went through all eighteen gears then wound it back down, looking for a wide drive to get turned around.

"Plan B," Gunny said. "We're far enough away they should all be out of your neighborhood. I'll take out as many as I can on the way back in. We stop at your truck and you guys hop over, then let's head back on this same path, kill any more that we can get before we run back up the mountain."

"They weren't in there, Gunny," Firecracker said over the splat of bodies bouncing off of the blade. "They were alive, I talked to them. I told them I was coming."

They were all quiet. Any number of things could have happened. She could have gotten scared and ran out of the house. She could have gone to neighbors for safety. Maybe she thought she needed to run to the store for milk. How do you tell a guy to forget about them, they were gone, when you really didn't know anything?

"Maybe she went over to her mother's place," Fire-cracker said as he stared intently out of the windshield, hope blooming in his voice. "She must of. It's only a few blocks from the house. Let's check there."

Gunny looked over at Lars, Stabby, and Scratch, a question in his upraised eyebrows. Shrugged shoulders, a nod.

"Okay, man. We'll go by there, but no screw ups this time. You guys have fresh mags? Swap out your empties, hurry up. Keep your eyes peeled for people waving at us in windows. If anyone is alive in that neighborhood, they should have enough sense to try to flag us down when we come back. These trucks ain't quiet and we made enough noise to wake the dead."

Stabby and Scratch groaned at the weak joke as they raided the box of loaded magazines in the sleeper. "Just when I thought there was some hope for you," Lars said and shook his head.

# 28

They decided to swing by mom's house since it was on the way, before they got to Firecracker's truck, just to see if there was anyone there. It would buy them a little time from the following runners if they did need to evacuate some people. Checking the mirrors and seeing they didn't have any followers in sight, Gunny brought the truck to a quick stop in front of the house Firecracker had pointed out.

The three were out of the cab and taking up defensive positions as Stabby took high watch from the truck, and Firecracker ran toward the opening door of the house. She was there! She was there! A dark-haired woman ran out onto the small porch and they embraced with whoops of joy.

"Let's go!" Gunny yelled. "Time for that later!" He was on one knee, scanning back the way they had come. Scratch fired off a single shot toward the front of the truck and Firecracker broke the embrace and ran toward the house to grab his kids. "Get in the truck!" he yelled at his wife, "I've got them!"

They were standing in the open door, his six-year-old

son holding his smaller sister's hand. "Come on!" he said, and swung his daughter up in his arm, grabbing his son's hand with his other and starting to run toward the idling semi.

Stabby was waving them on, yelling and pointing. "I see some coming! Hurry up, lads!"

Gunny heard the quick sound of rifle fire from Lars, but kept scanning his area, still nothing.

He heard Firecracker yell, "What are you doing? Get in the truck!" and took a swift look over his shoulder and saw the woman running back toward the house.

"I've got to get Mom, she can't walk!" she cried as she flew past her husband and back to the porch. Firecracker continued toward the truck to put his kids in, and Stabby jumped down. "I'll help her. Get them loaded up!" and he took off after her into the house.

The popping from Scratch's carbine was starting to get fairly consistent and he heard Lars' picking up the pace, too. Still nothing in his sector, still no followers catching up to them yet. He yelled back toward them, "How we doing, boys? Can you hold them?"

"Magazine," Lars yelled and there was a short pause in the sound of the rounds going off.

"Yeah, we good," Scratch yelled back then, "Magazine," himself.

"Ones and twos," Lars shouted. "We got this for now."

Gunny kept scanning, butt stock to his shoulder. He knew when they came in view from his direction, it wouldn't be in ones or twos. It would be a mob. He couldn't hear anything, but they didn't seem to scream unless they spotted prey. They would just be running silently, never tiring, never getting short of breath, and never getting a stitch in their side.

He saw the first one come around a slight bend in the road. A man with a bathrobe flying out behind him and wearing pajama bottoms, the slippers that had probably been on his feet long gone. Gunny sighted in through iron sights and squeezed, red mist flying out of the back of its skull as its feet flew up and out from under him.

"They're coming!" Gunny bellowed. "We've got to go!"

Now there were more and he was right. Not coming in ones or twos, but a bunched up mob sprinting for all they were worth, cutting down the distance between them quickly. Another fast glance over his shoulder showed him the children were in the truck, looking out of the window toward the house. Stabby was half dragging, half carrying an older woman and Firecracker was running back toward the truck with his wife in tow.

He breathed a sigh of relief. This was going to work. He sighted in on the crowd, who was starting to scream now that they had their prey in sight, and started popping heads. He ran through most of his magazine, dropping at least ten and causing the rest of the crowd to stumble and slow. They were only a few blocks away now and he yelled, "Let's go, to the truck!" at the top of his lungs as he let the M4 fall on its sling and sprinted back toward the others.

*"What the hell were they doing?"* Lars and Scratch were both shooting steadily toward runners coming in from the front, but Firecracker, his wife, Stabby, and the old lady were all still standing outside the truck, waving frantically at the kids inside.

Before he took three more ground-eating steps toward them, he realized what must have happened. The kids, looking out of the window toward their running parents, had pushed down the door lock. He kept running, aiming for the driver side door, but there were already five or six of them making a beeline for it and they would beat him there. He brought the carbine up to his shoulder at a full run and emptied the magazine, but none of them went down. Zero head shots.

He could hear Scratch yelling at the kids to "Get down, get down, get down!" He was going to shoot the window out, but they were too scared to move, just kept crying and reaching for their parents, not even realizing what they had done. It was too late. They were being surrounded. Even if the door opened right now, there wasn't enough time to get all six people into the cab before half of them were pulled down by the undead masses.

"Back to the house!" Gunny roared as he ran by them, grabbing the other side of the old woman Stabby was still supporting, and they both flew up the sidewalk carrying her, her feet barely touching the ground. Firecracker pulled his wife after them, with Scratch and Lars trying to keep the horde of zombies off of their backs. Gunny sent Stabby reeling off toward the living room with the old woman and was waiting with his shoulder against the door, ready to slam it as soon as Lars cleared the threshold. He no sooner got the deadbolt turned, when he felt the first impact against the door.

It wouldn't hold long, but probably longer than the windows. The house was full of them: big picture window in the living room overlooking the porch, big windows in the kitchen. Big windows in the bedrooms. All the curtains were closed and Gunny shushed everyone. "Don't make any noise," he whispered loudly. "If they don't see us, maybe they'll settle down. Forget we're here." The door shuddered violently.

The single-minded infected had seen them come in through it and they continued to try to follow. Gunny

DAVID A. SIMPSON

motioned toward the kitchen table, indicating to Lars and Scratch to bring it over. They hurried, quietly pulled the chairs away from it and hustled it back to him, settling it in on its side against the door and the first riser of the staircase. It was a little short, so they filled in the gap with a few books, kicking the last ones in tightly to form a solid barrier against the door, making it impossible to open.

The old lady lay on the couch, pale and strained from all the exertion and Firecracker was trying to calm his wife, telling her the kids were fine, the truck was armored, the zombies couldn't get in.

"Perimeter check," Gunny said. "Stabby, upstairs. Make sure they don't see you from any of the windows."

Lars and Scratch split off, going in opposite directions to circle the inside of the house and Gunny went to the back door, to see if there was an escape there. There wasn't. There must have been hundreds by now. All the zeds in the immediate area drawn to the gunfire and the mob that had followed the truck.

This was a disaster Gunny raged at himself. They had two close calls on just this one simple mission. Dumb ass mistakes had been made. By him, by Firecracker, by his wife. By the kids. He was going to get them all killed if the mistakes didn't stop. It all came back on him, though. He was the one calling the shots.

He knew Firecracker didn't have any combat time. He had never left the Green Zone when he had been in Afghanistan. The kids didn't know any better, and the wife...well, she was a civilian. She didn't know what they knew. Didn't have any experience. Now the safety of the truck might as well be a million miles away. None of them had radios on them. It was supposed to be a quick in and out.

They had plenty of ammo, more than enough to snipe the hundred or so outside then walk through the piles of dead to get back into the truck, but every shot fired would draw more toward them. They all carried M-4 variants, and they were loud. They couldn't blast their way out. The door shuddered again, but it wasn't budging. The ones swarming around the back of the house weren't really trying to find a way in, they were just the overflow from the undead in the front, still trying to go through the door.

Lars and Scratch came back, both started shifting magazines around in their pockets, moving empties to the off-hand side, making sure the loaded ones were where they wanted them, and facing the right way. They hadn't brought any extra ammo, just the loaded magazines. It was only supposed to take a minute, maybe two, to get them out of the house and into the truck.

"Indefensible," Lars said.

"Concur. Too many windows. They'll break sooner or later, just from the sheer weight of so many of them pressing against the house," said Scratch.

"Agreed," said Gunny as Stabby came quietly down the stairs.

"All clear up here," he said. "The truck's surrounded, but if the kiddies would get away from the windows, maybe go take a nap, those bloody rotter's will lose interest."

"Right. Hope they have the same courtesy for us. Let's get upstairs, fortify the stairwell, and hope they go away in a few hours."

Lars and Firecracker went to help the old woman up the stairs as his wife wrung her hands and quietly cried. Gunny felt for her. She had managed to keep her family safe for nearly a week and when the cavalry shows up to rescue them, her kids are locked in a truck surrounded by monsters and she's in a house about to be overrun by them.

He went over to her, to offer a few words of reassurance that the kids would be fine, the truck was impossible to get into, when he noticed the bandage on the old woman's leg. Her housedress had pulled up some as they carefully stood her on her feet to guide her to the stairs.

"Hold it," he said and changed his path from the wife to the mom. "What happened to her leg?" he asked, pulling the floral print dress up to the woman's knees. When Lars and Firecracker saw it, both of them quickly set her back down on the couch. Lars put the back of his hand to her forehead. "She's burning up," he said. She was breathing fast and shallow. Barely coherent. Gunny grabbed the bandage and ripped it off, exposing a half circle bite mark of infected flesh trickling blood, angry and red with black runners leading away from it.

"When did she get bit?" he whirled on Firecracker's wife, a little more forcibly than was probably necessary.

His eyes were angry and she hesitated, still sobbing.

"When?" Gunny asked again, dropping the old woman's dress back over her ankles. He stood to face the idiot woman who may have just gotten them all killed over an old lady who had already been served a death sentence.

"This, this morning," she stuttered. "She went out to check the mail and a little kid attacked her."

Gunny was stunned. How utterly ridiculous. They were all going to die because some ditzy old lady wanted to check the mail?

They were all staring at her with the same incredulous looks on their faces. "There was no one out on the streets when she went. We thought it would be okay," she said defensively.

"That junk mail cost her life," Lars said.

"Probably ours, too," Scratch added.

"But don't you have medicine?" she asked plaintively. "It was a small bite, nothing major."

There was the sound of breaking glass in one of the bedrooms, the big picture window overlooking the back yard would be Gunny's guess.

"Upstairs," he said and they didn't have to be told twice. Firecracker's wife was pulling against him, toward her mom. "She needs help," she said.

She just didn't get it. How could she? She hadn't seen what they had.

"Go!" Gunny said. "I'll take care of her." And Firecracker finally drug her up the stairs.

As soon as their feet went around the landing midway up the stairs, Gunny didn't waste any more time. The old woman was barely breathing, the poison killing off the last of her humanity. He flipped her roughly onto her stomach and pulled the Gerber from his leg sheath. He didn't hesitate, plunged it in at the base of her skull like the Sisters had shown him. It sank to the guard and he gave it a little jiggle before pulling it out.

"You coming?" came a stage whisper from up the stairs.

Gunny slipped over to the bedroom, peeking in from the side of the door. He wanted to know if they were coming in, or was the breaking glass just incidental to the milling crowd.

It wasn't incidental, there were many hands trying to claw their way in and he heard the sound of another window breaking elsewhere in the house. He ran for the stairs and as soon as he cleared the top, the boys muscled a mattress into the stairwell and down toward the landing, essentially erecting another wall. Next came box springs, and a dresser to wedge it in place, and by then the first floor was full of screaming infected, all rampaging up the stairs and trying to force their way to the living.

They all started grabbing whatever they could and filling up the stairwell with anything that wasn't bolted down. Firecracker's wife's face was still tear-streaked, but she hadn't asked about her mother. Gunny could only assume she was quickly schooled on the new facts of life in the few minutes it took him to take care of business downstairs.

When everything they could toss down the stairwell had been thrown into it, she ran over to the window looking out over the street, at her kids in the truck. They were still at the window looking out and she caught their attention and waved to them, trying to give a mother's comfort from fifty yards away.

Gunny did a quick look around the upstairs, at the horde below that could be seen out of every window. Maybe two hundred and they were still screaming and keening, drawing more.

"Can the boy read?" Gunny asked Firecracker.

"Some," came his reply. "Mary has been teaching them. Why?"

"They need to get back in the sleeper. Out of sight, out of mind. They should leave them alone if they just stay quiet."

"He reads Dr. Seuss, he knows all the words to most of them," Mary said.

"Make a sign big enough he can read. Tell him to hide," Gunny said. "That wall of junk won't hold them off of us for long. The kids can last a long time, there's food and water in the cabinets. The guys from the camp will come looking in a day or so, if we're not back. They'll find them."

He turned away before she could see the lie in his eyes. Nobody was coming after them. That wasn't part of the plan.

If two trucks and some of the best men, were lost on a simple rescue operation on the outskirts of town, Cobb wouldn't be sending anyone else on a suicide mission. He caught the eyes of the others as they stationed themselves at the head of the stairs, guns at the ready. They knew the truth. They had known there was a chance of this being a one-way trip when they volunteered to go.

It just seemed so stupid to go out like this. To have such a simple thing, a door locked by a couple of frightened kids, be their downfall.

The mattress below was slowly being shredded. The screaming horde would tear it apart inch by inch until they got to the stacks of tumbled furniture and start tearing it apart one piece at a time.

By then, the boys would be taking careful aim at heads and stacking up corpses for the rest of them to have to tear their way through, but they would. Slowly but inevitably, they would make it through all barriers placed in their way.

There was no running water, but the fresh water tank on the back of the toilet had a good four gallons in it and they all took turns, drinking thirstily from the toothbrush cup.

Mary had finished her sign, printed in simple words on the backs of animal posters that had been hanging on the wall. The kids were out of sight and hiding, waiting for rescue.

They had all circled around the upstairs rooms more than once, looking for a way out. The closest house was too far away to jump. Wishing for a helicopter didn't seem to be doing any good.

Mary had apologized so often, and with such heartfelt sorrow, they all felt bad about blaming her and kept telling her it wasn't her fault. Each one trying to come up with some way the whole fiasco was all their doing, and the responsibility should be placed squarely on their shoulders.

The boys kept trying to outdo one another to take the blame, and some of the reasons were bordering on ridiculous. Especially Stabby's. He had declared he was completely at fault because he had been distracted by the three Indians in silver tennis shoes teaching him sign language. As they quietly laughed at his antics, he suddenly stopped.

"Attic," he said.

"I looked. There isn't one," Lars said, realigning his magazines for the hundredth time on a night stand.

"Course there's one," Stabby said. "This roof ain't flat, now is it?"

"He's right," Gunny said and sprang up from sharpening his Gerber.

# 29

Gunny jumped up on the narrow banister at the head of the stairwell and balanced himself with one hand on the decorative newel post going up to the ceiling. He poked his Gerber through the drywall over his head. He smiled down at them, then started tearing out chunks of it, making a hole wide enough to fit through the two by sixes it was nailed to. It really wasn't an attic, just an insulated crawl space, only about four feet tall in the center. It would be hot and itchy with all the open batted insulation, but it was better than being dinner for a party of two hundred.

"It's good," he called down over the snarls and howls of the zombies. "Hurry and get up here before they break through. Maybe they'll give up if they don't find us."

One by one, they scrambled up the narrow opening with helping hands from above and below, until the last man was up and they covered the hole the best they could with strips of insulation.

The zombies were still battling each other and the stacked furniture, trying to get through, but they were packed so tightly, forward progress had nearly ground to a halt. With the ninety degree turn in the landing, the crush of bodies from below couldn't force through the improvised barrier. They were pushing against the support wall of the house, not the flimsy wall of cheap wood from heaped furniture.

"Maybe should have stayed down there a bit longer," Scratch grumbled. "It'll take them days to get through. And I'm allergic to fiberglass."

"Nah, mate," Stabby said. "It'll go like a dam bursting. Once they get a hand hold of a chair leg or sumpin', it'll all come crashing down."

Gunny hunchbacked his way over to the end of the roof and tried to see out of the aluminum gable vent. It was futile, all he could do was look down at the ground, the way the slats were. He pulled his knife out again and started working it around the edges, bending the soft aluminum frame away from the screws that had been shot into it years ago. It was slow work if he didn't want to make a lot of noise, but there was nothing else to do. One more avenue of escape, another chance to live five more minutes if they got out on the roof.

They hadn't been up there for more than half an hour or so and Scratch announced he had to take a dump.

"You couldn't have gone before?" Lars asked, working on the other gable end of the house.

"Please tell me you can hold it," Stabby said. "I don't want to be smelling Martha's cooking coming out your backside."

"I'm going back down," Scratch said. "I ain't planning on squatting up here with you clowns."

They pulled the insulation back from the hole in the ceiling, but what they saw stopped them. Hands had finally pulled the mattress apart enough to reach through, and they were scrabbling for anything to grab. The first of them was halfway through the pile, pulling and fighting its way to the top of the stairs.

"Crap," Scratch said, and quietly put the insulation back. Stabby snickered at his choice of words and got the bird flipped at him for his troubles. "I really gotta go, man," Scratch whispered, cutting a glance toward Mary, who was sitting next to her husband a few feet away. Calm now, talking quietly with Firecracker.

Gunny hunchbacked his way back over to the group. "Plan B," he announced.

"I thought retreating to the house was plan B," Scratch said.

"Okay, Plan C then," Gunny started, but was interrupted by Stabby.

"Wasn't Plan C barricading ourselves upstairs?"

"Fine," Gunny tried again, getting exasperated. "Plan D."

"Thought that was climbing up here," Lars chimed in, the three boys grinning.

"Would you friggin morons shut the hell up?" Gunny growled. "Next time I'm bringing Bastille and Bunny with me! Better than you useless tits."

That got them chuckling and Scratch finally got serious. "What's up, Boss?"

"The electric and phone lines run right over the top of the truck," he said. "All I have to do is shimmy out there on them, drop down on the roof, get in on the driver's side, and lead this pack off. If you stay quiet, they should all chase the truck. I'll get turned around up the road, do the zombie snowplow thing and pull up next to the porch. You guys just hop over and climb in. Can of corn."

"A what?" Stabby asked.

"Hillbilly vernacular for easy as pie," Scratch said.

They were looking at him like he'd lost his mind. "You got a better idea? Wanna stay up here and smell what Scratch is planning on leaving for us over in the corner?"

That got them falling all over themselves agreeing that it was a genius plan, best one ever, it should have been Plan A all along, and they started duck walking their way over to the end of the house.

They climbed out onto the roof as quietly as they could, the milling crowd around the house never looking up. Now that he was out here and looking at it, Gunny was having second thoughts about his idea. He wondered how long the horde would stay gathered around the house before they wandered off. Basing what he knew about them from the three days at the truck stop, probably never, unless they were drawn away by something. He wasn't going to stay cooped up in an attic for days with no water, in the hopes they would wander off on their own.

If they didn't, they would be doing this same thing in a few days, but weak from thirst and hunger. Best to do it now, they were all fresh.

He tested the wires going into the storm head, putting as much weight as he could on them without fully committing. They seemed to be solid.

He handed his rifle up to Stabby, then turned to Scratch. "If I fall, clear me a path. If I don't make it, don't let me become one of them." He looked directly into his eyes. He held his gaze until he saw the man nod, all jokes aside for the moment.

*"No guts, no glory,"* he thought, then triple checked his Glock, making sure it wasn't going to slide out of his holster. He eased out onto the wires, hooking his feet over the cable

just like basic training, and started to slowly move his way toward the truck.

He made careful movements, trying not to make any sudden jerks that might alert the horde to dangling meat just over their heads. The wire was starting to sag lower and lower the farther away from the house he got and the boys had all taken a knee on the porch, steadying their rifles and ready to start blasting if anything went south.

Gunny didn't look down, just ahead, hand over hand, sliding his feet, cutting down the distance with each pull. It had been a bunch of years since he had done anything like this, and holding onto a steering wheel all day long didn't do much for building muscles. His arms were already aching and he wasn't even half way. The cable was dipping lower, and he was still on the easy part of the crawl. Once he started going uphill, it was going to get a whole lot harder. He started the uphill part with the mass below him still trying to get into the house. From this vantage point he could see through the broken windows and it was already nearly full. The pull was getting harder, he really had to grip the cable and his arms were starting to get tremors. He lowered his head and looked.

Getting close, another twenty feet. Another twenty feet uphill, he corrected himself. The truck looked like a lot further drop from here, than it did from the roof of the house. Maybe twelve feet from the wire to the top of the sleeper. No biggie. By the time he dropped his feet and stretched out, only about four feet. His hands were cramping. He couldn't stop, he knew from experience. If you take a break, it's that much harder to get started again.

He forced the pain out of his head, concentrating on his next move, his next grip, the next slide of his foot. He inched the feet away and when he looked again, he was where he needed to be. He unhooked his boots and tried to hang on with just his hands, but his fingers didn't comply with his brain's commands and he slipped to the roof of the sleeper with a loud thud instead of a soft bump. He heard the kids inside scream and he cursed as he rolled over the edge, grabbing the rebar webbing welded over the window of the driver door.

It wasn't quite a controlled fall and he landed hard on top of the battery box, lost his grip on the mesh and fell off the truck backward, his foot seeking the lower step that he never had Tommy weld back on. He managed to get his head tucked so he didn't bash his brains out on the pavement, but he landed solidly on his back, his air rushing out in a whoosh. The milling horde was no longer milling, they had seen him land and disappear from their view, and the screaming started up again as they surged toward the truck. His crew on the roof of the house were helpless, they couldn't see what happened from their vantage point, let alone try to send lead downrange.

Gunny jumped up instantly, ignoring the pain and his narrowing vision, his lungs trying to suck in air, but unable to wheeze in more than tiny sips of it. He grabbed the door handle and it swung open with ease as he leapt back up on the battery box and into the cab, slamming it behind him before any of the undead could get their fingers in the gap. He sat on the seat, trying to say something to calm the crying kids, but it was all he could do to pull in enough air to keep from passing out. He had forgotten how much that hurt, getting the wind knocked out of you.

He hadn't felt this since grade school and the monkey bar incident, which left him in much the same condition. Except the recess teacher had come running over. And there weren't any flesh eating monsters trying to sink their teeth into him. It took him a minute, but when he was finally able to take a normal breath, he reassured the kids in his clumsy way and fired up the truck.

The horde outside redoubled their efforts to get to him, clamoring up the blade and climbing on the sides, hanging from the mesh protecting the windows. Gunny dropped it in third and mashed the pedal. The mass of zombies at least five or six deep in front of the truck didn't even cause the Cat to hesitate in the slightest. Gunny grabbed another gear, blew the air horn and started playing the role of the Pied Piper.

He drove slow enough and blasted his horn a few more times, trying to draw away as many as he could. He headed back out of town, in the opposite direction of the overlook, where the rest of the trucks were parked. He followed the same game plan they had before. Lead them for a few miles then hurry up and get turned around. On the way back in, crush and destroy as many as possible, chopping off legs and tossing them aside like empty beer cans at a Nascar race.

When he got back to the house about twenty minutes later, they all came running out of the front door before he could bounce up to the porch. It seems he had led nearly all of them out of the house, too. The boys had made quick work of the stragglers, Stabby still wiping gore off of his claws. Within minutes the family was reunited, they had Firecracker's truck and were heading back to the Overlook.

*"I hope my reuniting family story goes as good as theirs,"* Gunny thought, as he wound his way back up the mountain, *"just a few more days and I'll be there."*

When they got back and Gunny was hooked up to his wagon, he looked at his watch. The day was nearly gone, the sun getting ready to sink over the horizon. A quick rescue run had turned into an all-day affair, with them nearly losing both trucks, being trapped in a house, getting separated...the list went on of all the mistakes they had made.

Even with all they knew, they had nearly died just taking a trip into town. They were lucky all of them made it back. These things could not be underestimated again. They needed to set up some protocols for refueling, for any stops they made. This enemy was worse than the ones they all had faced in the Middle East. They had numbers and near invincibility, superior speed and strength, and were undeterred by anything.

They had zig-zagged their way back up the mountain, taking meandering routes to try to throw the followers off the trail. Maybe it worked. He understood why the ones on the freeway had kept coming mile after mile, they just followed the straight path of the big road. Maybe with all the turns they had made, there wouldn't be a huge horde coming at them from Salt Lake tonight. He got with Cobb and Griz when the 'glad you made it' and 'welcome backs' had been said. They had made one run with Scratch's truck back down the freeway, but the stragglers coming in from that way were just trickling in now, all of them broken in one way or another, crawling along on severed or shattered limbs.

They had set up sniper positions and had been brushing up on rusty skills, training those who had never fired long distance about windage and bullet drop. Kim was still the best shot, reaching out and touching them in the head at over a half mile, with an off the shelf pawn shop .308 and an inexpensive scope mounted to it. There wasn't even a discussion about leaving, they needed fuel and they didn't want to do that in the dark. They would roll at first light.

They doubled the guard to the front of the Overlook

and expected the worst, but by the time night fell, they still hadn't seen a mass of them coming up the freeway. The twisting, turning, and backtracking had worked. After dinner, as Griz had everyone tearing down and cleaning their weapons, the boys had regaled them with their overblown tales of harrowing escapes and death defying near misses around the campfire.

Stabby was hilarious at times, setting the mood with dark tension at others. He was a natural storyteller and Scratch and Lars were natural clowns, knowing the right moments to add their bits to the stories. It was hugely entertaining watching them, and when they had finished, Griz asked Gunny how much of it was true.

"All of it," he said. "Except for the part where everyone passed out from the smell of Scratch copping a squat in the attic."

"Even the high wire act over the horde?"

"Not quite the way he told it, I didn't try to walk over it with a pink umbrella for balance, but yeah. Even that."

Stacy was standing near him and after the laughter and the quiet applause died away with their triumphant return to the camp she said, "What he did was good for those kids. They can see now that maybe it wasn't as bad as they thought. Especially when he made the little boy into a hero, protecting his sister. Hell, they'll probably even remember it like that now."

"Yeah," Gunny agreed. "He's ate up, but in a good way."

# EPILOGUE

**D**aniel didn't make eye contact as he rigidly stood at attention on one side of the oak door leading into the conference room. He'd been warned never to look her in the eye. She would interpret it as an act of defiance. There was some kind of emergency meeting, and from the looks of the people who had come in as he was standing guard, it was something serious.

He didn't know what was happening in the world, and neither did anyone else in the barracks. He had just finished his first rotation, with two years of training in his platoon with the Force Recon Marines. They'd been rushed here a week ago with rumors of an imminent terrorist attack. He was in an expansive underground city somewhere in the Catskill Mountains, as near as any of them were able to determine.

They had no communication with the outside world and had been sequestered to a small area the whole time they were here. Even though there were plenty of enlisted men, the officers were told they would be standing guard for the meeting, even though it was demeaning to them. That is what the president wanted. Times had changed. They were some of the lucky, the chosen few, who had been hand-picked to serve as defenders for the survivors of the disaster, or so they were told.

No one had said exactly what the disaster was, but it must be severe. He recognized many of the people attending the meeting from seeing them on the news. Highly placed politicians and corporate heads of business.

She started screaming at them as she stormed through the door.

"How did this happen? How did they get control of the nukes? You guaranteed me it would be impossible!"

The door slammed behind her, and the rest of her tirade was muffled and indistinct. Daniel chanced a glance over to the other Lieutenant who was standing guard. He read the same look on his face. "What the hell is going on?"

He didn't know. He just knew this was a far cry from any kind of stories his grandpa Cobb, or his dad, had told him about the Marines.

# AUTHOR'S NOTE

There is much more to tell in the Zombie Road saga, but this seemed like a good place to end the beginning of the story. I hope you enjoyed it and will follow their journeys in the second book. If not, then you weren't left with a life or death cliffhanger on the last page and you can take comfort that they are all alive and well, with no imminent danger lurking over them.

Jessie and his friends have found a good place to go into hiding and as long as they stay put and don't do anything stupid, they will easily survive the zombie outbreak. Everybody knows teenagers never do anything stupid, so they should be just fine.

Lacy and her new friends are in a predicament, trapped in the high-rise with all avenues of escape infested with the undead. They'll probably think of something. Maybe they'll find an ample supply of food and all live happily until the zombies wither away.

Gunny and the crew from the Three Flags are well on their way to the safe haven of Lakota. I'm sure they'll arrive without further incident, all of the nuclear reactors will be safely deactivated, and he'll embrace his role as a politician. He'll send a helicopter to pick up his family. He'll make peace with the Muslims, start shaving, and wear a suit every day.

Or not.

One last thing: Indie authors live and die by their reviews. It helps others to decide whether to pull the trigger or not to make a purchase, or even download if it's free. (Or so I've been told. Since this is the first book I've published, I guess I'll find out.) If you enjoyed it, please take a minute or two to leave a review. Thanks.

There is a David Simpson Fan Club on Facebook if you'd like all the latest info or hang out with other fans.

If you would like to contact me, my Facebook is David Simpson. I'll have occasional updates on the next book I'm working on.

https://www.facebook.com/profile.php?id=100009128109716